KINGSCOTE

HEART OF INDIA SERIES

Silk
Under Eastern Stars
Kingscote

KINGSCOTE

LINDA CHAIKIN

BETHANY HOUSE PUBLISHERS
MINNEAPOLIS, MINNESOTA 55438

Cover illustration by Joe Nordstrom

Published by Bethany House Publishers
A Ministry of Bethany Fellowship, Inc.
11300 Hampshire Avenue South
Minneapolis, Minnesota 55438

Printed in the United States of America

For dramatic purposes, Felix Carey, son of William, has been portrayed as several years older than he actually was in 1800. Felix was in fact born in 1785 and was ordained in 1807.

Library of Congress Cataloging-in-Publication Data

Chaikin, L. L., 1943–
    Kingscote / Linda Chaikin.
        p.   cm. — (Heart of India ; 3)
    I. Title. II. Series.
PS3553.H2427K56   1994
813'.54—dc20   94–6788
ISBN 1–55661–378–4   CIP

To

Barb Lilland

"Iron sharpeneth iron;
so a man sharpeneth the
countenance of his friend."
(Proverbs 27:17)

LINDA CHAIKIN is a full-time writer and has two books published in the Christian market. She graduated from Multnomah School of the Bible and is working on a degree with Moody Bible Institute. She and her husband, Steve, are involved with a church-planting mission among Hindus in Kerala, India. They make their home in San Jose, California.

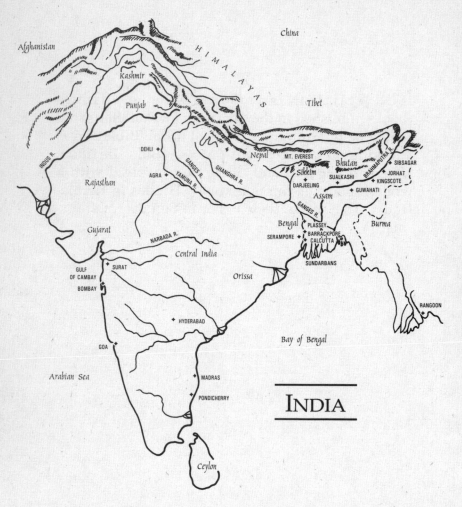

Prologue

GARDEN OF THE ROYAL PALACE, GUWAHATI, NORTHEAST INDIA

APRIL 1800

Major Jace Buckley's face was still stinging from Coral Kendall's slap. He watched the last glimmer of her silk skirts disappear as she walked quickly from view toward the maharaja's* lighted banquet hall ... and Doctor Ethan Boswell. Jace stood very still in the shadows of the garden trees, his arms folded across his chest, his blue-black eyes narrowing. He told himself that he would walk away emotionally unscathed, even as he had from other women.

Go after her.

The haunting stringed music coming from the Indian sitar as the musicians played in the upper gallery continued to throb in the fragrant night air closing in about him.

No, he decided with a stubborn determination that

*A glossary of Indian words is at the back of the book.

surprised even him. His jaw set. He would perform his duty to the colonel, learn what he could about Gem—then board the *Madras* and leave.

He turned abruptly, took the stone steps into the lower tiered garden leading down toward the Brahmaputra River, and walked the short distance to his military quarters near the British residency.

When Jace entered his chamber he tried to smother the memory of Coral and found he could not. He expressed his frustration over his emotional downfall by heaving the door shut with a bang. The windows rattled.

There came an exaggerated groan from the bunk. "Must you slam door, sahib? Ah! The treachery of romance is like goads to soul. . . ."

Jace recognized the unmistakable voice of Gokul and glanced sharply at the bunk. The presence of his old friend cheered him. He said lightly, "You are a welcome sight. Get up, you old thieving spy. Where is my coffee?"

Gokul struggled into his wrap. "Sahib, patience is the fruit of kings and wise men."

Jace walked to his wardrobe and flung open the door. "Any more news from the northeast?"

"Much. Very important."

"Why did you not come to me at once?"

A malicious glimmer showed in Gokul's black eyes as he scanned Jace.

"I fly to bring news to palace garden, but old Gokul is too much the romantic to interrupt. I see delectable English damsel in sahib's arms."

Jace turned to give him a level look. Gokul rubbed his chin. "That slap cracked silence like musket."

"Never mind. What news?"

Gokul sobered and glancing toward the open window went to close it. He drew near, his voice low and tense with excitement. "I discover Gem is alive and held prisoner by Warlord Zin."

Jace's breath caught. "Zin. . . . Then my suspicions were right. But why would Zin hold Gem captive? He has made no contact with the Kendall family for ransom jewels."

"That, sabib, I could not find out. I found my contact in Jorhat with knife in back next day. Old Gokul quickly decide it is time to make hasty departure. And so here am I and will make hot coffee instead."

Zin! As Gokul went to boil water, Jace mused over the information. He grabbed his leather satchel, throwing the things on the bed that he would need to take with him to the British outpost at Jorhat.

The memory of Coral also wrapped about his heart and would not let go.

Enough, he rebuked himself. He would think of her no more.

"I must think of some way to meet with the maharaja before we ride out with Sir Hugo Roxbury. There is little time, and I have no real plan. The rajput guards are thicker than cockroaches—" He flicked one of the pesky bugs off his gold-embroidered tunic before tossing the elegant garment on the bed. He snatched a white shirt from the wardrobe.

Again he thought of Coral. He must not indulge the strange sense of loss he felt. Mulling over an idea was the first step toward acting. And if he openly admitted his feelings to her, what was left?

"Ah, sahib," sighed Gokul. "Marriage is mysterious thing, full of splendor!"

Jace turned, his eyes narrowing under his lashes as he watched Gokul brewing the coffee.

In frustration Jace unwound the turban and ran his fingers through his dark hair. . . . Commitment, sharing, loving. If he admitted to Coral that he wanted her, it would mean coming into her presence without his armor. . . . Dangerous.

She would come to know his heart as she knew her own. If she should choose to do so, she could cut his heart from him and crush it in her small hand. The thought of being so vulnerable left him cold. Coral was too good to do that . . . or was she?

He stood for a moment thinking. And what of himself? Could someone so lovely and innocent trust herself to him? He would not hurt her emotionally with intention to do so, but then his moods were such that there were times when he did not even trust himself.

The great adventure of marriage: what did he know about it? Faithfulness was involved, of course. No problem there, he thought. Any man who ended up with Coral would end up with a prize for which dueling princes might fight; nor was there a problem with love, but what about commitment?

Commitment demanded his all. He must be there when she needed him emotionally, physically . . . spiritually.

Spiritually. The full-orbed meaning of the word stabbed through his soul like a dart. She belonged first of all to Christ. No man dare intrude without His permission.

Now why had he thought of that?

John Newton came to mind along with the books that the old ex-slaver had given him that rainy night in London. Jace had not planned to do so but had felt compelled to spend months aboard ship pouring over those volumes during the return voyage to Calcutta. He understood theology. In order to please Coral he could engage her in deep discussion. He believed he could even pray with her if she wanted him to.

He belted on his scabbard. He also knew that what was precious to Coral did not mean as much to him. Her will was yielded to Christ; his own remained in the hands of Jace Buckley.

First obstacle, he thought, and buttoned his shirt. The greatest obstacle. She deserved a godly hero like William Carey, or Charles Peddington. Yet . . . if he did want Coral enough to admit his feelings for her openly, could he convince her to marry him? He had never tried to convince a woman, any woman, that he truly loved her.

Gokul brought him a mug of steaming coffee, and his knowing smile caused Jace to smirk. He took the cup and turned away.

"One warning, sahib. Kendall family expect damsel to marry sahib-doctor."

Second obstacle, thought Jace. It would not be easy to convince Sir Hampton and Elizabeth Kendall to give their daughter to him instead of to Ethan. He would not allow himself to forget that Coral was a silk heiress. He had nothing to offer her but his intentions with the Darjeeling tea plantation.

Back off, Jace. Forget it.

He snapped his satchel shut and frowned. If he truly loved Coral he would stay away from her. What could he bring into her life but trouble? What of her school? Her dedication to God? She deserved Peddington.

Jace looked up at his military image in the mirror. *Yes, you might win the battle. But she would lose. Stay out of her life, Buckley. She belongs to the purposes of God, and you belong to the deck of the Madras.*

There came a rap on the door. Gokul shot him a glance. Jace slipped his pistol under his jacket, then nodded to him to answer.

An Indian servant stood there, unreadable, his turban

golden under the torchlight. "I bring a message for the major."

"Yes?" said Jace.

He salaamed. "Ambassador Roxbury regrets he cannot ride out tonight for Jorhat. The major is ordered to remain in Guwahati until further notice."

He backed away and left. Gokul shut the door and looked at Jace with caution. "The sahib-ambassador's delays smell of trap."

"Yes, but for whom, me or the maharaja?"

"Maybe both. You must be cautious, sahib. He is a clever man who knows what he is about."

"At least the delay will give me time to see the maharaja. Somehow I must gain a private audience. He must be warned of an imminent attempt on his life." He fixed a narrowed gaze on Gokul. "I need the garb of a royal bodyguard. Can you manage to produce one?"

"You turn Gokul into a thief, but yes, I manage."

When Gokul had left, Jace thought again of Coral. He snatched a piece of paper and wrote:

I would not write you this brief message unless I had certain proof. Gem is alive. Gokul has discovered his whereabouts. It is not safe to say more in writing. If all goes well, I shall return him to you by Christmas.

J. Buckley

He would have Gokul deliver the message to her . . . or . . . he might even ride to Kingscote himself once he had met with the maharaja.

He watched a large moth hopelessly beating its wings against the bright lantern.

If he rode there himself, his presence would inform Coral that he was only making an excuse to mend the final goodbye. Was that what he truly wished?

He watched the moth with growing irritation, then flipped it aside. It returned, beating its wings.

With a sigh Jace folded the paper and stuffed it inside his jacket. He would decide after his emotions had plenty of time to cool. He reached over and put out the lantern.

1

The night was hot and muggy as Jace left his quarters. The light wind from off the Brahmaputra River stirred the poinciana trees. He kept to the shadows as he walked across the cantonment in the direction of the Guwahati palace. What would he do when he got inside? How could he convince the guards that he must see their raja?

For weeks now, Jace's attempts to meet privately with the maharaja had been foiled. Spies were everywhere. He could trust no one in the palace, for Sunil was cunning. The prince would have worked long and hard to sow his seeds of mutinous discontent among those close to the raja before he felt the confidence to make an open move. Jace knew the assassination orders would come from Sunil. For Jace to trust any one of the royal guards or the important Indian officials meant risking his own life as well as the raja's. Who could guess who was loyal and who was not?

In these past weeks Gokul had gone into hiding, meeting with Jace late at night, and then only in disguise. Jace had long since abandoned any thought of riding to Kingscote himself. His message to Coral finally made its

17

way there in the hands of a trusted acquaintance who had slipped away, dressed as a sepoy on route to Jorhat.

Anxiously considering his options as he neared the palace, Jace knew that this was his last chance to contact the maharaja. Roxbury's plans had forced him to risk this meeting now. Tonight Sir Hugo would join him and the small troop that was in readiness to ride to the military outpost at Jorhat. There was little time.

A whisper of sound came from behind him in the trees. Jace stepped aside, turning to face the shadows, his blade lifted from its scabbard with a glint in the moonlight.

His emotions were on edge as he confronted the same lean and tough rajput guard who weeks earlier had been waiting at Jace's military quarters near the residency. The rajput had brought him the gold-embroidered black tunic, turban, and tulwar that he'd worn to the palace that night. They had been gifts from the maharaja's dewan. The dewan had surprisingly turned out to be Prince Sunil, the king's nephew and the younger brother of Gem's father, Rajiv.

The rajput now spread his hands forward, palms showing.

"There is no need for that, Sirdar-Buckley."

"I shall decide, Rajput. Step into the moonlight."

He did so, and his expressionless face was still, his dark eyes solemn. In a small gesture of respect, he gave a low tilt to his head.

"You are summoned to the residency. Ambassador Roxbury waits to speak to you about your military papers."

Jace had already dispatched the official papers to Roxbury concerning his fact-finding mission to Jorhat. What papers did he speak of, or was it a ploy to divert him?

Jace glanced casually into the trees. He heard nothing. Did other guards wait? He sheathed his blade but kept his distance, and his mind shifted to Roxbury. Suddenly his own plans had become more difficult to carry out.

If Roxbury had somehow guessed his plans to seek an interview with the raja, he would resort to anything to stop him, especially if Jace was right about the new ambassador's involvement with Sunil.

For a moment he contemplated breaking with Roxbury and riding to Jorhat with Gokul, but if he did, he would be court-martialed on his return to Calcutta. As much as he chafed at the military bit binding him, he could not bear that dishonor.

As major, and commissioned by the governor-general in Calcutta to command the small security force protecting Roxbury, Jace had no choice but to serve him.

Leaving the rajput, Jace's steps made no sound on the compacted dirt that led through the avenue of shade trees. Overhead the white moon was now blotted out by clouds.

Jace's thoughts reverted to the trouble that had come to him during an earlier summons by Roxbury before they had left Calcutta. He still felt anger when he mulled the incident over in his mind, for he had been certain then, and still was, that it had been one of Roxbury's tactics to thwart his effort to discover the facts about the assassination of Major Selwyn at Jorhat. In Calcutta, Roxbury had informed Jace that his orders to command the 21st at Jorhat had been changed by the governor-general himself, and that he would become captain of Roxbury's security guard.

Jace's mouth twisted with impatience when he thought about it. The very least of his personal concerns was Roxbury's security.

He could feel the rise in tension as he walked in the darkness. Like a riled cobra, danger waited its hour to strike. But from what direction would the attack come? From Roxbury? Sunil? Would conflict explode here in Guwahati or on the quiet road northeast to Jorhat?

His instincts were on edge as he paused in the uncanny stillness of the muggy night. Ahead was the newly built British Residency House, where Roxbury would set up representation of the Company. A light burned in the lower window, and through the split-cane screen he could see a figure pacing. Roxbury?

For several minutes he studied the situation.

Roxbury had wanted him killed in the ambush near Plassey Junction. He had not truly wanted him to be captain of his security guard, and no doubt found his presence here a threat to whatever his own plans might be. Now it was too late. They found their purposes head to head in conflict. The journey they would take together inland had always been suspect to Jace, and he had wondered if a bullet might not wait somewhere out there in the darkness on the road to the outpost.

He might wish that Roxbury's summons had come because of Jace's adoptive father, Colonel John Warbeck. Had the colonel been successful in convincing the governor-general in Calcutta to release him from service to Roxbury? Captain Gavin MacKay would have arrived at Government-House in Calcutta by now to inform the military of Harrington's suspected involvement in the mutiny at Plassey Junction with Sir Hugo.

But Jace knew there was not the slightest chance of that being the cause of the summons. It would take at least two months before MacKay arrived at Guwahati with reinforcements. It might take even longer if they had trouble putting down the rebels at Plassey. Until McKay arrived, Jace would remain in the sensitive position of reporting to Roxbury, who alone had the authority to change his orders.

The residency was ahead, bone white under the brass pagoda lanterns.

From where Jace stood under a poinciana tree, the golden lantern light fell across the garden, and there on the lawn was one of the large stone idols of the Hindu religion. He recognized Kali. One of her religious feast days was drawing near, and the carved idol was wreathed with flowers.

What was it that Gokul had written him in the message received at Jorhat?

"The raja may take sudden ill and die . . . and Burrasahib Roxbury is a worshiper of Kali. . . ."

Jace stared at the image, aware of something that had not crossed his mind until this moment. This was the British residency, and the cantonment was rarely used by Hindus, Muslims, Sikhs, and Mussulmen as a location to place religious articles. They considered all Westerners to be "Christian," even if many British were blind and deaf to the one true and living God.

So what was the image of Kali doing in the garden of the residency?

For the first time he noticed the figures of six or seven men stooped on the grass before the idol. They were talking in low, urgent voices among themselves.

Was the idol a sign that the British ambassador of the East India Company was a man to be trusted if a mutiny should break out? And would that make the residency safe from attack?

He heard footsteps coming from the opposite side of the road nearest the maharaja's palace. The boots rang on stone, taking no thought for the need of caution, and Jace turned his head to see who would take such small care at being seen. A moment later the figure of a man emerged from the trees. As the man hurried forward, his mind obviously on whatever had prompted him to rush to come to the residency, the moonlight shone down upon Ethan Boswell.

Ethan was the last person that Jace had expected to see. He watched the young doctor stride resolutely toward the gate, his head bent as though in deep thought. His steps alerted the small group that was gathered around the idol, and they were quick to jump to their bare feet, melting away into the darkness. All had left except one, and as he turned toward Ethan, Jace caught a glimpse of the Indian's face. He came alert. The man's long, ropelike dark hair was covered with gray ash, and he wore a rosarylike cluster of religious beads around his neck. A dark caste mark was on his forehead.

A sadhu, a religious holy man. What was he doing pretending to be the low-caste gatekeeper? Where *was* the gatekeeper? Had he melted away with the others at the sound of Ethan's steps? Had they not expected Ethan, but Jace himself?

The sadhu came forward to meet Ethan, bringing fingers to his forehead in greeting. Ethan would not know that this man was considered of high caste to his people. Jace felt that he had seen the sadhu before and tried to place him. Ethan passed through the gate, and Jace heard his steps resounding on the verandah.

It's just like Ethan to blunder his way into a situation, thought Jace.

The sadhu had disappeared when Jace neared the gate, and he suspected him to have gone into the courtyard, where he had heard a woman singing. He might follow, but it was Ethan who now commanded his attention. Wasting no time and not wishing to be seen, Jace took the path around the residency entrance and, following the wall for some distance, came to a secluded spot where the trees overhung their branches onto the dirt path. He jumped, catching hold of the wall, and pulled himself up to lie flat. Seeing that the garden below was empty, he landed softly in the soil where freshly planted bougainvillea vines were thick with crimson blossoms.

Lights blazed in the residency living quarters. Through a split-cane curtain, he looked into the drawing room, feeling no qualm at spying. Too many lives depended on learning the truth.

Ethan stood with his back toward the window, but Sir Hugo could be seen, his swarthy face showing hard and angry beneath the short-trimmed beard.

"You know better than to show up now. Buckley is due here any moment. Get out."

"Indeed, my very thoughts. I'll not stay in Guwahati. I've come to tell you I'm leaving in the morning for Kingscote."

Sir Hugo strode toward him. "I forbid it. You are needed here."

"Needed? Oh, yes, so I have discovered! But I do not take my oath as a physician lightly. Druggings are one thing; sending a maharaja to the funeral pyre is quite another."

Roxbury's hand whipped across the side of Ethan's face, jerking his head to the side.

"You fool!" came his hoarse voice. "They'll kill you in a second if you do not cooperate!"

"And you involved me knowing this?"

"I had no choice! You must go through with it, or we are both dead men. We are without sufficient troops, and left to Sunil."

"If Buckley is without adequate soldiers it was your wishes, you and Harrington—"

"Shut up, Ethan! You don't know what you're talking

about. If you don't cooperate with Sunil a dagger awaits you!"

"Yours?" came the angry sneer.

"You speak as a fool. You are my son! Do you think I want you floating down the river? I've plans for Kingscote, and for political authority here in the northeast. You've always figured highly in those plans, you and Coral."

"I want none of it." Angrily Ethan pushed past him toward the door.

"Ethan, wait," demanded Roxbury.

Ethan came out the door onto the porch, and Jace stepped back from the open window into the garden shadows. Ethan hurried down the steps and out into the night.

Jace had only a moment to decide. Follow Ethan? Force him to disclose all he knew? Or catch Roxbury now, when he was emotionally off guard?

Jace's boots rang deliberately loud as he came up the steps and entered the open door.

Sir Hugo jerked about and confronted him. There was no time to alter his expression, and for the first time Jace saw fear in Hugo's dark eyes, not because of Jace's sudden presence but because of Ethan. *So Ethan is his son, not his nephew.*

It was then that Jace understood. Sir Hugo Roxbury, despite all of his cruel ambition, did have family feelings and loyalties. Jace considered unmasking Roxbury, letting him know just how much he knew, not only about the maharaja but also the mutiny at Jorhat and Plassey; but he held back when Roxbury's agitated features swiftly composed themselves again as if by magic.

Ethan would be the man to confront, Jace decided.

Sir Hugo walked to an intricately carved black table and snatched up the decanter of wine, filling a glass.

"Ah, Major, I've been expecting you. My apology for delaying you in Guwahati these past days, but it was necessary. There's been a serious change in our plans. You may have heard by now about Hampton and Alex. Sit down, won't you? A glass of wine?"

Jace stood in a calm military stance, hands folded behind him, showing nothing. "No, thank you. I am on duty. I gather, sir, you speak of Sir Hampton's trek into the Darjeeling area?"

Roxbury turned, glass in hand, and gave him a probing stare. Jace knew that Hugo was wondering if he had seen Ethan hurrying down the path with a cut lip. Sir Hugo was a frightened man, and as such, he was even more dangerous. If he thought Jace had overheard, he would strike before he had intended to do so on the lonely road northeast to Jorhat. Not that he expected Roxbury himself to try to kill him. He would leave that to Sunil and his ghazis.

Jace stood, the image of disciplined loyalty.

Roxbury said, "Yes, Darjeeling . . . a treacherous situation, Major. The more I ponder it, the more my alarm grows. My brother-in-law is older than I and certainly no mountain climber. Nor, for that matter, is my nephew Alex. He's a musician, not an outdoorsman the way Michael was." He frowned. "I cannot for the life of me understand what prompted Alex to make the mountainous journey into Darjeeling." His dark eyes riveted on Jace.

The man has no conscience, thought Jace. *He lies without qualm. If Alex went to Darjeeling, he was lured there under pretense, even as Sir Hampton was snared into risking the trail. And Roxbury is the one who baited both traps.*

But Jace said casually, "Might he have gone there hoping to find me or Seward at the tea plantation?"

"I had not thought of that possibility, Major. Then you would know the route they would take?"

What a question. "I know it well. There is no house on the land yet, only a hut, but Alex knows that Michael and I were partners. I intend to see his brother's share go to Alex or one of his sisters."

"Hmm, that may account for his unexpected decision to go there. I'm worried about the weather; it will worsen with the monsoon season. Knowing they both could be lost in the rugged mountainous area near the eastern Himalayas is a matter of utmost concern to me."

"I understand, sir. You do well to have concerns. I've trekked that area several times, once with Michael, and I've experienced the terror of an avalanche."

Roxbury raised his glass and emptied it. Jace noticed a slight tremor in his hand, something unusual for the iron demeanor of Sir Hugo. So Ethan's refusal to participate in his plans concerning the maharaja had unsettled him. It was the first time Jace had seen Roxbury frightened, and watching him guzzle the liquor down was unpleasant. It brought back memories to Jace of his childhood and the drunken brawls aboard his father's ship.

Jace showed none of this, his eyes meeting Hugo's evenly. "Your concern for your brother-in-law is understood," he said briefly, observing Roxbury's reaction. "One slip, and a tumble down a mountainside would mean his end. I doubt if we could ever find him."

Hugo turned his head away and walked toward the window, but not before Jace had seen the small ugly flicker of victory in his eyes. If anything did happen to Sir Hampton and Elizabeth, Roxbury would become Coral's guardian.

"Hampton has a number of guides with him," said Sir Hugo. "In his letter he mentioned taking men from the village, but unless they are familiar with Darjeeling they are not likely to be of much assistance."

Jace knew from Seward that the guides had been procured by Natine, the headman at Kingscote, but could these guides from the nearby village be trusted? Jace believed Natine was serving Roxbury. All this Seward knew as well, and Jace trusted him to keep Coral under his watchful eye.

"You'll forgive me, Major, if the life of Hampton weighs more heavily on my mind than does the death of Major Selwyn and the attack on Jorhat. What is past is already done; their deaths cannot be averted now, but Hampton may need help."

Sir Hugo turned abruptly from the open window, where earlier Jace had stood outside in the garden listening to the angry exchange between him and Ethan, and looked intently at Jace.

He has just now noticed the window is wide open. . . . Does he suspect I was out there? That I heard?

Sir Hugo let the cane curtain fall back into place.

"I've thought all evening about this, Major, and I've made up my mind to send you to Darjeeling to look for Sir Hampton."

So. . . .

"Rest assured the investigation into the death of Major Selwyn will go forward. I shall proceed as planned to ride to Jorhat. The Burmese prisoner could have told us what we need to know, but the dewan has informed me that the scoundrel hung himself in his cell. Dewan Sunil is certain that the attack on Jorhat came from Burma."

Jace felt the conflicting emotions of anger and relief. Any report Roxbury would send back to the governor-general would be a cover-up of the mutiny. Colonel Warbeck would know this and not accept the report at face value, and Captain Gavin MacKay's troop would eventually arrive to reinforce Jorhat. Unfortunately, Mac-

Kay's troop would not arrive in time to thwart a mutiny against the raja.

Jace said deliberately, "In Calcutta you believed the outpost at Jorhat was not the intended target of an 'unknown enemy,' but rather Guwahati. His Excellency's life was in danger by ghazis who were displeased with the signing of the treaty with the East India Company. If I recall, there was even an attempt made on Sunil's life. If I journey to Darjeeling, taking the security guard with me, you will be left shorthanded."

"The danger here is real, Major, and I mean not to make light of it. As I said in Calcutta, Prince Sunil suspects the ghazis of plotting with a Burmese warlord named Zin to dispel any British presence in north India. Sunil protects his uncle the maharaja, using his own guards as well as his uncle's. But you are right. We find ourselves pitifully shorthanded. It is a curse that we must wait as sitting ducks until Captain MacKay arrives with the 13th. And I'm worried about Sir Hampton. I suggest you take as few men from the security guard with you as possible. The rest, I shall keep here under my command. Perhaps the ugly matter of Jorhat should wait until Captain MacKay arrives."

Although Jace knew Roxbury was planning his demise in releasing him from duty in Guwahati, he saw opportunity in the change of orders. It was now possible to make the secret journey into Burma to speak with Warlord Zin and to discover what he could on the way northeast by stopping at Jorhat.

That Roxbury would set him free of his military obligations deserved suspicion. A shrewd man, Roxbury would know Jace's advantage in escaping his surveillance. It was a risk that he would have mulled over but had evidently found needful. No doubt he wanted him far from Guwahati when the mutiny against the maharaja took place. Had Prince Sunil advised Roxbury to send him to Darjeeling, hoping to have him ambushed on the road?

"I shall meet you and Hampton at Kingscote after MacKay arrives," said Sir Hugo. "There may be trouble ahead for Kingscote from Burma, and we'll need to work together. Sir Hampton will need to sign a protection treaty for the family holdings with the Company if the land and hatcheries are to survive."

Jace was confident that Roxbury did not expect Sir Hampton to return to Kingscote alive. He did not expect either of them to return. . . .

When Roxbury would arrive at Kingscote, it would be to announce their deaths and to coerce the ailing and grieving Elizabeth Kendall into cooperating with all he had planned for the silk holdings. And Coral would be pressured into marrying Ethan, thereby granting Sir Hugo the extra authority he needed in the family dynasty to become its sole master. With Jace having been ambushed on the road to Darjeeling, there would be no one left who was strong enough to contest Sir Hugo.

Such were his plans, or so Jace was convinced. Roxbury, however, underestimated him. He would not die by some assassin's bullet on the road to Darjeeling.

There was much to do, and he must work swiftly.

"Then I'll leave for Darjeeling tonight," said Jace easily. "I'm pleased you're sending me, since I am certain I can locate Sir Hampton. Your niece, Miss Kendall, asked me a few weeks ago to search for her father."

Sir Hugo appeared pleased, and Jace imagined him thinking that he could use Coral for a witness in backing his decision to send Jace on an emergency trek into Darjeeling. Her testimony of concern for her father and brother would lend credence to the report he would later send to the governor-general when he explained the "unfortunate assassination of the maharaja and Major J. Buckley."

Someone waited near Darjeeling to kill him. Sanjay?

"I do not blame Coral for requesting your help in locating her father, Major. I doubt if we could find a better trekking man anywhere about. You shall also be commended by the governor-general for bringing me safely on safari to Guwahati. After the mutiny at Plassey and the death of your troops, you behaved honorably. I shall mention your action in my report, and I will recommend you for a brevet."

Jace kept a straight face. "Thank you, sir."

"You are quite welcome, Major. I wish you success in Darjeeling."

Jace gave a small salute and turned to leave. At the door he paused and glanced back. Sir Hugo had his back toward him and was again staring at the open window in concern. The corner of Jace's mouth turned into a smirk. He went out, closing the door behind him.

Jace stood for a moment on the steps, thinking, his hand resting casually near his sword, his gaze fixed ahead on the open gate. The muggy night caused his shirt to cling to his skin. A whiff of breeze coming from the Brahmaputra shimmered through the flowering vines and cooled his face. First, he would locate Ethan and force him to talk. As for Roxbury's orders, they could rot. Jace would now proceed according to his own wishes. When the hour came for him to be called before the colonel on charges of desertion, Jace would have proof of Roxbury's involvement with Prince Sunil in his mutiny against British interests in Assam and its treaty with the maharaja.

From a courtyard behind one of the servant's quarters, a woman's voice could be heard singing a quavering, nasal Indian song to the accompaniment of a sitar.

He heard a subtle sound ahead of him in the garden trees lining the residency stone wall. A lone figure, telltale in white, detached itself from the trees. One of the servants, thought Jace, until the man moved out into the shaft of moonlight that fell across the carriageway. The Indian was running toward the residency gate with bare feet that made no sound on the sunbaked earth.

Jace's suspicion warned that the sadhu had overheard Ethan's argument with Roxbury and then his own conversation, and was now on his way to Prince Sunil.

"You! Halt!" commanded Jace, running down the steps after him.

The sadhu turned his head. Confronting Jace in a major's uniform, the sadhu would normally have stopped—unless he had something to hide. The sadhu ran toward the gate. The gatekeeper was in his place and arose from the ground where he sat, salaaming low.

"Stop him!" shouted Jace in Hindi.

The sadhu said something to the lower-caste gatekeeper, who stepped aside, allowing him to pass.

Jace ran past the gatekeeper into the warm road that went straight past the residency toward a ghat on the river, but the road was empty.

He ran to the ghat, but any small boats usually tied there were gone. His eyes scanned the glassy waterway and he saw no movement. He walked back to the road, which was hemmed in on one side with a long line of dark shade trees. The sadhu had escaped into their secretive embrace. Tracking him now would be as unwise as walking barefoot among a den of cobras.

Jace paused, hands on hips, turning back to the river, trying to place the religious man in his memory.

Religious? Jace straightened, staring unbelievingly toward the trees. *That face.*

"Rissaldar Sanjay!" he breathed.

The man who had betrayed the 17th had shed his uniform for the masquerade of a Hindu holy man . . . or could it also be that Sanjay *was* a sadhu and the uniform had been a disguise?

He heard soft steps on the dust behind him, and when he turned, Jace had unsheathed his blade. The gatekeeper brought fingers to forehead in a low salute.

"Sneaking up on a man may yet cost your head," stated Jace harshly in the Hindi language. "The sadhu— who is he, where has he gone, what was he doing prowling the British residency?"

"No evil, Huzoor! Holy days are nearing. He came to call upon the Hindu gods for the festival."

"You lie. There were six of you groveling around the feet of the idol when I came in. Where are the others?"

"Huzoor, I lie not. I know not where the others are now. They have left to do their duties."

Jace murmured in English, knowing the man did not understand. "You take the English for fools. Well maybe we are, seeing how we allowed ourselves to be trapped here in Guwahati with nothing but a handful of fighting men."

The gatekeeper only salaamed deeply and drew back toward his post.

Jace left and headed in the direction of the palace grounds. The sadhu, whom Jace was now certain to be Sanjay, would inform Prince Sunil of what he had overheard between Ethan and Sir Hugo, but he probably wouldn't go directly to the dewan's chambers, knowing that Jace might have recognized him and could go there to confront him. Nor would Sanjay wish to implicate the dewan in the mutiny, for he couldn't be sure that Jace knew their plans.

No, thought Jace. He would waste time if he went to search for Sanjay now. Perhaps he would find yet another disguise. Where he was now was anyone's guess, but he might have circled back to rejoin the others who had gathered at the idol of Kali. As much as Jace wished to capture Sanjay, a confrontation must wait.

It was Ethan whom he must see first. Jace frowned. Ethan did not know how much danger he was in. He was foolish to have blundered into Sir Hugo's house and boldly inform him of his refusal to cooperate. He should have known that servants would overhear, that few could be trusted when a mutiny against the British hung in the air like incense offered to Kali. Even if they did not agree with the mutiny, few would prove so loyal as to side with the British if violence struck. The English were not wanted here, and the maharaja had displeased many by signing a treaty with Company officials.

Jace slipped through the trees and walked in the direction of the royal palace, its white stone with inlaid marble reflecting in the moonlight. He frowned as he walked, thinking of Ethan. Jace was not one to suddenly develop sympathy for Boswell, but he did sense a certain unease over the man's situation in Guwahati. Not that his own was much better, he thought. Aside from Gokul, and perhaps one or two sepoys from the outpost at Jorhat, he doubted the loyalty of the guard.

But Ethan was another matter. He knew what Sir Hugo and Prince Sunil had in mind for the maharaja. If Sunil heard about the disturbance he had made tonight at the residency, he would think nothing of killing a stubborn Englishman. Sir Hugo knew this and would strive to keep his iron grip on Ethan's resolution. Jace was determined that Ethan would talk.

The night air was heavy with jungle smells. His hearing was attuned to the noises of the river lapping the bank and the piping of birds. Cautious, lest an assassin's dagger find him with unexpected accuracy, he kept close to the outer trees.

The dislike between him and Ethan would most likely cause the doctor to rebel when it came to cooperation over the maharaja. Jace had not forgotten that night at the palace when Ethan had come into the garden and found him and Coral together.

Jace quickened his stride. No matter. He would make Ethan talk. Lives depended on it, and however either of them may feel about Kendall's daughter, they must cooperate. Ethan would bring him to the maharaja. But would Maharaja Majid Singh talk of what he knew?

Jace thought of the small stolen idol of Kali. Solid gold and embedded with sapphires, emeralds, and rubies, it was worth much. Although the maharaja desired its return, Jace would need it when he met with the local warlord, Zin, on the border with Burma. Convincing the maharaja to wait would prove a bit difficult, he thought dryly. And so would retrieving it back again from Zin when the warlord left his compound.

Jace's eyes narrowed. Before this episode of intrigue was over he might get himself killed. For one moment he found himself wondering what Coral would do if Gokul did end up bringing her news that Jace Buckley was dead. He absently rubbed the side of his face, remembering her slap the night of the dinner party, then rebuked his wandering mind. If he were to stay alive he must keep alert.

Jace figured that Sunil knew him well enough to know that he had the gold idol. Jace had always suspected that Sunil had worked with Zin and his son to steal it from the temple in Burma. It might have been Sunil who had killed Zin's son, Ayub Khan.

Sunil was also looking for the jewel-studded relic.

As Jace neared his quarters he saw a faint glimmer

in the window. It disappeared. Was Sunil foolish enough to send the rajput guard—or even Sanjay—to search his quarters?

Jace approached the door, hearing a faint rustle of garments. He lifted his sword from its scabbard and reached for the doorknob.

2

His silhouette in the open doorway with the moon-light behind him would prove a perfect target—not for one of Sunil's warriors bearing a sword, but for a dagger, the way of assassins, thought Jace. He knew well the ways of intrigue in the dark underworld of the East.

He stood outside his quarters and coolly sheathed his sword. Instead, with deft fingers he reached beneath his jacket sleeve and drew the deadly stiletto dagger from its concealed wrist sheath.

Jace flung open the door, hit the floor rolling, and stopped in a crouched position on the other side of the room.

A glimmer of dim light from a lantern under a rattan stool cast its glow across the floor matting. His gaze searched the room.

Wearing a black turban and jacket to keep from being seen, the assassin, tough and lean, turned to face him. With a whisper, the man hurled his blade. Jace had expected it and threw his stiletto with deadly accuracy. The assassin's two hands went up to grip the hilt protruding from his chest, and he fell to his knees.

Jace remained where he was. Outside, the river

breeze brushed against a shade tree, and a bird cackled.

He made careful search of his chamber, and swiftly packed his satchel and went out into the night. There was little time to find Ethan.

———

Ethan's nerves felt like dry thorns ready for the fire. Although he was alone in his bedroom chamber in the maharaja's palace, he continued to feel as if eyes watched him—unfriendly eyes. His chamber was on the second floor close to the king, to whom he was to give medical treatment. *Aside from a flare-up of gout, there is nothing ailing the maharaja,* he thought, his gray eyes cool.

Wearing a satin robe, Ethan sat cross-legged on a thick rug woven with blue and crimson silk. Directly in front of him there was a low marble table veined with gold. His slender hand held a feathered quill, which he dipped into a black and gold ceramic inkpot on the table beside the letter he was writing to Coral.

Again, he sensed eyes watching him and casually lifted his head, the lantern light catching the fair strands of his hair. He scanned the large chamber with its intricate stonework and inlaid marble veined with blue and gold. Woven hangings of Hindu idol-gods draped the walls. Ethan stared at them. Perhaps these were the probing eyes he felt. *Idols,* he thought, and some of the words from Psalm 135 came to mind. Coral had read a verse to him in Hindi, then translated into English while they had been standing near the great Hindu temple in Guwahati.

"Eyes have they, but they see not; they have ears, but they hear not. . . ."

He hoped the cold, lifeless eyes that stared down at him now were not peepholes for spies. The palace was large, and there were no doubt many secret chambers and passages throughout. Yet, Ethan saw nothing to validate his discomfort. He glanced to the side where an open verandah looked down on an inner court.

He set his quill down and arose, walking out on the verandah. The night was ominously still, the weather muggy. Would he ever become used to India's climate?

Beyond the inner court there was a wall with gate-towers, and torchlight reflected on a rajput guard. The palace itself was built on the half-circle bank overlooking the Brahmaputra River, and Ethan could see small lighted boats on the water belonging to fishermen or village traders.

Convinced that his feeling of apprehension was the harvest of his inability to persuade Hugo, he turned away from watching the night and went back inside his chamber to end his letter to Coral. He briefly informed her of his change of plans to not remain in Guwahati—"Matters have changed," he had written, "I will journey to Kingscote after all to set up my lab."

Ethan was signing his name when he heard a faint sound, like a groan. Silence followed. He strained his ears to hear something else, gripping the quill.

Where did the sound come from? The raja's royal chambers?

He stood, staring at the great intricately carved ivory door between his chamber and the hall leading into the raja's royal apartments. Ethan's heart pounded. His slim fingers moved slowly beneath the satin smoothness of his dressing robe to where he had concealed his pistol.

From behind him came a grating sound. He turned, pistol drawn, to face the verandah, and Major Jace Buckley climbed over the rail, casting a glance down to the inner court.

A prick of irritation stung Ethan. It was like Buckley

39

to slip past guards and scale the stone wall successfully.

His thin mouth tightened as he saw Buckley hesitate, a slight smile on his rugged face, his gaze dropping to the pistol in Ethan's hand.

Ethan's temper grew taut, and he deliberately kept the pistol aimed at him, his hand nice and steady. "I told you once I was a crack shot. You might have gotten a bit of your head blown off, Major."

"You've good reason to worry about your own. We need to talk."

Ethan could see a seriousness in Buckley's expression that sobered his own. He lowered the pistol.

"Keep it handy," said Jace. "You're likely to need it before this night is over."

Ethan watched as Jace glanced below in the courtyard again, made a signal, then threw a rope over the side of the railing. A moment later he hauled up a bundle. Evidently someone was below cooperating with him, but who? Surely not the rajput guard that Ethan had seen only minutes ago. . . .

Ethan walked to the desk where he had been writing the letter and sat down, picking up the quill. He said in a low voice, "Stay where you are, Major. Don't come in. I've a feeling we're being watched by a Hindu carving of an elephant mounted high on the wall. I've felt its eyes for the past hour."

Jace stopped at once and remained in the verandah shadows. "Finish your task, look as though you are going to bed, then turn out the lantern."

Ethan did so, grudgingly admiring his simple suggestion. "I heard the guard moan when you struck him. Someone else may have heard. Whoever is below aiding you had best be on the lookout."

"Gokul is an expert at deceit," came the dry retort. "You need not concern yourself. That letter—if it is to

Miss Kendall, forget it."

"I dare say!"

"Relax, old chum, it is her safety I'm thinking about. The less she knows, the better. If you intend to join her at Kingscote, simply show up."

Ethan was surprised that Buckley knew of his change in plans, but said nothing. As though he had changed his mind about what he was writing, Ethan picked up the paper and tore it into bits, then held his head in his hands.

"Good show," came Jace's quip. "Now off to bed like a good chap."

Ethan walked over to the large bed, drew back the satin covers, and climbed in. His eyes looked straight ahead to the elephant on the wall, and he felt an uneasy tingle on the back of his neck. With one hand he reached over and snuffed the lantern. Darkness swallowed up the chamber.

A moment later he heard Jace's light steps enter and cross to the other side. Ethan tossed aside the cover and was on his feet joining him.

"I was at the residency tonight when you confronted Sir Hugo," came Jace's whisper.

Ethan sucked in a breath but felt the major's iron grip on his shoulder.

"I'll have none of your self-righteous complaint at my eavesdropping. Men's lives hang in the balance—including ours. Even if I cared nothing for Sunil's assassination attempt on the raja, I care about my own neck. You'll tell me everything. Be quick about it. We haven't much time."

Ethan felt his indignation rise at the major's superior attitude, one that he had resented from the beginning, but he put a clamp on his feelings and let out a breath of resignation. "As you wish, Major," he whispered stiffly.

"As you know, it is said the maharaja has been in ill health. To the contrary, he is quite fit. I discovered that tonight."

"Was he suspicious of being poisoned by his physicians?"

"No. He said few words and seemed more intent on watching me."

"Then you were not alone with him?"

Ethan tensed as he remembered back earlier that evening. "No. The dewan was there the entire time."

"You mean Sunil?"

"Yes . . . until tonight I did not know he was the raja's nephew."

"You said the raja is fit."

"I made preliminary tests tonight. There is nothing wrong with him except a mild form of gout."

Ethan saw the major digesting the information.

"That will make it easier," said Jace.

"I do not follow you, Major."

"I think you do. I told you I overheard your words with Sir Hugo, so let's not waste time. There's to be an assassination attempt on the maharaja; we both know it. So does Roxbury. He's working with Sunil, for what reasons I've yet to discover, but I doubt if it is profound, only a matter of simple greed. You too are at serious risk now that you've refused to be the instrument of death. What did Sunil ask you to do, poison his uncle?"

Ethan flinched at his blunt questions. They came at him like hammer blows. There was no use denying what had happened. In any case, it was best he knew for the raja's sake. But Ethan refused to bring his uncle—*nay, my father*—into the quagmire of treason.

Ethan whispered tonelessly: "Sunil offered me royal treasure and authority in the palace if I would eliminate his uncle by means of a painless drug. There would be no suffering, no blood. He would die in his sleep."

"The drug being poison."

"Yes, a rare drug I came across in Burma. Sir Hugo knows of it."

"Like the one you used on Coral in London, and again at Manali?"

"If it were not that the noise would bring the guards, you'd be absent your front teeth, Major."

"Is that what you told Sunil?"

Ethan gritted, "I told him to take a swim in the river and make some hungry crocodile happy."

"Sunil, of course, insisted you participate in his plans."

"He did. Said that Sir Hugo Roxbury would see that I obliged, or we would both be dead before we ever rode out of Guwahati."

"You needn't concern yourself for Roxbury; he is in this up to his neck. It is you, old chap, who will soon be dead. I advise you to leave for Kingscote tonight. But first—bring me to the maharaja."

"Are you mad? No one is allowed in the royal chambers!"

"No one except his guards and trusted physician."

Ethan knew that he was the trusted physician, but how this helped to get the major into the royal chamber was beyond his understanding.

"It is out of the question."

"Where does that door lead?"

Ethan followed his gesture to the carved ivory door. "An antechamber. Beyond are the royal apartments— good heavens, Major! You cannot enter. What excuse could I offer for your presence? Besides, it is late and the raja will be asleep—"

Ethan halted, seeing that his argument was wasted. He watched, alert and curious, as Buckley knelt and undid the cord binding a small bundle. Ethan recognized a uniform worn by the royal guards, but this one went beyond the authority of the guard. The rich purple and black told him that this particular garb belonged to the maharaja's chief bodyguard.

"Where did you get that? Or need I ask?"

"Gokul has a degree in the clandestine."

Ethan had no notion who Gokul was, nor did he wish to meet the scoundrel. He watched Jace exchange his uniform for the royal garb and belt on his sword.

"Quick. Get dressed. And don't forget that pistol."

Ethan did so, watching as Buckley proceeded to fold the British uniform, tying it with the cord to take with him. Jace also was a master at the clandestine. Ethan remembered coming upon Coral in the palace garden, and he was certain she had come directly from the major's arms. The muscles in Ethan's jaw hardened. A man like Jace Buckley was a risk. Did Coral have feelings for him?

"I am ready, Major," he said flatly. "Let us hope your comrade Gokul did not leave a dead body lying about for the other guards to stumble across. We'll soon be amidst a swarm of tulwars," he said of the curved Indian blade.

"If we do, your repeated warning of being a crack shot had better be more than boast."

Ethan lifted his head. "You'll not be disappointed."

Jace looked at him, and Ethan thought he saw a faint grin. The major tossed him a scabbard. "How are you with the sword?"

Ethan caught it with one hand. "I'm a bit rusty on my fencing lessons, but I'll do my best should it come to that."

"Another thing. I was not the only one who overheard you tonight. Sanjay was in the garden."

Ethan was trying to notch the belt of the scabbard

around his lean hips. At the mention of Rissaldar Sanjay he paused. Buckley believed Sanjay had betrayed the 17th outside Plassey Junction.

"You do well to look worried," said Jace. "I suspect he will soon report what he heard to Sunil. When he does, Sunil will decide you are a risk to his plans. He will fear what he believes to be a nervous, uncooperative pawn. They are always a risk. Elimination is the safeguard."

Ethan tensed but said nothing. He had already suspected Sunil might feel this way about him. It was the reason for his change in plans and his decision to go on to Kingscote.

"Sir Hugo will have something to say to Prince Sunil," said Ethan after a moment.

"This is one time when even Sir Hugo is in deeper than he can swim out. He's come up against the world of Eastern assassins. He knows you are in danger; he'll do what he can, but he's likely to discover that his own sins are weights about his neck. What does the writer of Proverbs say—'A man's sins bind him in their own cord'? Roxbury's schemes have trapped even him."

"Sir Hugo is not involved in this treachery," Ethan found himself saying, but his lame excuses were hollow and he knew it.

"He was working with Harrington and Zameen in Calcutta and Manali. It was Sunil who sent Sanjay to Calcutta masquerading as a rissaldar from Jorhat, and Roxbury was in on it from the beginning. He knew about the mutiny at Plassey, and things went according to schedule—except that I survived the attack. I was meant to die with the sowars of the 17th. He wanted me dead. He still does. He and Sunil both expect me to ride out tonight for Darjeeling. I've no doubt that Sunil has another assassin waiting. This time they intend to make sure I remain lying on the road. And that goes for Sir Hampton too. He left weeks ago and I fear he's already dead."

Ethan felt the blow of his words. Coral rushed to mind. *If Sir Hampton is dead* . . .

Ethan had already guessed about Harrington and Zameen upon arrival at Manali. He had overheard Hugo talking with Harrington about a secret meeting they had undertaken at Barrackpore. Harrington had come in masquerade as an Indian to report to Sir Hugo from Prince Sunil that the ambush at Plassey was set. Harrington had been worried that he was seen by one of the Kendall daughters in the Canterbury House garden at the Christmas Ball, but Hugo assured him at Manali that he had not been identified. Ethan did not know for certain who had drugged Coral at Harrington's house, but he suspected his uncle. The drug had temporarily eliminated her from delving into matters that Sir Hugo knew would threaten them all. It had been a crude tactic, the second incident since the weeks that were spent at Roxbury House on the Strand, but his uncle often resorted to drugs in order to accomplish his plans. Ethan had gone along with the spider bite story to protect not only Coral but also her sisters. The scare had diverted them from becoming further entangled with Zameen, a man that Ethan thought to be more dangerous than even Harrington. He believed that Zameen served Prince Sunil. . . .

"Sir Hugo is like the cunning trapper who lures a den of cobras, only to fall in with them," Jace was saying. "If I were you, I'd be thinking about saving my own neck, and let him take care of his. If you don't, you'll end up bedding down with the serpents along with him."

"Rest assured, Major, I've every intention of saving my life. I have too many humanitarian plans for my medical research to see them foiled now."

"Yes, I am sure you do."

Ethan felt his frustration boil over at the smooth jab in the major's voice. He whispered harshly, "And as for your rendezvous with Coral in the garden, it will change nothing where she and I are concerned."

Jace turned his head and gave him a look that Ethan believed would have felt as sharp as a dagger.

"Get one thing straight, Ethan. Whatever there might or might not be between Coral and me is none of your business, and that includes our so-called rendezvous. Let's go."

Ethan stiffened. "When this predicament has spent itself, Major, I think there will be only one decent recourse left for both of us, and that is a duel."

Jace gave a short laugh. "You are actually serious."

"Indeed."

Jace paused, cocking his head as he scanned him. "A gentleman's way out of a sticky mess, no doubt."

"Exactly, Major. It is the decent way such matters are resolved in Europe, or have you been so long in India you have forgotten the code of honor among gentlemen?"

Jace smirked. "I've not forgotten, Doctor. But you see, India offers the easiest solution of all."

Ethan felt uncomfortable under the mocking gaze. "And what, Major, might that be?"

"I could simply leave you for Sunil. He'll lop off your head with his tulwar and save me the trouble." Jace walked to the door leading to the antechamber.

Ethan felt his face flush and was glad for the darkness. "You dare make a jest!"

"If it will make you feel better, Doctor, I promise to take you up on your offer. That is, should I decide to eliminate Coral's most vocal suitor. I've no question in my mind but that I would win."

Ethan stood in silent anger. The man's arrogance was not to be borne. "I would not count on that, Major."

"If we do not soon meet with the maharaja and leave this palace, neither of us will be around to see Miss Kendall happily married to Charles Peddington," came the jibe.

———

Jace's thoughts had already sought out every possible escape route, every stratagem, every ruse. Yet none were sure, and he wondered what information the raja would decide to give him, if any.

The door into the antechamber opened and Jace followed Ethan inside. "Be careful," Ethan said in a low voice as they neared the door into the royal chambers. "The guard is as wary as a reptile."

While Jace stood in the shadows, Ethan knocked on a second door made of heavy timber bound with straps of iron. The door opened, and a huge, powerfully muscled man stood there with a massive sword. Ethan gripped his medical bag and began to make a great fuss about the necessity of seeing the raja *immediately*.

"Be gone. His Excellency will not see you again tonight."

"I must see him. His health is at risk."

The guard began to shut the door with a scowl.

Ethan surprised even Jace by putting his foot in the door and raising his voice: "Close this door on me and you shall be called in question by Dewan Sunil! The Prince has solicited my medical knowledge to tend to his uncle and I insist you open up at once."

Jace reinforced his move by stepping forward and speaking rapidly in Hindi. "Step aside! You waste the physician's time."

The guard came alert when he saw Jace in the garb

of the chief bodyguard. "Where is Atool?" he demanded, reaching for his tulwar.

Jace drew his blade and stepped back, point lifted. "You dare threaten your new commander? I am Rajendra, appointed to be chief bodyguard by His Excellency Sunil."

The guard's cold eyes probed as if to know Jace's heart. "Where is Atool!"

"Dead," gritted Jace. "A fool who committed treason against Prince Sunil."

A noticeable twitch of surprise, then uncertainty over his own position showed in his face.

"Unlock the door *now.* If not, I shall delight to spill your innards on the floor," said Jace.

The guard warily stepped aside. "Move," ordered Jace, gesturing toward the royal ivory door veined with gold.

The guard turned a key in the lock and the door opened. Jace glanced at Ethan, who took the advantage and swiftly passed into the chambers.

"Who comes?" a tired voice called out.

The guard started to speak, but Jace's voice speaking Hindi overrode his. "A man you can trust with your life, Excellency. I bring news for your ears alone. I come in the company of the English physician Doctor Ethan Boswell."

The maharaja gestured the guard to silence. "Your name?"

Jace took a risk, but it seemed the only way to assure an audience. "Javed Kasam."

In the silence that followed, Jace suspected that he had the maharaja's alert attention, although he could not yet see him.

"Kahn, light the lantern then leave us."

The guard did so, then shut the royal door behind

him. Jace heard the key turn in the lock. Was there another exit from the chamber?

In the golden glow of ornate lanterns, Jace saw the Maharaja Majid Singh sitting on a dais. The old king was pale, but his black eyes were lively and suddenly interested in the two men. "Step forward, Javed Kasam."

Jace neared the imposing platform knowing that Singh was aware of who he was, and that the past disguise of Javed Kasam identified him as a member of the underworld of Eastern intrigue. He was quite certain that the gold idol of Kali was also much on Singh's mind.

"What is the nature of your news from Burma?"

Truth must be his guard. "I have not yet met with Zin."

"Ah?" The maharaja's fingers tapped upon his silken knee.

"I must go into Burma as quickly as time permits me, Excellency. Since Roxbury has released me from my duties as captain of his Security Guard, I shall leave tonight."

"He released you from your position? Why?"

"His motives are suspect. I would advise you to not trust him, nor your own nephew, Prince Sunil."

If his words shocked him, Singh did not blanch. He studied Jace with attention.

"The British military has sent me to discover the true motive behind the mutiny at Jorhat. While the governor-general's ambassador insists Burma was behind the attack, we have reason to suspect intrigue."

"By the use of *we*, do you mean to imply the British government at Calcutta?"

"I speak of myself and Colonel John Warbeck. Roxbury has deceived the governor-general. I believe he is working with your nephew to have you killed."

The maharaja remained calm, and only his eyes

showed his internal rage. "I see you speak the truth, Major Buckley. I believe you can be trusted. So I shall confide that such news has long been known by me. I am outnumbered by men loyal to Sunil. A power struggle goes on within the palace, and my life is in question. The struggle may go yet farther, reaching even into the palace of Raja Singh in Sibsagar."

"Your Excellency, you have a treaty with the British government. The troops assigned to me for security purposes have been killed in an ambush designed by your enemies here in Guwahati. I have no more than six or seven soldiers I would trust with plans for your protection. I suggest you do not contest your nephew, but leave the palace to him and his followers until British troops arrive in force under Captain MacKay to put down the mutiny and secure your throne. You must leave Guwahati tonight."

"I have made secret plans already to leave for Burma."

Jace showed surprise at the mention of Burma. Singh saw it and said, "He is my enemy, but I have no choice but to go there." He stood.

"Have you men in the palace loyal to your throne?"

"Not as many as I first thought. Khan, my guard, has discovered much by pretending loyalty to Sunil. I have a dozen rajputs, no more. Sunil has inflamed the ghazis against me by convincing them I have brought in the Western religion to insult the brahmins. Many of the brahmins have been quietly preparing for a mutiny under Sunil. I can do nothing to stop it."

"We must leave Guwahati tonight, Excellency. The guard at the door, can he be trusted?"

"Khan, he would die for me."

"Have him send word to those rajputs loyal to you to prepare supplies and horses. We will meet them outside the gate near the river in an hour."

51

"An hour!"

"There is no time, Excellency. A spy for Prince Sunil will soon report to him that the English physician would not cooperate in your death. Knowing Sunil, he will take no chances. He will strike at once with his assassins."

The maharaja frowned but nodded agreement. He sighed. "As your British poets declare, Major, uneasy is the head that wears the crown. An hour it shall be. I have a personal attendant I can also trust. He will prepare me for travel."

Jace thought of the gold idol of Kali. He also thought of Gem, and as he did, it was Coral's face he saw—her green eyes, and her intense pleading. He had trusted the maharaja with the truth, and in return the king had confided in him. Now he must also make good his vow to Coral, whatever the risk to himself. "One thing more, Your Excellency. Rajiv was a friend of mine. I cannot forget that someone commanded the assassin's dagger to be used on him while he took quiet refuge from your displeasure on the Kendall lands."

"You are mistaken. It was not my wrath he fled but Sunil's. I gave no order for his death, nor for the abduction of his son, Prince Adesh."

"Then I am correct in believing the child has royal blood, despite Jemani. He is not an untouchable."

"Prince Adesh is heir to my throne." The maharaja was weary and ashen as he slowly lowered himself into his seat. "It was Sunil who first loved Jemani, and he sought a wedding to take place with her, but she did not trust him and fell in love with his older brother. Sunil tried to have Rajiv killed here in Guwahati after the marriage, and it was then that both he and Jemani disappeared."

"And the family of Jemani?" asked Jace cautiously.

"I do not know. Perhaps from a brahmin guru in Rajasthan, but I cannot vow to this. After Rajiv and Jemani left Guwahati I searched for them but knew not where they were, and I suspected them both dead, that Sunil had them assassinated. It was then that news arrived to me secretly that Rajiv was masquerading as a man of low caste on the Kendall plantation near Jorhat."

Jace thought of Kingscote, of Coral, and his unease mounted. "May I ask who sent you that information, Excellency? It may be important for the lives of others involved."

The maharaja shook his gray head. "I do not know for certain. It was unsigned."

"It came by a messenger?"

"Yes. I did not speak with him, but somehow I believed the message was sent from Kendall's Kingscote, or very near the border. There are Burmese renegades hiding in the jungle who often prowl the road. It has been suggested one of these Burmese soldiers sent the message."

Jace wondered . . . *Burmese renegade? But who! Warlord Zin is far from a petty rebel living in the jungle.* And the news only heightened his concerns for Coral. Sir Hampton was not there to protect his wife and three daughters. *But Seward is there. . . .*

"Sunil must have discovered about the secret message sent to me and arranged Rajiv's death."

Jace masked his tension. If Sunil knew that Zin had Gem. . . . The question must be asked.

"Then Prince Sunil has discovered where Prince Adesh is?"

"Sunil? No! Sunil searches for him this very moment. It is the reason I must go to Burma to Warlord Zin!"

"Then you know that Zin has Prince Adesh," said Jace with masked surprise.

"Yes. It was Zin who had him abducted, perhaps with

the help of renegade sepoys and Burmese infiltrators who are enemies of the English on Kingscote. The warlord has held him these years as ransom. If I do not pay handsomely as he requests, he threatens to alert Sunil, to turn him over for the highest gift of rubies and emeralds. I could do nothing but capitulate." The maharaja leaned forward anxiously. "I must go to Zin. Both I and Adesh are at risk from Sunil. From the wealth of the house of Singh I will buy protection from Zin and his warriors. I am in no position to bargain my own terms. But at least I have secretly sent the best of our scholars to train little Prince Adesh to rule after me. Zin allowed this. He has grown fat on my riches."

"And Sunil? He does not suspect?"

His smile faded. "No. He thought Adesh dead until recently. I believe he received secret information that the boy is alive after all and sought by the Englishwoman. Sunil has been searching diligently. He went to Zin asking questions, offering great prizes for information, but Zin is also clever and greedy. He will continue to play us one against another until he is certain to receive the highest prize for the prince. I have been paying him well; yet my own spies have reported seeing Sunil with Zin on the Burmese border. That is why I must go there. Not only for my safety but for little Adesh."

Jace was thinking of Zin. His friendship was weak at best and easily bought for the highest bid. Gem was far from being secure. And when Sunil found out for certain that Zin had the child . . .

"This is most amazing news, Your Excellency. Gem Kendall alive and in Burma!" breathed Ethan.

Jace had nearly forgotten Ethan was in the chamber. Evidently so had the raja, for he looked sharply in the doctor's direction, his eyes cold.

"There is no such child as Gem Kendall, Doctor Boswell. Rajiv's son is Prince Adesh Singh, heir to kingship in Guwahati. Nor is my grandnephew to embrace the foreign religion of the West. I regret Sahib Kendall's daughter involved herself in matters that were none of her own, but she shall not have him back as her son."

Ethan flushed under his tan and started to protest, but Jace interrupted him with a warning stare. "The maharaja is right, Ethan. Miss Kendall was in error. She thought she was adopting an orphan, a mere untouchable, born from a humble maid and a friend . . . but Gem is royalty and as such she could not adopt him."

"I beg pardon, Major. But from what Miss Kendall has confided in me, Jemani entrusted her son to her at death. The law will have something to say about this—"

"This is not the time to protest the fate of the maharaja's grandnephew," Jace gritted, angry that Ethan would risk the raja's cooperation by throwing his allegiance to the side of Coral. "I advise you send for Khan," said Jace.

When the burly guard had received his secret orders and went to implement them, the maharaja left the chamber to ready himself for the journey to Burma. Jace turned on Ethan. "Do me a favor, Doctor. Keep your opinions to yourself in the presence of the raja. Don't you realize if Singh believes I want to find the boy for Coral's sake that he'll cease all further cooperation with me?"

"The man is obnoxious. Gem legally belongs to Coral under the laws of adoption. I'll not stand by and see her treated with scorn. If Gem is alive, then I shall go with you to rescue him."

Jace measured him, his irritation growing. Ethan was like a grain of sand in the eye. He remembered the confrontation over the sacrifice to Kali on the river safari and how it almost cost them the boats. "When it comes to risking my neck, I work alone. I advise you to get out of Guwahati while you still have your own. Leave the matter that concerns Coral to me."

"You would like it so, would you not? But when it comes to Coral, I have more to say about what concerns her than you do, Major. If Gem is alive, then I shall lend my hand to help in his rescue."

Jace's irritation grew. "You are rather late, aren't you? In London you worked with Roxbury to try to force Coral into accepting the child's death."

"Are you insinuating I deliberately tried to deceive her about his fate?"

Jace answered with a cool smile.

Ethan flushed. "I truly believed the boy was dead."

"And Coral was emotionally ill," quipped Jace.

"We've no time to waste debating. All that is in the past. I was wrong. I've asked her to understand my dilemma, and she has. I'm coming with you to Burma."

"As I said, I work alone."

"Don't be so arrogant, Major! You need another man; you're hopelessly outnumbered. I'm doing this for Coral, not for you. . . . It so happens that I proposed marriage to her after what happened between you and her in the garden."

Jace's eyes met Ethan's evenly. His jaw set.

"She accepted," said Ethan. "That was the main reason I informed Hugo tonight that I am leaving in the morning. We intend to marry immediately."

Immediately. The word left Jace stunned. Coral wouldn't marry Ethan in order to hurt him—or would she?

Pride kept him from probing, for he believed Ethan's boast just might prove true. He felt a sudden anger toward Coral. She might have at least waited until he returned from Burma, but instead she had agreed to marry Ethan on the very night he had held her in his arms and kissed her. "Congratulations," he said flatly.

"I am pleased to see you are wise enough to accept the news without calling for a duel."

"As I recall, the 'code of honor among gentlemen' already demands that we have one. Have you changed your mind?"

Ethan scanned him. "Are you saying that is what you wish?"

"If Miss Kendall wishes to spend her life helping you dissect bugs on Kingscote, far be it from me to send you to an early grave," he said flippantly. "No. Let her marry you. Sorry I won't be around for the wedding. After Burma, I have an appointment with the *Madras*."

"I'm pleased you see it that way, Major."

"A suggestion, Doctor: If you treasure winning Kendall's daughter, you had best pack your bags and ride to Kingscote tonight. It is going to get ugly before the matter of the raja and Gem is over."

Ethan smiled thinly. "You think I am unwise enough to retreat to Kingscote so you can be the hero who brings Gem home? You do not deceive me, Major. You want the accolade of victory on your own brow, hoping to change her mind about me."

"The only accolade Kendall's daughter is interested in lies within your grasp. If you were wise you'd ride out tonight. Start building her school on Kingscote and there's not a man who could turn her against you. But come to Burma and you will take on more than you're capable of handling. You are a doctor, not a mercenary soldier."

"She already knows I support the work for the children. I've promised to aid her with my medical knowledge. But since I'm to be her husband, I'll not sit back now and allow you to be the one to rescue Gem."

Jace felt a strange dart of jealousy. It angered him

that Ethan's boast could goad him like this. *She agreed to marry Ethan without so much as a second thought.* "As you wish, Doctor. But get one thing straight. My sword is committed to the survival of the others first. You are on your own."

"As I keep telling you, Major, I am well able to take care of myself."

"Yes, I know, you are a 'crack shot.' I hope you speak the truth. I should hate to leave you in some hastily dug grave between here and Burma."

Ethan's gray eyes went hard and cold. "It may be *your* unexpected fate, Major. An ironic twist to come at the end of our unhappy drama. I shall, however, comfort Coral and graciously acclaim you to be the hero after all. I could afford to do so, since I will be the one to walk back to Kingscote to her." Ethan turned his back and walked to meet the maharaja.

Jace saw that the raja was dressed for travel, wearing the rugged warrior's dress of a rajput with a belted sword. His somber attendant carried only one bag, but his grip on the handle alerted Jace to the importance of its contents.

Jewels, no doubt. He thought of the gold statue of Kali but said nothing yet. If the maharaja had too much on his mind to remember, the idol would benefit his meeting with Zin. Jace intended to use it to buy Gem's freedom.

A moment later the guard Khan arrived. Jace studied him, wondering if he could trust him. The maharaja did, but kings could be wrong about their closest guards; only they never lived long enough to tell about it.

Khan spoke low in the native tongue. "Everything is in order, Excellency. The warriors are now with the horses waiting by the river."

Jace turned to the maharaja. "Let us leave at once before Sunil has time to make plans. By morning there won't be one of us alive."

3

The maharaja trusted Khan explicitly, so Jace resigned himself to do the same. Yet he watched him carefully. The guard led them through a secret passage to a
stone-flagged chamber where other warriors waited.
Jace felt the penetrating eyes and immobile faces. They
did not seem readily disposed toward Ethan, perhaps
wondering if he could fight if it came to that.

Khan handed each of them a black cloak. He glanced
at Jace's sword, noting that his hand rested there. Jace
suspected he was remembering his threat at the door of
the royal chamber.

Horses awaited them as promised, and a second
guard of men. Jace made it a point to study each man's
face. He would not be deceived again by Sanjay.

The alley down which they rode was unpaved, and
the horses made no sound. As they neared a postern gate
it opened, allowing them to pass, then silently closed
behind them. Jace rode guard beside the maharaja, with
Khan on the king's left. Jace had to respect the old king,
who was willing to risk his palace and crown to Sunil
during his absence in order to protect not only his own
life but Gem's—or had he best begin thinking of Gem

Kendall as Prince Adesh Singh?

He imagined Coral's pain over future events. Whatever may happen in Burma, her relationship to Gem would never be the same. She could never go back to the time in the Kendall nursery when she had looked upon the baby as her own son.

Saddles creaked in the night, a breeze stirred from off the wide, dark river. The moon was setting over the Brahmaputra, and the night was still. Too still, thought Jace. He glanced into the darkness but saw nothing. Then a lone figure emerged from the trees and rode toward them. Some of the guards drew swords and reined in their horses.

Gokul came riding up, his dusty white turban showing in the moonlight. Seeing the maharaja, he salaamed, then his eyes searched the group of warriors for Jace. At last he recognized him wearing the garb of the chief bodyguard.

Jace maneuvered his horse forward from the others and rode to meet him. "It is time you finally arrived, old friend," he said in a low voice. "I was beginning to believe temptation had won the day. Did you have trouble?"

Gokul pretended an injury to his feelings. "Sahib! Would I steal gold statue of Kali and leave you in what—how do you say?—'tight spot'? Nay, Kali is safely wrapped in sacred cloth so she cannot crawl out. All set for Zin to see and drool over like a starving jackal."

"What took you so long?"

Gokul looked indignant and rested a hand on his soft belly. "Sahib, you hide treasure in a bird nest high in banyan tree. You dare ask poor Gokul with belly what takes me long? I was made to scheme, to sell goods at the bazaar, to spy, and not as you English say—'shimmy up tree'—to loot bird's nest."

Jace smiled. "Never mind. No one must see you give

it to me now. If you let anything happen to it—"

"Sahib! I guard it with my life."

Jace knew that he would. He grew sober. "Gokul . . . do not look now, but do you see the man who is the maharaja's trusty guard? His name is Khan. What do you know of him?"

Gokul reached into a cotton bag tied to his saddle and drew out a bright orange mango. He bit into it, and as he spat out the skin, his shrewd black eyes drifted casually over the fierce fighting rajputs with their long faces and dark beards, his gaze coming to rest on Khan, seated on the horse next to the maharaja. "He has served His Excellency for three years, and I can find no suspicion. He is loyal. So are all these rajputs. We have good company for the ride to the Burmese border, sahib."

Jace briefly explained about Sanjay and the danger of his reporting the conversation between Ethan and Sir Hugo to Prince Sunil. He briefly mentioned the assassin he had confronted in his quarters.

"Dark news about Sanjay. You will play hard battle to snare so slippery a fish, sahib. If you think to bring him to Calcutta to face rifles of the military for treason, it be best to kill him now, here. Sunil will—"

Jace was not listening. His tension suddenly mounted. His heart began to thud in his chest. He raised a hand to silence Gokul, all the while straining to hear off in the distance. The sound came from the royal stables . . . where the maharaja kept the war elephants. . . .

That noise. What was it? He listened in the darkness. The sound grew louder. Gokul heard too. He straightened in his saddle, his eyes darting to Jace. The others began to understand. The maharaja stirred and looked about. The captain of the rajput guard gave a shouting command. In unison they drew their mighty horn bows and reached for arrows. Jace unsheathed his sword and wished instead for cannon! A battle was about to break forth upon them. One that they could not hope to win, or even escape. Death rode the wind.

Someone had betrayed the maharaja by sending word to Sunil of his intended escape. What had first been planned as a secret assassination by poisoning the raja in his sleep had turned into open conflict. Sunil intended to have the maharaja slain before he could escape Guwahati.

The sound they heard were elephants coming, not the docile females used around the women's quarters but first-rank war elephants—mammoth size, known as "full-blooded," selected from young males who had demonstrated endurance and an even temper essential in battle.

Jace rode swiftly to the maharaja and Khan. "Make for the river. I and the rajputs will try to gain you time. You will have only minutes, so go!"

"It is too late," said the maharaja, his dark eyes calm and unafraid. Swiftly he removed huge ruby and emerald rings from his hands and pressed them toward Jace. "These must be protected! They are the royal rings and now belong to Prince Adesh. Care for his life, Major Sahib-Buckley. He is the hope of his people!"

"Khan!" the maharaja shouted. "The chest! Bring it to safety!"

Khan turned instantly to obey, but it was too late for any escape. The elephants were looming like great terrible monsters in the moonlight, their armor glinting as they came.

Jace shouted for the loyal rajputs to make an outer wall guarding the backward escape route of the raja. It would mean their death, all of them. The elephants were invincible. A well-trained war elephant could be valued at a hundred thousand rupees. Experienced commanders had been known to declare one good elephant worth five hundred horses in battle.

Jace heard Gokul ride up beside him. "Leave, Gokul! You are no soldier! Take Ethan and find Roxbury." He turned and shouted at Khan. "Bring the raja to the river! Now!"

They turned to ride, but Sunil's warriors were coming from three directions at once. Jace and the others had only a flash of warning before they heard the sound of trampling elephant feet, of earth ripping, of tulwars clashing in the moonlight, of the trumpeting of the brave warrior-beasts, which were thrilled with battle.

There was no time to reach the river in an attempt to escape. Nor was there any hope. Jace gripped the handle of his sword as a force of steel-armored elephants advanced, their armor glinting in the torchlight. Jace glanced about him, looking for an opening for the maharaja to ride through. There was none. Sunil knew exactly what he was doing, and he would show no mercy now. The rajputs guarding the maharaja could not retreat under the crushing feet of the elephants.

Then they would fight to the death. They would fight honorably for their king, but the clash of their tulwars would prove useless against the armor of the war elephants. Sunil's men were undercover. The war elephants rumbled toward them, their trunks grabbing the maharaja's rajputs and hurling them beneath their crushing feet. The screams of men mingled with the trumpeting.

The ancient rajput war cry sounded from the loyalists defending the maharaja: "RAM! RAM! RAM! RAM!"

Sunil's elephants carried steel howdahs, in which the warriors rode, with arrow slots to allow the archers to aim and shoot without standing. The maharaja's fighting rajputs fell from the screaming horses.

The maharaja, where is he? Jace looked for him but

could not see him in the chaotic attack. Had Khan some-how been able to harry him away?

Then he saw him—just as the elephant grasped him from the saddle and flung him to the ground beneath its feet.

A musket shot was fired from the long barrel of an Indian matchlock, and Jace felt a blow sear his forehead, leaving his brain ringing. Stunned, he felt himself spin-ning out of control into hot blackness. For a moment his ears were filled with the noise of battle, yet he could see nothing. He felt something wet and warm running into his eyes, mingling with sweat. For a moment his head felt on fire. Darkness consumed him, yet he was con-scious.

"Sahib! This way!"

The muddled voice belonged to Gokul.

Into his darkened vision there sprang up tiny flames. It took a moment to understand that the flames were real; they were torches. He could see again, but the mov-ing forms ahead of him appeared like shadows. He ran a hand across his eyes. His vision continued to clear. . . . Rajputs were fighting with two and three arrows in their bodies, their curved swords slashing as they fought on as though possessed, unaware that their maharaja was dead. In the confusion and darkness the battle raged.

Gokul was beside him, his dark eyes fierce and deter-mined. "Sahib! There is a way! Will you die also? Flee for the sake of all tomorrows!"

Jace looked into the sweat and dust-stained face of Gokul. He could not answer him. He would not flee. Though all was useless, his fighting spirit seemed to merge with the rajputs and he could not turn his back on the warriors. One of Sunil's men rode toward them, lifting his tulwar to take the head of Gokul. For a moment Jace's emotions screamed rage, then turned heavenward in a cry of petition. *God Most High! Not Gokul—please! Do with me as you will! But do not take him! He is not ready for eternity!*

Jace's sword could not stop the slicing blow. As though the scene played out before his eyes in slow motion, his own hand reached for the pistol on his saddle. But the Indian warrior moved a second ahead of him in the attack. As he swung the curved blade for Gokul's head a pistol fired from somewhere in the hot night; a small flame leaped, landing with deadly accuracy between the eyes of the Indian warrior. He appeared to freeze, then the tulwar fell from his hand as he slid from the side of his armored horse.

Jace knew that he had not fired that shot. He turned his head and saw Ethan calmly reloading his pistol from where he had taken partial shield in a tree limb.

But as if in mockery, an arrow whizzed, striking Gokul in the back.

Jace grabbed the reins of Gokul's frightened horse, intent on making for the riverbank. It had taken the near death of Gokul, and now the arrow, to breed new sanity into his emotions. He rode beneath the tree where Ethan straddled a limb, slowed, and reached up as Ethan grabbed hold. They raced into the night, leaving the agony of the ugly ambush behind.

At the river they could hear the elephants. Jace had no recourse but to stop and take refuge in the grasses. The arrow must be removed. He and Ethan knelt in the grass, breathing heavily as they laid Gokul on his stomach. He was unconscious, and Jace feared the arrow was tipped with cobra venom, or any number of Indian drugs—which he could not survive.

"It does not look good, Major. I think your friend is in ultimate decline."

Ultimate decline . . . what a way to put it. At that

moment, and since the pistol shot rang out, Jace felt a grudging respect for Ethan.

"Poison?" Jace found his dull voice inquiring. His own mind was again weaving in and out of mental darkness. His head throbbed.

"I do not know . . . I cannot say for certain. We'll know soon enough." Ethan listened to the old man's heart. He frowned and slowly shook his head from side to side as though he had no answer.

All of a sudden Jace was flooded with emotions he thought no longer existed within him, emotions that had died in his youth. Now they broke within like the bursting of a dam—pain, loss, gut-wrenching loss that tasted like gall in his mouth. Death, hell, and the grave pointed a bony, accusing finger.

A voice seemed to come from far away: *Death is swallowed up in victory. The choice is yours to make. Choose life. Rebuke the harvest of death.*

Where had he heard those very words before? Had he read them? The Scriptures of course . . . where were they?

His hand, stiff from battle, fumbled under his tunic to touch Michael Kendall's Bible. No one knew he carried it everywhere he went. He touched it, but could do no more than feel the cool leather. Thoughts of Michael brought a little whiff of breeze like a summer's night in youth when friends and loved ones were gathered. Laughter seemed to ring out—

But the harsh wind blew them away. He felt sweat sting the cuts and abrasions on his face. From Guwahati, the distant sounds of death, terror, and elephants trumpeting blew toward him. Dimly, and without emotion, he was aware that other Indian guards must have joined the fighting on behalf of the maharaja, not realizing that their gray-haired king was dead. But in all the world of

68

India at that moment, there was only one friend his heart reached out for. Gokul. The man who had been both servant and father, peer and friend. He was losing him, losing the last person who had been in his life since childhood.

Jace stared down at him. *What will I do without you, old friend? Goldfish will miss you,* he wanted to say, giving in to a torrent of raw emotion. His vision was clouded, and he closed his eyes tightly, trying to refocus.

Gokul could never be replaced. Despite the jesting that often went on between them, despite their differences that often got Jace into tight spots—such as when Gokul had leased out the *Madras* to John Company— Gokul's loyalty was real, real enough to die for Jace, and Jace would risk his life for the old munshi who had befriended him as a boy escaping slavery in China.

Jace listened to the labored breathing that was soon to fall silent for all eternity. *Eternity.* How that word unexpectedly lashed through his heart, bringing pain. With a reality that brought tears, Jace tasted the threat of eternal separation that would come between them, realizing he had done too little for the soul of one who was a true friend.

Tears were strangers to Jace, yet they came calling, despite his struggle to hold them back. His jaw clamped, and his hand formed a fist until his nails cut into the flesh of his palm. He had not tasted salty tears since he was a child watching helplessly behind a rock as his father was beheaded on the beach by a Chinese warlord. Now that the flood of emotion had broken free, he could not stop it.

Helpless to rescue Gokul from eternal blackness, he reached out and laid a hand on his head. His gaze met Ethan's, whose face was wet with sweat, and a strange look of understanding showed in his eyes.

"Sorry, Jace."

Jace was oblivious to Ethan, to anything. He wearily leaned and rested his dark head against Gokul's, hearing his labored breathing becoming more and more weak.

Ethan stood, staring not at Gokul's still body in the dried grass, but at Jace. Then he turned and walked to the Brahmaputra River, knelt, and drew handfuls of water to splash against his face.

Strange that I would think of Coral now, thought Jace. He yearned to embrace her, to forget all the loss and ugliness.

Jace wanted to pray, not only for Gokul but for himself—to open wide his own heart to Christ in confession of his self-will, of his refusal to let go of the reins of his life to the One who had so majestically and wisely designed the universe. Too often he had chosen to back away from Him. Too often he had refused the call. A call that he knew had been unmistakable. Sometimes it had come as gentle rain in the English countryside, speaking with the voice of spring flowers, patiently wooing, patiently understanding the struggle of a carnal will that clenched fists like a child and begged to be left alone to play a little longer. Sometimes the call had come like the monsoon—fierce, overwhelming, warning of a precipice, of a fall that would leave him splattered like quivering flesh on the rocks of hell's destruction.

How could he pray? How could he plead for Gokul when his own disobedience tasted like the sweat and tears on his lips? Words from Proverbs came to mock him: *Because I have called, and ye refused . . . I will also laugh at your calamity.*

As a deadness of resignation to his own worthless state settled over him with the mugginess of the night, hope from above came on the gentle flutter of the wings of grace.

Come . . . come to Me . . . come and let us reason to-gether, saith the Lord. . . .

As though transported back to London, to the room in John Newton's house with the fire bright and warm in the hearth, Jace could hear the rain on the window-panes; he remembered sitting there with the Olney Hymnbook open before him while John Newton and Seward spoke of God's grace . . .

"Amazing grace, how sweet the sound that saved a wretch like me. I once was lost but now am found; was blind, but now I see. 'Twas grace that taught my heart to fear" . . .

He thought: *And grace my fears relieved!*

. . ."How precious did that grace appear the hour I first believed."

Jace opened his eyes, but he could not see clearly enough to even recognize Gokul.

4

Brahmaputra River

Jace awoke with the first chatter of birds in the branches. Strange that they were singing before the sun came up. He stirred, hearing the river lapping the bank below. His muscles were sore after the fighting in Guwahati, and for a moment he remained where he awoke.

Footsteps sounded, coming near, then stopped. "All is not dark, Major. Your Indian friend will survive." The voice belonged to Ethan.

Jace raised himself to an elbow and squinted up, expecting to see the doctor's weary smile, and was greeted instead by a blurred figure with as little color as London fog. Jace could feel dried grass brush against his hand as Ethan stooped down beside him.

"Something wrong?"

Jace ran a hand across his eyes, as if to wipe away cobwebs, slowly remembering now, recalling how they had escaped Guwahati after the assassination of the maharaja and had fled to the Brahmaputra. Gokul had been sorely wounded by an arrow containing a poisonous drug, and he himself had been grazed by gunshot—

Jace became still. The gunshot.... Except for a throbbing ache between his eyes, he had thought little about it when Ethan had treated the wound. He remembered that his vision had dimmed in and out like starlight obscured by clouds. He had been too worried about Gokul to make much of it at the time. He had witnessed this before in soldiers with head injuries. Sight usually returned in time, and last night before falling asleep exhausted, he had expected that by morning his vision would clear.

His brain felt bloated with pressure. He looked toward Ethan.

It is nothing, thought Jace, trying to silence the pang of fear. *It will go away. It must.*

The more he strained to clear his vision, the more the fear of being trapped like a tiger on a short chain wrapped its cold bands of iron around his heart. For a moment the thought flashed—*suppose I never see again?*

Trapped! He experienced the icy grip of fear, fear that he had never known when facing swords, guns, or wild animals. Then he had been in control, confident, free—now he was vulnerable!

He felt Ethan gripping his arm. "Good heavens, man! What is it? Do you have pain? Where?"

The urgent concern in his voice jolted Jace back to reality. He touched his head and the small bandage across his forehead. "The gunshot is all. I'll be all right."

"It's only a graze," came Ethan's voice.

Jace knew that Ethan sensed his alarm and was watching him intently.

"Unfortunately, the shot took the side of your head where you were wounded at Plassey. You have a concussion. If the pain is bad I can give you a bit of opium—"

"It's not the pain. I can't see. The idea makes me feel trapped. . . ."

Ethan went silent.

"They have a name for it, I think," said Jace.

"Yes. Can you see this?"

Ethan held something before his eyes, but Jace could barely make it out. "Your hand?"

"Good! Stay calm. Periods of dimmed vision often follow head wounds like yours. It will pass. Keep telling yourself you are in a wide open field. You can see for miles. If it helps, imagine the deck of your ship, the expanse of the ocean, the sky, the gulls soaring."

Jace envisioned it all, yet the fear that he would never *truly* see it again brought the curtain down.

He did not like the silence growing between him and Ethan, for Jace knew he watched him through the eyes of a physician, and it fed his uncertainty.

"Easy, Major."

Ethan's almost kind voice tended only to provoke him. He listened to the grass rustle around Ethan's boots as he stood, and Jace imagined him frowning down upon him as though he were a small boy with a skinned knee. The idea left him smarting.

"It's only temporary," said Ethan again. "You're not helpless. You can see well enough to distinguish objects, so you are not blind."

"How temporary?" gritted Jace impatiently. "There is Burma! Sunil will be looking for us, for Gem!"

"I do understand, Major! I do not know how long it will last. Hours, days perhaps."

Days . . . he could bear that . . . but what if it were weeks, years!

"You are a doctor, there ought to be something you can do to snap me out of it. Drugs, another impact on the head, anything."

"Don't be absurd! You touch that concussion and you may indeed go blind!"

Maybe that's what he wants, thought Jace, his hand clenching into a fist. *No . . . I'm behaving like a fool.* He let out a breath.

"You need rest, Jace. So does Gokul. Danger from Prince Sunil is real, but your condition is also real. Ignoring it will make it worse. This is one time when you must accept the fact you can do nothing but wait."

Wait. The most difficult word in any language when urgency nipped at your heels like hungry rats. Yet sanity told him Ethan spoke the obvious. He could do nothing until his vision cleared.

"We've one choice as I see it, and that is to wait at Kingscote until you can see well enough to journey to Burma," said Ethan. "Didn't you say you would need Gokul? He, too, must recover."

Jace thought of Coral. He would rather die by the tulwar of Sunil than have her see him like this. He did not want her sympathy. He would not take refuge at Kingscote. Layers of frustration mounted inside him. He pushed Coral from his mind and forced himself to think of Gokul. His friend had survived the night. Jace saw a glimmer of gratitude in his dark sky. "How did he make it? The arrow was tipped with poison."

"A question I shall never be able to answer, yet he is awake and determined to ride to Kingscote. How about you—can you get up? Can you ride?"

He would ride if it killed him, but not to the Kendall plantation. "If you wish to go to Kingscote, do so. I've friends in Sualkashi. Gokul and I will take our leave there."

Jace stood and felt Ethan's hand steady him. He resented the need of his support and wanted to pull away.

"Neither you nor Gokul are in any condition to journey alone to Sualkashi."

"We'll manage."

"Major is right," came Gokul's weak voice from somewhere in the river grass. "I am well . . . only very tired . . . I will be his eyes to reach Sualkashi. We will make it, sahib-doctor. Major and me, we face many hard places together before. This one, we will make also. The friend he speak of in Sualkashi, he is my brother."

Ethan did not argue, and Jace believed it was because he was pleased to have him away from Coral. Well, the idea also suited him just fine.

"Very well, Major. I'll saddle your horses."

Ethan returned in a short time, and Jace saw his and Gokul's shadowy figures moving about and Gokul being helped into the saddle. Ethan walked up to where Jace leaned against a tree.

"I've put medication in your saddlebag. You may find it helpful. I've included a salve and fresh bandages for both of you, and some mangoes I picked this morning before you woke. Godspeed," he said, and Jace heard him turn to leave.

"Ethan—wait."

The shadowy figure stopped.

"Coral already knows Gem is alive. I sent a message. But it is important you say nothing of what you overheard last night between me and the raja. If Coral learns the truth, that Sunil is closing in on Gem's trail, she will be prompted to act before I can reach Zin. Any blunder now will ruin the chance I have to save him from Sunil."

Ethan hesitated. Jace knew that he understood the *blunder* included anything that he and Coral might plan together.

"I hear you, Major. But if Sunil discovers where his nephew is before you are able to go to Burma, it will mean the boy's death."

"I'm aware of that. Give me time. If you do not hear

from me or Gokul—you are on your own."

"Understood. I know your friendship with this warlord offers you the best opportunity."

"If something happens and you feel it is imperative to act, take this with you." Jace felt inside his jacket for a map of Burma and handed it toward the shadow. "If you go, proceed cautiously. The monsoon often washes away sections of the road, and avalanches are common. And whatever you do, do not journey by way of the British road. Take the route I've marked."

"But wouldn't the road be the obvious and quickest route?"

"It would," said Jace dryly. "Except Sunil and his assassins will be traveling along that road."

Ethan's response came stiffly. "Thank you for the warning."

Jace heard Ethan's steps crunch across the grass to where the horse waited. Soon the thud of hooves died away.

Jace remained leaning against the tree. In the branches a monkey jabbered. He imagined the Brahmaputra gray in the early light of dawn; he listened to the caw of mynah birds, to the whooping of long-legged cranes, and somewhere the water lapped against the bank.

His sight would come back. It had to.

But what if the worst happened to him? What if God permitted permanent blindness? What if losing his sight was God's way of teaching him important lessons he had refused to learn when strong and free?

Yet a flicker of hope shone like a singular candle in the dark empty mansion of his soul. *I am not totally blind. If the Lord wished to seal me in blackness in order to bring light to my soul, He could have already done so.*

Perhaps this experience was a warning, and God

wanted his attention—

Newton's hymn echoed and reechoed through his mind. *I once was blind, but now I see....* His fingers touched Michael's Bible inside his inner pocket next to his heart.

He heard Gokul riding toward the tree, bringing the horse. He remembered that Gokul had almost died.

Newton was right. Amazing grace.

"Well, friend, thief, and spy," Jace said. "Christ has granted you a reprieve. Last night the earth opened her jaws to swallow you inside her hellish bowels. You might have been eternally digested by now."

Jace imagined Gokul's black eyes glinting as he stopped the horses and leaned to press the reins in his hand.

"Ah, sahib, old Gokul is wiser than you think. He learns quickly. Fleshly delights only whisper, but pain shouts. He is ready to listen to words William Carey brings to Mother India."

5

Kingscote

India's hot season continued to build toward its crest, leaving those on Kingscote feeling listless, and tempers were short. Even at dawn it was wretchedly hot. Coral pushed her damp blond hair away from her face and remembered dully what her father had once said: "The hot season is the time when murders are made and suicides mount."

Once again Coral's memory strained to recount the message in her father's letter received by her uncle, Sir Hugo Roxbury, at Guwahati. What had he written?

The situation on the border with Burma grows more dangerous. . . . Yet I've no choice but to leave the matters here with God and journey to Darjeeling to find Alex. Word arrived by courier that he is missing.

The days inched by without word as they waited for the sound of horse hooves on the carriageway, while all about them the tensions of danger and war gathered like the heralding clouds of the monsoon.

Coral was anxious to move ahead with plans to complete a wooden structure for the school before the rains came and the ground turned to mud. Once the rains began they would continue until what India called "the cool" was ushered in.

Jace had pressed her to wait until her father returned, but who knew how long he would be gone? Any hope of soon hearing horses in the carriageway was unrealistic, and so she turned her energies into convincing her mother to allow her to begin the school project.

"If we delay until Father returns it will mean waiting until next year to build. When you said you'd discuss the school with him, you thought he'd be back with Alex by now."

Elizabeth's worried thoughts about Hampton and her son were visible. "Yes, I did expect them back by now."

"And planning and building will give us something to fill our hearts while we wait."

Coral could see that the thought of the school filled her mother with the same excitement. Now that Elizabeth was growing stronger from her long illness, she too needed a worthy goal in which to refocus her energies. "I suppose Hampton will not be overly upset if we begin now."

Coral was quickly out of the chair and beside her mother. "Let's take the ghari this afternoon and decide on the location. I was thinking of the clearing near the silk hatcheries. If we start today we can have a structure built before the rains."

Several days later, Coral sat at her father's big desk and began to construct on paper her idea of how the school should look. The morning was gone before she paused to scrutinize her plan. She heard the familiar sounds of the servants moving about the dining salon, preparing the table for the noon meal. The smell of baked bread wafted through the room, making Coral realize how hungry she was and that she had only taken tea for breakfast.

She frowned at her drawing. It wasn't quite what she had visualized in her mind, but then she had never claimed to be an architect. She paused, hearing a slight noise behind her.

Coral's back was toward the door and she turned, half expecting to see one of the girls announcing lunch. The door remained shut. She stood, then noticed a piece of paper had been pushed under it. Quickly she picked it up, looking to see if she could catch a glimpse of the messenger, but the hall was empty. A breeze came to rattle the cane blind on the open window.

Coral read the words in Hindi, written by a hand struggling with grammar:

Sacrifice to dread Kali. Meet me in back near smoke-house after lunch.
—A friend

On Kingscote? Who would be so bold after strict orders from her father all these years? Coral debated showing the note to her mother but changed her mind. Whoever had left the note had chosen her as a confidante instead of going openly to the memsahib, probably knowing full well that Elizabeth would be outraged.

Someone trusts me to protect their identity, she decided, heading for the dining room.

———

Seated at the large table spread with the crystal sparkling and the chinaware from Canton filled with a variety of English and Indian cuisine, Coral waited until she could make an excuse to leave. Her sisters, Kathleen and

Marianna, were discussing Cousin Belinda's marriage to Sir George and who among the nobility might be invited by Aunt Margaret and Granny V.

"Wouldn't it be grand to be able to attend the wedding in London?" said Marianna. "Or better yet, if the marriage could take place here."

"With Burmese soldiers prowling the outskirts of Kingscote?" mocked Kathleen. "Yes, how grand indeed." She looked across the table at her mother. "Is it true there was another infiltrator shot last night?"

"Yes, but before your father left he took care to assign his most trusted mercenaries to defend the plantation borders. And your father will be back soon," said Elizabeth, trying as always to ease their concerns.

Coral imagined Burmese soldiers prowling the plantation. But soon Jace would be arriving at the British outpost near Jorhat. He knew the danger; he had warned her about it that night in Guwahati. Surely he would alert the commander there to send some English troopers to check on Kingscote. Yet he believed that Seward was here, not searching for her father in Darjeeling, and he trusted him explicitly.

Kathleen was frowning thoughtfully. "About Belinda's wedding in London ... I'm surprised she didn't write Alex about her fate before leaving Calcutta."

"Yes, she did not want to marry old George, did she?" said Marianna.

"She only moaned and groaned the entire time we were in Calcutta," said Kathleen. "I wonder if Alex received a letter or a small box from her when the shipment of mail arrived with Granny V's letter."

Why is she asking that? wondered Coral. She recalled her cousin's fiery infatuation with the Kendall sons, first Michael, then Alex. With Alex, Belinda's interest had exceeded that shown in her youth for Michael.

"There was no letter from Belinda in the sewing box when I found the one from Granny V," said Marianna.

"I was so ill at the time I cannot say for sure," said Elizabeth. "If there was a letter Alex would have received it before going to Darjeeling. If it is important to you, Alex would not mind if you looked in his room."

Kathleen said nothing and took a second cup of tea.

Watching her, Coral came to the conclusion that something about Belinda and Alex troubled her sister. The noon meal ended, and once her mother and sisters went their separate ways, she left the back door and walked across the yard in the direction of the smoke-house.

The outbuilding, made of stone and smelling of curing meats, was nearly deserted when she arrived, and she walked around to the back entrance, where some trees formed the outer growth of the jungle. Several empty wagons were nearby, but the workers were still away eating their noon meal.

Coral stood, glancing about, smelling the odor of smoke. She waited for the approach of footsteps but there were none. "Hello?" she called out into the stillness. "Anyone here?"

A twig snapped, not from the direction of the smoke-house but the jungle. She turned quickly, her eyes searching the shadows of the trees.

The branches moved, and Preetah, Natine's niece, stepped out nervously and beckoned Coral to follow her into the jungle trees. Coral believed she could trust the young woman; after all, Natine was her father's head servant. Casting a glance over her shoulder to make certain no one had followed her from the house, Coral picked up her skirts and sped after the Indian girl.

In the cloistered shadows smelling of damp earth and ferns, they paused, breathless. Coral saw the fear in Preetah's brown eyes and felt the girl's fingers close tightly about her arm. Preetah glanced off toward a little-used trail that wound deeper into the jungle. "It was I who slipped the note beneath door."

"You must tell me everything."

"No, you must see, and hear—for your sake."

Coral felt a tingle. What was it about Kali that the girl thought so important that Coral must hear for herself? She remembered back to the river journey and the tiger attack. After the death of one of their hired guides, the others had believed a sacrifice to appease their vengeful god a necessity. She had no wish to look upon the scene now on Kingscote land, but she must learn who was involved in order to report it to her father when he returned.

Minutes later Coral followed her through the trees, uncertain of their destination. Birds twittered and a cackle of jungle noises closed in about them.

They had walked for some time. She felt insects about her face and slapped them away. Remembering when Jace had rescued her from the horrid spider that had lodged on the back of her neck, she glanced up into the overhanging branches, but saw only a bird in emerald plumage flitter away. A short time later, they stopped, and Preetah gestured for silence.

Coral saw the glow of a small fire among the distant trees. They crept up silently, the dense jungle growth shielding them. Ahead, a number of trees had been chopped down to make a small circular clearing where a fire was flickering in the breeze.

Coral stooped behind the trees and heard voices. One of them she recognized immediately. *Natine!*

There was a religious man—a sadhu—with him and two other men, none of whom she recognized. Coral saw a small altar built, and nearby a goat waited to placate Kali.

She turned her head away as the bleating of the goat died at the hand of the sadhu. Suddenly she froze with horror, hearing her name mentioned. She listened, not daring to breath, her heart pounding. The village sadhu was signaling her out as an enemy of Kali.

Preetah tugged at her arm, and they slipped cautiously away.

On the brisk walk back to the mansion, Coral was silent and Preetah was grave, clutching her long head wrap against her chest.

When they arrived back at the smokehouse, Preetah turned to face her. "The sadhu and Natine are against the presence of the English in Assam. Many in the village agree. They speak secretly of a great battle that will come, when the new maharaja in Guwahati will purify the land of all feringhis. If you seek to serve your God by building the school, I do not know what will happen on Kingscote."

Before Coral could respond, the young woman stepped around a tree and disappeared into the dense jungle. Was Prince Sunil the new maharaja the people in the village looked to in order to drive out the English?

Coral awoke to the sound of the punkah fan located on the wall near her bed. The bedchamber was warm and still with late-afternoon shadows, and for a drowsy moment she lay there contentedly watching the delicate flutter of the mosquito netting.

Her mind was heavy with sleep as her eyes fell on a tiny figure standing on a peacock-feather stool pulling the fan cord. The child's long ebony pigtails hung down her back like two shiny ropes. She was wearing an embroidered blue tunic that reached to her knees. Beneath, she wore tight-fitting yellow pants. It was Reena, Preetah's small sister. Both girls belonged to Natine, who was their uncle.

After what Coral had witnessed the week before with Preetah, Jace's warning about Natine set her on edge. She found her curiosity about Natine's political beliefs growing with the passing weeks.

"You do not need to keep pulling the punkah, Reena. Your arms must be tired. I am used to the heat. Why not come here and tell me about your uncle Natine. He is a respected leader, isn't he? Has he many friends in the village?"

Reena shyly climbed down from the peacock stool and, with an embarrassed smile, lifted the netting and looked at the bed. Coral beckoned her to come, and the child crawled up as if accomplishing some impossible task.

"Tell me about Natine. What does he do when he visits the priest and the other men in the village?"

Reena tensed and glanced toward the door. "I go now, Missy Coral."

Coral realized she had moved too swiftly and had set the girl on guard. "No, you need not go yet. You can help me understand about Kingscote. I've been gone from home a long time. I expect you and your sister know everything that goes on around here?"

Reena smiled and lowered her eyes. "Mostly Preetah. She is a close friend with Yanna, who works in the silk hatcheries."

Yanna . . . how long ago it seemed when the small child had come running to her with the message that Jemani had gone into labor. Yanna was now a Christian, baptized by Elizabeth Kendall.

Coral was relieved to learn the two young women

were friends. It was good that Preetah had someone like Yanna to turn to for advice.

"Do not tell our uncle they are friends. He has told my sister to stay away from Yanna because she serves another god, but she brings hot broth to Yanna for her little friends. It is a secret. If Natine finds out what Preetah does to help Yanna, he will send us both away before memsahib can stop him."

"Little friends? Why are Yanna's little friends such a secret?"

Reena glanced toward the door. "They have sweating sickness. My uncle says let them die first as sacrifice to crocodiles to stop all the sickness. Kali is angry. It is why the sickness spreads on Kingscote, even though memsahib is better now. Uncle said they would die. Maybe Sunday, maybe Monday. He does not know my sister helps Yanna bring them food. He says they will now be thrown to the river crocodiles on festival day."

"Throw them to crocodiles! Are these children from Kingscote?"

"No, the village."

So that was why Natine did not fear to offer them to the river god as a sacrifice!

"Where are they now?"

"Do not ask!"

"If children are sick they must be cared for. I need to know where they are, Reena."

"But Natine will punish Preetah for helping Yanna."

"I won't let him. Tell her I will go tonight when she brings the food to Yanna. Tell her to send me word of when and where to meet her."

When the girl had gone, Coral's thoughts raced back to the sadhu. Involving herself would be a risk, but how could she stand by and do nothing, allowing children to die?

Before going down to dinner, she opened her Bible and read Psalm 91, then prayed for those on her heart. Mentally she placed each one, along with herself, in the "secret place of the most High."

The words penetrated her mind: "There shall no evil befall thee."

6

Night softly touched the Brahmaputra River, and in
the jungle perimeter around Kingscote the growl of a
tiger could be heard. Coral was dressed for the secret
excursion into the jungle, and her heart beat with odd
little jerks as she waited expectantly in her room. She
stood up quickly from her bed as the soft tap sounded.

She crossed the thick Isfahan rug and opened the
door. Reena stood there with her dark eyes appearing
even rounder as she put her fingers to her lips and beckoned for Coral to follow.

She sensed the urgency in the child's manner and
knew that their plan must be carried out before Natine
returned from his meeting in the village. Without a word,
she followed her down the back stairs of the mansion to
a seldom-used storage room near the cooking quarters.
They could hear Rosa humming as she pounded and
rolled the fresh dough for the next morning's breakfast.

Preetah met them, holding a jug of hot broth, her face
tense. "I cannot go, Miss Coral. Natine did not go to the
village tonight as usual. Please, you must take the broth
for me. Yanna waits in the trees."

Outside in the warm night, Coral left the back porch

and walked across the dusty yard, carrying the large jug of broth. Yanna waited, a shadowy figure in her dark sari. Farther ahead and amid the thick trees surrounding the yard clearing, the two-wheeled trap called a tonga was parked.

Yanna was surprised to see her, but her delight sprang into a smile. "It is you! How glad I am!"

Coral heaved the jug into the cart, taking care not to spill its contents, then climbed in behind Yanna. The tonga creaked forward into the blackness, and the hooves of the ox lumbered over the ground, kicking up the dust. The night was sultry, and Coral raised a hand to push back damp tendrils of hair from off her neck where they'd fallen from her chignon. She glanced about, seeing jungle trees silhouetted against even blacker shadows, trying to hold down her apprehension.

She admired Yanna's courage. Elizabeth had taught her well, after the death of Jemani. Now, a silent bond formed between them as they shared the same determined spirit to save the children.

Yanna leaned close and whispered, "It was Preetah who first told me about the four children. They are untouchables from the village. She was in the ghari when Natine brought them here and left them beside the river. They were to be thrown to the crocodiles on the festival. I hid them in the jungle, since I could not bring them to the bungalows." Yanna scowled. "Natine is watching me. He has become bold since the illness of memsahib. He must not know Preetah helps me. Without your father's presence to rule Kingscote, she has no one."

"I will do what is necessary to see she and Reena are not involved. As for the children, we can't leave them out here in the jungle another night. I heard a tiger prowling."

Yanna gave a nervous glance into the trees. "I have

heard it for two nights. Angels have protected them so far. Each night I come here I feel my heart in my throat, wondering if I will find them."

"Then there is no one else involved?" Coral asked.

"No one else. If Preetah did not smuggle food from the kitchen, I would have little. Even if the other untouchables wished to help, they dare not. And the others do not want to come even if they could. Many agree with Natine." Yanna glanced at her warily. "He has spent much time in the village where the new sadhu holds meetings. He is against the English presence in Assam."

Alert, Coral asked, "When did the sadhu arrive?"

"Three years ago. He is from Sibsagar."

Sibsagar was northeast of the Jorhat outpost, and the great capital of Assam. It was strange that a sadhu would leave the ancient city for a small village. She might have told Yanna about seeing him with Natine in the Kali rite but did not wish to involve her more than she already was.

The jungle thickened. Night wrapped about them. Coral held to the seat to steady herself as the trail wound deeper into the solitude. Perspiration made her clothes stick to her, and her stomach tensed when Yanna at last brought the ox to a stop.

Coral saw the outline of a shelter built of dried branches, leaves, and dirt. "Hand me the lantern."

A moment later she was down from the seat and stooping before the opening of the small lean-to. She thrust the dull yellow light inside, and dismal sobs filled her ears. Coral's throat constricted and she swallowed hard. "Oh, Lord," she whispered, and momentarily shut her eyes against the pathetic sight that greeted her.

Four small, skinny children huddled together, naked except for the blanket Yanna had brought them. Large brown eyes stared at her with apprehension, while their breathing came in rasping chokes.

"Do not be afraid," she told them in Hindi. "I am your friend." She turned to Yanna. "It is a miracle the tiger has not come by now," she said. "My conscience will not permit me to leave them out here like this. I must do something."

Yanna knelt beside her, her eyes anxious. "But where can we bring them without Natine finding out?"

"You are right about the silk workers—who would take them in when they fear Natine? But who cared for them in the village before they became ill?"

"An old woman, Ila, but she is dead. She was sick long before they were. And no one else will bother with un-touchables who have no relatives. That is why Natine brought them to the river."

"Do not fear Natine," said Coral.

"Be careful. I have heard Natine listens only to your uncle from Calcutta, Sir Hugo Roxbury."

"Who told you so? Preetah?"

Yanna looked uneasy. "Yes. Everyone whispers of war and mutiny. Preetah says she heard the sadhu mention your uncle in the village meetings."

Jace had warned her that Natine may serve Roxbury. "Sir Hugo is my uncle, but he is not the master of Kings-cote, no matter what others may think," Coral assured Yanna.

While Yanna fed the children, Coral walked toward the tonga to think. If only there was someone to help her. Wearily she stood. Sounds coming from deeper in the jungle closed in about her emotions like a fort. *Fort. . . .* The word took on an image in her mind like a glimmer of hope in the thick darkness. Jorhat . . . Major Jace Buckley. . . . He would be there by now looking into the matter of the assassination of the British officer. He could not have gone to Burma yet, and Jorhat was not that far away from Kingscote.

Would he come? Could he leave his command even for a short time? Was she also searching for an excuse to get in touch with him again after their last meeting in the palace garden?

"We need a friend, Yanna. Someone strong, someone equal to Sir Hugo who can help me stand against his schemes until my father returns with Seward. I must send someone to the Jorhat outpost. Is there anyone among the workers I can trust to ride there?"

"There is Thilak. He guards the hatchery. He is a good man."

"Then I must speak with him tonight."

With that decided, Coral's heart felt a little lighter. She turned her attention back to the children. So, was this to be the fate of the untouchables—to slowly die while weakness stole the life from their bodies, or to wait until a wild beast came upon them?

If I do nothing, then what am I? thought Coral. *How can I claim to be a follower of Him?*

When they had been fed she told Yanna, "They may yet die, but if they do, they die in a warm bed with at least one person to comfort them. Help me get them in the back of the tonga. I'm taking them where I know they'll get proper care—the dispensary."

Admiration shone in Yanna's eyes. "There is no need to risk more trouble. I will do what my heart told me from the first. But I let fear stop me. I will take the children to my bungalow and care for them there. Everyone already knows I am a Christian, and if there is trouble for me among my friends, it must come. Thilak will protect me."

Coral was deeply moved. "Are you certain you wish

to take the risk now, Yanna? Perhaps we should wait until my father returns."

"I am certain. I live in the bungalow once belonging to Jemani and Rajiv. There is room for the four children."

"Then I will speak to my mother about it. But the children are too ill now. I must take them to the house, to the dispensary, where they can be cared for by Rosa."

"Then I shall come and help nurse them if you wish. I do not think Rosa will touch them since she is of higher caste."

Kingscote lay in sleepy stillness when they arrived near the hatcheries. Yanna jumped down from the driver's seat to return to her bungalow, and Coral took the reins. She waited until Yanna ran off into the darkness, then flapped the reins, and the ox treaded forward.

The light flooding the windows of the mansion reminded Coral of gleaming candles in St. Paul's Cathedral in London. A sense of reality flooded her heart.

There was nothing to fear. No one in earth or heaven could harm her unless God permitted it, she thought. Scripture verses memorized now winged their way across her mind. *My times are in Thy hand. If God be for us, who can be against us?*

No force could harm her here, safe in the company of her mother and sisters. And soon Jace would arrive. The petition to the idol was folly, and while Satan's power may lodge in Kali's image, the righteousness of Christ flanked her with armor.

7

Ahead, the light in the mansion burned. Coral left the ox and tonga under the trees and climbed down, lifting the blanket to cover the children. They whimpered but didn't cry aloud. Perhaps they had long ago learned that no one responded to their tears. No one at all. Dark, empty eyes stared up at her. "It is all right," she said in Hindi. "I am your friend. I will come back in a few minutes to help you." She hurried across the dusty yard, and then up the steps to the back porch. She threw open the door and walked into the brightly lit kitchen.

Piroo, the head cook, was asleep in a chair snoring loudly, the Kingscote breakfast all laid out and prepared to cook in the morning. Hearing her enter he came awake. Coral's perspiring face streaked with dust, with strands of hair hanging loose from the heavy chignon, caused the older man to struggle to his sandaled feet.

"Miss Coral! You are hurt!"

"No, no I'm quite fine, Piroo, but, I'll need hot water, milk, and sweet tea. Find Mera and tell her to awaken Jan-Lee. I'll need four more beds and blankets in the dispensary—and children's garments. Hurry."

Before he could ask questions, Coral pushed past

through the door into the lower hall. Her mother's health had not been strong that day, and she refused to add to her burden. She might awaken Marianna to help, but she was sleeping tonight in their mother's chamber. Coral hurried down the hall to Kathleen's room.

Her sister was asleep, the satin coverlet pulled up about her neck. Coral's mouth turned up at the corners ruefully. *She almost looks angelic*, she thought. *Let us hope she behaves as such.* She pulled the cover aside. "Kathleen, wake up, I need your help in the dispensary."

Kathleen groaned, stirred, and with her voice dulled by the pillow, mumbled, "Hmm. . . ? Coral, don't . . . bother me. . . . Leave me alone."

Kathleen burrowed down in the bed again. Coral pulled the coverlet off. "Get up, Sis, I need your help. There are four children . . . very sick. Please, Kathleen!"

Kathleen responded to the alarm in her voice. She rolled over and stared up at her. "What? Is it Mother?"

"No. Four children. They have the fever. Come, I need your help."

As though she did not hear Coral correctly, Kathleen stared up at her, scowling. "Are you daft? Children? Whose?"

"Orphans, you goose! Get up! I need your moral support. Natine will be angry."

Kathleen moaned and covered her face with her palms. "Natine! I'm beginning to wish he would mount an elephant and ride off to the Himalayas!"

"Not much chance of that—unless he returns with war elephants. Get up."

"Coral! Do you realize we're all alone here? With Mother about to have a relapse of the fever, and Father gone—"

"The major will come soon. I will send Thilak to Jorhat."

98

Kathleen crawled out of bed, reaching for her silk dressing gown. "Marvelous, but the message he sent about Gem said he would be gone until Christmas."

"I am hoping he is still at Jorhat. Wait for me in the dispensary sickroom, will you? I'll be there as soon as I write the major a letter. Yanna's friend will ride to the outpost tonight."

The servants watched in silence as the children were carried into a large back chamber that Elizabeth used as a dispensary. Containing beds and medicine, it had been her mother's first project as mistress, and one that had proved invaluable. As Coral went there to join Kathleen, she pretended not to notice Natine waiting at the end of the darkened hall, watching.

Mera stepped aside, troubled, as Coral entered the large room housing a number of beds. She knew that Mera feared she would ask her to help wash the children before putting them between the clean blankets.

Coral smiled at the old woman for whom she carried a deep affection. "It is all right, Mera. You best get some sleep. Kathleen and I will tend to them."

Mera's expression betrayed her relief. "I called for Jan-Lee to help you, my child. She comes now, sahiba."

If only Jace would come, thought Coral.

Deep night lay upon Kingscote. The flame on the candle burned low. Her eyes felt like sand, and she was physically and emotionally exhausted, but pleased. Already the Lord had used her to prolong the lives of four children. Instead of going up to her room, Coral rested on one of the empty beds.

Untouchables, she mused sleepily. The lepers of the caste system. Christ could touch lepers and make them whole; how much more were little ones on Kingscote precious in His sight?

Coral found her eyes closing and sleep dragging her

mind off to captivity. She dreamed of Kali, goddess of destruction. . . . The hideous four-armed idol with protruding tongue stood on a dead man and wore human skulls on her girdle like beads on a string. Coral awoke with a start.

Dawn had broken, with no relief from the draining heat. Coral looked out the window toward the dusty road, remembering that day so long ago now, when Major Jace Buckley rode in with a small troop of sowars from Jorhat to hunt the tiger. Gem had been born that night, when the monsoon broke . . . and Jemani had journeyed home to heaven. Coral felt a cloud settle over her soul as she remembered, and she desperately wished to see Jace riding now toward the house in the company of trusted sowars. The road was empty. She turned away, leaving the dispensary to take morning tea with her mother, and arrived at the door just as Preetah was coming out.

"Memsahib insists she is much better. She is dressed and taking tea on the verandah."

Elizabeth Kendall looked thin and pale, but smiled cheerily as Coral kissed her cheek and drew up a white wrought-iron chair to the table.

"You are up early, Coral." Elizabeth set her Bible aside and poured her daughter a cup of tea. "Scones? They are your favorite. Mera sent up lemon honey."

Coral shook her head no and looked across the railing toward the river, a sullen gray. To ease her mind she concentrated on the elephants being led down the road for their morning wallow. "Something must be done about Natine."

Elizabeth, in the midst of preparing her hot scone, paused and studied her daughter's face.

In low tones, Coral explained about the happenings of the night before.

"If you had awakened me I would have insisted the children be brought to the dispensary. You did the right thing, especially with a tiger roaming the perimeter. I had better see the children myself and make certain their ailment is the fever. There has been no sign of cholera this year, but we can take no chances."

"Yanna is willing to share her bungalow when they recover. She can put them to work in the hatchery, and they can be our first students in the school."

Elizabeth was calm but alert. "Natine knows better than to offer a sacrifice to the crocodiles on Kingscote property."

Coral did not tell her about the sadhu who had spoken her name to Kali. Despite her mother's determination to carry on as mistress, Elizabeth's health continued to trouble her, and Coral feared a serious relapse. Some things must wait for her father's return.

"Natine will deny everything, of course," warned Coral, "then question Preetah to see if she was involved in telling me about the children."

"I'll not mention her nor Reena. But I will need to confront him with this."

———

The children's fever eventually broke, and Coral knew they would live. They were emaciated and withdrawn, never smiling, never talking. They watched Coral mutely as if they were caught up in a nightmare. She tried to make friends with the four little faces staring at her with wide dark eyes, but received no response.

One morning after Coral had recounted in the Hindi language the story of Jesus touching and healing the leper, the boy named Ajay was the first to smile shyly up at her.

"Burra-sahib very good, sahiba."

Coral smiled at her success and reached a hand to the side of his face. "Jesus is more than a Burra-sahib. He is Lord of all, and just think, He loves *you*, Ajay."

Ajay covered his face with both hands and giggled shyly. His laughter provoked the other three to giggling, and soon the mattress was filled with merriment of laughter while they struggled to hide their faces under the sheet. It was hard to get them to calm down after that, and thereafter her relationship with the children was guaranteed.

"We never go back," they kept saying as if questioning her, afraid that she would return them to the village. "We never go back to Ila or hut."

"Ila dead," said Mona sadly to Ajay.

"We never go back," he repeated. "We stay with Sahiba Coral and Yanna."

8

Not long after the children's recovery, the sound of horse hooves outside the window on the carriageway brought Coral quickly to her feet. She opened the door and sped from her father's office into the large hall, her eyes expectantly on the front door as Rosa came to answer the knock.

Coral stood anxiously, her hands pressed against the sides of her skirts.

Was it Jace? Had he had arrived in answer to her request sent through Thilak?

Ethan entered the hallway, holding his familiar medical bag, and did not see Coral standing off to the side near her father's office.

"I am Doctor Ethan Boswell, a relative of the Kendall family," he told Rosa. "I've just ridden in from Guwahati."

Coral recovered from her surprise. She had been so certain it was Jace. Ignoring the twinge of disappointment, she picked up her skirts and hurried toward him across the polished wood floor. "Ethan!"

He turned quickly at the sound of her voice and, seeing her, removed his hat and set his bag on the floor.

Coral stopped short. One glimpse of his face, now soiled from sweat and dust, shouted to her of dark news. His wheat-colored hair was disheveled, his lean jaw tense. His usual formal dress was soiled and sweat stained, his jacket ripped at the shoulder seams, and there were dried bloodstains on the frilled cuffs of his shirt.

In two long strides Ethan was before her, catching up her hands into his and holding them so tightly that Coral nearly winced. She looked searchingly into his gray eyes. She had never seen him look so hard and remote.

Her eyes fell to the dried bloodstains, stark and ugly on his frilled cuffs—cuffs that belonged in the elegant parlor of Roxbury House in London, and she felt a dart of fear. "What is it, Ethan, what's happened? Are you hurt? There's blood on you. . . ."

"There has been a rebellion in Guwahati."

Coral listened, her nerves taut as he explained how he had been expected to deal treacherously with the maharaja by quietly poisoning him under the guise of medical treatment.

"A fine way to keep the British government from suspecting anything," Ethan said. "Having signed a treaty with the maharaja, the East India Company could have come to his aid."

By now Ethan's arrival was known to the rest of the house, and Elizabeth appeared on the stairs, with Kathleen and Marianna hurrying down the stairs after her.

Coral was left to her anxious thoughts as Ethan walked to meet them.

He had said nothing of the major, and Coral could hardly contain her impatience. She glanced out the front window facing the carriageway, but there was only one horse, the Indian boy now leading it to the stables to be fed and watered. She heard her mother greeting Ethan, worriedly asking of his condition and the trouble at Guwahati, yet somehow maintaining that gracious demeanor of courtesy she always displayed. She asked of Hugo's safety, and Ethan's voice went stiff.

"I am certain Prince Sunil would not dare harm the British ambassador. It would damage his relationship with the East India Company and weaken his position on the throne."

"Yet if Prince Sunil resents British incursions into Assam, would he not attack all the English presence in the north?"

Coral heard her mother's question and turned to see Ethan's response. He was tense, as though holding back feelings for Sir Hugo he did not wish on display.

"The major feels Prince Sunil is not yet strong enough militarily to risk driving the English out of northeast India, but will wait. He will first seek to rally his people around him by appealing to their religion. He may even seek to make some manner of appeasement toward Calcutta in the assassination of his uncle, as though wishing to make good the treaty signed with the Company."

"But the major thinks that Sunil will eventually attack the feringhis?" Elizabeth continued.

"Yes," said Ethan. "But before the troop under Captain MacKay arrives, Sir Hugo stands to offer the best hope of protection for Kingscote. I feel certain we'll be hearing from him soon."

"Hampton would be pleased to know of the major's presence in this dangerous situation. I do hope he felt free to make use of Kingscote on the way to the outpost at Jorhat?"

Then Jace was not injured . . . thought Coral, a sigh of relief escaping from her.

"I regret to say the major declined Kendall hospitality."

Coral came alert.

"Oh. I am disappointed," said Elizabeth. "He has other quarters?"

"He and an Indian friend named Gokul were both slightly wounded, nothing to be concerned about, but the major felt strongly inclined to seek the solace of a certain family in Sualkashi."

At the mention of Sualkashi, Coral's memory confronted a vision of the lovely Indian girl. Her fingers dug into her palms as she watched Ethan intently from where she stood at the window. *Inclined to seek solace elsewhere, was he? He prefers that Indian girl's company in his emotional pain instead of facing Coral Kendall again.*

"An English family?" inquired Elizabeth casually.

"No. Indian I believe."

"Sualkashi?" Marianna turned to Coral, wrinkling her pert nose. "Why, we stayed there the night you were ill. Remember, Coral? That is where you said that Indian girl was rude to you. I wonder if—"

Kathleen casually turned her head toward Marianna. Marianna looked suddenly confused, then ashamed, and her eyes darted quickly across the hall to Coral. She hastened to recover her blunder but only made it worse.

"Oh, yes . . . so it was the same family . . . but I'm sure she and Major Buckley are merely friends."

Coral made no sound. Her heart was pounding. Ethan did not look at her but said stiffly, "The girl is related to the major's Indian friend. A niece, I think, was what Gokul said. Gokul informed me that the reason the major went to Sualkashi was because he intends to marry the young woman as soon as he is relieved from his military duty. From what Gokul said, the marriage plans were rather sudden."

"Major Buckley is getting married?" gasped Marianna. "Why, I never thought he would."

The unexpected announcement caught Coral unprepared. The malicious bite of jealousy clenched its teeth into her heart before she could guard herself. Her stomach tightened into furious knots. *The knave! And after all his drivel about desiring little except his freedom and his miserable ship to take to sea again!*

The realization stung. *I couldn't influence him to give up his adventurous life, but a young Indian girl has been able to secure a marriage proposal.*

"You said the major was injured?" asked Elizabeth.

"Only a scratch."

"Well, that is some good news. Both Hampton and I thought well of the colonel's son."

"I did not realize you were acquainted with him," remarked Ethan.

"He's worked for Hampton hauling silk to the markets in Spain and England. We first met him during a tiger scare some years ago. Michael thought of him as a brother."

"A pity Michael lost his life on Buckley's ship."

"Yes. . . . I received a letter of condolence from the major while he was still at sea. It showed much insight. I was pleased to discover that the colonel's son is a Christian. But enough of this, you must be exhausted after your long ride. We've kept you far too long from the rest you need."

Elizabeth slipped her arm through his and turned him toward the stairs. "The horrid happenings at Guwahati will not be easily erased from your memory, but a good day of rest in bed will make you feel much better. This is one time, Ethan, when I shall don the role of physician."

"You are most kind, Aunt Elizabeth. I am only grieved

to have arrived in this condition and be the bearer of dark news."

Elizabeth led him slowly up the stairway. "I'll have Mera bring hot tea and something to eat. You can tell us what happened in detail when you are up to it in a few days. There is so much news, one hardly knows where to begin. I suppose Hugo received Hampton's letter about your cousin Alex in Darjeeling?"

"Yes, on arrival at Guwahati. Is there news?"

"I'm afraid not, and with the monsoon building, my concerns grow."

"If you do not hear from Hampton soon, I must insist on going there to search for them."

"We must not even consider anything so risky now. It's enough you've arrived safely, and I'm able to meet Hugo's nephew. He and Margaret have written so much, we feel we already know you. And, of course, Coral has spoken so well of you. We both are in your gratitude, Ethan. Coral seems completely recovered from the tropical fever, and I am well on my way back to good health. What a godsend to have a physician in the family, and soon a son-in-law, at that."

"Your words bring me deep satisfaction. . . ."

Their voices trailed away as they disappeared down the upstairs corridor. Coral stood stiffly looking after them. Little of their friendly discourse had sunk into her mind, for her thoughts would go no further than Ethan's announcement about Sualkashi. Not until her mother and Ethan were gone and the hall silent did she realize Kathleen and Marianna were watching her.

"I'll, ah—tell Mera to send the tea up to Cousin Ethan," said Marianna and left quickly for the cook room.

"War elephants," said Kathleen thoughtfully.

Something in her voice caused Coral to pay attention.

"The maharaja would have many," said Kathleen. "I'm surprised the fighting wasn't much worse than Ethan suggests."

Coral frowned. "The maharaja was killed. Sunil is now on the throne. How much worse could it be?"

"The major only received a 'mere scratch' is the way Ethan put it."

Coral caught the suggestion in her sister's voice. Was a mere scratch cause for Jace to seek recovery at Sualkashi? It was not like him to pamper aches and pains, and even less likely that he would set aside the secret mission into Burma, especially with the maharaja slain and Sunil as the usurper of the Guwahati throne.

Coral had a notion that Kathleen suspected her feelings about the young woman at Sualkashi, and she questioned Ethan's report in order to soothe her. The feeling of dislike between Ethan and Jace was mutual, but Ethan was not deceptive like his uncle, Sir Hugo. Ethan would not deliberately sow seeds of conflict to place Jace Buckley in an unflattering light.

Coral felt her feelings toward Jace harden into resentment. "I see no reason to think Cousin Ethan would deliberately hold back the truth as he saw it. As far as I'm concerned the matter is over."

When Kathleen made no further comment, Coral felt that her emotions had betrayed her, and she wished to get away, to be alone. She grabbed her straw hat from a stand in the corner and pulled open the front door, calling over her shoulder, "Jan-Lee says the children we rescued will recover. In a few weeks they will be on their feet. Yanna has offered to take them. I'm taking a ghari to the hatcheries to make arrangements."

The wind cooled her face as she chose to ride in the outer seat next to the ghari-wallah, but nothing cooled her emotions. Like kindled coals wanting to burst into flame, her thoughts went in all directions.

Sunil was now the self-proclaimed maharaja. A ripple of fear ran down her back. What if he came to Kingscote with Indian warriors searching for Ethan? Did Sunil know Gem was alive? And if he did, would he search for him? Had Jace abandoned his quest to bring Gem home by Christmas?

She fumed, her eyes narrowing under her lashes as the ghari bumped along the rutted road toward the silk workers' huts in the mulberry orchard. How could Jace sit in Sualkashi when there had been a mutiny in Guwahati? Would his sudden decision to marry the girl put a complete end to all other commitments?

Kathleen was in doubt, but Coral, who felt she had known him far better than anyone else, found her thoughts muddled by jealousy and a rage of which she had not known she was capable. Jace had abandoned them all for solace in the company of Gokul's smug-faced niece. Gem was at risk of being located by Prince Sunil, yet Jace did nothing to warn her.

The least he could do is tell me where Gem is so I can hire mercenaries of my own to free him, she thought bitterly.

He had led her to think she could depend on him, depend on him for honor and strength of purpose, even if he had made it clear that he would eventually leave India for the *Madras*. Now he had chosen to walk away from everyone and everything, in the darkest moment of all.

If Sir Hugo had been the bearer of the news instead of Ethan, she might have good reason to question it, for she remembered all too well the lies he had spoken about Jace in London.

Derelict in his duty. Drunk in his cabin when Michael was swept overboard.

But Ethan! Would he lie so blatantly in order to turn her against Jace? He did not like Jace, she knew that. But she could not imagine Ethan cunning enough to lie to her about Sualkashi, knowing she would one day find out.

"Unless he thinks I shall be so outraged with Jace that I'll marry him now."

She straightened her straw hat, frowning. But if it was a lie, where was Jace?

And Sir Hugo . . . where was he? Maybe Ethan was wrong and he had been killed in the fighting. Anything might have happened once the ugly torch of mutiny was lit in Guwahati. Sunil may not have planned for Hugo's death, but some enraged Indian, jealous for the worship of Kali, could strike out at any Englishman in sight.

Or was Hugo even now working with Sunil to carry out whatever plans they had in mind from the beginning?

She shaded her eyes and looked toward the clouds. Her fevered mind raced ahead to her father at Darjeeling. *What can be done to stop him from meeting whatever vile trap is set?*

Her eyes spilled over with tears of frustration as the burdens coming from so many directions at once overwhelmed her.

Rest in the Lord, wait patiently for Him.

The words scattered across her soul like seeds of new life, bringing hope. How unwise to allow herself to forget God. Soon she would be rushing about in a tizzy like some startled old hen, squawking and carrying on as though the entire safety of the coop depended on her.

Coral unexpectedly laughed at herself. The old sun-baked ghari-wallah stole a side glance at her. Coral looked off toward the silk workers' huts.

Jace marrying Gokul's niece! She lifted her chin and folded her arms tightly. He wouldn't do that. She remembered too well what had happened between them in the palace garden.

She sat up straight. *I'll write him, that's what. I'll have Thilak deliver a message to Sualkashi.*

Coral felt surprised at her decision, and at that a strange satisfaction stole over her. She would not simply retire from the scene like some scared rabbit afraid of the Indian girl. Unless—

Unless she had been right about what happened in the garden after all. Maybe Jace Buckley kissed all women goodbye that way.

Her eyes narrowed again and her fists clenched in her lap. *I'm glad I told him what I thought of his knavish ways!*

No, she would forget Jace. She would proceed with her own plans for the school, and now that Ethan was here, she would get him to help her construct the wooden structure before the rains.

Coral's mind drifted back to that night in London at the chapel when she had read William Carey's treatise on world missions. The burning desire to teach the children about Christ had come with a calling that could not be silenced. She had surrendered her future that night to the Lord. She was so sure that He had placed the burden on her heart. How then did Jace fit into all this, or did he?

The truth of her situation hit with force. She had no right to Jace until she knew that they belonged together as one. If she could not follow a man's vision, far better to be single and to pursue the cause on her own heart.

A calm came over her soul. God *was* guiding her, but not her only, He had a plan for Jace too. The thought startled her.

What was that plan? Would Jace surrender to it? She knew that his knowledge and confidence in God went much deeper than he would say. Jace would be a man worthy of any woman to follow if he ever became dedicated to the purpose of God.

Coral became still, knowing that God desired the best for them all, if only they would submit to His purpose. The one thing she could do for Jace, perhaps the greater thing, was to pray fervently for him. She would make it a daily matter of concern, then leave him with the Master Designer.

9

Despite the problems that loomed, Coral's spirits felt lighter than they had in weeks. Ethan had taken on the medical work in the dispensary, and more surprisingly, he had shown unexpected interest in the school project.

She awoke early. Her eyes took in the horizon, a hazy brown from the dust in the atmosphere on the plains of India, but sunrise on the Brahmaputra remained gold. *A perfect day for building a school,* she decided with a smile.

One of the workers walked across the lawn and Coral leaned over and called, "Send to the stables for a ghari. I will need to take a drive today. And have Rosa send someone to awaken Doctor Boswell. I want to go right away."

The boy pointed down to the riverbank. "Doctor is already awake, collecting bugs in net."

"Then tell him I wish him to come to the house at once."

As the boy ran off toward the river, Coral changed into cool muslin and came rushing down the stairs, tying her wide straw sunbonnet under her chin.

Ethan came through the front door carrying his

prized samples, and for the first time since his arrival there was a look of relaxed pleasure on his face.

She cast him a smile. "Already gathering samples for your medical lab?"

"I've never seen such a rich bounty of specimens."

Coral stepped onto the white verandah and shaded her eyes. Ethan gave his samples to the boy with strict orders for their careful handling and came up to stand beside her.

"The monsoon," she said, and started down the steps toward the waiting ghari. The driver opened the door. "Come, Ethan, don't be so slow."

"Do you expect it to break today?" he laughed, then held up his smooth hands and grimaced. "The very thought of soiling them with hammer blows and wood slivers fills me with loathing."

Coral laughed as Ethan dismissed the driver and helped her onto the open front seat. She spread her skirts, adjusted her hat to protect her from the already blazing sun, and pointed toward the other side of the plantation. "We've already chosen the location for the school, but Mother also wants your opinion."

Ethan climbed up beside her and touched the horse with the whip. The horse trotted off across the carriageway onto the dirt road that divided the plantation. On one side were the acres of mulberry trees and hatcheries; the other side contained the workers' settlement of low buildings plastered with mud.

"Stop here, Ethan." She waved an insect away from her face.

Some of the children were bold enough to salaam to her. Coral smiled and reached down to the basket of sweet treats she had brought, when Ethan's low voice interrupted. "Wait, I believe we are about to encounter a bit of trouble."

She looked at him, wondering what he meant, then followed his gaze to the Indian foreman, who yelled in Hindi for the children to stay away from the ghari. Behind him walked a sadhu with a shaven head and a white caste mark painted on his forehead. He was the same priest Coral had seen in the jungle.

"I wonder what he is doing here?" she tried to say casually.

"The priest? I was up late last night when the butler named Natine returned from the village. He had this insufferable guru with him. I confronted him at once, demanding to know what goes. He said his niece is to be married on the plantation in a few weeks."

Coral grew uneasy. Was the wedding of Preetah a ploy to secure the sadhu's presence among the workers? He would contest her plans with the children, not publicly but in private.

Coral sat in the heat staring at the sea of faces and uselessly swatted insects. If she openly confronted the man now during the beginning of the religious festival, she would accomplish little and only alienate the workers further from her own cause.

She heard a low din of conversation break out among the elderly men as they congregated together watching, keeping their distance. The priest paused, and the foreman approached the rig and salaamed to Coral and Ethan.

"Greeting, sahib, miss-sahiba, do you wish words with me?"

Coral sensed that Ethan was about to reprimand the foreman, so she moved quickly to avert him. Her gloved hand came to rest on Ethan's wrist. "Jai ram, friend Hajo. This is Doctor Ethan Boswell from England, a cousin of mine. I'm taking him on a tour of the silk plantation. Pay us no mind. You may proceed with your work."

The Indian foreman stepped back. "Namaste, miss-sahiba, sahib."

He walked away. The priest stood like a statue in the dust and heat, and Coral watched until the foreman walked up to him and the two went away together, the workers following.

Wearily she pulled off her hat and fanned herself. Foiled, she thought. The silken strands of her hair caught the sun's rays. She turned to Ethan and he sat watching her. Coral pulled out the picnic basket she had intended to share with the children. With a rueful smile, she said, "It's not the prettiest weather for a picnic, but would you care to share some lunch?"

Ethan took up the reins, his eyes smiling with good humor. "Do you have some pleasant cove in mind with the sea breeze and a few gulls soaring above us?"

"Now you are beginning to sound like Major Buckley."

She felt Ethan's glance as if the mention of Jace's name had altered the mood.

"This is one time the major and I agree. But unlike his adventurous wanderlust, I'm not apt to mount the deck of a ship and disappear for two years. And," he added with a thin smile, "I'm willing to build your mission school."

Coral turned her head and looked at him from beneath her hat. "Yes . . . and I'll not forget."

Coral walked in the direction of the clearing, calling happily over her shoulder. "This is the location we have chosen. What do you think?"

Ethan walked to where she stood waiting for him.

She stood staring as if she could envision the completed project and hear the laughter of the children. All else was swept from her mind, as if by some refreshing heavenly breeze.

"The ground is high enough here so the rains won't wash the school into the river," Ethan commented. "We won't need to clear the ground or worry about trees."

Coral envisioned the bungalow standing with firm foundations and filled to overflowing with children singing in the Hindi language the song her mother had written:

> "Saviour of all Nations,
> Shepherd of young and old,
> Guide us with your Words of light,
> and make us all one fold. . . ."

Coral took hold of his arm. "Ethan, I can see it now, bursting with children memorizing Scripture. One large room will be sufficient to start with. Eventually we'll have several rooms, and a kitchen too, so we can serve hot meals. But now, I'll be content with a roof and four walls."

"We?" asked Ethan quietly, his hand tightening on her arm.

Jace barged into her mind, but she laid a hand on Ethan's. "I've no choice but to turn to you. Help me get the school going and I shall always be in your debt. The four children are enough to begin the class, and the priest has no jurisdiction over them. They were abandoned to death on the river, and now, what I do with them—what *we* do with them—is no concern of theirs. Soon others will see that what I teach is beneficial. When the adults see the untouchables able to read and write when they themselves cannot, and healthy and happy—they'll know the school is not cursed by Kali."

Ethan smiled ruefully and held out his hands.

Coral looked at them. They were the hands of a physician, smooth and slender.

"These are not quite the hands of William Carey," he said.

"At the moment they are all I need." She took them into her own and smiled up at him. "If you're willing to sacrifice them to help me start the school, I can only be grateful."

His gray eyes sobered. "You may discover my reason is not altogether sacrificial. Someone once told me the best way to win your heart is to build your school and support your interest in the untouchables. I think he knows you very well indeed."

Coral smiled. *Seward*, she thought. "Then you best listen to him."

"I intend to. And as I told him, I make no apology for whatever means brings me success."

"Success?"

"Tomorrow," he said, placing a finger over her lips, "we start the school of Coral Kendall."

———

Coral was eagerly counting the days as the mission school took shape. Daily she ventured forth in the ghari to see how Ethan was progressing with the walls and roof, sometimes in the company of her mother and sisters, and sometimes alone. She involved herself in the work and was enjoying every moment of it.

Coral became a familiar sight in the ghari and in the company of Ethan, whom the Indian men watched curiously. They knew he was a physician, and they were puzzled at his new behavior. Coral was pleased that he chose to get on well with the workers' children and with the untouchable orphans, and now that the priest had unexpectedly disappeared from sight, there were few who bothered to call the children away. The bolder children ventured forth to watch the carpentry work and to wait for sign of Coral's ghari coming down the road from Kingscote, for she began bringing them sweet cakes from Piroo's oven. The baskets were quickly emptied as she made new friends.

Ethan emptied the skin of water, then tossed it aside. "What is *my* reward for all my muscle aches and splinters besides a daily ration of lemon water?"

"Sunstroke," she teased. "Don't you know better than to work during the noon hour? You are supposed to be inside the school resting and waiting for me to bring your lunch."

"I expected you to swoon and tell me how wonderful you think I am."

"Caution. The Lord may let your roof fall in."

"I'm almost done with the roof. Splendid, is it not? Sir Hugo would be amazed if he saw me now!"

"I wonder where he is?"

"Is the physician a carpenter, or not?"

Coral shaded her eyes and looked up. Ethan stood there, his white Holland shirt glued to his skin with perspiration and wearing a huge straw hat. She laughed. He looked anything but the Ethan Boswell she had known on the safari northeast, collecting bugs and butterflies for his "crow's nest" on the wooden barge.

"I wouldn't trade your hammer for all the jewels in the Taj Mahal!"

His eyes turned a warm gray. He climbed down to meet her. "I do have jewels for you, Coral. They are at the house. I ask for your permission to give them to you tonight. It is a necklace. I have waited to give it to you . . . hoping you would wear it as a 'bond' of our growing affection. One day soon I hope you will become my betrothed."

Coral thought of Jace and the Indian girl at Sualkashi
that he would marry.

"Yes, Ethan. One day soon. . . ."

———————

Coral's days were packed with excitement as she anticipated her success in teaching. At last the day arrived
for the dedication of the school. Elizabeth, Kathleen, and
Marianna sat on chairs under the shade of umbrellas
held by the children Ajay, Hareesh, Mona, and Kirin. Jan-
Lee and her young daughter, Emerald, were also there,
and Yanna, who had long ago given up fear of Natine in
order to align herself with the memsahib whom she loved
so dearly.

At the conclusion of the brief ceremony, with the
school now dedicated to teaching the Scriptures to the
untouchables, Coral offered a praise to the Lord for His
faithfulness and added: "And thank you, Lord, for Ethan
in making all this humanly possible."

When the ghari returned to the house with the others,
Coral remained behind with Ethan while Ajay and the
children who were with Yanna bravely stepped inside to
have a look at the new "shrine" that somehow was to
involve them. They saw nothing exceptional, only a large
bare room with woven bamboo mats for the rug. But the
Bible Coral brought had been placed on the table at the
front of the room, and they stared at the black holy book
with awe, thinking that the words from heaven would
not be read to them in the feringhi tongue, but in sweet
Hindi.

"I cannot believe my first class begins on Monday,"
she said. "I'll bring my desk down here, too, and some
cushions for the children to sit on." She walked about
the room, smiling. "You've done a wonderful job, Ethan,
but it does look dull in here, doesn't it? Kathleen is mak-

ing some posters, and I think the Christmas story will be perfect to start out with."

"Christmas, Miss Coral?" asked Ajay, puzzled.

"You'll find out soon," she said with a smile.

Sualkashi

Devi made the morning tea and carried it to the salon in her father's house, where both Gokul and Major Jace Buckley had been staying for the past weeks. As she entered quietly, she saw that her cha-cha was still asleep but that Jace was up and dressed and standing before the window. She stopped. The split-cane blind had been rolled up.

A glimmer of light from early morning fell upon the rattan table where she had left the Bible belonging to Michael Kendall. The other books were also there, given to Jace in England by John Newton. His vision had not permitted him to read them for himself, and her uncle could barely read English and had not been able to help him. But she had learned English well. She had sought to please Jace Buckley from the moment that Cha-Cha Gokul had brought him to meet his family in Sualkashi. That had been many years ago, and Devi had still been a girl in braids. Now she was a young woman of marriageable age, yet she had delayed her father's ambitions to marry her off to a rajput guard at the maharaja's palace in Guwahati, hoping that Jace would at last tell her he loved her.

He had not told her so. She had imagined his affection all these years, she thought sadly, watching him. He would never tell her the words she wished to hear, for she now knew beyond all doubt that it was the young Englishwoman who had stayed in her chamber that he desired. He had not told her so, but she could guess. How it was that she knew this, Devi could not completely explain even to herself. Yet she was certain since his arrival here that he thought much of the Englishwoman from the silk plantation called Kingscote. He had not mentioned her; he spoke little, only asking Devi to read the holy book to him and other books about the Christian beliefs.

Not that Jace had ever given Devi any reason to think he would marry her. He had never so much as hinted he wanted a relationship with her. Once, when he had come here on his way from Kingscote to ship Kendall silk to Cadiz, she had taken it upon herself to let him know she wanted him. She had been waiting for him in his room, seated on the matting in the dim shadows when he came in. She remembered back, and now felt nothing of the shame she had felt then when he refused her and sent her away. He had never treated her as anything more than a friend, as Gokul's niece, and yet she had hoped. The hope was in vain.

During these weeks at her father's house, he had wished her presence each morning but only to read to him. Now she knew even that desire had slipped through her fingers. *He can see now.* She knew he could, because she had watched him too long, too deeply not to notice the change in his stance. She even thought she knew what was going through his mind as he watched the splendor of the sun rising over the Brahmaputra River.

Quietly she placed the tray down on the low table, but this time instead of pouring the cup of coffee she knew he always preferred instead of tea, she walked softly up behind him to also look out the window. A smile touched her lips as she looked at him and saw his expression, but his gaze remained riveted upon the glory of the golden dawn, the splashes of vermilion, of topaz on the horizon, and still farther away the great white clouds that had not yet decided to drench India.

No, he did not see her. He did not even know she stood there, so engrossed was he. *He thanks his Christian God,* Devi thought, and felt nothing. *He believes this God has done for him what no other deity could ever do . . . take the darkness from his eyes.*

Jace had told her there were no other deities, only the one true and Living God, the Creator of the universe, but she held fast to her Hindu beliefs, for it was a way of life she knew, the only one. To give up her religion was the same to her as giving up India, and how could she give up her customs, her life?

Jace thinks his God has restored his sight. Has this one named Jesus answered him? She looked away from Jace out at the new morning.

"Look—over there!"

She had pointed to the east where pink flamingoes with wings tinged with black flew in a column, their colors merging with the light of the sun breaking like a flood over the distant mountains.

"How splendid the sight," she said.

If he spoke, she did not hear his words, but rather *felt* his reaction. For that moment they stood without moving, watching the color, the light, the graceful movement of their wings soaring high into heaven's freedom.

That moment would have been complete if she had felt his hand reach over and find hers. His answer did not include her. He turned from the window as though he were a part of that freedom. His excitement seemed to grow as she turned also and watched him go to the Bible, the books, and lift them from the table and look at them. The Bible went inside his tunic—next to his heart—she noticed. The books went into his satchel. His clothes were swiftly removed from the drawer and packed. He was putting on the black and silver jacket of his British uniform. He belted on his scabbard, called out to Gokul in a calm but strong voice.

The door flew open and Gokul entered as though having waited for this moment expectantly. One look at Jace and her cha-cha's hard brown face opened into a grin. "It is time, sahib?"

"Yes, it is time, old friend. The horses?"

"They have been made ready each morning, sahib, just waiting."

"We need wait no longer. Let us ride."

Gokul laughed so jubilantly that Devi couldn't help but join in, especially when Jace looked at her and smiled. Caught up in the excitement she ran across the salon and picked up his hat.

Almost shyly now she came up softly and handed it to him. "Goodbye, Jace."

His smile slowly faded. Gently his hand reached, lifting her chin to look into her eyes. Devi told herself she would not cry. And she did not. She lifted her head proudly.

Wordlessly the blue-black of his eyes said goodbye for the last time. Then his hand fell away and she watched him leave the room.

Gokul hung back, saying something softly in Hindi. Devi nodded. "Yes, Cha-Cha, I know, I understand him. It is *her* he wishes." Her eyes hardened for a moment. "If she does not run to him when he goes to her, tell her Devi says she is a fool."

Outside the house, the doves were cooing in the mango trees, and Devi thought that the day shone bright with an expectation all its own. She watched until their horses were out of sight. Then with a dignity that was part of her Indian culture, she went to find her father. She would calmly tell him that she was ready in her heart for him to arrange the wedding with the rajput.

———

Jace paused astride his horse to read the message delivered earlier to Gokul by a rajput friend.

Danger. Sunil has discovered the whereabouts of Prince Adesh Singh—the child you call Gem. He will seek Warlord Zin himself, or send others to pay jewels to have the prince turned over to him. Sir Hugo Roxbury is also aware of Zin and is your enemy. Take heed. Roxbury left for Kingscote plantation yesterday.

Jace scowled. Sunil knew! Somehow he must reach Zin before him! How many days ahead of him was Sunil? He turned the reins of his horse to ride from Sualkashi.

"Ill news, sahib?"

"Yes. Sunil is on his way to Zin. But we must go first to Kingscote. Roxbury, too, will know. I must alert Seward to possible danger where Miss Kendall is concerned."

10

Coral felt the eyes of disapproval from the silent silk workers as she arrived in the open ghari for the first day of the mission school. They stood in small groups watching her; young boys and girls hung back, some looking at her with wide eyes from behind trees and bungalows. Coral could only imagine the words of warning to stay away from miss-sahiba that had filled their ears recently. The sadhu was nowhere in sight, nor, of course, was Natine. They were too subtle in their disapproval to confront her openly. The warnings against attending the "feringhi's shrine-school" were propagated at night behind closed doors.

The first class opened as planned, although on a much smaller scale than Coral eventually intended. For one thing, she had yet to arrange the hours of schooling to coincide with the same time periods that the children were not at their duties in the hatcheries. This was not an oversight in her planning but was due to her mother's yet frail health. Eventually, Elizabeth Kendall would call for an assembly of all the workers on Kingscote and explain not only the purpose of her daughter's school but enroll the children whose families wished them to attend. Coral was under no false impressions and knew few if any of the Hindus would immediately come forward, but she anticipated that, in time, when the parents saw the success of the other children, they would relent. There would always be the majority who turned their backs and ordered their children to stay away from miss-sahiba. Coral's main hope was for the numerous abandoned orphans who were under the Kendall family's jurisdiction, most of them untouchables.

The memsahib, as Coral's mother was called, had long ago arranged for certain women who were also untouchables according to the Hindu religion to oversee a group of ten children who had no parents or relatives. All these untouchables Coral felt certain would eventually be enrolled, and that would require an even larger structure.

But for now Coral was content. The school was built, and the first class would be held before the rains.

Yanna had arrived early, bringing the four children they had rescued from the crocodiles. They now lived with Yanna in the bungalow once belonging to Rajiv and Jemani. The children, freshly scrubbed and warned into good behavior for miss-sahiba, were bright-eyed as they anticipated a great adventure. They sat cross-legged on the floor of plain matting.

For her first lesson, Coral told the story of Jesus and the children, using colorful sketches that Kathleen had made to visualize the Bible story. The children were all eyes as Coral emphasized how the disciples of the Lord Jesus had sent away the parents with their children, scolding them, and telling them that the Lord was "too busy" with more important matters.

Coral spoke in Hindi: "But Jesus was displeased with His disciples. 'Allow the children to come to me and do not forbid them.' And he picked each child up in His arms and blessed them."

The children leaned closer to stare at Kathleen's drawing showing small children climbing happily into the arms of the Lord. Then the children looked at each other and grinned. The little girl Mona giggled, and Coral sensed her delight.

Soon Yanna passed out cups of milk and the frosted sweet breads that Marianna had struggled the night before to shape and bake in the form of children.

They sang and clapped to Elizabeth's song:

"Saviour of all Nations,
Shepherd of young and old,
Guide us with your Words of light,
and make us all one fold. . . ."

Then class ended, and Coral knew that from henceforth she would have at least four faithful students.

She left the bungalow with the children clamoring to get into the ghari for the ride back, Yanna reprimanding Ajay for shoving Mona out of the way to take first position. Coral squinted at the hot sun, tying the ribbons of her hat beneath her chin. Taking the reins, she lightly touched the horse and it moved off down the road, the inevitable layer of dust kicking up behind the wheels of the ghari.

Thank you, Lord.

The afternoon heat was sweltering; not even a light breeze afforded relief. Ajay sat beside her on the seat, still holding the remains of his child-shaped sweet bread, although only the head remained on the napkin.

"Burra-sahib say school is cursed," came the unexpected remark.

"Natine?"

"He say it, Missy Coral. He told others if they go,

much punishment will come to us all by earth and sky. Mulberry leaves will fall from trees, and a great wind will carry Kingscote Mansion into Brahmaputra River. All the Kendalls will drown."

Coral kept her tension from showing. It angered her that Natine would frighten the children this way. "Natine has no power to speak such terrible things. Pay him no mind, Ajay. The words you learned today, they are good words. They bring hope, joy, and light to our hearts. They tell of the Lord who controls the Brahmaputra River, and all rivers."

"Including the holy Ganges?" he breathed, brown eyes wide.

"He is Master over all His creation."

The little boy looked doubtful. "You mean no wind will come to destroy, no fire to burn and kill the silkworms?"

Coral felt a tightening in her spine. Fire. The night that Gem had been abducted there had been fire. Was Natine's remark a coincidence? Frowning on her school was one thing, and she might put up with the inconvenience in the hope of winning his respect if not his heart, but scaring the children with visions of destruction was quite another matter.

She might tell Ethan, but she thought better about doing so. Unlike Jace Buckley, who knew India, who understood the sometimes insurmountable differences between the Indian and English culture, Ethan was often impatient and sometimes too anxious for confrontation. If she went to him with Ajay's information he might, as Jace put it, "blunder into the situation and ruin it."

She frowned, thinking of Jace Buckley. There had been a mutiny in Guwahati resulting in the death of the maharaja. Her father should have sent some message back to the family by now. And what of the safety of Gem?

Yet the major remained with Gokul and his family in Sualkashi.

Suddenly Coral felt a desperate longing for the stalwart presence of her father. Instead she became aware of the little boy Ajay watching her, and she tried not to show alarm, for concern that he might think her fear was due to the power of Shiva, the dark god of the Hindu religion.

"The Lord Jesus is more powerful than all the idols of all the world's religions," she told him. "He can still any storm, silence any raging fire."

But what of her own faith in His authority? Did she truly have confidence that He would protect them all from the many snares that lay like hidden traps?

She did, and yet . . . she dare not presume upon the Lord, knowing that better Christians than she had faced fire, sword, and martyrdom for the honor of bearing His name. How could she complain with simple trials and testings?

"But the truth is, Ajay, the Lord does not always answer our prayers in the way we expect, or ask."

"But why, miss-sahiba?"

"Because His plans are wiser than ours. And even in what we think is failure, there is victory."

He seemed satisfied, then: "But if the Christian God is more powerful than Shiva, and also very good, then why let wind and fire come so Natine can say Shiva is better?"

Coral smiled down at him. "I see you're going to become my star pupil. Your question has provoked the thoughts of great religious men. The living God is so wise, so good, that all His ways are higher than our ways, and all His thoughts are higher than our thoughts. Whatever He allows in the lives of His children is for a wise and good purpose. Even hard and bitter things are permitted to come, not to harm and destroy us but to teach us many things."

"What things?"

"Things like having patience in all our troubles instead of complaining, trusting Him in the darkness when we cannot see our way out, learning how to wait in hard circumstances when it seems the answer to our prayers should have come yesterday."

"Even if Kingscote burns down and silkworms all die? Will you still have school for us?"

Dear God, do not let me be insincere with the child when it's so easy to be pious. . . .

For a moment she couldn't speak. As they rounded the turn in the road and the warm hush of the jungle wrapped about them, Kingscote Mansion loomed ahead of them in the distance, white and serene against the setting blaze of ruby sky, and the poignant sight of her home arose to test her words of faith. For as she looked at Kingscote she imagined it turned into charred rubble before her eyes and the blackened ashes swept away in a great wind—the wind and the fire of Natine's threats.

She could not go on. Coral stopped the ghari and sat there for a moment, staring ahead. The sun beat down upon her. For a moment it seemed to Coral that she was not only tasting what it would be like to lose her home, her family, all that she held dear and precious, but even Jace—he was not here when she secretly yearned for his strength—although she could never admit it to him.

Gone. Everything dear. Was the school worth it? Was anything worth her forging ahead, ignoring all the signs of trouble?

To speak bravely of suffering and loss with ringing words of faith when all goes well is one thing. To taste the bitter gall and swallow it is quite another.

She remembered a past vow of surrender to whatever

134

purpose God may have for her life, whatever the cost. In answer, she had seen Gem torn from his nursery bed and carried off screaming in terror into the darkness, to what? Death? Suffering? She had not known his outcome, and fear expected the worst.

How easy for you, Coral Kendall, to make brave speeches in the sunlight. But how realistic of you to tumble to defeat in the trial! It was too easy to feel alone, empty of His grace, in doubt of the outcome.

She thought again of her defeat when she had first lost Gem. After these years the pain was gone. Even his face had begun to slowly fade as she saw the faces of so many other children, all with needs equal to his. But at the time of the loss, the foundation of her faith in God had seemed to crumble beneath her feet. God, if He was there at all, had seemed deaf to her cries and uncaring to her pain. She had yielded to seasons of bitterness. *What would I do if everything that means so much goes up in flames?* she thought, horrified.

There was no answer, only the steady beating of her heart.

Ajay was not looking at the white mansion of Coral's birth but at her face, and his brown eyes seemed to be entranced with a lovely sight. Coral felt his sticky fingers reach out and shyly enclose her hand. She turned her head and looked down at him. Ajay was not as beautiful as Gem; he had an old scar running across his cheek to his lip.

"Miss Coral?" came the urgent question repeated. "What if all silkworms die? No more silk, no more Kingscote forever?"

Ajay squinted against the sunlight as he stared up at her, and it seemed her answer would either bring the end of the world, or secure its foundations.

Faith, like a tiny seedling, unwilling to die—that

could not die—had reemerged like new growth after a frost, unscathed by the blast, growing and green and alive forever. She smiled at him. The Lord had graciously come to her like sweet rain on the mown grass.

Ajay's hand was squeezing hers, and she looked into eyes guileless and anxious to trust something, *someone*, for the first time in his life.

"Even if Kingscote burns down and the silkworms all die, school begins tomorrow at eight A.M. sharp. And I expect you to be there."

Ajay grinned. "Yes, miss-sahiba."

As Coral turned the horse-drawn wagon into the front carriageway, the voices of the children in the back called out excitedly. She followed their gestures down to the Brahmaputra River.

"Miss Coral, dekho! Topiwallah!"

Coral looked and saw a boat docked, and baggage was stacked on the bank. A familiar Englishman with heavy shoulders and a neatly trimmed short dark beard stood in black broadcloth, a wide-brimmed Spanish-style hat covering his thick ebony locks. Around him were a dozen rajput warriors in colorful but masculine garb.

"Sir Hugo!" gasped Coral. So her conniving uncle was alive and had decided to come to Kingscote directly from the British residency in Guwahati. Her fingers closed more tightly about the horse's reins. The indomitable presence of her uncle was the last thing she now needed to add strength to the trouble she was already having with Natine!

From the looks of his trunk and baggage, she guessed that he had come for a long stay.

Coming out on the front verandah with Elizabeth Kendall, Ethan also saw his uncle. He left the steps and walked down the sloping lawn to meet him at the riverbank. From the side of the house, Natine, leading two

136

male servants in white, also walked to greet Sir Hugo.

Coral only stared off toward the river, shading her eyes to get a better view, half hoping that she was seeing a mirage in the glittering sunlight. Manjis in white loincloths were unloading still more trunks and crates containing what she guessed to be books and medical supplies belonging to Ethan. At least Ethan would be pleased at his uncle's arrival. The medicine he had been forced to leave behind in Guwahati on short notice had been a cause of vexation.

Would Uncle Hugo have brought any information on Major Jace Buckley?

She sat, too preoccupied to climb down from the wagon seat. The heavy trunk and numerous bags and crates were being loaded onto an elephant's back. She was still mulling over the untimely arrival of Sir Hugo when Natine's niece Preetah emerged from the shadowed shrubs next to the verandah and slipped up to the side of the wagon where Coral sat. She took note of her secret friend Yanna in the back with the children, then her gaze swerved anxiously to meet Coral's.

"Sahiba, is not that man, the one they call Sir Hugo Roxbury, your uncle?"

Coral could see her concern and wondered what Preetah may have heard about the new British ambassador from Calcutta.

"Yes, my uncle, and Ethan's. Sir Hugo is memsahib's brother-in-law." Coral searched her face and saw only tension. "Yes?" she encouraged. "What about my uncle?"

"I must speak to you alone, sahiba, tonight."

As Coral was about to press for more information, the girl turned and hurried back into the house. Coral turned and looked at Yanna in the back of the wagon. Yanna too was grave but shook her head. "What concerns Preetah I do not know. You must do as she asks."

Coral had every intention of meeting Preetah. But now she thought of greeting her uncle, and it gave her no pleasure. He had arrived on the same day the school opened. And what will he say when he learns it was Ethan who built it?

Sir Hugo and Ethan were walking up the lawn toward the mansion, and Elizabeth had come down the steps to greet him warmly. Hiding her frown, Coral climbed down from the wagon, and drawing in a small breath walked to meet him.

"Why, Uncle Hugo!" she cried. "What a wonderful surprise!"

———————

That evening after the lavish dinner to welcome Sir Hugo was completed, Elizabeth gathered the family members in the large parlor that on festive occasions doubled for a ballroom. Tonight, as Natine and Preetah served refreshment from Viennese crystal, light from the chandeliers fell on the marble floors with their ivory-colored Afghan rugs. Coral sat on the divan made of polished mahogany with muted rose velvet cushions and watched Sir Hugo pace.

He had already told them what had happened in Guwahati, filling in the information that Ethan would not know about. The maharaja was dead, he stated again. Sunil was now on the throne and desired peace with the East India Company. "He claims no prior knowledge of the assassination of Majid Singh."

Coral knew that both Ethan and the major believed that Sunil was behind the entire ugly affair. She avoided looking at Ethan now for fear of giving her own feelings away and instead concentrated on Sir Hugo. He certainly appeared believable, his dark brows knitted together, his eyes somber.

"What will the Company do about the mutiny?" asked Elizabeth. "Will the treaty signed with the maharaja be honored with Prince Sunil?"

"It's my opinion they will not want to give up their foothold in Assam and will decide to work with Sunil. But until troops arrive from Calcutta we are in a precarious situation."

"You don't expect Sunil to attack Kingscote?" asked Elizabeth dubiously, and Coral wondered how much her mother actually trusted Margaret's husband. But from her poised expression Coral could tell nothing. "After all," continued Elizabeth, "we pose no threat to whatever Sunil's ambitions to rule the area may be."

"We're not out of danger yet," said Hugo. "Sunil resents the English presence, and his followers number in the thousands. Despite earlier gratitude for the Company's support when Burma had ambitions to incorporate Assam, he has changed and now wants us out of the northeast." He looked at Elizabeth pointedly. "No matter how Hampton feels about Company jurisdiction over the Kingscote silk enterprise, he would have done well to listen to me when I and Margaret were here last. Had he done so instead of demanding his independence, there would be sufficient Company soldiers here to avert any attack from Sunil or Burma."

Elizabeth's expression hardened, and Coral knew her mother resented Hugo's accusation against Hampton. It was Marianna who spoke up, her blue eyes wide. "You mean we're likely to be attacked?"

"There is no reason for undue alarm, dear," said Elizabeth. "Kingscote has always stood in the way of risk. It is the reason your father hires mercenaries to patrol our borders. We have men now."

"Thank God," said Hugo and walked to the window where a slight breeze entered. "But it is not enough, Elizabeth. I do not care to alarm you and the girls—"

"We are not alarmed," came her calm voice. "As I said, Hugo, we've faced danger many times. If it comes to an actual attack, we all know what to do. Hampton has trained us well since the girls were only children. I only wish he were here. As I said earlier, we should have heard from him and Alex by now."

Coral was watching her uncle. Her past experiences with his carefully planned schemes gave her an advantage the others did not have. Ethan, too, knew him well and undoubtedly saw behind his attempts to frighten Elizabeth into whatever cooperation he wished from her. Coral could see that Hugo was impatient with Elizabeth for remaining calm in the face of the fears he raised, but he was able to keep his irritation masked.

"I dislike to say this, Elizabeth, but Kingscote is in danger. The English military is to blame for this predicament! Even now Jorhat has less than twenty British soldiers. The rest are native sepoys and sowars!"

"Captain Gavin MacKay and Major Buckley would have arrived months ago with troops had it not been for Plassey Junction," said Kathleen, her eyes snapping with sudden temper. "If I recall, Uncle, the major's troops were all massacred in a mutiny, and he was severely wounded. We all barely got here alive!"

Coral expected her mother to speak her sister's name in a warning tone, but she did not. Coral, afraid that Sir Hugo might suspect Kathleen of knowing of his involvement in the Plassey mutiny, turned on her as though upset. "Really, Kathleen, I'm surprised at you." She stood to her feet and walked over beside Ethan, who had his back to them all, looking out the window. She laid a hand on Ethan's arm protectively. "Everyone knows that Major Buckley was to blame for Plassey. He hates the military and did little to protect his men. If we are without sufficient troops at Jorhat now, it's partly the major's fault."

Kathleen looked at her as though she had lost her mind, and even Ethan turned and stared down at her. Coral glanced at Sir Hugo. As she had hoped, he noticed how she had come to the side of Ethan, and how her hand rested possessively on his arm. "Even now the major has turned his back on the lot of us to pursue his own selfish aims," she finished.

Sir Hugo came alert, his dark eyes fixed upon her. Ethan seemed a trifle surprised, but there was a glimmer of triumph in his gray eyes.

Coral turned toward her sisters. Kathleen dropped her eyes to her lap and Marianna glanced at her mother. Elizabeth showed no expression, and Coral wondered if she guessed what she was doing.

"Well, at least Gavin will arrive soon with the 13th," spoke up Kathleen. "I'm sure the revolt at Plassey has been brought under the British control by now."

It was the first time Coral had seen Kathleen boast about Gavin MacKay. Usually she had little good to say of the military, for fear of becoming a soldier's bride and living with Gavin on one of the frontier outposts belonging to the Company.

"Yes, they should have gotten through by now," agreed Ethan.

"What is this about the major turning his back?" came Sir Hugo's voice, casual but definitely interested.

Coral felt a moment of glee. It wasn't often that she managed to divert her uncle from his own purpose. "After the maharaja and his guards were killed, the major seems to have cut all ties to his military responsibilities," said Coral.

"You mean you have not heard from him?"

Coral was about to say he was in Sualkashi, but

Ethan said casually, "He went to Darjeeling to search for Hampton. He should have been back by now."

The room went silent. *Why would Ethan say such a thing?* wondered Coral.

Sir Hugo turned to Elizabeth, who sat still and appeared rather pale. "You are wise enough to know the reasons; we all do well to worry about Hampton."

"If only he were here. With the rains coming, he and Alex will be in desperate straits," said Elizabeth.

"Yes, so I've been thinking, Elizabeth. There is little I can do here now. I'll leave you a few of the rajputs, then take the others with me. I've come to the conclusion that it's worth my risk to ride to Darjeeling to search for Hampton. I intend to leave in the morning."

The thought brought mixed feelings of joy and fear to Coral. Her eyes caught those of Preetah, who unobtrusively had brought in a tray of hot coffee and tea. Coral remembered the girl's request to speak with her tonight.

"You mustn't go alone, Uncle," Ethan protested. "I shall ride with you."

"There is no need. I have the rajputs—"

"Every extra man will help," came Ethan's cool interruption. "The journey will prove too dangerous, especially for you. You don't know India."

"And I suppose you do?"

Ethan appeared to ignore the slightly caustic tone.

"There will be mud slides and flash floods, and Darjeeling could be washed out," he said.

Coral felt a nervous qualm in her stomach. "Are you sure you should go, Ethan? Uncle does have the rajputs."

He turned to her, his gaze trying to conceal his concern. "I was going anyway, just as soon as my work here was done. I've only been waiting. Perhaps I've waited too long."

She wondered what he meant, but the answer was

not meant to be spoken aloud.

Elizabeth was quick to show her relief and gratitude. "I can spare a few extra men from the hatchery if you think they can be of help."

"You best keep them," said Sir Hugo. "Kingscote may need them far worse before this is over." Sir Hugo's expression hardened as he turned to Ethan. "Very well. Then we will leave first thing in the morning."

"I shall be ready." He turned from Hugo's cold gaze to Coral, his tension showing. "Excuse me, but I've some packing to do before I ride out in the morning. I will need a fresh supply of medicine if Alex is ill with the fever."

Coral watched Ethan cross the room and go out into the hall, then call for Natine, inquiring if the elephant had brought the baggage up from the river yet.

Elizabeth moved toward Sir Hugo, taking his arm and assuring him of her relief now that he had arrived. While they were taken up in a discourse of their own, Coral slipped from the parlor and came into the wide hallway, the lantern light shining on the red stone. She stood there, thinking. Preetah could be in the cook room, but if she went there now Natine might see them together.

As though emerging from nowhere, Preetah's small sister Reena appeared, her eyes wide and dark with the thrill of her secret mission. She glanced about, and seeing no one other than Coral, whispered, "Go down to river! Preetah wait there for you now!"

Coral gave her a pat and sent her on her way. Glancing into the parlor, she saw that Sir Hugo was occupied with her mother. Another glance up the wide stairway proved she was alone. Quickly she opened the heavy front door and stepped out into the sultry night.

11

Standing on the wide lawn looking down toward the dark water, Coral saw the slow-moving river ripple like darting silver fish in the starlight. The landing ghat appeared deserted, but she expected Preetah to be waiting there in the shadows. She lifted the hem of her billowing skirts to keep from tripping and sped down the lawn, feeling the sod sink beneath her slippers.

Nearing the bank, she listened to the soothing lap of the water. A melancholy call of a night bird echoed from the trees on the other side of the river. Soon a shadow disengaged itself from the boats, and Preetah stood nervously, her head draped in a dark chunni. Seeing Coral, she beckoned, and Coral followed her onto the ghat.

The girl appeared uneasy, glancing about as if expecting her uncle Natine to loom in the night and catch them in some conspiracy. "I fear and have affection for Natine, but I cannot keep silent, sahiba, especially now that Sahib Roxbury arrived this day. I—I must tell you what I heard in the village."

Coral tensed. "Yes?"

Preetah stepped closer, still glancing up the lawn where the mansion's windows were golden against the night. She whispered, "I fear because everyone thinks your brother Alex is somewhere in Darjeeling, perhaps lost, perhaps ill. But he is not there. I overheard Natine speak to the priest while I was in the house of a cousin. Alex Kendall is not in India but has left for England."

Coral did not move. Dazed, at first the girl's words made no impression, like falling seeds lying dormant on the cold earth. *England!* What was he doing there? When had he gone? Why didn't her father and mother know this? Why had they not seen him leave Kingscote?

Her mind raced backward to that last evening she had spent alone with Seward in her father's study. Seward was wary about the message that had been delivered to her father.

Jace and I, we be thinking Alex could not have the fever. It is very uncommon to the climate of Darjeeling.

The next deduction was obvious: If Alex was not ill, if he was not in Darjeeling, if he was in England, then the message delivered to her father was a lie to lure him away from Kingscote. But why? Was there to be some attack on Kingscote by Sunil and the ghazis opposed to the English presence in Assam? Was Sir Hugo helping them for lucrative reasons of his own?

Deliberately keeping her voice calm, so as not to frighten the girl more than she was already, Coral asked, "What exactly did you overhear Natine say when you were in the village?"

"Sahiba, I swear I did not know about your brother before your father left with the men from the village to trek east—"

"Wait, when did you hear this—when were you in the village with Natine?"

"When I went with him to see the priest about the marriage to Pravin."

"Three weeks ago!"

"Oh, sahiba, forgive, but I was so afraid, especially after I helped with the children brought to the dispensary, after what we saw in the trees! I feared to tell mem-sahib what I heard, feared she would go to Natine at once. He would know I overheard, that I spoke!"

Coral fought to keep her anxiety under control. And no wonder Preetah was afraid to tell Elizabeth, thought Coral. If Alex was not lost in the mountainous region as the messenger had informed her father, then both Jace and Seward were right. Someone had lied in order to lure her father away! And what of her brother's ring shown to her father as evidence?

Her father's letter to Sir Hugo at Guwahati had mentioned several skirmishes with Burmese infiltrators along the border of the Kendall holdings. Perhaps Sir Hugo was speaking the truth about an upcoming attack on Kingscote, and the enemy had wanted her father gone during the conflict. Or were there more devious plans at work?

Her heart pounded as her mind sought for answers. Could there be a plan to harm her father? Or was it Alex? Who would have sent the false message? Prince Sunil? Sir Hugo? Perhaps Hugo was working with Sunil. . . . But if that were true, why would Hugo warn them tonight of an imminent attack? His worry had appeared genuine, but then, when it came to the workings of her uncle, how could she be sure of anything?

Her meeting with Jace in the palace garden at Guwahati came to mind. At times Jace appeared preoccupied with concerns he had not been willing to share with her. Those troubling suspicions must have been about her father.

I was right to insist Seward leave Kingscote to search for Father, she thought.

But many weeks had already gone by. Anything could

have happened, and since Seward himself had gone there alone to search for her father, he too might be in danger.

Coral's first inclination was to go immediately to her mother. Yet Preetah was right. Her mother would confront Natine, perhaps even Hugo. What could she do if her own brother-in-law were involved with Sunil?

"You are right," said Coral. "My mother would confront Natine. She might go to Sir Hugo too, and he would only deny everything. He has a way of making us all appear imaginative fools driven with girlish hysteria. He would demand who his accusers were, and that would mean I must identify you."

"Natine, I do not know what he would do if he thought I told you what I heard. When he is angry, sahiba, I fear his face."

Thinking back to their excursion into the jungle trees, Coral, too, shuddered.

Ethan was the only one she could turn to now. He had insisted on going with Sir Hugo to Darjeeling. Did Ethan suspect his uncle of plotting against her father? And why did Hugo wish to journey all the way to Darjeeling to search? Was it a ruse to later convince her mother and the family that he had been worried about Hampton? If something did happen to her father, then he could be the one to return in sad spirits bringing the dark news and pretending he had gone out of his way to locate him.

"The words Natine and the priest spoke, did you hear them all? Hold back nothing."

"I was visiting relatives to make final plans for my marriage to Pravin. I had gone to the other room to sleep on the mat with the other girls, all cousins. They were soon asleep, but I could not. I heard other men from the village come quietly to talk to Natine in the next room. The priest was with them. I did not hear all they said, for they spoke in low voices, and it was this that worried

148

me, for I heard the name of your father."

Preetah drew her chunni about her throat and glanced nervously toward the darkened lawn between them and the lighted mansion. "The priest ask Natine what will happen when the burra-sahib's son returns to Kingscote from England and memsahib learns Alex left a letter before going away. 'They will know he was never in Darjeeling,' he said. 'What then of the message? What then of the ring? How will you explain this to the memsahib?' Natine said the feringhi ambassador will explain everything to the memsahib. Not to worry, for by then Sahib Roxbury would be new burra-sahib of Kingscote."

Coral's hands went cold and she tightened them into fists against the sides of her skirt. Yes, Sir Hugo would be certain to have adequate answers. He always did.

Coral's mind flashed back to London to the times she had been so ill. Jace was right. She had been drugged in order to control her. And the letter she had written to the major soon after Michael's death, asking about the charges made by her uncle—there was no doubt now in her mind that Hugo had destroyed it. He feared Jace and did not want him around. And how much had her uncle been involved in Gem's abduction? Was it not he who had found the other child's body in the river? Who had helped to deceive the family into believing Gem was dead until Jan-Lee had discovered the scar on the child's foot? Hugo had been on Kingscote the night the sepoy took Gem and the fire was started in the silk hatcheries.

Coral's anger seethed. If Sir Hugo dare harm her beloved father she would . . . she stopped, her breathing coming rapidly. Yes, she would go to Ethan. But what could he do alone?

"You did well to come to me," said Coral quietly to the girl. "Say nothing to anyone. It's important that neither Natine nor Sir Hugo realize we know the truth. Perhaps Seward was able to locate my father in time . . . and if they return soon, there is hope we can stop whatever is planned."

"Yes, but what I say is not all. I have this." Preetah reached under her chunni and came out with a folded piece of paper glinting white in the starlight. "It is the letter from your brother. After I heard he left it for your father, I looked in my uncle's bungalow." Her voice shook. "It was there."

The letter! Coral could not read the words in the starlight even though she recognized Alex's handwriting. "I will not forget your loyalty, Preetah."

"I must go now quickly. They will miss me."

She watched Preetah slip away into the darkness. Coral walked back toward the lighted house, concealing the letter from Alex in her bodice. As she neared the front lawn, she became cautious.

Inside the hall, she heard voices. A brief glance through the archway into the parlor showed the family was there as she had left them earlier. Her mother and Sir Hugo were in conversation, and Marianna sat on a settee doing her embroidery, but from the stilted movement of her hands Coral could tell she was nervous around their uncle. She had never forgotten her terrifying moment in the garden at Barrackpore when she had heard the conversation between Hugo and Harrington.

What was Marianna thinking now? Did it cross her mind that the man whose demise they had spoken of might be their father?

Kathleen was not in the parlor. Coral dimly wondered where she had gone. As she climbed the stairs and went down the hall she noticed a light under the door of Alex's room. She suspected Kathleen was in there for reasons of her own, but Coral had too much on her mind now to find out. The person who could do the most good for her father now was not Kathleen but Ethan.

Ethan was in his room still packing when she tapped. He seemed surprised to see her, but Coral motioned him to silence. "Come down to my father's office after the others leave the parlor. I must talk to you alone."

He nodded, curious but alert, and Coral went past the other chamber doors to her own room to read the letter from Alex. As she stepped in, closing her door, she stopped abruptly. Her eyes confronted a large bronze urn sitting in the middle of the room. Inside, she glimpsed the charred remains of a small black book—

"No! Not the Scriptures!" She rushed forward and knelt. Despair welled within. The Hindi New Testament that she had received at William Carey's mission station in Serampore lay in ashes.

Her hands formed cold fists. *Natine!*

The bamboo rattled in a light breeze, and she looked up toward the open verandah doors. Had she not bolted them earlier?

Slowly she walked forward, and her gaze fell on the lock. *Broken.* She stepped out and looked across the lawn toward the river. Maybe not Natine. The sadhu perhaps?

She shuddered to think anyone might find her chamber so accessible. Or was the broken lock only to mislead her? Sir Hugo had arrived today. Yet she could not see her uncle staging the dramatic episode of burning her Scriptures and leaving them as an omen in the middle of her room.

She slipped out and came to the stairway. Now only a dim lantern glowed in the parlor. Her mother and sisters had retired, and she supposed that Sir Hugo had also. He and Ethan were to rise early the next morning for the ride to Darjeeling.

Coral listened tensely, then went softly down the stairs into her father's office. It was not that late, and

Mera and the other servants were still up and attending their duties.

In her father's office she shut the door and heard the gilded clock in the Long Gallery chime. She counted . . . six, seven, eight.

Outside the open window she heard a distant noise. Horses on Kings Road? She decided it must be only the elephant boys moving the beasts to their stables near the hatcheries for the night.

In the sanctuary of her father's office, she lost herself in the big leather chair, holding one of his favorite books on her lap, drawing comfort from the items that reminded her of his fatherly strength.

"If only you are safe, Father. What will the family do without you?"

She leaned her elbows on the scarred mahogany desk, resting her head in her hands, listening to the distant sounds, yet not distinguishing them in her anxiety. She must have sat there without moving for some time before she heard the office door open quietly. She was expecting Ethan, and yet felt a nervous tingle at the back of her neck. She feared to turn, almost certain she would see an angry ghazi.

"I saw the light, my dear, and thought I better look in."

At Sir Hugo's voice she stiffened. Anger flooded her chest, for she was now certain he had heaped lies upon her for the last years. Yet she must play dumb to his present workings, for if he guessed the truth were known he might implement whatever plans he had more quickly. She thought of her burned Scriptures.

"I was reading, Uncle."

"You must not worry about your father and Alex, my dear. I've confidence Ethan and I will be able to find them."

"Yes. Perhaps they have rendezvoused at the tea plantation belonging to the major and Seward," she said, forcing herself to casual conversation. "Alex may have decided to buy into the enterprise of raising tea, in memory of Michael. We know how much the Darjeeling project meant to him. I believe Seward mentioned there is a dwelling on the land now . . . they intend to build a mansion, to make the plantation into another Kingscote."

Did she sound normal?

"Then I shall find a tour of the holdings of interest."

She said nothing, hoping he would withdraw before Ethan came downstairs.

"Ethan informed me of the good news. No need to tell you how pleased I am. A pity the wedding could not be a double celebration in London with your cousin Belinda and Sir George. Grandmother Victoria would be so delighted."

Coral's heart pounded with confusion. What had Ethan told him? She stood from the chair and turned to face him for the first time.

Sir Hugo's dark eyes were alive with pleasure, but his smile teased her, forcing itself into a rueful grin. "After learning of the bungalow school, which Ethan foolishly risked the anger of the Hindus to build, news of your engagement eased my kindled displeasure."

Her lips tightened. One evening at Kingscote and he was already behaving as its new master.

"Really, Coral!" he said with a wince that came off as insulting. "I do hope your willful spirit becomes tempered with marriage. Perhaps children of your own will squelch some of your lust for excitement and daring."

She found his ugly choice of words to describe her interest in the untouchables demeaning.

"But we'll forget this dreadful mistake, my dear, and

celebrate your wiser decision to marry Ethan. I confess, I was beginning to worry over the delay. You are getting on in your twenties now, and it is past time to turn your attentions to family and home."

"Kingscote is my home," she said, holding back a look of fury that caused her voice to shake.

"Of course. And so is Roxbury House. I hear your sister Kathleen wishes to return to work in silk design. I think it a wise idea, especially with Belinda and George there now. Not to mention your aunt Margaret. I mentioned it to Ethan tonight. We should have the wedding here at Christmas, and a trip to Europe for a honeymoon—if Napoleon ends the war! It might interest you to know that I've made fruitful contact with his government, and they are enthusiastic about importing Kingscote silk into Lyons."

Coral could not speak. She tried to keep from shaking with anger over his bold audacity.

Marriage! She had not told Ethan she would marry him soon; she had only agreed to accept the necklace as a form of engagement. Whatever love she had for Ethan— if indeed it was that—was held captive in a sea of confusion by unwanted memories of Jace Buckley. She had been wrong to hint to Ethan she might marry him soon, wrong to accept the necklace; yet she had been furious with Jace and jealous at the thought of the Indian girl at Sualkashi.

She touched the ruby and diamond necklace at her throat, and when Sir Hugo came to brush his lips against her forehead, she turned hot with embarrassment, knowing she had failed miserably and had misled Ethan.

"You—you must not think we have set a date," she stammered, angry because she had backed herself into a corner.

"Nonsense, my dear. There is no reason to wait. Elizabeth is also pleased. And of course, Hampton will be as well, as soon as he knows. If all goes well, he will know soon enough. Ethan and I will leave for Darjeeling in the morning. You best not stay up late; you are looking a trifle wan. Good-night."

The door shut behind him. Coral stared at it.

A Christmas wedding, indeed! She threw the book down on the desk with a thud. How dare Ethan mislead him into thinking the matter settled!

She knew why, of course. The school. Hugo must have been furious with him at the news, and Ethan had appeased his uncle by bringing up the necklace she had accepted.

She reached behind her neck with the idea of unlatching the clasp when there came a small tap on the door, and it opened. Ethan stepped in, his face taut. "Was that Uncle talking with you?"

Coral put a clamp on her temper. "Yes," she quipped. "He's cutting the wedding cake a bit soon, is he not?"

Ethan flushed under his tan. "I am sorry about that, Coral, but—"

"Sorry? After you've announced our Christmas wedding?"

He sighed, and she folded her arms tightly, her eyes narrowing. "You'll have to disappoint him. I am not ready for that final step. I—"

"Good heavens, Coral! Will you hold me off until we have gray in our locks? Besides, I cannot tell him now," he said. "We are leaving in the morning. It must wait until we return, unless I can talk you into keeping your promise."

"I made no promise, Ethan. You are being unfair. But making me feel guilty will not force me to marry before I am ready."

"Will you ever be ready?" he snapped.

She turned away from his bright, frustrated gaze. "I do not know."

He said something under his breath and walked stiffly to the open window, pulling aside the curtain to allow in the night air, but the night was still and hot.

"Blasted India. I am sick of the heat, the dust, waiting for the monsoon."

"Ethan, I must talk to you about Alex. It was why I asked you to come here. I didn't intend to speak with Uncle, or begin an angry discourse over our future. The future must wait until matters with my father and the mutiny at Guwahati are settled. And then there is Gem. . . ."

"What about Alex? We are leaving in the morning to search."

Her heart began to race again. "Alex is not in Darjeeling."

Stunned, he stared at her. Coral produced the letter. "It's from Alex. He wrote this before leaving Kingscote weeks before my father ever went to Darjeeling. But Hampton never received it. They disagreed about his future here on Kingscote and evidently came to harsh words. Alex apologizes in the letter for the things he told my father, and informed him he was going to England to sort things out in his own mind. What 'things' he wished to sort out, Alex doesn't explain, but evidently he thought father would understand. Alex promises to return with his decision next year."

Ethan was amazed as he held out his hand for the letter. She gave it to him. "Ethan, he is not in Darjeeling. You do understand what this implies?"

"Yes. Where did you get this letter?"

She hesitated. Then told him what Preetah had overheard in the village. He showed no surprise, but she did detect a resolve of purpose that worried her.

"I'll find Hampton. Do not worry."

She took hold of his arm, her eyes searching his. "You already knew Alex was not there."

"No. But I've suspected your father may be in trouble since I left Guwahati."

"Guwahati? But how! And why! Who told you?"

She listened as Ethan explained how her uncle had altered the major's orders for the purpose of sending him to Darjeeling, but that Jace suspected that men loyal to Sunil waited in ambush.

"Is that why you stopped me from saying he was at Sualkashi tonight?"

"Yes. The major requested I say nothing. He gave me a map. If I did not hear from him in three weeks, I was to go on alone to Burma to find Gem."

She searched his eyes. "You kept it from me."

"Buckley insisted."

His flat tone alarmed her. What else had he withheld from her? Was Jace's injury worse than Ethan had earlier implied? "Why wait three weeks?"

"He has his own mission to Jorhat and Burma, but I insisted I wished to be involved in Gem's rescue."

Gem's rescue. The words brought excitement. Then Jace had not forgotten, nor changed the plans he had informed her about in the garden.

"I want the truth. Is Uncle Hugo involved in a plot with Sunil? How does it implicate my father?"

"Good heavens, Coral! Do you expect me to know the dark weavings of his mind?"

He turned away from her. *Dark weavings.* She mulled over the words, and they only provoked her alarm and suspicion.

"I think you know more about Uncle than the rest of the family," Coral ventured.

"And what is that supposed to mean?"

"It was Uncle who pressed for this marriage long before we ever met in London."

He turned, his gray eyes growing tender. He took hold of her shoulders. "Yes, but the moment I saw you, I knew I agreed. Had he been against it, I'd still desire you to be my wife."

"You know his mind. He looks on you as a son."

"Does that make me guilty of his ambitions, or that I am partner to them?"

"Where my father is concerned, no, but—"

"Had you asked me in London if Hugo was capable of planning assassinations I would have been outraged. After Guwahati I can only say I do not know."

Icy fingers of alarm gripped her and a sickening feeling settled in her stomach. Roxbury House in London . . . the time Sir Hugo had blatantly lied about Jace being negligent as captain of his ship . . . Hugo had made her think Jace was guilty of Michael's death. The drugged state that she had been kept in at the family house on the Strand until she appeared to accept his explanation that Gem was dead . . . Hugo had tried to convince her she was bordering on insanity. Only his unexpected call back to London to receive a new position as ambassador to Guwahati had caused him to voyage to Calcutta without first pressuring her into marriage with Ethan.

What was it that her uncle truly desired so badly that he schemed and lied for? To be master of the family silk dynasty? What political ambitions in Assam were included in his plans?

Whatever drove Hugo, he was willing to arrange the untimely accident of her father in the mountainous regions of Darjeeling to grasp it. Yet men murdered for far less than riches, esteem, and political power. Thieves killed on the streets of Calcutta for a handful of rupees.

What was it that Jace had once told her about Sir

Hugo? " . . . *Greed and ambition can make devilish masters. . . . I think your uncle has an appetite not easily satisfied. . . . It is his nature to disapprove of making an Indian
child a silk heir. Especially if that position contests his
own. . . . You must be extremely cautious.*"

Her revulsion must have shown in her expression, for
Ethan took her hands into his, holding them too tightly
in the heat of his anxiety. "Darling, don't look like that.
You must not let Hugo know you understand. Dear God,
I do not know what he might plan if he thought that you
and I would not marry." He swallowed and awkwardly
patted the side of her face. "Please, darling, I'll find
Hampton. I promise. Perhaps it is best I leave tonight
ahead of him. That will give me a day's advantage. Don't
worry."

His words only partially settled into her consciousness. Ethan was not involved in Hugo's plot. But what
about London? What about those horrible days when he
and Hugo worked together to convince her that Gem was
dead?

Lies. Had Ethan obeyed Hugo and used his medical
knowledge to control her for Hugo's purposes?

As she searched his eyes, she could not find malicious
deceit. There was the mission school. . . . He had risked
Hugo's anger to build it for her. And there was her illness,
which he had successfully treated, as well as helping her
mother recover. Ethan was not all dark like Uncle Hugo;
he was also light, and the two natures appeared to come
into constant conflict . . . perhaps because of the hold
that his uncle had on his life for so long in England. He
was beginning to change now, to become his own man,
to resist Hugo's bidding.

She touched the rubies and diamonds around her
throat. "Ethan, there is something I must know about
London, about the house on the Strand."

A flicker of consternation showed in his eyes. "Coral, do not ask."

"Why?" her voice tremored, but she was calm. "I have the right to know the truth if you are to be my husband. How can you ask me to trust you in the future if you will not tell me the truth now about the past?"

"Because the past is over. It can only destroy the future if we allow it."

"I will always wonder. The time we were in London . . . when I was so ill and having those nightmares about Gem. Did you knowingly drug me in order to do as Hugo asked?"

"Do you think I would ever deliberately harm you? I am not only a physician, I cared for you even then. I have always done what I believed was for your best welfare."

"Your denial is evasive. Did you drug me to keep me from going to the director of the East India Company about Gem?"

"I tell you, no."

"What of Manali? Was Jace right about the spider bite? Was it also one of your Eastern drugs learned from your stay in Burma?"

"Darling Coral, I swear it isn't true!"

"But you have always done what Hugo wanted!"

"No! No!"

"It is he who wishes us to marry. And you agree because you have your own purposes for being here. The lab! The miserable mosquito lab! Your research means more to you than the life of my father!"

"Not anymore—"

"Not anymore? But it was true in the beginning?"

"Yes! But I tell you I love you! I would do anything for your happiness, anything! Did I not build the school?"

"For what purpose? To obligate me to marry you now

160

that Hugo has arrived? If my father is dead, he is my guardian, and between you and Hugo, you think you can control me. Building the school was just a way to make marriage to you more palatable. Tell me the truth, Ethan!"

"All right! I built the school for reasons of my own—to please you, to win your love. Is that so despicable a cause? I am not as religious as you are, but I approve of the work you want to do with the children. I did not deceive you for other ambitions. I meant what I said about respecting your spiritual convictions, and I'll do whatever it takes to keep my father from hurting you!"

As though struck, Coral took a step backward. She choked, "Your father?"

Ethan paled and turned his back. When he spoke his voice was dull and quiet. "Yes. Would God it were not so, but it is." He turned, his eyes blazing. "But I am not his puppet, not anymore. I'll do what is best for you, for us, for Kingscote—for Hampton. I'll find him!"

Her mind reeling, fear latched hold. "No. Do not go with him! I put nothing past him now. Nothing."

"He would never harm me," Ethan said wearily as his shoulders sagged, all energy spent. "What he does, he does for me, as well as for himself—and the family. Sometimes he truly believes he is doing the right thing. I know that's hard for you to accept, but it is so. Hampton's refusal to work with the Company, your school. Hugo has monumental dreams of greatness in Assam that will spread not only to London but Paris, Madrid, Rome. He thinks Hampton will ruin it, that his ambitions are too small and narrow. Sunil has promised Hugo a treaty for all Assam, and access to Burma, if he cooperates with his plans to rule in place of the maharaja. Hugo has been working with him. I confronted him in Guwahati; he knows how I feel about what is happening, but he would never harm me if I stood in his way. However, we have reason to fear for the others . . . Hampton and Buckley—my father will do what he must to win."

Her heart stopped. "Jace? What about him?"

Ethan shook his head as if he could not talk and walked away from her.

New suspicions fed her fears. "Hugo wishes to have Jace killed? Is that it? *That is why you stopped me tonight from saying he was in Sualkashi.*"

"Yes."

"Then he was expected to go to Darjeeling after the mutiny?"

"Yes. Jace felt certain an assassin waited for him on the road. Probably one of Sunil's rajputs. Hugo was involved in the plan. It was he who changed his orders in Guwahati at the last minute. He sent him to Darjeeling to search for Hampton."

"But he did not go!"

"No," he said flatly. "Jace is too clever to believe anything Hugo says. He came straight to me with news of the plan to kill the maharaja. We worked together to save him. We were almost out the gate when Sunil attacked with the war elephants."

Weary now, Coral walked to her father's desk and leaned against it. She heard him come up behind her, taking hold of her arms.

"I'm ashamed to be his son, but I love you. Please, Coral, do not hold me to blame for my father's sins. I'll find Hampton. I'll bring him home safely."

The depth of his anguish touched her heart with pity, and with something else—perhaps a wish to solace him. He looked so miserable.

Her lack of argument must have fed his expectations, for he grasped her, holding her tightly, burying his face in her hair. "Coral . . ."

Above his voice she could hear horses. "Ethan, no—"

He held her, kissing her, oblivious to all else. She tried to push him away, hearing the voice of Rosa in the outer hall. And then the door opened. Over Ethan's shoulder she faced Major Jace Buckley. He paused, his cool gaze taking them in from head to foot.

"Jace!" she breathed.

12

Ethan heard Coral's startled response and turned around. He showed no surprise, nor alarm at being caught with Coral in his arms. If anything, he seemed smugly pleased that Jace Buckley would find them together. As she sought to step back, distressed, Ethan's hard fingers grasped her waist, holding her close to his side, as though he possessed her.

"Ah, Major. Good evening. We were not expecting you."

Jace's brittle gaze held Ethan's. "Evidently not." He looked past Ethan to Coral. A familiar smirk touched his mouth, but there was no humor in it. "Miss Kendall. My apology for interrupting too soon."

Too soon? Confused by his words, she flushed with embarrassment and could say nothing. But his next statement, smooth with meaning, she did fully understand. "Had I intruded a moment later, I would have fully expected to hear a ringing slap."

Coral felt the dart pierce her heart. She turned away.

"You might as well know, Major," came Ethan's almost victorious tone. "Coral and I are betrothed. The marriage is to be held here on Kingscote this Christmas.

She wears the ruby and diamond necklace of engagement. And now, Major, I assume you are here on business about Burma?"

Coral whirled, her hand going to the necklace. She saw Jace's gaze fix upon the glimmering jewels.

"My mistake, Doctor. Congratulations," came Jace's calm but precise voice. "I shall wait in the hall. I have come for my map."

"The map, ah, yes, of course, Major. I shall get it at once."

Jace stepped out into the hall; Ethan followed, crossed the floor, and took the stairway up to his room.

Coral stood in her father's office, her heart hammering, her hands cold. If Ethan had been facing her she might have made good the ringing slap of which Jace had hinted. She remained without moving, hoping against hope that Jace would come into the office. Even a cynical remark from him would have been appreciated at the moment.

He did not come.

She stood there, her nails digging into her palms, waiting. The front door opened and closed, not with a bang, but so quietly that her heart wrenched.

He was willing to leave matters as they appeared.

But of course he would. He was going to marry the Indian girl anyway.

Before she realized it, Coral caught up her skirts and rushed from the office into the hall. Rosa stood in the shadows, probably wondering if she was to prepare a room for the major. Coral drew in a breath, opened the front door, and stepped out into the night.

The porch was empty. She glanced about for Jace and saw him farther down the carriageway, mounting his horse. Another man on horseback was beside him. That would be his Indian friend Gokul.

Coral flung aside her pride and hurried down the steps. She hesitated only a second, then rushed down the cobbled drive toward Jace, who was turning his sweating horse in the direction of Kings Road, and Jorhat.

A slight look of surprise crossed his face as he reined in his slow-moving horse and half turned in the saddle to look down at her. "Miss Kendall?"

His voice spoke to a stranger, as though his eyes had never seen her before. Coral's throat tightened at his rejection and she wanted to say, *"Be as you once were, Jace, when you cared about what I did. When you felt opinionated enough to tell me I was wrong!"*

Quietly she said, "I hope you've recovered from your injury."

"Yes, thank you."

She searched his face. *There must be something left of that moment in the garden.* But he only looked down at her with eyes that refused to be searched, watching her without emotion.

"You are riding on tonight to Jorhat?"

"Yes, as soon as Ethan delivers my map."

Even the way he pronounced Ethan's name held none of the usual challenge. Coral knew she must not make a fool of herself. It was now clear that Ethan had told her the truth about Jace and the woman at Sualkashi. With as much grace as she could manage, she murmured quickly, "Goodbye, Major. A safe journey."

"Goodbye, Miss Kendall. Thank you."

Coral turned and walked back up the drive to the steps and into the house. Inside she met Ethan coming down the stairs with something in his hand. Coral said nothing to him and took the stairs up to her room.

———

Astride the black horse, Jace watched Coral walking

away. The sight of Coral in Ethan's arms still left him feeling cold and angry. He jammed his hat on his dark head and glanced up at a lighted window he suspected might be her bedchamber. His blue-black eyes narrowed.

"Ah, sahib," came Gokul's mock sigh. "I am disappointed in you."

Jace gave him a cold glance. "I'm in no mood, Gokul, so just keep silent."

"And sahib says he knows women," Gokul softly chuckled.

Jace flapped the horse reins across his gloved palm. Gokul continued, casually taking fruit from the cotton bag tied to his saddle. He polished the skin, held it up to the starlight to check it for its sumptuousness, then bit into it. "Is my belief, sahib, that if you let a woman like *her* escape, you received more in concussion than short loss of vision." Gokul looked at him with a smile. "I shall impart my wisdom, sahib."

Jace continued to flip the reins, growing more irritated by the moment. His eyes narrowed as he watched Gokul relishing his fruit with too much noise.

"I wager one share in tea plantation that English beauty could be had by you if sought. Yet you let her fall like ripe fruit into hand of irritating doctor." Gokul shook his head as if in disbelief. "You should not ride off tonight, sahib. Stay."

"You dream, old man. She's going to marry Boswell this Christmas."

"Yet she comes running after you. Most satisfying, I would think. Why you think she come to side of your horse all polite and pretending nothing of feelings? You too busy pretending you do not feel. But old Gokul, he took long look at young woman and see something worth fighting doctor for in eyes. Very nice eyes. Green like soft emeralds—"

"Your tongue wags too much. Silence, here comes our gallant gentleman."

Gokul chuckled and threw the core of his finished fruit into the darkness. He felt satisfied, certain he had accomplished his goal.

He was right. Gokul rubbed his face to hide a grin as he heard Jace say in an even challenge to Doctor Boswell: "I've decided my horse needs rest and food. And I'm ready for a bath and a decent bed. Tomorrow will be soon enough to be about my business."

"As you wish," came the stiff reply. "But remember, sir, we made plans to deliver the boy from Burma together."

Jace had no intention of allowing Ethan to come with him. "The map." Jace held out a gloved hand. Retrieving it from Ethan, he swung himself down from the saddle and tossed the reins to an Indian boy waiting by the side of the house. Jace was watching the lighted window and saw the verandah doors open and a woman step out into the cloistered shadows. He knew without being told that it was Coral, that she had probably wondered why the horses had not ridden away. He walked slowly toward her verandah and paused beneath it, looking up. He knew she saw him. She stepped back and went in. A moment later the door shut.

———

Perhaps the cause of her nightmare was prompted by seeing Sir Hugo again. Hurtful, frightening memories seemed to leap back into flame from smoldering embers; perhaps it was bred from the fear that lodged in her subconscious over the safety of her father. Maybe it was seeing Jace again and feeling the emptiness as he prepared to ride out of her life.

Whatever drew the dark foreboding to her mind,

Coral found herself tossing restlessly as snatches of the old nightmare that had once plagued her came stalking. . . .

Somewhere in the darkness a tiny helpless child was calling her, and she left the front steps of the porch to find him. Urgency pressed her forward toward the familiar trees. Suddenly the jungle erupted with flames; all Kingscote was on fire and the heat was unbearable, touching her skin and blackening the air with clouds of smoke. The child was trapped amid the flames and Coral was alone, trying to grasp him from certain death, but he remained ahead, just out of her grasp.

"Gem!"

Then Coral became aware that someone else was with her struggling to grasp the boy. She could not see his face, but she knew they battled together until they were ultimately torn apart by the fire. As he disappeared she saw him. Jace! Then she stood alone again with the fire everywhere. She had lost them both. She could see them receding farther and farther from her grasp as the fire of death sucked them away—

"Jace!" she called into the emptiness.

She sat up in the darkness of her room, her heart slamming in her chest, her skin wet with perspiration. She held her head in her hands, closing her eyes tightly.

As the trauma faded with reality, a flash of dry lightning streaked in the distant sky, followed by the deep rumble of thunder.

Coral looked around and realized she had not undressed for bed but had fallen asleep on top of the satin coverlet. She remembered suddenly that she had not heard Jace ride away. Earlier, she had heard Rosa talking as she had led him to a chamber in the hall not far from her own room. The idea that he had decided to stay piqued her curiosity, but after his cool reception in the carriageway she did not intend to ask questions. Perhaps the monsoon was ready to break, and he had wisely decided not to ride on.

She tried to push away any notion that she had been the cause for his unexpected change of mind. It didn't matter. In the morning they would all ride out for their various destinations, their rendezvous with time and events: Sir Hugo and Ethan, Jace and his friend Gokul.

She went to the verandah and opened the doors to see if the monsoon was arriving. The night was still and she stepped out. Not too many hours had passed since Jace had arrived, for as she scanned the sky, the location of the moon told her it was somewhere near midnight. The sky was yet clear; the rains had not yet come. And yet . . . something was wrong. . . .

The sky in the direction of the workers' bungalows glowed with a splash of crimson, etched with an unnatural haze—what was it?—black smoke! Not the silk hatcheries! Not again!

From the adjoining chamber, Jan-Lee threw open the split-cane shade and leaned out. Her young daughter, Emerald, was quickly beside her, wearing a long white nightgown, her waist-length braids showing dark against the white gown. "Missy Coral!" the girl cried. "Fire! Fire!"

Coral's fingers tightened around the verandah rail as she stared off in the distance at the billow of acrid smoke drifting from the direction of the hatcheries—no, not the hatcheries—

Her bedroom door flew open and Coral whirled to face Kathleen, whose expression of alarm mingled with sympathy. "It's the school!"

For a moment Coral wanted to weep. Her eyes met Kathleen's in wordless understanding. In a frenzy they both bolted down the hall and raced for the stairs. A bedroom door flew open but Coral did not stop. She and Kathleen ran for the kitchen. Kathleen fumbled to unbolt the door, flinging it open so wildly that it smashed into the wall. Down the steps they raced into the back garden, into the night.

Somewhere between the stairway and the back porch, Kathleen, far stronger, had surged ahead to the stables. Coral was forced to pause in the sultry night, trying to catch her breath. In the distance the red glow of fire reflected against the sky.

Too late, it's too late—the flames would swiftly consume the wood and thatch roof. All their work, gone.

Kathleen came riding on the old horse kept near the kitchen outbuilding, her skirt flaring, and her hair flying as wildly as the horse's mane. Even in that swift instant, Coral was amazed to see Kathleen's determination emerge, drawing her own up out of the pit of depression. Kathleen grabbed for Coral's arm. "Get up, hurry!"

Coral grasped the pommel with both hands, but they were sweating and slippery. She managed to swing herself up behind her sister as Kathleen slapped the reins and clapped her heels against the horse's side. With a shower of dust they galloped in the direction of the mission school.

As they rode nearer to the fire the horse became frightened and whinnied, pulling back nervously. Kathleen steadied the reins and turned the horse from facing the fire, unable to ride closer. Coral stared at the burning structure. The flames appeared to cackle mockingly and dance victoriously, casting billowing smoke and cinder about them.

Coral bit back her rage and bitter disappointment, sweat joining her tears as she dashed a hand across her face. They could never put it out—never! The hard-won mission school was dead! Years of planning, all their work and prayers, going up in smoke!

She turned her face away from the foul fumes, her throat burning from a gust of smoke that blew against them. Kathleen rode some feet away. By now a number of Indian workers appeared in silent groups, watching, no doubt believing that Kali had brought judgment on the shrine of the feringhi's religion.

Coral climbed down from behind Kathleen, her hand grasping the saddle for balance as she stared toward the burning ruin.

Kathleen's voice tensed as she leaned over her from the saddle. "If you cry, so will I, and I won't be able to stop—"

"I am not crying," said Coral. She began walking slowly across the dusty ground in the direction of the smoking rubble. Flames continued to spurt up from charred wood, bursting forth, then dying into smoke.

Coral heard another horse ride up and Jace asking Kathleen what happened.

"Someone set the mission school on fire!"

"Mission school!"

"Ethan built it. Coral has held classes for several weeks. It's gone!"

Coral heard the workers talking excitedly among themselves, then Jace's commanding voice ordering them in Hindi to leave.

Kathleen turned her horse, and seeing Major Buckley walking toward Coral, she flicked the reins and rode back toward the house. As she trotted down the road, she saw Ethan rushing to the fire, his shirt yet unbuttoned. There was a rifle in his hand. He stopped and stepped to the side of the road when Kathleen rode up.

"The school?" he asked.

"Yes, there is nothing left—no, Ethan, don't go there.

Coral wishes to be alone, and there is nothing more to be done."

"I cannot leave her out there by herself! Someone started it, and whoever it was may still be there!"

"She is not alone. And you'll receive no answers from the workers even if you threaten them. Whoever did it will be protected. Let my mother ask the questions. They respect the memsahib."

Seeing Ethan's expression harden as he began to ask further, she said firmly, "Yanna is with her."

It was true, for Kathleen had seen the girl running from her bungalow with the children to see if the fire was spreading.

Kathleen leaned toward him, extending a pleading but restraining hand. "Please. Coral wishes to be alone. We best get back. The others will have heard us leave the house and will want to know if we are all right."

"You are certain she is taking the loss well?"

"Yes. Come, I'll put water on for tea and coffee. It won't be much longer before you and Uncle Hugo will need to start out for Darjeeling."

———————

Jace stood watching Coral as she faced the smoldering ruins of the small mission school. Her hair was mussed, and there were traces of smoke and ash on her dress. She had never looked more noble, more beautiful to him than she did now.

With cool determination he thought again of the reason he had stayed. Gokul's goading remarks had snapped him back into reason—he would be a fool to leave without telling her how he felt. He would contest Ethan for Coral Kendall with the same commitment he had previously given to other causes that maintained his adventurous freedom.

If necessary, in order to have her, he would pursue her across the continent of India and beyond. He would defeat Ethan. For that matter, he thought, his emotions now confident and contained, he would win over any other man who might stand in his way.

He understood what devastation she must feel over the burning school. He was not thoughtless to her pain, but there could be another school, the next one built of stone. He would see that she had it, and despite the danger, he would protect her even if he had to hire English mercenaries to guard her while she carried out her heart's purpose in serving Christ.

But there was more on his mind, which he believed to be crucial. Like the smoldering ruin that held her captive to discouragement and defeat, Jace believed that what they secretly felt for each other must be seized and secured before the kindled flame of all that was noble in love was also destroyed and left in ashes. For unlike the school, if they lost each other because of pride or fear, they could not rebuild—not if he rode away. . . .

It mattered not that she might be engaged. The engagement was wrong. The one thing that mattered to Jace was that he knew he loved her. His old friend Gokul had helped him understand the reason behind his earlier determination to ride out without contesting Ethan. Walking in and seeing her in his arms had caught him off guard, and the pain had penetrated more deeply than he had thought possible. Angry that she could hurt him, and at himself for failing to preserve his immunity, he had wanted only to protect himself. In the past he could walk away from a woman. Once at sea, or on some risky adventure, he would forget all about her. Not this time, and he felt relief, even delight. He had found a woman who could fill his life's void, who was noble, strong in godly pursuit, and pure. One that set his heart pounding, one for whom he loved enough to lay down his life.

————

Coral heard Jace walk up behind her, and turned.

The warm glow of the diminishing flames flickered against the handsome cut of his features, and the familiar blue-black eyes were intently fixed upon her. Amid the rubble he stood as the one reality that could rekindle her shattered emotions. Her cold heart began to beat again, pounding in her temples.

A familiar slight smile touched his mouth. He studied her. "I have never yet fled from a battle. When it comes to the only woman I want, I will not walk away. I've decided to stay and contest Ethan for a worthy prize."

Her breath caught in silence. For a moment their eyes held, each searching for truth, and as the realization of their need for each other became known, it drew them together at the same instant, forcing a decision that promised a love too strong to be denied any longer.

Coral moved toward him at the same moment his hands enclosed her arms, drawing her, and it seemed she belonged in his embrace, that it was home for her heart. Her head fell back to receive his kiss, and the world disappeared about her with all its ugliness and ruin.

I love you, she wanted to repeat over and over. *I love you. I love. . . .* She heard the words spoken, but not by her. Jace was breathing them as he held her.

"I once convinced myself I would never become vulnerable to any woman. I was wrong. My armor is off, and I confess I need you more than anything else this world can offer," and with those words he was kissing her again and again.

"Answer me," he whispered, looking down into her eyes.

"Yes . . . yes—"

"Yes, what?"

"You are the one I love, Jace."

It was several minutes before he released her, and all the strength had gone out of her. She clung to him desperately, oblivious to the night about them, of the smell of smoke, of sputtering wood.

He looped his finger about the necklace on her throat and lifted it, his dark eyes narrowing at the jewels. "Gaudy, and boasting of financial power. Boswell has garish taste in jewelry. I find it repugnant . . . you are much finer than this. It stands between us like the vaunted wealth of the Kendall and Roxbury family, boasting of what I do not have to give you."

Her heart pounded with expectation. "So it gets in your way, does it?" she whispered.

"It reminds me of a religious medallion to ward off an 'accident.' And I rather think that Jace Buckley is the accident."

"What would you like to do about it?" she asked softly.

His eyes held hers, then he took her shoulders and turned her around. Coral smiled as she lifted her hair and felt his fingers unclasp the latch.

A moment later she turned to face him and Jace held up the necklace to dangle in the firelight, and rubies danced like flames of their own, the diamonds flashing like starlight.

He lifted her chin and turned her eyes away from the necklace to meet his gaze. A brow went up.

"Right now there is little on the Darjeeling land except the beginning of a house and a few miserable tea plants."

She smiled at his persistent dislike of tea.

"But someday—if Seward, Gokul, Jin-Soo, and I are successful, it might be different. Notice I say 'might.' It will take years before we can become as superior in tea as Kingscote is in silk. At present, I cannot offer you rubies and diamonds."

She reached a hand to his, and with her fingers, she blotted out the twinkle of the jewels, her eyes holding his, and loving the glimmer of warmth she saw in them.

"You are certain you mean this, Coral? You are the only woman to whom I would ever risk my heart."

She was thrilled, but could not resist— "What about that Indian girl?"

"What Indian girl?"

"At Sualkashi. That day you brought me there when I was ill. The next morning she was very smug. Too smug. She called you 'Jace'—and there was a gleam in her eyes when she said it. It was very intimate."

"Ah, sweet jealousy. Coming from you, I find it very satisfying. But there was never anything intimate between Devi and me. A certain damsel masquerading as Madame Khan had already filled my mind with her presence wherever I went."

Confusion and pleasure swept through her at the same time. "But Ethan said—" She stopped.

His eyes hardened. "Just what did Ethan say?"

"It does not matter now. I understand the truth."

"But you might not have. I shall demand the truth from him."

"No. Please do not."

"Is that why you accepted the necklace, because you thought I cared for Gokul's niece?"

"Yes, although I never actually told Ethan I'd marry him, but he seemed to think so."

"At Guwahati he insisted you had agreed to marry him after you left me in the palace garden. I do not know if I truly believed his boast, but I was afraid you might have agreed after that stinging rejection," he said wryly,

178

touching the side of his face. "I guess you know you gave me something to think about when you walked away."

"I saw the Indian girl in my mind, and . . . well, became furious that you would tell me goodbye."

"I doubt if I could have stayed away. I implied as much in the message about Gem."

"Yes, and you are here now, and nothing must be allowed to come between us. But Hugo thinks I'm going to marry Ethan. They have actually been audacious enough to plan a Christmas wedding."

His mouth turned with thoughtful sarcasm. "Then I suppose he will demand his duel after all."

"Duel?"

"Never mind," he said with a smile. "It is you and me I want to discuss. I respect Elizabeth and Sir Hampton, but they are likely to favor Ethan as a son-in-law more than an adventurous sea captain. Just how deeply are you willing to commit yourself to me before I face the lions?"

She reached both hands and drew his dark head down until her lips found his, giving him all the assurance he needed.

The necklace slipped from his fingers and fell into the hot dust, and Coral felt his arm enclose her.

"Then we have a bargain, Miss Kendall."

"We do, Major."

"When?"

"Well. . . ."

"As soon as I return from Burma."

"But I will need to make plans for a grand wedding, and though I shall vow to die before I marry Ethan instead of you, I fear you will yet need to speak to my father and mother, and then there will be a wardrobe to make—"

His arms tightened about her. "Oh, no, mademoiselle,

none of that runaround you gave to Boswell for the past few years. Now that our minds are made up, I have become an impatient man. You will become Mrs. Jace Buckley as soon as I return from Burma."

She smiled. "Yes . . . just as soon as you come back to me."

"That is one thing you can be sure of—I will come back."

13

Jace took her arm and walked her away from the rubble to where his horse waited, but Coral was not anxious to get back to the house. She would never fall asleep after everything that had happened. *I am actually going to marry Jace*, she thought, and looked at him possessively. Major Buckley, the captain of the *Madras*, and Javed Kasam, all belonged to her heart. Marriage with Jace surely promised to be exciting.

"Do you still have the golden monkey?"

"Goldfish and Jin-Soo are both anxiously awaiting your arrival in Darjeeling. You do not mind if Goldfish sleeps in the same room with us?" he asked innocently. "He has a few habits that are hard to break."

She gave him an amused glance. "I suspect the captain of the *Madras* does too."

"Jin-Soo will take to you immediately," he went on smoothly. "He'll insist that his ginseng tea is just what is needed to make you strong and healthy." He held the stirrup for her foot. "Ride?"

Coral shook her head and slipped past him toward the road, calling over her shoulder, "Let's walk back. I still have so much to tell you."

She was thinking of Alex and the letter Preetah had found, but before turning to more serious matters she said innocently, "You do realize marriage to me will make you Sir Hugo's nephew?"

Jace cocked his head and looked at her.

Coral smiled and walked ahead of him. "I forgot to mention his new interest goes beyond silk to tea."

Jace grinned as he took the horse's reins and followed her on the dusty road that led the short distance to the mansion.

As Jace and Coral walked together, their mood turned as somber as the dark and silent road that hemmed them in on both sides with mulberry trees. Coral began to explain everything that had happened on Kingscote since they had parted in Guwahati, including Seward's search at her insistence and Ethan and Sir Hugo's trek the next morning with a dozen rajput warriors to Darjeeling.

"But why Alex went to England remains a curious thing," she said.

"Maybe not so curious."

"Why do you say that?"

He did not explain but asked, "Does Roxbury know you have the letter?"

"No. I only received it tonight from Preetah. I did show it to Ethan. That was the reason we met in my father's office. We had been . . . discussing matters when you arrived." She glanced at him, wondering if he understood that it had not been her intention to be in Ethan's arms. Evidently he was satisfied, for he let it pass.

"Tell me about the school. What was Roxbury's reaction?"

She thought of her uncle coming into the office earlier that evening, and shuddered. "He knows Ethan built it. The misconception Ethan gave him of an engagement has mollified him temporarily. I do not know what Uncle will do when he learns about us."

His slight frown told Coral that he was more disturbed over what Sir Hugo's reaction would be than he was over Ethan's. "Say nothing until I return from Burma. I will worry less about you that way."

"But how! Ethan will notice I've removed the necklace."

He looked thoughtful. "Roxbury is leaving at dawn with Ethan. That is not too long from now. Can you avoid them both for the rest of the night?"

"Yes, if I go in the back way I suppose I can, but eventually I will need to tell Ethan. He is likely to return before you arrive from Burma."

"When your father and Seward arrive I'll have less reason for concern." He frowned down at her. "Until tonight, I thought you were safe with Seward here guarding you."

"He felt bad about leaving, but I encouraged him. We were both so worried about my father."

"With good reason. But I have confidence in Seward. Between him and Hampton, they have a chance to survive." He stopped on the road and faced her. "It is best I do not return to the house. I'll locate Gokul and ride out tonight. Any trouble with Ethan must wait, lest Roxbury be alerted. Ethan is of the Old School and will insist on settling differences in a duel."

"You are not serious!" she said, horrified. "A duel?"

"My dear girl, are you so naive of the ways of Europe's gentlemen?"

By the tone of his voice she could not guess if he were being serious or cynical.

"Ethan will think nothing of showing up on the front lawn with pistol and sword in hand. My concern," he said dryly, "is that his temperament will prompt him to act at four in the morning. I would rather sleep by the side of the road than be rudely awakened."

"A duel is out of the question—it is absurd!"

"What! The beautiful damsel sought passionately by two men is offended by such knightly display?" He smiled and folded his arms. "You mean you do not want me to fight to win your hand? Or are you afraid Ethan will shoot me?"

His jesting nettled her. "I'm quite certain you can take care of yourself in duels, but I prefer a more civilized approach."

"Duels are a noble part of Europe's foundation, and any lord in England will tell you so. And if her ladyship required one more noble deed in order that I win her hand, you would hear my voice on the lawn calling Ethan out."

She smiled and studied him. "Would you, really?"

He lifted a brow over her seeming pleasure.

She changed the subject. "I have a notion Ethan got the necklace from Sir Hugo at Guwahati."

"Does Roxbury usually trek across India with a satchel of jewels and other bangles?" he asked dryly. He removed the necklace from his jacket. "You better take this now."

She looked up in surprise, then felt the cold jewels pressed into her palm. "I suppose I should return it to him. I will as soon as he returns from Darjeeling. He should know right away it is over between us—and, I am quite angry with him over his deception," she said, thinking of Sualkashi. Another suspicious thought entered her mind. "Ethan said you were only slightly injured in the rebellion."

"He did not explain?"

"I suppose I should have pressed him, but when he

said you had gone to Sualkashi to marry Gokul's niece, I wanted to forget—"

"That is what he told you! No wonder he sought to coerce you into a quick engagement. He thought you might just be ready. He knew I would come to Kingscote for the map within three weeks if I regained my sight."

Startled, she searched his eyes. "You lost your sight? But how?"

He touched the side of his head and said wryly, "After being struck on the skull several times, including at Calcutta when that miserable thief stole my Mogul sword, my vision was affected. I'm all right now, but I need to avoid another concussion."

Ethan had lied to her!

"Never mind me, I want to know what you've been up to while I've been at Sualkashi studying theology."

Theology? She did not take his remark seriously and let it pass, going on to tell him about the children Yanna had rescued from the crocodiles, and how she had brought them to the dispensary. "Along with Jan-Lee's daughter, Emerald, the four children were my only students. Now I've lost both the school and the Hindi Scriptures."

He regarded her. "The Scriptures from William Carey?"

"I found them in my room earlier this evening— burned."

"Natine."

Her heartbreaking loss returned with vivid clarity.

He drew her to him. She thrilled at the look of determination she saw in the blue-black eyes.

"Every end brings a new beginning," he said. "We will get new Hindi Scriptures. By now Carey may have translated them into Assamese. You can have both! We will build again, Coral. Next time in stone. It won't stop the ghazis, but it will discourage a hastily lit torch. And next time we will try building in a less confrontational spot. They see a school in their backyard as a religious shrine. It was bound to be a goad. We do not want to challenge them with an impression of superiority but in meekness instruct those who oppose the light. Next time, why not build closer to the river near the elephant walk? You'll attract more children, and being closer to the mansion will make it appear to be more of a Kendall enterprise."

She noticed he used the word "we" when speaking of rebuilding, and her heart beat with joy. "I should have thought of that—near the elephant walk. And I should have expected trouble from Natine after I witnessed the religious sacrifice to Kali."

He looked at her swiftly. "On Kingscote?"

She explained about her excursion into the jungle with Preetah.

"Are you telling me Natine and this priest from the village threatened you?"

"Not threatened exactly," she admitted cautiously. "But I heard my name mentioned."

"Which is quite the same thing, and dangerous." He took hold of her shoulders. "You never would do as I asked before, but I must insist you listen to me now, Coral, especially with the school burning down."

"Of course, Jace, anything you say," she said sweetly.

He gave her a questioning look, then went on. "What did Natine say to you about the school?"

"He was upset, but that did not surprise me. He told me the East India Company would control Kingscote if I persisted in spreading Christianity among the workers. He seemed to think the Company could stop me. I insisted they had no jurisdiction here, that neither I nor Sir Hampton would be ruled by the Company's ambitions in Calcutta. You know how they are against William Carey holding public meetings and distributing leaflets among the people."

She did not like the gravity in his eyes, for it only convinced her that Natine truly did serve Sir Hugo, as Jace had already told her in the palace garden.

"So Natine appeared confident of the Company's intervention if you persisted?"

"Perhaps it is only a hope of his."

"I think not. He would not risk saying that if he didn't have assurance from someone."

"Sir Hugo?"

"I'm sure of it. You haven't forgotten amid everything else that Hugo wants control of the silk enterprise? His new position as ambassador for the Company enables him to interfere here. And with your father called away to Darjeeling, Roxbury intends to become the new master of the Kendalls, as well as the Roxburys in London. Except for you, there is no one left to oppose him."

"My mother will never turn Kingscote over to him, even if something did happen to my father."

"Your mother is a strong woman. You are very much like her. But your uncle will do what he feels he must to gain power. I do not know what he has planned with Prince Sunil, or for that matter with Natine, but while I am gone you must promise me to do nothing to provoke either one of them."

He pulled her against him. "I want you here in one piece when I return."

His concern only awakened hers. "Ethan said you suspected an assassin on the road to Darjeeling."

"Do not worry about me; it is you who must be cautious. I'm almost tempted to take you with me."

"To Burma? I have had quite enough of crocodiles, spiders, and tiger attacks, thank you. I'll be well enough here. And my mother and sisters will need me with them." She touched a palm to the side of his face. "The next journey I take with you will be to Darjeeling."

His strong hand enclosed hers. "Your father made certain to hire mercenaries to watch the borders of Kingscote?"

"Yes. We had a man killed recently. But surely they will not get through to the mansion."

He frowned. "I do not suppose you can use a pistol?"

She smiled. "I can. Father taught us all years ago. Does that surprise you?"

"Nothing surprises me about Coral Kendall. Keep it loaded—and don't get sentimental. Shoot point-blank if it ever comes to it, understood?"

She shuddered and nodded. "But it will not come to that."

He said nothing and looked down the road. "Coral . . . before I go, there is something I need to tell you about Gem."

She noted the change in his voice at once and bolstered her courage. "Yes?"

"Did Ethan say anything to you about the maharaja?"

She shifted uneasily. "He mentioned his death. The message you sent said Gokul discovered where Gem was being held."

"Yes. But it was the maharaja who shared the truth. Gem is alive, but there is more. Are you ready to hear and accept it, however it may disappoint your own plans for Gem?"

Somehow she had sensed the truth would not be what she had long hoped for since arriving home to Kingscote.

He hesitated. "Gem is heir to the throne at Guwahati. That is the reason Sunil searches for him. As long as Gem lives he is a threat to Sunil's ambition to become the maharaja."

Coral made no sound. Dazed, she listened as Jace explained the details of what he had learned in Guwahati, and of how Sunil had sought the hand of Jemani in marriage.

"And Jemani?"

"We do not know her blood. We think she came from a princely line in the south. You adopted a baby," he said softly, "but he could never be truly yours. Gem belongs to India. His title is Prince Adesh Singh."

Despite her best effort, tears welled in her eyes. She blinked them back. "Adesh—yes, I like that name."

He belonged to India. The words repeated themselves.

Jace reached inside his jacket and drew out a cloth. As he opened it in the starlight she saw gold, emeralds, and rubies.

"These rings belong to the maharaja. Sunil would kill to possess them, for they are the royal rings of the family dynasty. They belong to Prince Adesh."

His use of the Indian name was deliberate, to build a wall between her and the child she knew as Gem.

Coral remained silent, not trusting herself to speak. She watched as he folded the cloth and placed it back inside his jacket. She swallowed. "I feel proud that God allowed me to save his life. We must save him now too, Jace!"

He drew her into his arm. "Yes. I am sorry to hurt you," he whispered. "You could consider contesting his right to the throne, but I doubt if you will gain any help from the East India Company. Sunil is on the throne now, and he is no friend of the English presence in Assam. When troops arrive from Calcutta they will seek to overthrow him. The Company will see young Prince Adesh as the key to their hold in north India. Because of past ties with you, they will expect the boy to be sympathetic to the English."

Coral concentrated on the steady beat of Jace's heart beneath her ear. She had lost Gem, but she had Jace. Together they would have a new life in Darjeeling. In time she would have her own son. *Jace's son.*

And Gem? Melancholy stole over her heart. She would never forget the child of the monsoon. And as though a wind stirred, bringing back that night so long ago, her memory found its way back to Jemani and the little hut. Visions of the birth of Gem played before her with rich clarity. She could see Jemani's lovely face, hear her words as if repeated in the night wind:

"Jesus," whispered Jemani so sweetly that Coral's breath had paused. She watched Jemani's lips move softly into a sigh. Again Coral seemed to feel her fingers, hear her whispering, "Take . . . my son. His godmother— you promised—no untouchable. . . ."

"No untouchable indeed—a prince!" Coral repeated as she rested the side of her face against Jace's rough jacket. With those words she realized that Jemani had been trying to tell her that Gem did have royal blood, but she had died before she could explain.

In her memory she felt the rain, remembered carrying the baby to the ghari to bring him to the Kendall mansion. She could see Jace in the rain too, hear his smooth voice warn: "I dislike the idea of a girl ending up with a broken heart."

She came back to the moment, aware of the still night. How long they stood there she did not know. He simply held her, and she took solace in his love.

She raised her head. "Where is Prince Adesh?"

"Burma. Zin has him. Indian gurus have been schooling him for the throne."

She felt a stab. She had taught him of Christ, but how much could a small child be expected to remember? Very little. Did he even remember her?

"Listen, Coral. A rajput friend sent word to me at Sualkashi that Sunil has discovered where his nephew is. Gokul and I have little time if we are to stay ahead of him. Sunil has the loyalty of the maharaja's army, and he will try to stop us."

Suddenly she remembered the nightmare, and it brought cold fear. She held to him tightly, her eyes wide and pleading. "Do not go!"

He showed faint surprise, then smiled, but his voice was kind. "After all the zeal and prayers you have expended to locate him, and how you begged me to return him?"

"We'll hire mercenaries to find Gem. Stay with me, Jace. It was you in the awful dream!" she whispered.

"What dream?" he asked gently. "The one you had so often in London?"

"Yes, yes, only this was far worse, for *you* were in the fire with me. You disappeared. Both you and the child slipped from me into the flames and were taken away—Jace, I am afraid."

"Since when do you interpret prophecy from nightmares? Darling Coral, you've had a traumatic day, and you fell asleep disturbed. It is natural you would have a bad dream."

"No, no, you were with me helping to save Gem, just as you have been all these long months. And in the dream you had him in your grasp—only neither of you could escape. Please! Do not go. If anything happens to you I won't be able to stand it!"

"Coral!" He held her tightly, soothing her hair. "It was only a nightmare; it was not real. I will come back. Nothing can keep me from you."

"This time it was different. Both of you were in danger."

"Perhaps I was always in the dream, but you weren't

aware of it until tonight. Finding Gem has filled our sub-conscious thoughts. I do not believe the Lord is terrifying you with nightmares. Does not the Scripture say He speaks through His word?"

"Yes, you are right, only—what if it is a warning?"

"I am already alert to danger and the traps of Eastern intrigue. This is one time I do not need handwriting on the wall. God gave me a mind, and He expects me to use it. I'm aware Zin is a dangerous man. And Sunil will kill me if he can. But I am not going to give him the oppor-tunity."

He lifted her face to his, and the glint of confidence in his eyes brought her courage.

"I expect to come out of this alive, and with Gem. India needs him, and I have faith enough to believe he will always think of you as his mother. He will want a relationship with you even if he does sit on the throne. Whatever happens on this excursion, the Lord is Sover-eign. Is this the brave young woman who was willing to face Sir Hugo, Natine, and a host of ghazis to build a mission school? God is answering the prayers you have invested in Gem. Will you let fear steal your peace and paralyze you at the very gate of victory? I don't think so."

His knowledge and confidence in God went far deeper than she had hoped. Coral's voice quavered. "You never spoke like this before. You are right, your armor is miss-ing, and I like it."

"I'll come back," he said again softly. "Now that He has brought us together, we will trust Him with our fu-ture."

Her eyes closed tightly, and her palm clenched. *Please, Lord. Let our lives merge into one, and with your light shining upon us.*

She raised her lips to meet his as he bent to kiss her

goodbye, and they held each other. Then he loosed her grip and turned to mount the horse while she stood watching.

He looked down at her, and Coral stared up at him, holding back her anxiety. Then he rode away, and she watched in the darkness until his shadow disappeared and the horse hooves left no sound on the wind.

Gone. She shivered, folding her arms across her chest and looking up past the tree branches toward the sky. The dark clouds were building.

She turned quickly and ran from the road onto the carriageway. There were dim lights glowing in the lower half of the house. By now Ethan and Hugo would be preparing to leave to search for her father. She must slip past them unseen, reach her room safely and bolt the door. If Ethan came and knocked, she would not answer. And when they returned with her father and Seward, she would tell him she loved Jace Buckley.

14

Except for the golden glow from the lanterns in the front hall and ends of the stairway, the house was concealed in darkness when Coral slipped through the servants' door near the cook room.

From the back of the mansion, she made her way quietly to the stairway, surprised that the family was not up waiting for her, yet relieved to be able to escape to her room.

Did Kathleen and Jan-Lee not inform the others of the fire? Had no one else heard her run from the house except Jace? Yet, if her mother was awake she would be here waiting for her with words of encouragement.

Evidently her mother's health had caused her to sleep soundly through the confusion, Coral decided, and Kathleen had not awakened her. But where were Ethan and Uncle Hugo?

She glanced cautiously about as she came to the wide stairway, then began to quietly mount the stairs. As she reached the fourth step, the door to her father's office suddenly opened. Light showered across the red stone floor. Her heart flinched as she paused, expecting to see the foreboding shadow of Sir Hugo framed against the light.

Coral let out a sigh of relief. Ethan stood there, carelessly attired in an open white shirt, his sandy hair tousled. He looked almost boyish as he walked swiftly to the stairs, but upon seeing his agitated expression, she knew his mood was far from being harmonious. She did not like the look in his usually quiet gray eyes, and as he moved closer to the bottom stair, the lantern light revealed a crafted leather holster, worn over his left shoulder, housing an ivory-handled pistol.

Jace was right, she thought with alarm. *Ethan is a man of irrational moods*. Where had she ever gotten the notion he was a gentle physician? He was a man of impatience and rash judgment when confronted by obstacles threatening his expectations.

She became aware that she was clutching his engagement necklace, and unobtrusively moved her hand into the billowing folds of her skirts.

"Are you all right, darling?"

The word of endearment came unnaturally, as though to bind her.

"Yes. Only tired and weary. I am going up to bed. Good-night, Ethan."

She mounted the stairs, feeling his overly anxious gaze.

"What were you doing so long with the major? You have been gone for two hours."

She already felt irritation toward him because of his deceit, and her voice was harsh. "Are you accusing me of impropriety?" Seeing the flicker of pain and anger, she sighed and added more kindly, "I do not wish to talk now. You too should get some rest before leaving with Uncle."

She turned, hoping to escape further confrontation, but his mood turned to frustration.

"Kathleen told me you were with the native girl. She lied to me. You were alone with the major. I suspect he sought to turn you against me."

Her nerves were taut after the evening's traumatic events. She turned sharply to look down at him, prepared to accuse him of his own lies, but bit them back. "Do lower your voice. You will awaken the household."

"They will hear soon enough of your being alone with Buckley on the dark road to the hatcheries. I know he plans to come between us. He took advantage of you in the palace garden. You must stay away from him, Coral. He is a scoundrel and no gentleman."

Her face was strained and pale, and the jewels dug into her sweating palm. She could have flung them at his feet, asking if his lies were marks of the gallantry he insisted Jace did not have.

Suddenly, Ethan no longer reminded her of the physician she had come to think well of in London. She was discovering hints of temperament that reminded her of Uncle Hugo. No, Ethan was not as dark, nor as calculating, and he was unable to remain cool the way Sir Hugo did.

She wondered why she had never noticed this before. Had she been too occupied guarding her heart against Jace? Or was it because Ethan had not yet shown his capacity for deceit? His opportunities had improved since arriving at Kingscote. He now considered her his betrothed, and he was willing to insist she had vowed. He would expect a Christmas wedding and pretend injury when refused. Jace threatened the fulfillment of what he considered to be *his*, and that provoked him to irrational behavior.

But was that so unusual? Ethan had also tended to be unreasonable on the river journey. There had been the quarrel with Jace over the sacrifice to Kali, and the insistence of taking the barge and his medical supplies against the advice of those more experienced than he.

Perhaps these quirks were small enough in themselves, but were they not typical of his temperament? Far worse was his recent threat to duel with Jace. And what of his lies to her about Sualkashi and withholding the truth from her about Jace losing his vision? These, she thought, were far more serious.

Disturbed, Coral came down the stairs and brushed past him into her father's office. At least in here, his voice would not be heard throughout the house. The last thing either of them needed was Uncle Hugo coming down.

Standing at the window, she turned as Ethan entered and shut the door. He faced her, pale and stiff, and was about to say something when his eyes reached her empty throat.

The engagement necklace—she gathered the loose strand of gems more fully into her palm.

Ethan gathered his emotions into a dignified demeanor. "The major and I shall settle this disagreement as two gentlemen. Where is he?"

Her emotions snapped. "He has left. And for your sake I am glad. You are behaving immaturely."

"I think not. I shall not be dishonored."

"Dare you speak of such injured honor when it is you who have lied to me? The major had more than a light wound in the rebellion. He lost his sight! Ethan! How could you keep anything so traumatic from me?"

Her urgent demand stripped him of his offended arrogance, and he stood without making a sound. Then, as though coming out of a daze, he turned away.

"For Jace to think he might lose his vision was a terrible dilemma," she said. "He thrives on adventure; he is a soldier, a sea captain. Had he truly gone blind he would forever remember visions of the sea he loves, the wind, the stars. . . . He would be the most miserable of men. Yet you refused to tell me."

"I had my reasons," he said dully. "When he was wounded near Plassey you insisted on going to him. Believe me, I feared for your future if the major got his way."

"I see. I am far better off with my future in your hands—and in Uncle's. It doesn't matter that you both have become adept at deceiving others."

"Do you think I wished to deceive you? I didn't plan it, but when I arrived you were so obviously concerned for him. In order to protect you I found myself resorting to methods not altogether honorable. But I knew his loss of vision was only temporary. There was no reason to alarm you when you already had enough concern with your father."

She doubted his reason for keeping silent.

"No, Ethan, you feared I would send a message to him if I knew, that I would learn how you also lied about his marriage to the Indian girl at Sualkashi—no, do not bother to explain."

"Jace has his sight back just as I knew he would! What of me? How long did you expect me to wait for your answer? Until he decided whether or not he loved you enough to ask you to marry him? I could not bear to see you running after the likes of him. You are a Kendall. It is only right you should marry me. It is the wish of Sir Hampton and Elizabeth."

Coral thrust forth her hand displaying the flashing necklace. "No, and I'll not marry you to please the family. I too was wrong, and I am sorry. I should never have accepted this from you. Now you must understand there is nothing more between us."

"Do not be hasty, I admit it was a mistake on my part, a foolish one, one I'll never make again. Do give me another chance to prove myself."

"No. I fear you find it too easy to revert to lies and deceit to manipulate people and situations for your own ends, just like Sir Hugo."

He flushed with anger and embarrassment. "But you will think nothing of throwing yourself at Buckley! A man who is nothing, who has nothing. You cheapen the Kendall name and behave like some dockside girl—and I am certain the major has known many!"

Her slap cracked the silence. The mark from her hand showed visibly on his cheek. As though shocked from his behavior, he looked stricken, defeated. He groaned, sinking with dejection into her father's chair, head in hands.

"Dear God, why did I say that. I did not mean it—I swear I didn't, Coral. Your decency and character is above reproach. I—" he stopped.

Coral could not speak.

"I am sorry," he choked.

Her rage left her as quickly as it had come, leaving her weak. She laid the necklace on the desk, then turned and opened the door.

Ethan stood in anguish. "Coral, wait—"

She felt calm now, and looking back over her shoulder said, "I am going to marry Jace Buckley as soon as he returns from Burma with Gem. And if anything happens to my father, I shall order both you and Uncle off this property, even if I must hire mercenaries to do it."

She turned and walked briskly across the hall to the stairway, determined to pay him no heed as he followed her.

"Coral—" He paused on the stair, looking after her with agony.

Coral turned, her expression without sympathy. "Enough lies. Enough deceit. I've had little else from either you or Hugo since I set foot in London. There will be no more. My mind is made up. You might as well leave Kingscote and return to London. The masquerade is over."

"Never mind Kingscote, never mind marriage! I won't have you think I'm involved in any of this rot! It is your respect I want now, nothing else."

Coral would not stop, nor did she look back as she went up the stairs, her shoulders straight.

Ethan stared after her, his stomach in knots. His sweating palm balled into a fist. Hugo had provoked him to this.

Sir Hugo . . . his uncle . . . his father.

Father! What a miserable jest! Hugo had left domineering scars on Ethan's soul from the moment he had taken him away from his mother as a boy.

"The woman he pushed in the dirt," he murmured, his heart thudding in his chest so loudly he began to breathe heavily. "That was *my mother,* whether she bore me out of wedlock or not. Yet he pushed her into the dirt without a thought, the way he does everything that stands between him and what he wants. He had better plans for marriage than my mother . . . he saw an opportunity to marry Margaret Roxbury, a wealthy cousin. He has broken every rule, schemed to destroy Margaret's relationship with Colonel John Warbeck in order to marry her, not for love, but for a hefty stake in the Roxbury and Kendall silk—and he won."

Ethan stood there in an emotional daze, staring blankly up the empty stairway. Much of what she had accused him of was true. He had aided Hugo's schemes at first; his dream to possess the wealth and position to pursue his medical research had been too strong to resist. When Coral arrived in London so ill, he had cooperated with Hugo. He always did, except in Guwahati. Now he had come to love her; yet there seemed to be no hope of winning her love in return, nor even her respect. Coral was right. He was becoming like Hugo.

"Deceit learned from my father," he whispered. "I resorted to it too easily. And if I had gotten by with it, would it have bothered me? Like Hugo I could resort to other deceits to get what I wanted. I would become to Coral what Hugo was to Margaret, hating myself all the while, and lying my way through to protect myself from being unmasked. Yes . . . I have learned well from my father."

Yet Coral was too wise to be manipulated by either of them.

As he stood there thinking, he did not hear the muffled steps behind him in the darkened parlor, where the wide double doors stood open. Someone had been alerted by the arguing voices—and had come to listen.

The steps behind Ethan quietly retreated, unnoticed.

15

There came a sudden jerk to the side of her bed, and Coral awoke with a start, staring into the darkness. What time was it? Who was there, or had she only jumped in her sleep? She was surprised to find that her heart was thudding.

This is foolish. There is nothing to fear. Ethan and Hugo had ridden out with the rajputs the previous morning.

The odd sensation of alarm persisted. For a moment or two she lay still, trying to identify what had awakened her from a sound sleep, and wondered that she should feel so tense.

Another sound ... the wind rattling the bamboo shades on the verandah doors, but she heard nothing more from the sleeping house.

The night was muggy, smothering her behind the mosquito netting that was drawn closed about her bed. Then, somewhere in her room, she heard a floorboard squeak. Every nerve in her body came alert, and she had to force herself to sit up, trying to breathe quietly so she could strain to listen.

She eased one hand out from beneath the netting,

moving cautiously, and reached to the bedstand to light the lantern. Another swoosh of wind coming from the direction of the wide, dark river made the shades snap, and also sent the netting around her bed fluttering. Coral let out a sigh of relief. It was only the wind. She must have left the verandah doors open before going to bed— *But I thought I latched the doors.*

She was certain she had done so, since the dry lightning signaling the monsoon kept her awake with its blinding flashes.

With the lantern now lit, she took her silk dressing gown from off the mahogany bedpost and wrapped it about her. The polished floorboards felt cool beneath the soles of her feet as she stood there for a moment feeling the wind. Wind was unusual at this time of year, she thought.

Again she wondered what time it was and decided that she had been asleep for several hours and that it must be nearing two in the morning. With the sheen of the lantern light illuminating the room, she walked to the verandah to shut the doors, wondering that her head felt a little odd. She recalled the lemon drink she had enjoyed with her mother and sisters before they all retired for the night, but decided that she was being overly suspicious because of past druggings. She felt a qualm, thinking of Ethan. She had been hard on him, perhaps too much so.

Coral tightened her dressing gown about her and reached to close one side of the double doors against the night, feeling a chill crawl up her back as though unfriendly eyes watched her. She turned quickly and glanced about the shadowed bedchamber and saw nothing unfamiliar.

"I'm overreacting to all the strain of these last days," she murmured to herself aloud, adding ruefully, "Dear

Uncle Hugo is gone. There will be no more druggings."
In the darkness of uncertainty, she murmured, "When
my spirit was overwhelmed within me, then thou knew-
est my path," quoting Psalm 142:3.

She paused to take a deep breath of night air, hoping
to settle the queasiness in her mind. Maybe the lemon
refreshment they drank had spoiled. Perhaps her mother
and sisters were feeling the same symptoms.

The wind had stilled as suddenly as it had risen, and
nothing moved outside the verandah on the estate
grounds. Deliberately she stood a moment longer to
squelch her unease, and looked up at the beads of white
stars that were strung across the black velvety sky. And
Jace . . . where was he now? Did he think of her as she
thought of him. . . ? Below, the silhouette of coconut
palms lined the edge of the lawn down to the river that
lay still like glass, reflecting the starlight. From somewhere in the distant jungle came the familiar sounds of
wildlife.

Sometimes the birds sound positively eerie, she
thought, listening to their cackles and hoots, almost as
if they mocked her attempt at a positive outlook on the
future.

She closed the other side of the verandah door, shut-
ting out the jungle sounds. This time she would slide the
lock into place to make certain the wind could not blow
them open again.

She turned and something caught her attention. It
was her red and brown rattan basket where she kept
personal items: her King James Bible from Granny V, a
number of letters, some from her deceased brother, Michael, mementos belonging to Gem's baby days, and the
precious ebony cheetah that Jace Buckley had given to
her in Calcutta aboard his ship. A faint smile touched
her lips as she remembered.

She stood looking at the basket . . . strange. It was sitting on her bed, inside the mosquito netting. Had she set it there when she retired? No, it had been on the rosewood chair by her wardrobe.

She climbed into her bed and lifted the lid on the basket, setting it aside. She was about to reach inside the familiar hollow when there came a slithering movement from within. A hissing sound spat its rage, filling her ears.

Coral froze. A head lifted—the flat head of a cobra, its beady eyes immediately fixing upon her. Slowly the head moved from side to side. Coral wanted to scream but went weak with terror. Trapped! The cobra had already been riled. There was no way to climb out of bed without moving the feather mattress or pulling aside the netting. She was certain any movement from her would provoke it into striking.

Don't move, she told herself.

Then she heard it. The floor squeaked. . . .

Someone was in her room! Whoever had planted the cobra had been there all along. Had the rattan basket been placed on her bed while she stood on the verandah? But she had seen no one—

Her wardrobe, of course. No wonder she had felt unfriendly eyes! And whoever it was had come to make certain the deadly work was accomplished—

Coral screamed, but her voice sounded only a feeble protest. Drugged—the lemon drink before bed was working. . . .

The cobra's hiss filled her ears like a reverberating curse, the cold coils came unwound, the flat head darting in a momentary flash. The fangs sunk deeply into her arm and held. She gasped.

The cobra drew back, slithering across the cover and under the mosquito netting, leaving two small punctures in her arm. Her dimming vision watched in a sickening daze as its body slowly disappeared off the bed onto the floor matting.

She reached a hand to her arm. She must make a tourniquet, lance it, let the blood run to keep the poison from reaching her heart, but she could not move. Within minutes now it would all be over. . . .

Death was coming to silence her, to mock and smother her protest, to swallow her up in waves of darkness . . . no one to help . . . no one till morning. Too late then. In a few minutes she would sink into a stupor and die. . . .

She imagined herself moving from the bed, straining to toss aside the covers, to move the netting, to stagger to the door, into the darkened hall, screaming for help. But she could not—

Coral thought she was floating away. Kingscote was receding, and she was alone. She found herself in a valley, walking slowly. As she walked, the valley grew narrower and the shadow of death fell across her path. The sides of the mountains, reaching steeply toward a pale sky, closed her in, blocking out the sunlight. Yet there was no fear, only a sweetness of soul that promised the walk would not disappoint her, nor would it hurt. A gentle wind beckoned.

But unexpectedly, Coral found the sweet wind was catching her up and taking her back, back down the shadowed valley from where she had first come, and her eyes fluttered open and she heard her voice filling her mind and she was yet laughing and saying: "I saw Him, and He smiled at me . . . no, I don't want to wake up. I do not want to come back! No!"

Coral gasped, awake. She was in her bed at Kingscote again. She stared into the fearful face of Natine's niece. Preetah was sweating and breathing heavily, and her eyes were wide. Her hair was disheveled as though she had been in a fierce struggle. There was blood on the side of her face above her eyebrow, as though she had been struck, and her sari was torn.

"Coral, oh, thank your God, you are not dead!"

"I d-don't want to come back. . . ."

"It is well now, you rest in sleep. You will be very ill for many days with a great fever, but your God will help you. And memsahib is coming to you soon. She is trying to wake up now."

Preetah had awakened Elizabeth Kendall, shaking her by the shoulders, as she refused to respond and only moaned. It had been Preetah's words that had shocked her awake.

"Memsahib, wake up. It is your daughter Coral. She is bitten by a cobra and is dying! Wake up!"

Elizabeth was out of bed, grabbing the bedpost to support herself as Preetah ran back out calling for Kathleen.

Elizabeth lost her balance again and grabbed hold of the bedpost. Each step was laborious. She must reach Coral. . . .

I've been drugged, she thought with alarm.

She closed her eyes as her brain whirled and her stomach turned. She inched her way to the door, finding herself treading water that dipped left and right.

"Heavenly Father, help me! Help me reach Coral—"

She leaned her head against the post, drawing in deep breaths, trying to clear her mind.

Footsteps. . . .

Elizabeth opened her eyes, expecting Kathleen or Jan-Lee.

It was Natine.

Through her blurred vision she could see that his usually immaculate white jacket was soiled with something dark—blood. He was out of breath and in great agitation.

"Sahiba, we have chased the intruder away, Preetah and I. He went through verandah. A rajput, I think. I have men out searching the grounds hoping to trail him."

Elizabeth stared at him.

Natine watched her, his face strained, his hands folded tightly against his chest as though in pain. "Memsahib, can you hear me? Go back to bed. All is well. I kill the cobra with burra-sahib's military sword hanging in hall." He held up the bloody sword in proof. "Preetah has cut and already bled Miss Coral's arm. She will live, though very ill. Go back to bed, sahiba. You too are very ill."

Could she believe him? Dare she? Coral had warned her about the major's suspicions, but would Natine go so far as to attack her daughter with a cobra?

Natine may be innocent. Perhaps there had been an intruder in Coral's room who planted the cobra. The rajput that Hugo had left to guard them . . . and had there not been an intruder the night Gem was stolen from the nursery?

"Miss Elizabeth," came Jan-Lee's urgent voice as she ran into the room from the shadowed corridor. "I bring strong medicine to make you better! Drink all of it!"

Elizabeth felt a cup pressed to her lips. The odor was nauseating. She tried to push the cup away, but Jan-Lee was insistent.

"It will make you vomit, but you must. It will help. Trust me!"

"Do not listen, sahiba!" cried Natine. "She lie! It is more drugs!"

Natine was beside Jan-Lee, thrusting the cup from her hand. It fell with a clatter, spilling the contents.

"Vile beast!" Jan-Lee shouted at him. "What have you done?"

Elizabeth knew her faithful ayah too well. She tried to focus on Natine. "Who placed the cobra to kill my daughter!"

Natine's mouth tightened. "If sahiba thinks I would do so much evil, it is best I leave Kingscote for the village and not come back."

"You speak well, Natine. Return when Sir Hampton arrives."

Her eyes blurred, the room was spinning, and she could not see his expression. His voice was growing distant, but she thought she heard his voice unexpectedly break with emotion.

"I am innocent, sahiba! I am faithful to the Kendall family! It is not I!"

Elizabeth's brain weaved to and fro. Cobras—yes, they were everywhere now. She could see them crawling, slithering all over her floor, crawling toward her bare feet.

She clenched her teeth, shut her eyes, and her soul cried out to God. Elizabeth took a step and staggered, but Jan-Lee caught her, easing her down to the floor. Jan-Lee cradled Elizabeth in her lap as if to protect her.

"You!" she hissed at Natine. "I know the truth! Evil shall come upon your head, Natine."

"You speak like crazy old woman, Jan-Lee. Am I fool to bring a cobra to Coral's room?"

"You hate her. You knew the sepoy who stole Rajiv and Jemani's son that night. I have told Coral the baby was not Gem, because of the scar on his foot. She ask me again as soon as she come home, and we talk many hours. I take her to little grave out in the family cemetery, but she did not weep, because she knows—we both know it is not Gem."

Natine walked toward her, still holding Sir Hampton's sword. "You croak like a frog from the stagnant pool, words you know nothing about. I knew sepoy, yes. He served Rajkumar Sunil at Guwahati. I say nothing to Miss Coral because to search for Rajiv's son would mean death to her and many Kendalls. I knew who Rajiv was— a prince—and Jemani too has royal blood. Rajiv confided in me," he boasted. "He thought me a friend. It was I, Natine, who sent warning to maharaja that Prince Sunil would take Rajiv's son. It was I who warned him in time so he could save the boy!"

"You lie," said Jan-Lee. "And when Sir Hampton comes, I will tell him all. I was fool not to tell him everything at once. No more will I be fool."

Natine hissed at her. "It is *you* who sneak about in masquerade as faithful ayah. You have them all tricked, but not me. You are Burmese, an outsider to both English and Indians on Kingscote."

"You are insane on your own evil drugs. You drugged them tonight. You placed the cobra."

"No. And it was not I who put the dagger in Rajiv's heart, nor helped Sunil take Gem from Miss Coral, though I knew for her to take the child would only mean much trouble. I tried to warn, but no one would listen."

Jan-Lee sucked in her breath and stared at him. "No one believes your lies."

"It is Burma who fights Assam. The Burmese soldiers cross our border and fight skirmishes with English outpost! Do you not send secret messages to Burmese soldiers now attacking the borders of Kingscote? You are loyal to Burma."

Jan-Lee's face contorted with a dart of fright. "I am loyal to Miss Elizabeth, to Coral. I would give my life for them."

"No. I know your secret, woman. I know who you are.

You have venom in your heart for us all. Only Burmese Warlord Zin do you serve. Is he not of your family blood, Jan-Lee?"

"They will never believe you. I have deep affection for Elizabeth, for Coral—I have held her in my arms; I have wept when she was ill; it was I who nursed her when she was ill with fever after Gem was abducted. When she was in London, it was I who wrote her the truth about Gem being alive."

"If you are so loyal, then why is memsahib going into brain sickness? You fool everyone but me."

A moaning sound came from Elizabeth.

"You heard her order! She bid you go! Take your evil Kali and go from Kingscote!"

Natine turned with grave dignity and walked to the door. He glanced back over his shoulder. "I go. But I will come back. And when I do, I will have proof you are the betrayer."

Jan-Lee cringed at his threat. "You plot to destroy me to make yourself look innocent. But what proof you may bring will turn to ashes."

"I have friends in village, so think before you try to have me silenced and thrown in river. It may be I have one of your letters."

He went out, leaving the door open.

Jan-Lee followed him into the hall, her face ashen. She watched as his white turban disappeared and he went down the stairway.

She ran back into Elizabeth's bedroom and struggled to carry her back to the bed.

"What is it? What is wrong?" cried Kathleen, appearing in the doorway. She watched Jan-Lee struggle to lay her mother upon the bed. Kathleen felt drowsy, but Preetah had forced her awake, daring to dump water on her! Preetah had refused to talk and seemed to be on the verge of hysterics. "Go to memsahib," she kept repeating.

Kathleen rushed into the darkened room as her mother began to thrash about on the bed. She grabbed hold of her. "Mother!"

Kathleen crawled on top of her to hold her down by the shoulders. "Jan-Lee, go for Coral!"

"She will not come to help this time. She was bitten by cobra."

For a moment Kathleen could not think. The emotional blow felt like a dagger between her shoulder blades. Cobra! And her mother—what was going on?

"Jan-Lee! Do something!" she cried, wrestling to hold her mother down.

Jan-Lee fell to her knees, weeping, and Kathleen glanced over to see an old broken woman. The ayah's sobs mingled with the throaty noises Elizabeth was making, and Kathleen knew real fear. Through her own sweat she could see the face of her mother, white, her lips bared back and her teeth gritting together.

Kathleen wanted to faint, to go tearing from the room, screaming at the top of her voice. She would run to Coral, but Coral, always the steady one, could not help her. Their father was gone, Alex—even Jan-Lee was overwrought. Where is Marianna?

Her mother had broken from her grasp.

No one to turn to . . . alone.

"Lord, help me! I don't know what to do. Just help me!"

A logical thought came to her mind, bringing a breath of calmness. "Okay, one thing at a time," murmured Kathleen, and as if in a daze, she went to work, grabbing the top sheet and tying her mother to the mattress until the fit ceased.

While she worked, she prayed continually, but her words were only His name spoken again and again. A peace had come to guard her heart like sentinels of angels with drawn swords. *We're not alone.*

Jan-Lee lingered beside the bed, where Elizabeth was now unconscious and still, yet breathing laboriously.

Kathleen knelt on the floor, hands clasped on the bed, her head bowed.

Jan-Lee stood and, leaning over the bed, brushed her unsmiling lips across Elizabeth Kendall's forehead. Without a glance at Kathleen, she then appeared to take on swift energy. She jerked and ran toward the door. "We need doctor. I trust no one here to go with news. I go myself. I need horses for change on long ride."

"Yes, have one of the manjis take you by boat to the village tehsildar. He may know what to do about the drug."

"The village is not to be trusted. I must ride hard and overtake Doctor Boswell."

Kathleen's mind staggered at the dilemma facing them. Unless Ethan was found, there was no one to distinguish the drug used on her mother. Who would do such an evil thing? Natine? A rajput loyal to Prince Sunil? Did someone want them *all* dead?

16

Marianna's pale brows inched together above sober blue eyes. Her reddish blond hair was drawn into a smooth chignon, giving her the appearance of maturity. Her anxious gaze scanned Coral's face, flushed with high fever. Seeing the perspiration around her golden hair, she wrung out the wet cloth and proceeded to cool her face and throat.

Marianna had awakened that morning from a deep slumber, her tongue feeling thick and fuzzy, and no amount of scrubbing could take the strange taste from her mouth. . . . "Whoever planted the cobra drugged us all, to keep us from hearing Coral's scream and from coming in time to bleed the venom from her arm," she murmured. That someone had done so, and used a more potent drug on her mother, sickened her.

She thought of her mother, sometimes writhing in her bed, sometimes yelling out aimlessly, then lapsing off to sleep. Marianna shut her eyes tightly to block out the image. It would be too easy to sink into feelings of fear and despair. This time she must stand without the strength of Coral and her mother. Yet her decision to be strong rose to mock her. *Silly little Marianna, with no courage or convictions of your own.*

Her mouth set. No. She was no longer a child, but a young woman, and she must mature. She had spent the days in prayer for her mother and sister, and now she must leave them in the hand of their Master.

Yet the question demanding an answer came again. Who would do such a thing? There was no way a cobra could slither unseen into a second floor bedchamber. She glanced toward the bedroom door, but what did she expect to see? Any enemy would appear no more dangerous than the loyal servants who calmly went about their duties. How loyal were they, even those she had known since childhood?

It was Natine, of course, who else?

There was nothing more to fear, for he was no longer in the house. Her mother had ordered him off Kingscote until their father returned. Natine had gone to his relatives in the village, yet his niece Preetah had remained.

"But is it possible Natine was innocent, that he was telling the truth?"

Marianna thought of the rajput guard whom Natine had accused. Uncle Hugo had left the big, handsome, dark-bearded Indian in the house to protect the women from Burmese infiltrators or even Prince Sunil. Natine had accused the rajput, who had now disappeared . . . or was he somewhere about the estate grounds—or even in the house?

Thunder grumbled in the sky above Kingscote. Marianna left the side of Coral's bed and went to shut the verandah doors.

Uncle Hugo. . . . Marianna remembered back to the Christmas ball at Barrackpore when she had blundered into a clandestine meeting in the garden between her uncle and a mysterious Indian in a yellow turban. Coral had long since ceased to discuss the incident, and Marianna wished to forget it. Now those uncertainties about her uncle were rekindled.

A brilliant flash of dry lightning startled her. She drew the heavy velvet drapes over the split-cane shades on the doors and turned to look toward her sister to find the bedroom door ajar. Her breath caught.

"Who is it?" she demanded nervously.

Preetah stepped quietly through the door, not looking at Marianna but toward Coral, who moved restlessly in her fevered sleep. "Yanna says that Thilak has returned from the road going east without news of Jan-Lee."

There were reports that scattered Burmese infiltrators had been seen on the road, and the risk of travel was now greatly heightened. Since Thilak, the head Indian worker over the hatcheries, was a friend of Yanna's, Marianna had sent Thilak to catch up with Jan-Lee to protect her on the road.

"Thilak says she is now far ahead, but does sahiba wish for him to arm some workers and try to find her anyway?"

"No, I suppose not. As he says, Jan-Lee will be far ahead. Perhaps by now she has caught up with Doctor Boswell."

Preetah nodded hopefully and moved softly toward the bed to look at Coral. "Mera comes to take your place now, Miss Marianna. You need rest. And Yanna asks if she may come to help with memsahib."

Yanna was deeply attached to Elizabeth Kendall, and Marianna was relieved that the girl wished to come and assist Kathleen. She gave her permission, and as Preetah turned to leave, Marianna recalled how she had wanted to speak with Preetah alone about the cobra.

Images of having come into Coral's bedchamber and finding Preetah soon after the attack were recalled by Marianna with vivid horror. As she had entered through the door with her mind yet dull, Preetah had been frightened and bolted upright from the foot of Coral's bed, where she had taken vigil. Preetah's sari was torn, there were dark stains on the front, and bruises showed on her cheekbone and above her right eyebrow. Perhaps more frightening than anything to Marianna was the desperate look in Preetah's eyes, as though she might have expected someone else to return.

Marianna had then seen Coral, with her skin a sickly ashen color, twisting and turning about and muttering in her sleep, her arm bandaged.

"She has been bitten by a cobra. It was necessary to cut her arm and allow the blood to run to get rid of the poison. I used permanganate crystals in the wound. I also give a small amount of opium for pain and sleep," Preetah had told her.

The rest of the evening had seemed a nightmare. The nature of their mother's illness was bizarre. Only later did Marianna learn from Kathleen of the seriousness of Elizabeth's condition.

Now, as Marianna watched Preetah, the girl looked nervous.

"May I go now, sahiba? Yanna waits outside for permission."

It was not Marianna's nature to be confrontational. Usually she remained in the background, willing to be uninvolved. Perhaps it was best for the present if she played the silly girl everyone thought she was. *If only Major Buckley would suddenly ride up!* she thought. *He would take care of everything.* But the vain wish to hear horse hooves on the carriageway was silenced by another roll of thunder.

Marianna straightened her shoulders. "Do not go yet, Preetah. I must talk to you about last night."

Preetah's brown eyes grew remote, and Marianna recognized her tension.

"It is time you told me what happened."

"What happened?"

"Yes, the cobra. You saved my sister's life, and the family will never forget. You've not told me how it was that you came just in time. A few minutes more and—and Coral would have died from the venom."

Preetah flushed, pleased, yet her smile quickly faded as she became cautious. "Miss Coral's God watches over her. He had me come."

"Yes, I believe God has more plans for my sister, and that He did have you come. But what would your uncle say if he heard you? You are afraid of Natine."

"It is custom to fear my uncle. I have no father in the village—he died of illness. I and my mother both are grateful to Natine for family care. I must not offend Natine. It was he who spoke to your father about my position here."

Marianna took a risk and said, "Yet you did more than offend your uncle when you fought him to save my sister's life."

Preetah glanced to the door but remained dignified. "Fought against my uncle Natine? I do not understand."

"Yes, you do, Preetah. In order to lash Coral's arm and drain the venom, you had to fight off Natine."

"No, sahiba!"

"Yes, your sari was torn, there was blood on it, and those bruises on your face are from Natine."

Preetah turned pale; her fingers dug into her sari. Marianna drew in a breath and continued, surprised at her own persistence. "There was no intruder, and the rajput did not place the cobra."

"The rajput is gone, as Natine vows. He ran away! That is proof."

"The rajput serves my uncle, and I have an uneasy feeling he is yet about, watching us. Yet I do not think he placed the cobra. You were very brave to risk your life to save my sister, and she and the memsahib will reward you well, and your mother in the village. So you need not fear Natine anymore."

Preetah shook her head wildly. "Words of kindness and reward are taken with gladness, but you are wrong— it was not my uncle."

"Who then?"

Preetah's breathing came rapidly and she jumped to her feet. "You are wrong!" she said simply. "Please, I must go now."

"Did he insist you allow the venom to do its work? And when you would not, he tried to stop you from helping Coral."

Preetah stared at her, then covered her face with trembling hands. Her shoulders shook as she began to weep, holding in her sobs, and she lowered herself into a chair.

"Do not be afraid. No harm will come to you now that he has gone to the village. And soon my father will return with Seward and Alex. Tell me what happened, Preetah, I must know. It might help my mother!"

"Yes, it was my uncle. I—I was late going to bed, because I was helping in the kitchen. I—I saw him put something in the lemon water, though he did not know I saw him, and I was going to empty the pitcher outside before I brought it to the memsahib and your sisters, and was only waiting for him to leave the kitchen. But he did not leave, and Mera brought the refreshment. Later I did worry when I remembered the priest."

Marianna was shaking. "P-priest?"

"From the village. He came to Kingscote early in the morning before the doctor and Sir Roxbury left. He talked with your uncle before he talked to Natine."

"Sir Hugo talked to the priest?"

Preetah nodded. "And the priest brought something to Natine in a basket. When they had all gone from our bungalow, I peek inside the container and saw the cobra. But I did not know what Natine would do! Later, after the lemon refreshment it came to me and I greatly feared! The light was on in Miss Coral's room when I came, and I heard a noise, so I knocked. Miss Coral did not answer, and so I entered and saw the cobra, saw the fang marks on her arm—then I saw Natine on the verandah. Uncle always carries a knife and I begged him for it, but he would not. I fought him for it and screamed for help and Jan-Lee come running down the hall! He heard her and was afraid and angry, and I was able to get the dagger. He ran out past Jan-Lee and I remember no more, except I flung myself onto Miss Coral's bed and tied her arm tightly with scarf, then I cut and bleed her. . . ."

Preetah looked up, her face pale and wet with tears. She stood, taking hold of Marianna. "When memsahib ordered him off Kingscote he searched for me, to make me come with him, but I hid!"

Marianna was trembling, seeing the entire ugly scene played out in her mind. She barely felt Preetah's fingers digging into her arm.

"Natine fears I will talk to your father when he returns from Darjeeling, so he had my mother send for me, saying she was ill. But I did not go to the village as she asked."

"When did you get the message?"

"This afternoon, but I will not leave Kingscote. If I do, he will never let me come back. And what I say about your God watching you, I speak with good feelings. I have learned about His way from Yanna. Natine suspected it so, and knows I helped rescue the untouchables from the crocodiles. I fear to go home to the village."

"Do not leave the house," said Marianna. "He will not dare come back now. The drug used on memsahib, think hard, Preetah! If you can tell my cousin Ethan when he arrives with Jan-Lee, he may know what to do to help her."

Preetah closed her eyes tightly and shook her head. "There are many. I have thought about what it could be. I have searched our bungalow and found nothing. Maybe he got it from the priest."

Marianna did not wish to say what frightened her. Or perhaps from Sir Hugo? He knew all about bizarre Eastern drugs.

"But I will keep thinking, keep searching to tell doctor when he comes."

There was a light knock on the door, and Mera poked her head in. "Yanna waits anxiously downstairs. She wishes to guard the memsahib, she says."

"Yes," cried Marianna with relief. "Tell her to go to my mother's room at once."

Thank God for our Indian friends, thought Marianna.

"I shall take vigil for Miss Coral now," said Mera, gently laying a hand on Marianna. "You rest, little one. You lose weight and grow pale. There is hot tea and cakes waiting in your room. You eat, then go to sleep till supper."

Marianna nodded gratefully, touching her hand to the side of Mera's wrinkled face, and turned to leave the room with a backward glance of concern toward Coral.

They had ridden several hours before Ethan understood that Sir Hugo had no intention of going east toward Darjeeling. Ethan had studied the map belonging to Major Buckley well enough at Kingscote to know that they were riding northeast.

What lay northeast? The British outpost of Jorhat?

The change in their destination came as a surprise, although Ethan would have been the first to admit that journeying to Darjeeling on a mission to locate Sir Hampton was the last deed of gallantry on his mind. Yet he had expected Hugo to go there, if only to impede any rescue effort.

Why was his uncle riding toward Jorhat? Surely he did not expect to find the major there? Ethan suspected that Hugo knew of the major's mission to the borders of Burma to meet with Warlord Zin, although he could not guess how he had discovered it. Somehow he had known the night of the fire that Buckley would not go to Jorhat to inquire into the military mutiny that had taken Major Selwyn's life.

Did he know that the Indian prince Adesh Singh was with Warlord Zin?

As they rode, Ethan cast a side glance at his uncle. Sir Hugo's dark eyes were preoccupied with the thick jungle growth along the Brahmaputra River. Yet Ethan did not think he was concerned for tigers.

He expects to meet someone.

Of perhaps even greater concern than his uncle knowing about the major's mission was whether Prince Sunil knew of it. If he did, Sunil would have Indian warriors prepared to stop the major, and they would kill him.

Ethan's jaw set tightly, and he refused to think about what Jace's death might mean to Coral—and yet he did consider. Would she forget Buckley? Would she in time turn to him again?

Prince Sunil would also have the Indian child put to death, thought Ethan. *No, I will have no part in the filthy business.* He had lost respect for himself, and he had none left for Sir Hugo. Whatever the future held, dark clouds loomed over any prospects for happiness that he might have had with Coral, or for that matter, with the Kendalls on Kingscote. His hope of a research lab on the plantation was ruined, for even if Coral proved gracious enough to permit his presence, Ethan knew he could not be content seeing her married to Buckley. If there was any hope of beginning anew, he must find it elsewhere. And when he did, he would not carry the blood of either Buckley or Gem on his conscience.

Whatever Sir Hugo was involved in, Ethan made up his mind—his own fingers would not dip into the bowl of blood.

The rajputs made primitive camp for the night. Ethan was unfamiliar with the area between Kingscote and Jorhat, but he guessed they were far from the nearest village. But if Hugo did not expect to find the major at Jorhat, what was the purpose of going there?

But perhaps Jorhat was not their destination. Where, then? He wished he had used his time at Kingscote to learn more of Assam.

Ethan kept back from the light of the campfire, and when he did not watch the rajput warriors, he watched Sir Hugo. Beneath Ethan's jacket his pistol waited, loaded, and he kept a rifle across his legs. Beside him, as though guarding a satchel of gold, sat his leather medical bag.

Sir Hugo came from the darkened trees up to the fire, and the kansamah handed him a vessel of hot broth. Ethan could not read his expression beneath the well-trimmed dark beard, but he noticed his eyes were fixed on the rajput in command of the other warriors. The rajput walked up and spoke quietly, and Sir Hugo answered in fluent Hindi.

Ethan frowned. Being a novice of the language was a

disadvantage. He watched the rajput mount his horse and quietly ride away into the darkness. The faces of the other warriors told him nothing.

How much did the rajput fighters know? He decided they were sworn to Sunil's loyalty and would carry out Hugo's orders to the death.

Ethan knew that he was alone, outnumbered, and up against some scheme that he was not capable of thwarting. Sir Hugo was not a man who easily faced defeat. Just how did Hugo look upon him since his refusal to cooperate at Guwahati? His uncle talked little, and there were times when Ethan wondered if he knew that his loyalties were no longer with him to use and shape as he wished. If he were to oppose his uncle in whatever plan might be underway, he must not let him suspect. . . . And yet Hugo had brought him on the journey knowing that the day would come when he would know they were not in Darjeeling and demand to know why and what they were doing.

He had told Coral that Sir Hugo would never harm him. Was he certain? Whatever Hugo had planned, the fact remained that he was his son.

As dawn broke, they continued riding, and by nightfall they had journeyed still deeper into the jungle frontier. The purple twilight around them was loud with the shrill call of birds and monkeys. Ethan recognized some of the wildlife he had seen on the safari to Guwahati with the major: the small spotted chital deer, monkeys, pelicans near the river, and now and then he spotted a rhino. How long could he convince Sir Hugo he did not know they traveled northeast? And if he could continue the ruse, what would he learn? So far he had discovered nothing. If the rajputs did speak English, they pretended they did not. And his uncle hardly spoke but was consumed with thoughts of his own making.

Perhaps the time had come to openly confront him as to their destination and its purpose, thought Ethan. He looked at Sir Hugo and found his dark eyes and countenance pensive.

Jan-Lee, her face resigned to defeat, drew the reins on the sweating horse with its heaving sides. There was no one on the road now. It lay gray and empty and deep in dust, and the silence of dawn magnified every small sound: the shudder of the horse's mouth, the startled shriek of some bird, and Jan-Lee's own uneven breathing. It seemed to her that her progress must be audible a mile away, and that her first hope of overcoming the memsahib's nephew was now impossible.

If the doctor and his uncle Sir Roxbury had traveled this way she would have come upon their tracks by now, leading to some wayside camp, for she had ridden through the night, gaining the distance while they would have stopped to eat and sleep. Her dark eyes searched the road again for fresh tracks, but she found none that convinced her that they had recently passed this way. Why she did not find what she searched for was curious, yet to go on was useless; she would kill the horses and waste precious hours. If memsahib was to be brought help from the evil of the eastern drug Natine had used, then she must look to another source, a source she did not doubt would have the knowledge, but she would risk much to contact him.

Jan-Lee's usual stoic face was lined with care. Dust and sweat left streaks, and her black eyes flickered with internal anguish as she considered her next action—for it might mean her end, and the end of her own Emerald now safely in her bed at Kingscote.

Dawn was breaking with the first pale wash that

brought the dark silhouettes of trees to green and the distant mountains to purple.

Her hand tightened on the reins. The man she must now seek had the knowledge of Eastern drugs, but in seeking his help, she unmasked her face to her own detriment and that of her daughter. It was for Emerald's sake that she had worn the mask. Yet if she must face shame and even death for the woman who had shielded her these many years, she would lift her face up to the glare of angry scowls and hisses.

But would he lay aside his sword long enough to come with her to Kingscote as a friend when he was now a secret enemy? And if he did come, would the Kendall daughters receive him into their English sanctuary? Would he not be seen as a spy who had come to search out their defenses? And if they should accuse him, or question him suspiciously, would he not see his great honor shamed and turn in anger to leave, only then to attack with great fury?

Fear showed in her face as she turned from the direction of Darjeeling and gazed behind her, seeing in her mind the shadowy borders of Kingscote plantation and the beginning of the thick jungle where Burmese infiltrators came and went unnoticed, except when they attacked in secret ambushments.

17

Burma
Fortress of Warlord Zin

The ancient map once belonging to his natural father, Captain Jarred Buckley, had again guided Jace and Gokul safely across the treacherous border into steamy Burma. The secretive trails crisscrossing the thick jungle brought them to the little-known environs of the Burmese warlord, Zin.

It was noon, and the jungle was hot and humid. Traces of sunlight filtered through thick foliage of glossy green, while overhead, the intertwining branches were vibrant with the high screeching of birds. A flash of wings showing brilliant plumage flitted among the branches, and small brown monkeys chattered excitedly.

Gokul climbed down from his horse to walk ahead, and though confident, he maintained the vigilance of a hungry tiger stalking its prey. He stooped to his haunches and studied the rich damp turf smelling of rotting leaves. There were no horse or elephant tracks, only large army ants converging on a tree beetle that had unfortunately crossed their path.

229

Jace unloosed his pack from the horse and lowered it to the earth, drawing out the clothing that suited the identity he was adopting. The garb had been carefully chosen, for the only way that he might enter the stronghold of Zin was as Javed Kasam.

He dressed quickly while Gokul watched the road. First came the soft undertunic next to his skin, then the English supple chain-mesh shirt carefully hidden by the Eastern outer tunic-jacket of black, worn over heavy tight-fitting trousers. Lastly came the gift from Warlord Zin. Jace knelt and untied the cloth covering. He removed the present he had not worn since his days in Burma. It was an engraved warrior's vest of leather, mounted with a silver and red dragon the size of a man's hand. The sides of the vest were looped tightly with steel rings. The other gift was a Burmese dagger in a wrist-sheath. His own blade he kept in his left boot top. Lastly came the scabbard housing a tulwar.

He picked up his silk turban and stared at it. He touched the side of his dark head and grimaced. He would prefer his old British helmet. He laid the silk aside and opted for the rajput helmet that Gokul had wisely retrieved at the last minute. Made of leather, it was held in place by a colored headband; this was dyed with indigo and embroidered with silver tigers the size of a thumbnail.

Jace walked up to Gokul, who was busily adding the finishing touches to his own masquerade as a guru. He painted the three white brahmin caste marks on his forehead and added a scholar's turban. Jace's mouth turned wryly as Gokul produced fake pearls and a large ruby, which he proceeded to mount onto the front of his turban. He turned to Jace, his dark eyes twinkling mischievously.

"Ah, sahib, you now look upon an enlightened master of India."

Jace folded his arms. "I am awed. I suppose you are at one with the rhythm of the universe."

"But indeed! I am Swami Gokul Sankar—or maybe"—he paused thoughtfully to rub his chin—"Punditji—or should I be his holiness Sri Baba of Lankali?"

"I thought you might be the incarnation of Vishnu." Jace walked to his horse and swung himself into the saddle. He smiled.

Gokul hurried after him, his hand spread across his soft belly. "Actually, I am a Vedantic scholar who has come to teach the maharaja's nephew, Prince Adesh. I shall lecture the prince on meditation to bring him deepened awareness of the divinity within."

"You are certain," said Jace, "that it is divinity, and not a greedy nature that you have discovered within?"

Gokul grinned and patted a hand on his protruding belly. "For only thousand rupees, sahib, my wisdom will deepen your awareness also."

"I am certain, Guru, that in answer to your wisdom, confusion will be rife, and chaos and anarchy will reign supreme."

The last traces of lavender twilight were giving way to a canopy of darkness when they arrived in the city. Icy stars looked down, their cold glitter soon blotched by a low-lying halo of smoke ascending from the town's cooking fires.

Jace and Gokul entered through a seldom-used packed dirt street that was inlaid with square tiles made of Burmese wood. They walked in on foot, leading their horses by the reins, keeping close to the trees.

They approached the homes of shopkeepers, clerks, and poor merchants who could not journey far for their goods and did not fare as well as rich caravan traders. Huts with walls of dried mud and roofs of palm branches lined the narrow road. Beyond, the road opened into a large square that was the noisy marketplace. Even as darkness settled, a number of slow-burning torches were lit, and the babble of hawkers, arguing women, and the merry voices of children filled the sultry air.

Old men, their narrowed eyes empty of expression, sat on their haunches, smoking opium pipes. Near the market square there were stables, and Jace noticed young girls with baskets, gathering manure cakes to use for cooking fuel.

The night breeze drifted to him, heavy with smells of food cooking over fires and the moist jungle that enclosed them.

As he and Gokul neared the center of the city, the scene was drastically altered from one of poverty to wealth and power. Structures of intricate Oriental carvings rose up like small palaces. Teakwood gates opened onto arched bridges that fanned over fountains and pools containing bright-colored fish that darted like jewels under the bronze lanterns. The air was now perfumed with the scent of flowering vines that crept over iron fences. Here the houses were two-storied, their roofs elaborately carved, and screened by wide-spreading trees.

Jace looked upon homes belonging to the wealthy commerce traders who sold to both the Dutch and English East India Companies, offering ivory, teakwood, emeralds, pearls, and Chinese tea.

The narrow streets were a maze of alleyways and avenues with the poor and the slaves performing menial tasks or errands for their rich masters.

He and Gokul were now in the heart of Zin's city, and the wide street merged under an arched bridge of ebony stone; a red dragon gazed down upon them as they passed beneath into a wide plaza with a high wall.

They arrived as the evening fires were being lit in the tall stone idols. Brown-skinned boys in loincloths shimmied up teakwood poles, carrying torches. As they thrust the torches inside to ignite the fires, flames spilled forth like lava from the gaping mouths of stone gods with fat bellies and monkey-gods with fire dancing in their empty eye sockets. Jace carefully noticed the sentries, posted atop the pagodas, looking down on the wide square. They carried the curved sword and the deadly bow with quivers of bamboo arrows. The arrows, he knew, were used more swiftly and with greater accuracy than a rifle shot.

As he casually led his horse forward through the plaza under the dancing firelight, he saw the immense pink sandstone palace-fortress with ferocious royal tigers of marble—the palace of Zin.

The Burmese guards on the steps were wearing black headbands and knee-length leather tunics over loose-fitting trousers of black, and their broad faces and almond eyes showed not a hint of congeniality.

"Getting past the guards will prove next to impossible, sahib."

Jace did not wish to publicly announce the presence of Javed Kasam, for he had enemies, and who knew how many of his old foes were now serving Zin?

"Over there, sahib . . . do you see as I?"

Jace followed Gokul's glance. Standing on the front steps inside the entranceway, a man stood turbaned, wearing conspicuous jewels that gleamed against his bronzed skin. He was an official or guard and stood blocking the inner salon. Before him, there were two plainly clothed men bowing and hastily laying out their wares for him to scrutinize with a cold eye. No doubt the man's task was to screen the valuables being offered for sale by the traveling merchants before showing them to Zin.

Jace watched as the man gestured one of the two aside impatiently. The other must have offered something of interest, for he motioned for a second guard to come and show the man and his wares inside the salon.

Several other merchants were lining up at the steps and Jace and Gokul saw their opportunity.

"Shall I go, sahib? Do we dare risk the jeweled idol of Kali?"

"Stay with our horses and our prize. We will need it, I think, before this venture is over." His eyes were fixed on the official. "I shall risk something else to his greed."

In line at the steps behind the merchants, he heard the impatient dismissal of one disappointed merchant after another.

"Nay, fool, do you think His Excellency has need of English wool here in India's heat? Return it to the miserable feringhis."

When Jace mounted the steps, the official turned to him with impatience, but it swiftly turned to wariness as he scanned him, seeing that Jace was no humble merchant to be scorned. The black eyes took in his weapons, then noticing the dragon on his leather vest, came to meet Jace's gaze.

"I wish to speak with Zin."

The man hesitated, then for reasons of his own he chose to ignore the dragon. He raised a hand sparkling with rings to gesture him aside. "Zin sees no one. I am his eyes. Have you some item worthy of His Excellency? If not, others wait."

"I must see him."

"He has canceled the daily durbar."

"Tonight, then." Jace stood there, one boot resting on

the next step. He glanced past him into the well-lighted salon.

The official's eyes turned cold and speculative. "I think that is quite impossible. His Excellency is having dinner with important guests. As for tomorrow, he will not be here then."

"He is leaving?" Jace was alert.

"His Excellency's plans are his own and not subject to idle discussion. As I said, he has given orders that no one disturb him."

"I must. It is important." Jace held out his palm. As the official's eyes dropped, Jace lifted the cloth above the royal rings of the deceased Maharaja Majid Singh, and the heavy emeralds and rubies appeared to catch fire and gleam in the torchlight coming from the fat-bellied god who sneered down from his pedestal.

"Where did you get *these*?"

"My information is for Zin alone. If he leaves tomorrow, then I will see him tonight."

"Perhaps . . . I might arrange it, however difficult, but I will need to show him the rings first."

Jace met the man's lusty eyes and smiled faintly, but his deft fingers covered the rings with the royal cloth and returned them securely inside his jacket.

The official forced a smile as he turned toward the salon and signaled for a guard. "He may wish to see you. Step this way. You may wait in the salon. Whom shall I say has come to speak?"

"Javed Kasam."

18

When Jace stepped inside the large audience hall, he found that he was one among several who waited to see the warlord. Some were French, others looked to be Portuguese, and all the merchants had something worth the time and attention of Zin. The pompous official who guarded the front steps had done well.

Bronze lanterns brilliantly illuminated the marble floor with colored stone dragons and black cheetahs, but it was the dozen muscled guards surrounding the Burmese warlord who commanded Jace's attention. Shirtless, their black trousers were loose fitting and belted with gold, and each belt supported a scabbard with an Oriental curved blade.

Would he be able to convince Zin that the maharaja had commissioned him to become Gem's new bodyguard and that Gokul was to be the child's official swami? If Zin had heard of the rebellion at Guwahati and knew that Prince Sunil was now on the throne, the cunning Burmese warlord would not willingly surrender Gem— Sunil would offer him much to eliminate the rightful heir.

Jace scanned the audience hall, looking for the warlord.

He tensed. Zin sat on a divan of teakwood covered with red silk. He was not alone. Two Indian men in white turbans conversed with him. As one turned, his face became clearly visible. *Sanjay!*

Jace's former rissaldar-major turned and stared directly into his eyes. He was not masquerading as a native sowar in the Bengal army, nor as the guru whom Jace had seen outside the British residency in Guwahati the night of the rebellion. Sanjay was dressed in the garb of a high Indian official, yet he bore a scabbard with sword.

Would he recognize him in the role of Javed Kasam?

Jace casually turned his head away, but too late. A start of confusion showed on Sanjay's face, then astonishment. Sanjay pointed with triumph. "That man! Seize him! He is an enemy!"

Zin gave some silent command to his dozen warriors, and suddenly Jace was confronted with drawn blades. The guards spanned out, crouched in striking position.

Jace stepped back, holding his weapon. The merchants withdrew to the wall, nervously clutching their wares, giving Jace a clear view of Zin on the crimson divan.

"Is this the manner of welcome you give me, Zin?" called Jace. "I am disappointed. Especially when I bring news of a certain item desirous enough to have caused the death of Ayub Khan."

At the mention of his dead son, the warlord slowly stood, his broad face hard and ruthless. His black eyes flickered over Jace, then recognition struck. He walked forward, and his warriors stepped aside to form an aisle of drawn blades glinting in the light.

"So. The *Cheetah* returns to confront Warlord Zin!"

Jace did not move as their eyes held steadily, then Zin

unexpectedly gave a short laugh. "What is this! Have you turned an honest merchant that you come into my presence in the company of such as these?" And he gave a gesture to the wary merchants who watched from the wall.

"Send them away," Zin told the official. "I will see no more of their treasures tonight. Well, Javed Kasam! What have you to say for yourself?" He grasped Jace's forearms Roman style, grinning wolfishly, his bold black eyes laughing in malicious humor over the incident.

Jace gripped Zin's shoulder with his left hand, yet retained his blade with his right and glanced toward Sanjay. "I have come for that traitor's head."

Zin looked across the audience hall at Sanjay with sudden interest, and caution.

Sanjay watched Jace, and though he did not relent, his uncertainty showed. He glanced toward the open doorway that led onto the steps, but there were guards standing there now, their weapons drawn. Sanjay then looked toward an arch leading off into another section of the palace. A big Burmese man stood there, arms folded across his oiled chest, a black cloth about his head.

"You are a man who respects daring," said Jace to Zin. "I challenge my enemy to a duel. Here, and now."

Zin's eyes glinted like a hungry wolf, for his appetite feasted on a good fight. He chuckled, then turned grim. "You came to the border of Burma to challenge this man? Why do you seek him?"

"Because he is a traitor, and many good men are dead because of him."

Sanjay stared at Jace with hatred. "He lies! His Excellency calls this man by the name of Javed, but he is a feringhi. His name is Buckley. I would remind His Excellency how the arrogant English are also his enemies here in Burma."

Zin cast Sanjay an impatient glance. "I need be reminded of nothing. But this man is no Englishman."

"He wears the uniform of the English military beneath his disguise."

"Do you think me a fool? I know his blood! But to me, he is Javed Kasam, and he will remain so until I know he is truly my enemy."

"He is a sworn enemy of the new raja of Guwahati. If His Excellency is a true ally of Sunil, then you will arrest the feringhi."

Zin, an ally of Sunil. Jace knew he must move forward in his mission with caution. The warlord must know of the rebellion at Guwahati and the assassination of the old maharaja. Had Zin somehow been involved in supporting Sunil? If so, what of Gem?

Danger loomed its deadly head like the shadow of a cobra. The warlord was watching him now with less friendliness, his look speculative.

"You know my past," said Jace. "Let it speak for itself. This traitor Sanjay will say anything to save his head."

"Whom do you now serve?" asked Zin. "The English? Another? Yourself?"

If Jace withheld the truth, Zin would soon know. His chances fared better by speaking plainly. "I am a major in the British Bengal army, but I did not willingly seek it. It was my father's plan, one I felt obliged to accept for the return of my ship."

"You come for no other reason than for this man you say is your enemy?"

"There are other reasons. I have mentioned Ayub Khan."

A tiny flame of greed sprang up in the warlord's eyes as he understood that Jace might have the long-sought-for and coveted idol. He said nothing, for it was not a matter to speak of publicly.

"I have also been sent by the Maharaja Majid Singh," said Jace. "I and the swami," he said of Gokul, who stood unobtrusively to one side.

"The maharaja is dead," said Zin with no emotion.

"Yes. Assassinated by his own nephew Sunil. As for this man," said Jace, looking at Sanjay, "he will answer to the British military in Calcutta for the mutiny at Plassey, or he may save himself a tedious journey by accepting my challenge. What will it be, Sanjay? A duel here and now with the possibility you may kill me and go free, or the firing squad at Fort William!"

Sanjay's eyes spit his hatred, and he seemed about to step forward to accept the challenge. But the second man, who had kept silent until now, stood up. He was older than Sanjay, with gray hair and a certain dignity, and he appeared to be some manner of bureaucrat. Jace did not recognize him from Guwahati but judged him to be one of the maharaja's men.

"Both I and Dewan Sanjay are here on imperial business for the new Raja of Guwahati. Who is this feringhi mercenary to threaten the dewan of Sunil?"

Dewan! Jace's eyes fixed angrily on Sanjay. "So that is the position Sunil promised you for your bloodthirsty treason at Plassey."

Zin was alert as he studied Jace, Sanjay, and the government official with him.

"A duel is unthinkable, Excellency!" warned the older man.

Zin pretended disappointment as he grinned at Jace. "So speaks the Burha Gohain of Guwahati. But—the prime minister is correct. I cannot allow harm to befall Sunil's dewan, despite my sympathy for your earnest desire to confront your enemy. My reputation as a host would be ruined if either of you drew blood from the other. It is unthinkable, friend Javed."

Jace knew it was not his reputation that concerned the warlord. The fact that he was a ruthless leader to be feared was well known. He hesitated only because he was yet uncertain on which side he wished to align himself. Zin saw an opportunity for gain, and like a serpent smelling a rat he would wait; he would play one against the other for the highest gain to himself.

"Arrest him," demanded the Guwahati prime minister. "He is an enemy."

The Burmese official who had guarded the entrance unexpectedly stepped toward the warlord and whispered something.

The official must have mentioned that Jace held the royal rings of the old maharaja, for Zin seemed even more pleased at having opposing sides together under his jurisdiction. He turned toward the prime minister and Sanjay.

"You say Javed is an enemy. Whose? Mine or yours?"

"Any enemy of Sunil is yours as well, Excellency."

"It is I who shall decide, Burha Gohain, no one else." He gestured to his warriors. "Take them all away. I shall decide later who is friend and who is foe of Warlord Zin." He offered an official smile that was about as friendly as the mechanical obedience of his deadly warriors. "You are all my guests until I have wearied of your company."

The warriors moved to escort the furious prime minister and Sanjay from the audience hall.

Jace, too, felt a warrior's hand grasp his arm, but he jerked free and stepped back, his blade still in hand. The guard's eyes showed no emotion, only fanatical dedication to the Burmese warlord.

"Javed Kasam, you will go peaceably," came Zin's friendly voice, but it was absent of warmth. "Later we will speak alone without interruption." He turned to the guard. "Treat our comrade carefully. He is an old friend from the past. We have the same heartbeat—he once worked with my son to rob a Hindu temple."

Jace might have winced at that testimony. It was only half true. As the guards sheathed their blades in unison, so did Jace.

"I have come, Excellency, for the grandnephew of the maharaja."

Zin's black eyes mocked with amusement. "Which raja? Which uncle of Prince Adesh do you represent?"

Jace searched his face. Were there more than one? Certainly he did not speak of Sunil. "Maharaja Majid Singh of Guwahati has been assassinated. I seek to fulfill his dying wish. He authorized me to become the prince's bodyguard. And I bring the wisest man in the East to be his swami." Jace spread a hand and stepped aside. Gokul moved forward with all the grandeur of a king, his head slightly bent as though too holy and profound to be bothered by the mundane situation that had almost caught him up in bloodshed.

Jace managed an expression of grim dignity. "I present the Swami Gokul Sankar Punditji—his holiness Sri Baba of Lankali."

Gokul kept his eyes on the floor. With wolfish humor, the warlord scanned him. "Truly the wisest man in the East?"

Gokul did not answer. Jace stepped to the side of Zin and said in a hushed voice, "He is the Vedantic scholar who has come to lecture, to bring a deepened awareness of the divinity within."

Zin's hard, cynical gaze came to meet Jace's. Jace remained unreadable.

"And the royal rings of Guwahati? My official tells me you carry them for Prince Adesh."

"We must talk alone."

The warlord gestured a guard. "Take both Javed Kasam and his guru to a chamber." He turned to Jace. "We shall dine together, and talk."

Guards were everywhere as he and Gokul were escorted away. What could he do? How could he convince Zin to turn over Gem—and if he could not?

Inside the chamber, Jace expected trouble over his weapons, but to his surprise the Burmese made no attempt to disarm him. He was not certain how he would have reacted if they had. The door shut behind the guards, and a heavy bolt slid into place.

Gokul tossed aside his holy beads and sank wearily onto a cushion. He glanced about the chamber, watching as Jace went to the one window.

"Trapped. It is too high to escape, and if we could, Zin has posted some guards below."

"Sahib, I think we are in much trouble."

———

Zin lounged in a silk kimono against cushions at the far end of a long room whose doors were shut and guarded from the outside. A table was spread before him, and Jace and Gokul sat on either side of him. Servants brought in bowls of food, and women went about filling their glasses from bronze urns.

"In memory of my son—and your friend, speak freely," said Zin.

Jace wondered just how freely he should talk. Zin was now in control, but was there some way to gain a slight advantage? He must be alert, looking for any possibility.

"I can only imagine the lies the assassins have told you in order to have you turn over Adesh to them."

Zin waved an airy hand flashing with gems. "They spoke of a small rebellion among the Rajput Royal

Guard who favored Sunil."

"A rajput would die before becoming anything other than what caste tells him he is—a warrior. The royal guard were all loyal to the old raja and died without flinching under the feet of war elephants."

"You fought with them?"

"The maharaja knew of Sunil's treachery. He wished me to bring him here to Burma, to you."

"To me! I have been no friend to Majid Singh since I had the child abducted by traitorous sepoys from the English silk plantation near Jorhat. I have received modest payments from Guwahati with the promise I would not turn him over to Sunil."

Jace saw his opportunity to discover if he was correct about Roxbury, and Sir Hampton's headman, Natine.

"How you managed was clever. The diversionary fire in the hatcheries, the untouchable killed and thrown into the river for Natine to find—how much help did you get from the English ambassador?"

Zin's white teeth bared into a humorless smile. "There is no reason to shield the Englishman. I will tell you what happened. It was he who arranged the unfortunate accident of the untouchable, who informed me of the time to attack the plantation. He has his own ambitions."

"To control the Kendall silk."

"Yes, and a safe escort through Burma into China to open new trade routes. I will protect his future caravans passing through my territory. He is a hard man, one who bargains well. If he were not an Englishman but a warlord, I would have reason to see him as my chief enemy in Burma. He is the kind of man who eliminates his contenders."

"Yes—he works well with Sunil. Both men would use

an assassin's dagger to guarantee the success of their purposes."

"It is business between us, nothing more. What he wishes to do will also fatten my treasury, so presently we flow together smoothly down the same stream. But the future? Who knows."

"And what has Sunil promised Roxbury?"

"The protection of the plantation from the ghazis who wish the English presence out of Assam. In return for Sunil's help, the ambassador has convinced him that the Company would not interfere if he rebelled against his uncle and had him killed."

This, Jace had not expected. It did not seem wise of Roxbury to promise what he must know he could not deliver. The British military would fight to overthrow Sunil to place the maharaja's grandnephew, Gem, on the throne.

"A mistake. Roxbury will be arrested for treason against the British king, who made a treaty with the maharaja."

"Obviously the ambassador thinks he can deceive the East India Company about his own involvement. Those who know him to be involved will be dead when the English arrive. A warning to you to take to heart, Javed. You have proven to be his worst goad."

"There is one thing that bothers me. And that is why Sunil should care whether or not the Company accepts his rightful claim to the throne. He works with the ghazis, whose one aim is to rid Assam of the English. It is their wish to liberate all India of the feringhis."

Zin smiled. "I am surprised you would need ask such a question, Javed. You know the workings of intrigue. Today's friend may become tomorrow's enemy. Once on the throne with his power established, Sunil will then rid himself of the ghazis he now needs to place him there.

In the future, it will be more advantageous for Sunil to have the goodwill of the East India Company."

"By advantageous you mean that in the end, wealth and trade is the language of all races and creeds. Sunil believes he can gain more by working with the English—at least for the immediate future."

Zin waved a hand. "It is a matter of practicality."

"The ghazis would not agree," Jace said, hoping to find out about Natine. "The kotwal on the Kendall plantation has motives of his own, fired by religious fanaticism."

"You speak of Natine? That fool! He is no friend to the Burmese." Zin frowned for the first time, showing that the Indian man somehow angered him when others, more dangerous, did not. Jace wondered why, but at the moment he was more interested in Natine's workings with Roxbury. All information would be turned over to the governor-general in Calcutta.

"If he has aided Roxbury, it was not out of interest in trade," Jace prodded. "Roxbury must have promised him something important, something that would appeal to Natine's dedication to the Hindu god Shiva. Natine has helped him gain Kingscote by arranging the death of Sir Hampton Kendall in Darjeeling."

Again the warlord frowned. "I know nothing of that. But Kendall has proven a strong enemy to Burma. Even now he has mercenaries on his land to fight our infiltrators."

Jace believed him about not being involved, yet he was concerned, and stated evenly, "I plan to marry the daughter of Sir Hampton Kendall. No harm must come to them. Kingscote must remain as it always has in the past, as a separate province from either India or Burma."

There was no reply. Jace knew the silence meant that the warlord would promise him nothing. Zin changed the subject. "Why did the maharaja wish you to bring him here to the prince? We were enemies."

"He had few choices. Sunil gained the loyalty of his palace officials and the army. Prince Adesh was the old raja's last hope to stop Sunil from coming to the throne. He figured that he could offer the son of Rajiv, for Rajiv was loved." Jace was suddenly thoughtful. "I begin to doubt if those in the palace government who plotted with Sunil knew he killed his brother. They may have turned back to the maharaja had they known. As it was, the old raja could do little except wait and hope for the arrival of the English troops I was to bring. What he did not know was that Roxbury thwarted our arrival by the mutiny at Plassey. No doubt Roxbury had Sanjay stir up hatred for the English among the sepoys at Plassey."

He was certain Zin already knew all this, but the warlord behaved as though he did not. Jace was sure Zin's scheming nature was already busy at work wondering on which side to align himself.

Jace took a risk and produced the royal rings from the house of Singh.

Zin's eyes fixed upon them.

Jace realized that Zin could have his warriors take them by force, but he did not think the warlord would. Not yet. Not until he was certain in his own mind with whom he would ally himself in the battle for the throne.

"At his death, the maharaja entrusted the rings to me, along with his grandnephew." Knowing that Zin might let Sunil know he had the rings, Jace then added, "Sunil will want them to strengthen his claim."

Zin ate in silence while Jace watched him over his bronze goblet. Finally Zin spoke. "The prime minister and Sanjay bring me news that Sunil will pay much to have Adesh turned over to them."

And, of course, it was Zin who now had authority over Gem.

"Sunil will indeed pay whatever he must," said Jace. "But dealing with Sunil is like bringing starving hyenas to your table. They will eat what is there, then think nothing of eating the master who fed them. Sunil will also kill Adesh with no remorse."

"The prime minister and Sanjay speak not of his death but of his crowning."

"They lie to your face. Once in their hands, the boy will be slain. If not by them, by others waiting in Guwahati with Sunil. Come, Zin, I want the child. What is your answer?"

Zin emptied his glass, then held it out to be refilled. "What will you and the Kendall woman give me for his life?"

Jace restrained his anger. "Leave her out of this."

Zin smiled. "She must be beautiful indeed for Javed Kasam to venture into marriage. But the child can never become only her son, though he may be spared Sunil's dagger."

"I am aware of that. I will take him to a place of safety until we can place him on the Guwahati throne."

"By 'we' I assume you speak not of her but of the English in Calcutta."

"The British will not be expelled from India. Nor will they leave Assam. They will fight. They will send as many troops as are needed to secure the northeastern frontier. If you are unwise enough to align yourself with Sunil, there will also be fighting with Burma."

Zin sighed. "You are right, but Burma will not be intimidated."

"Then there could be a future war between England and Burma."

"But not between us, Javed." He smiled coolly. "Unless you insist on fighting for England. Somehow I cannot see Javed Kasam doing so."

"My only interest is a quiet departure, bringing Adesh with me. If I cannot put him on the throne, I would at least save his life. I would smuggle him to England. I leave you another thought: Sunil is untrustworthy and dangerous. Once on the throne, he would think nothing of turning against you if you get in his way. Ask yourself this, Zin. Who would you prefer on the throne of Guwahati: Sunil or Adesh?"

Jace could see by Zin's expression that he had already thought of this.

"How much will you offer for the grandnephew of Majid Singh?"

"The stolen idol of Kali."

Zin's eyes came alive. He drummed his fingers on the table, all the while staring thoughtfully at Jace. "Then you speak the truth. It is you and not Sunil who has it."

"Did he tell you otherwise?"

Zin did not answer.

Jace said, "Sunil seeks it. He had a rajput assassin in my chamber at Guwahati, hoping to find it."

"It is worth more than its gold and jewels. It will buy power from the Hindus who trouble me here in Burma."

"It is indeed worth much. It is worth the life of Adesh."

Zin's black eyes regarded him. Suddenly he smiled, slapped his palms together, and was boldly unashamed of his greed. "It is. Do you have it?"

Jace smiled and folded his arms. "Excellency! Would I, Javed Kasam, deceive such as you? Where is the son of Rajiv?"

"Safe. I shall have you and the swami visit him."

Jace remained calm but tense. "When?

Zin gestured his broad hand toward a loitering servant. "Send for the guard. My good friend Javed Kasam would see Adesh." He looked at Gokul with a condescending smile. "You too, Swami Gokul Sankar. It is good you have come from the maharaja. The royal scholar who has taught the prince has become ill and died only ten days ago. There has been sickness in the palace."

Guards entered, and Jace saw the Burmese official who had screened the merchants.

"You called, Excellency?"

"Is the prince awake?"

"He is asleep, Excellency, and his nurse is with him."

Zin nodded. "Take Javed Kasam and his swami to the chamber of Prince Adesh. They would see that he is well and safe. Prepare for his departure as well as my two noble guests," he said gesturing toward Jace and Gokul. "And the prime minister and Sanjay?"

"Bolted within their chambers, Excellency. And threatening to bring the entire army of Prince Sunil against you for treachery."

Zin sighed. "It may be that I must kill them so they do not reach Sunil." He looked at Jace. "You are certain you do not have mercenaries waiting in the jungle?" he asked with a mocking tone, for they both knew that Zin would have sent out scouts to search.

Jace smiled wryly. "You already know I have come alone. There are few I would risk my identity to as Javed Kasam. I would not wish to alert his many deadly enemies. At the moment Sunil is enough." Jace turned to follow the official out of the chamber.

Zin stood. "You have forgotten the idol, Javed."

"Excellency, would I be unwise enough to deliver before I first see the child? I will keep my side of the bargain as soon as we are safely out of the city."

Zin gave a soft chuckle. "Nor is Zin a fool. What if you

do not deliver but ride on with both Adesh and the idol of Kali?"

"You have fierce warriors and swift horses. You know I am alone except for the swami. You would overtake me before I ever crossed the border into Assam. Nor do I have reason to betray you. You must know I wish to have Adesh far more than the treasure, or I would not have risked coming to bargain."

Zin searched his face. "I shall take your word."

"And I shall take yours."

Zin gestured to the Burmese official. "Bring him to Adesh."

19

Jace followed the Burmese official to another section of the sandstone palace. They came to a door guarded by two warriors whose faces were hard masks. The official produced a key and slid back the bolt.

"Wait, I will tell Adesh Singh's nurse who you are, and to awaken him."

"We will take him at once and ride with speed. The nurse must stay."

"She will be most upset. She has been with him since he was a small child."

Jace thought of Gem being abducted from the Kendall nursery. "I can only take the prince. Tell her she may follow later to Jorhat and leave her name with the military commander. I will communicate with her when it is feasible."

The official stepped inside and returned almost at once. "Prince Adesh is awake. Come!"

Jace stepped into the chamber, Gokul behind him. He stopped short and reached for his sword, but it was too late.

Sanjay stood there with warriors holding deadly curved blades. Sanjay smiled with triumph.

"Welcome, Major-bahadur," he mocked the military term of honor. "I have been waiting. Did you truly think the warlord would betray Sunil? Ah!—do not draw your blade, Major. One flick of my finger and these warriors will attack. Not that I would not delight to see your head roll across the floor."

The door shut behind him. Jace heard it bolt. He turned toward the Burmese official, who spread his hands. "My apology, Javed Kasam. I am under orders from His Excellency. He has requested that you yield your weapons."

Jace kept his fury bridled. His voice was toneless. "Zin planned this?"

The official bowed slightly. "Would I dare lead you into a trap without his orders?"

Sanjay took a step forward, obviously impatient that the official was moving too slowly. "Kill him," he ordered the main Burmese guard standing near Jace and Gokul.

"It is like a coward to have others kill for him." Jace glanced at the guard. "Sanjay is responsible for the deaths of a hundred fighting men, each one worth ten of him. He can do nothing but plot and lie and give orders to kill."

The guard showed no emotion. Was he alive? wondered Jace dryly.

Sanjay turned angrily to the official, who stood with dignity, hands behind him.

"Stop him. Silence him now. You have your orders to kill him. Do it!"

"His Excellency will decide when and how he dies, Dewan Sanjay. There is another matter between them of which you know nothing. It will be settled first."

The idol. Was Zin mad enough to think he would turn it over to him? It would rot first! Nothing would make him talk now.

"What of Rajiv's son, Prince Adesh?" demanded Jace. "Has Zin no honor that he would lie to me and allow this piece of lice to kill a child?" he gestured to Sanjay. "At least allow the swami to see the boy, and go with him."

"The swami shall not go," said Sanjay.

"Do you also fear an old man with a soft belly?" mocked Jace.

Sanjay walked toward him as if to backhand Jace, but the guard stepped forward.

"Are these guards loyal to Sunil or not?" asked Sanjay angrily.

"Dewan Sanjay must know they are loyal first of all to His Excellency," came the official's calm voice. "As for the Swami Gokul Sankar, he cannot see Prince Adesh. The boy is ill."

"It may be that Swami Gokul Sankar can help to relieve the prince's suffering," said Jace.

"No!" snapped Sanjay. "Any man with the major is not to be trusted. He could be in disguise."

"You would know well of disguises," said Jace.

"I will look upon Adesh," said Sanjay. "He is to be prepared to ride out in the morning."

"No, while Sanjay will not fight a man, he will thrust a dagger into a child!"

"That, Javed Kasam, is none of my affair," said the Burmese official, his demeanor unchanged. "His Excellency has already agreed to release Adesh to the dewan and the prime minister in the morning. Come," he said to the smug Sanjay. "You may look in on Prince Adesh and his nurse. She will journey with him."

"Very well." Sanjay walked briskly to the door but looked back at Jace. "One day I will see you dead—I have vowed to Kali."

They went out, leaving Jace and Gokul alone. Again the door was bolted shut. He heard the sound of their feet walking away. Silence enclosed them.

Jace unleashed his emotion by kicking a stool and sending it smashing against the door. "Filthy curse! What a fool I was to trust Zin!"

"He is a cunning tiger, sahib. But Sanjay is a vicious cobra. Prince Adesh will never reach Sunil."

With frustration and anger Jace leaned his arm against the stone wall but could find no words. He uttered something beneath his breath. And Coral! How could he face her, knowing he had failed to save the child's life?

———

Outside in the hall, the Burmese official led Sanjay to the chamber of Prince Adesh. He unlocked the door and opened it wide, stepping aside for Sanjay to enter.

Sanjay entered boldly, his eyes sweeping the royal chamber. A Burmese nurse cringed away, frightened. "Please, mighty one! He is but a child!" She made an attempt to throw herself between Sanjay and the sick child in the bed. "Please!"

"Silence, woman! He will not die yet! Prepare him and yourself to journey at dawn."

"But Prince Adesh is ill with high fever. Moving him will—"

"If he is not ready at dawn, it is you who will die."

Pressing her fist against her mouth to silence her frightened sobs, the woman lowered her head in fearful obedience.

Sanjay turned and strode out. "Bolt the door," he ordered the official. "I want guards here."

"There is no possible route of escape. There are no windows in the chamber. Zin has been most careful. And the nurse's fear of punishment has made her fully obedient."

"Nevertheless, I want guards."

"It is done."

———

Jace could not sleep. He paced his chamber restlessly, thinking, praying, yet no ideas came to him. His call through the door to the guards went unheeded. So did his pounding, until he realized it was futile. As deep night settled over Burma, he could not sleep. Somewhere out there Sunil waited for Gem. And this time there was no one to prevent the boy's death. *No one*, he thought wearily, going to the window to look below into the torchlight, *but God.*

Had he failed because of pride? Had he not sought the Lord's blessing on his dangerous venture? But he had prayed! Why then? Why the stark, brutal face of failure?

His forehead rested against the cold iron bars. He shut his eyes. *Jesus, Son of God, perhaps you have permitted this because I have been slow to follow you. It was never a question of my not knowing who you are, or the meaning of your sacrifice for sin—it was a matter of obedience to your Lordship. . . .*

His hands closed tightly around the bars, and he felt the sweat on his forehead. "But at Sualkashi . . . I surrendered to your will. My life and my plans are meaningless without you. Your purposes are the only thing worth living for, dying for. I do not know what you may want of my life, but for whatever purpose, it is yours."

Overwhelmed, he could not think. *Lord, it is my honor to yield to you.* Dawn broke over the dark jungle, and Jace watched silently through the window as guards brought horses and a palanquin for transporting the prince. Minutes later he saw the warlord come out with his guards. Next followed the prime minister and Sanjay, followed by the Burmese nurse carrying Gem.

Jace watched as they were placed inside the covered palanquin and the others mounted horses for the ride to meet Sunil. Sanjay looked up toward the window and must have seen Jace standing there for he said something to the warlord.

Zin looked up at the window, his bronze face hard as he replied. Whatever it was pleased Sanjay, for he mounted his horse and rode off behind the palanquin without looking back.

"They are gone?" It was Gokul's sad voice.

"Yes."

"Do not grieve, sahib. We did what we could. And will not the True Master look with pity on the spirit of the child when he dies?"

"He will."

20

Northeastern Frontier

Ethan knew they were now somewhere between Jorhat and Sibsagar, the capital of Assam. They had arrived after dark at a little-used public rest house called a dak-bungalow where the tea was weak and lukewarm, and insects crawled on the walls.

The dozen rajputs belonging to Sunil, but now serving Sir Hugo, waited in the dark jungle near a narrow dirt road.

Ethan walked to the open window, where the night cloaked him in sultry heat. He turned, his nerves ready to snap, and glanced at Sir Hugo, who sat at a small table puffing on a hookah while tracing his map with an eyepiece.

Ethan had been able to discover little of his uncle's mission.

"We have journeyed miles out of our route. What can be more important than going to Darjeeling? Yet you sit for hours pouring over that wretched map!"

"You heard what the rajput told me when he arrived tonight from Kingscote."

"I saw the man, yes, but you know quite well I do not know Hindi." He jammed his hands into his trouser pockets. "I am able to pick up only a few words here and there."

Sir Hugo regarded him with a dark gaze. "Perhaps it is best you do not ask questions. The answers may prove unpleasant, to say the least."

Ethan was all too familiar with Hugo's baiting suggestions, and became cautious. "If there is dark news, Uncle, I wish to know it."

"Sit down and stop pacing like a trapped animal."

"It is Hampton, isn't it! If so, I am not entirely surprised. We have wasted weeks wandering like vagabonds while ignoring the serious matter for which we began this journey."

"It is not Hampton. The rajput arrived from Kingscote with news."

Outside in the hot darkness insects buzzed and crickets chirped. Ethan's gaze fixed on his uncle. "What ill news did the rajput bring?" he pressed.

"You might as well know what has brought us here. I have come to convince the Raja of Sibsagar to make peace with his son Sunil. If not, Sunil will go to war."

Ethan stared at him blankly. He knew nothing about Sibsagar except that it was the capital of Assam. He had heard about tension in the family dynasty between Guwahati and Sibsagar, and that squabbles had nearly led to a state of war.

"Assassinating his uncle and seizing the throne at Guwahati was not enough for Sunil, I gather?" snapped Ethan. "He wishes war with his father as well!"

"Sunil is an ambitious man. But there will be no war. Sibsagar will make peace in order to save Gem—or should I say Prince Adesh?"

"Gem!" Ethan walked toward him.

Sir Hugo stood, rolling up his map. "The boy is alive, and Sunil has discovered his whereabouts in Burma. Gem is of royal blood, not only from Rajiv but also from Jemani. She was related to the Raja of Sibsagar before she maried Rajiv."

Ethan's lips tightened, but he said nothing. So they had found out about Gem. They had located him, and now had him. Then what of the major? Had he failed in his attempt?

Ethan thought of Coral, and tension gripped his emotions. "It is a curse that Sunil has found him. He has no qualms about slaying his brother's offspring if he feels the child is a threat!"

"Your sentiment is foolish, the chatter of a woman. I am here to avert bloodshed. The death of a child is not the type of thing I would involve myself in."

"Rot! I'll have no part in this. I will not stay! Nor will I journey to Sibsagar. I am leaving in the morning." He walked toward the beaded divide. "I shall go to Kingscote."

"You will go nowhere until the matter which brought me here is complete," ordered Hugo. "Your rash behavior could ruin everything. I will have audience with the raja, promising to produce Prince Adesh, and you will journey to Sibsagar. Not because I need you, but because I do not trust you to keep silent."

Ethan turned, his face pale and taut.

Sir Hugo's black gaze glittered with wrath as he strode toward Ethan. "Do you think I do not know you informed Coral of my previous deeds in London? You might have had both her and your medical research if you had kept silent. Now it is too late for both of you."

Ethan's heart thundered in his chest. "What do you mean, both of us? What about Coral?"

"I was in the parlor the night your emotions turned

you into a blabbering fool, the night Buckley arrived. You destroyed in minutes what I had carefully planned for years! The entire matter of marriage was settled. I had convinced even Elizabeth to hold the wedding at Christmas. You need not have feared Buckley, but you panicked. You confessed to Coral that we drugged her in London, and that you were carrying out my wishes. It is too late now, for Coral. She is dead." Sir Hugo turned away. He went back to the table and sat down, picking up his hookah.

Ethan sucked in his breath. His stomach seemed to come up to his mouth. "Dear God—you didn't—"

"Pull yourself together, Ethan. Do you think I'd eliminate my own niece?"

"Yes! Yes!"

"You see?" said Hugo wearily. "You panic too easily. You nearly got me killed in Guwahati by your foolish outburst. That is why I cannot allow you to leave. Actually I was quite fond of Coral. . . . She outwitted me on several occasions. I should have had her as a daughter instead of Belinda. But alas, fate pulls so many ironic jests, does it not?" he scanned Ethan, his eyes mocking and malicious.

Ethan could not speak.

"She is dead," Sir Hugo repeated. "Elizabeth too. Natine has a most venomous temper when riled. He believes Kali has ordered their destruction. Shiva is a jealous god. The persistence of Coral and the sentimentality of Elizabeth in allowing the school was enough to provoke the attack by ghazis from Kingscote and the village. Did not I warn you in London?"

"Y-you allowed that fiend to kill them?"

"No! Don't you remember that I ordered a rajput to stay to protect them? Somehow Natine and the village priest arranged an accident with a cobra. The best way we can vindicate their unfortunate deaths is to see to Natine's when we return."

Sir Hugo drew on the hookah and the water gurgled. "Natine and the priest are far too risky to leave alive. I will order the rajputs to see to both of them on our return. In the meantime, you must gather your wits together. There is always Marianna . . . you might think of marriage to her. Without her parents and Coral she'll most likely have an emotional breakdown. You can be there to soothe and make her better. She will come to understand that you are her one source of strength."

Ethan stared at him. *The man is insane.* He turned swiftly and left the room. Outside, he went to the bushes to relieve his ill stomach.

How long he knelt there sick he did not know. He stared into the dark grass. He saw a mammoth bug crawl by and watched, feeling too dazed to move. He had told himself he was angry enough to break with Hugo after he had watched Coral climb the stairs and out of his life. He had thought he could cut the python from around his soul, a python that was slowly squeezing him to death. He could not. Now tormented by the death of Coral, the new plans of Hugo to marry him to Marianna left him angry. *How can I break free of Hugo?*

"God," he rasped into the tropical night, "help me. . . ."

He came alert. Horses! He scrambled to his feet, damp with sweat, and stared intently into the darkness toward the road. Armed riders were nearing, guarding a palanquin. Ethan's head turned sharply toward the dak-bungalow. Sir Hugo came out, followed by rajputs, and walked toward the road to meet them.

The entourage had stopped, and several armed men were dismounting. Ethan's trembling fingers touched the loaded pistol beneath his jacket, and he stumbled in their direction.

He arrived, stopping a few feet back to hear Sir Hugo speaking with an older Indian official. Another Indian stood near the door of the palanquin. With a start of surprise, Ethan recognized Sanjay.

"Where is the boy?" demanded Sir Hugo.

"With the nurse inside the palanquin," said the older Indian official. "He is ill."

"Turn him over to me. Once the raja realizes we have the prince, he will abdicate his throne to Sunil in order to save the child's life."

"An error, Sahib Roxbury!" came Sanjay's harsh voice. "He must die."

"Do not be a fool. The raja does not yet know of Jemani's son. If you slay him we have nothing with which to bargain."

"The house of Singh cannot be trusted. It was he who made the treaty with the feringhis—he, and the Maharaja of Guwahati. We will slay the prince now," said Sanjay.

"Slay the child and I will kill you," came Sir Hugo's voice, deadly calm.

Sanjay's eyes, hard and cold, were riveted on Sir Hugo.

Hugo gestured to the rajput guards, who stepped forward, their hands resting on their tulwars.

"You make a mistake," said Sanjay. "Letting Adesh live will mean ultimate defeat. Even if he leaves India, one day Adesh will return, as a man with a mighty army."

"Turn the boy over to the rajputs," commanded Sir Hugo. "They have been sent by Sunil to guard him until he arrives with his army."

Sanjay's angry gaze swept the others, then he turned to the palanquin. He opened the door and said something to the frightened Burmese nurse, but she would not leave the seat where the boy lay ill, covered with the royal blanket.

What happened next froze Ethan with horror. Swiftly Sanjay produced a dagger and plunged it repeatedly while the deafening screams of the nurse filled his ears. He then drew a pistol and shot the boy as the rajput guards converged on him, striking with their tulwars. He sank to the dusty ground, where they grabbed him, dragging him to the side of the road to die.

Ethan threw himself past the others into the palanquin in a desperate but futile attempt to save the child. He hesitated in confusion when he turned the boy over, ripped off the head covering, and saw his face. *He is Burmese! This cannot be Gem!*

He stared at the boy's almond-shaped eyes and lighter-hued skin. His eyes darted to the nurse, and he saw the signs of death coming upon her. Her eyes seemed to plead with him to remain silent about the boy's identity.

"Any hope?" cried Sir Hugo from outside the palanquin. "Is he alive, Ethan? Can you do anything?"

Ethan fumbled to cover the child with the blanket. His mouth was dry, and he tried to swallow.

"No. Prince Adesh is dead."

Jace heard a key turn in the lock, and the heavy bolt slid back. The Burmese official stood there, expressionless.

"His Excellency has called for you."

Jace's chill gaze swept him. "My weapons, where are they?"

A guard stepped from the hall.

"This way, Javed Kasam," he said calmly. "You also, Swami Gokul Sankar."

They followed the official into the warlord's chamber. Zin sat cross-legged on cushions, eating a sumptuous meal, and looked up when they entered. Seeing Jace's expression and brittle blue-black eyes, Zin chuckled and waved him and Gokul to join him at the table.

"Come, sit. You are my guests. But, we have made a bargain, Javed Kasam. Where is the idol of Kali?"

Jace refused to sit and stood in a military stance, his hands behind him. His even stare brought a mock wince from Zin, who looked at his official and said with wry humor, "Our guests are angry with us."

"Perhaps, Excellency, you best tell him the truth before you return his weapons."

Jace glanced from Zin to the official and saw a slight smile. He came alert. "What truth?" he demanded.

Zin finished draining his bronze goblet. His black eyes glinted. "The boy given to the Dewan Sanjay is the child of the Burmese nurse. He is expected to die from his illness. He would have been pleased to know he gave his life to save his beloved friend. Prince Adesh Singh, however, is well. This ruse of mine was necessary. But if the Burmese boy does not die, and they discover they have been tricked, they will soon return—and you had best be gone."

Stunned, Jace could not speak. His mind went back to the deceit played upon Coral. After Gem's abduction a child's body was found in the river, wearing the garments of Gem, including the gold cross.

Zin smiled, his black eyes glinting with amusement. "Adesh has been sent where they will never think to search," said Zin. "He is with a feringhi. A 'Christian' feringhi at that! His name is Felix Carey."

Felix! The son of William Carey in Serampore, thought Jace, astonished.

"The young Englishman is here in Burma translating the Christian holy writings into Burmese," said Zin. "Prince Adesh is safely held at the Carey compound. If you and the swami leave now, you will be well on your way before they return."

"Zin, I—"

"No need to tell Zin how clever he is." He smiled wolfishly and stood. "Simply produce the idol of Kali as we bargained."

Jace smiled. He glanced at Gokul, who also grinned. Jace nodded, and on cue Gokul turned his back and lifted his robe. When he turned around again, his stomach was flatter, and he presented Jace with the gold idol glimmering with precious emeralds and rubies.

"Ah. . . ." sighed Zin.

With a faint smile Jace placed it amid the tropical fruit bowls on Zin's table, adding a ripe mango for Kali's crown.

Minutes later, belting on his scabbard, and receiving a rough drawing from the Burmese official of the location of the compound, Jace turned to leave the chamber when Zin's sober voice stopped him—

"There is more we must discuss, Javed."

Caution. . . . Jace turned with a narrowed gaze.

Zin was grave and thoughtful, as though troubled, and motioned him to sit.

"There is much you do not know. Sunil's ambitions go further than Guwahati. He will war against the royal house at Sibsagar and rule both thrones."

The mention of Sibsagar brought new feelings of apprehension. Jace lowered himself to the cushions. Sibsagar's dynasty had ruled the Brahmaputra valley since the eleventh century. There had been many kings, and one of them had assumed a Sanskritic name—Singh.

His successors had also adopted the name and married with the maharajas of Guwahati. Sunil too would have his eye on the ancient city of the old Ahom kings. It was from "Ahom" that the name "Assam" had come. For Sunil to have his seat of authority in Sibsagar was in keeping with his ambition and pride.

"But why will he risk battle now? If he were wise he would wait to consolidate his rule in the south and move northeast when his military is stronger."

Zin looked at him evenly. "You do not know. Jemani is the daughter of the Raja of Sibsagar. If Sunil does not destroy the child you call Gem—then there will be one maharaja over all Assam."

For a moment Jace did not speak. He had always suspected that Jemani might have had royal blood, but somehow he had gone along with the assumption of the old Maharaja of Guwahati that she had come from some petty prince ruling a district in the south.

"Sunil will strike at Sibsagar while he has opportunity to gain military support from Burma."

Jace gave him a sharp look. It was the first mention of Burmese involvement in Sunil's plans. It all began to make sense to Jace now. The mutiny at Plassey, the massacre of his troops, even the earlier attack on Jorhat when his friend Major Selwyn was killed. Sibsagar was now isolated from military help, and Sunil and the Burmese government found it beneficial to work together.

"The British Bengal troops at Jorhat will not be enough to defeat Sunil," stated Zin. "The prime minister of Guwahati came to Burma not only about the child but to appeal to my government to join forces with Sunil. Together they will fight the king of Sibsagar to rid Assam of the English presence."

Jace thought of Coral and Kingscote. If fighting

erupted, they too would be at risk. His frustration mounted, but he must not let Zin know how weak they were. What could he do without adequate troops!

"He has come to you also?"

Zin measured him. "He has."

"And what was your answer?"

Zin looked at him gravely. "I have accepted."

In the silence, Gokul stirred uneasily, glancing from Zin to Jace. But Jace showed no expression.

"It is also true that you have informed me of your plans, and the plans of the others. You would not do so if you felt at peace in what you do."

"You give Zin more conscience than he has. I tell you only because I am a friend of Javed Kasam." His eyes were grave. "I do not wish you killed in battle by my warriors. Is it not enough I have told you where to find the child? Take him and return to Calcutta! Take the Englishwoman you love and go! The internal conflicts of the dynasty are not your burden."

"As Javed Kasam I might agree. As a major in the British military I speak for more than myself. If there is to be an attack on Sibsagar I cannot walk away. There are English soldiers at Jorhat, and I cannot desert them."

Could the gathering together of the Burmese warlords somehow be halted by convincing Zin to withdraw and to counsel the other warlords to do the same?

Zin, however, would not be easily convinced, nor did Jace think he could frighten him, yet it was his duty to stand for the Company.

"You disappoint me, Zin. I vowed in writing to the governor-general that it was not Burmese troops who attacked Jorhat and killed Major Selwyn. Colonel Warbeck did the same."

"Javed, would I be unwise enough to attack the English on my own initiative? I knew Selwyn was your friend. The attack was Sunil's doing, along with renegade Burmese from the jungle around the Kendall lands. It was Roxbury who approved the attack, offering important information. Selwyn, however, was not supposed to have been killed. Roxbury knew Calcutta would look on his death as reason to send more troops."

"And the colonel did," said Jace. "They were massacred near Plassey. Yet British reinforcements will arrive from the south. We have a treaty with the Raja of Sibsagar to come to his aid against any attack from Burma."

"Javed, you too must know how we Burmese feel about Assam. The territory belongs to us."

"Both India and England disagree."

"And you? Do you also disagree? Do you believe that English blood should dictate who rules the land?"

Jace lifted the cup of strong black tea and drank to mask any personal feelings he might have.

"I represent the British government."

"Javed Kasam is independent. He also was born here."

"I was born on an East India ship," he said dryly. "A pirate's vessel to be exact."

"Yet you have walked among us, as one of us. You have been a friend to many, whether Indian or Burmese."

"Whatever I may think of the policies of the East India Company, I am now their representative. Any attack on Sibsagar will be deemed an attack on the good word of His Majesty King George."

Zin sighed and shook his head. "Your honor is your death, Javed."

Honor? Was it that? Or was it the thought of Coral and her school on Kingscote, or perhaps all the English yet in Assam that kept him bound to his British uniform.

"If Sunil rules Assam, there will be more at risk than your ambitions, or even my life. I begin to see that for

270

the peace and well-being of Assam, Rajiv and Jemani's son must reign. Perhaps this was the reason for his survival . . . if he had not been taken by the Englishwoman, even for so short a time, Adesh would not have survived to claim his birthright."

Zin looked at him a long moment, then gave a light bow of his head to show the discourse was at an end. They had not come to agreement.

Jace stood. "I leave you with one thought. Who would you feel more secure with on the throne of Assam—Sunil or Adesh? Adesh will not come seeking you in Burma, but Sunil will never be satisfied with what he has. He will always want more."

Zin was thoughtful. Jace turned and walked out, followed by Gokul.

———

After Jace was gone, Zin pondered his words as he picked up the idol of Kali and turned it over in his hand. "What do you think?" he asked his official. "Does Javed speak wisely?"

"He does, Excellency. I too believe Assam and Burma will know better rule under Adesh. Sunil is a ruthless man."

"Ah, he is indeed." Zin removed a pearl-handled dagger from under his sleeve. "If Sunil will kill his nephew, a winsome child like Adesh, how much more easily will he put an assassin's dagger into the back of Zin!"

He threw the dagger for emphasis, and it stuck fast into the wooden table.

"Then does Your Excellency not wish me to prepare for your journey to the battle of Sibsagar?"

"I shall stay comfortable here after all. And I shall counsel the other warlords to do the same. If Sunil cannot take Sibsagar with ten thousand warriors and many elephants, he is too big a fool to reign Assam. And—send a wedding gift for Javed Kasam to Kingscote."

"Your Excellency?"

Zin beckoned to have one of his treasure chests brought to him.

Minutes later he pulled out a prized Mogul sword. His black eyes gleamed, then he sighed. "Such a sword. It is worth much. Javed will remember this delectable prize from Calcutta. A pity he had to be struck on the back of the skull. Alas! I shall make amends and send it back. We shall make him think I retrieved it from some thief at a bazaar. Who knows? I may need Javed Kasam sometime in the future."

"A wise idea, Excellency!"

Jace and Gokul rode from the sandstone palace and out under the arched bridge of ebony stone with its red dragon gazing down upon them.

Jace paused on the road, where the noon sun bore down on the reddish earth. Troubled, he frowned to himself, disturbed by the thought that the military at Jorhat was oblivious to the danger closing in about them. There were British and Scottish soldiers stationed there. Not many, perhaps twenty, yet they were fine soldiers.

And Kingscote was less than a day's journey from Jorhat. It would take little for the fighting to erupt beyond the walls of the outpost to ensnare the four Englishwomen alone in the mansion. . . .

And beyond Kingscote, on the road south to Guwahati, even at this minute Sunil would be preparing for war, gathering his thousands of warriors, his war elephants and war machines for the long march northeast.

"Your horse faces east, sahib, but your heart looks toward Jorhat."

Gokul faced him as Jace thoughtlessly flicked the end of the horse's reins against his palm. "Zin was right, sahib. Prince Adesh is safe with missionary Felix Carey. Each day and hour he stays, the more he knows of God. This is good. Sunil and Roxbury will not search there." He chuckled. "And if Zin's trickery went undiscovered, they will not search for him at all."

Jace agreed. Neither Sir Hugo nor Sunil would look for Gem.

"Not much time," said Gokul. "Our moments are like few raindrops caught in cup before it stops. My advice? Seize them! Is not sahib under military honor to alert the troops at Jorhat of grave danger?"

"Are you asking me to lead a death charge of some fifty men against war elephants?"

Gokul grinned. "Not with the promise of wedding to lovely English damsel."

Jace smiled faintly and turned his horse south, toward the military outpost. With only a handful of soldiers, what could he do? There was no hope of Captain MacKay arriving in time, even if his troop was near Guwahati.

"There is little to be done, Gokul. We can warn Jorhat, and see that the women on Kingscote are safe until Mackay arrives."

"It is enough, sahib."

But was it? There must be some way to stop Sunil short of storming his palace to duel him, but what?

He must alert the Raja of Sibsagar.

Darjeeling

The toe of his boot rested on a rock that he prayed would not dislodge from the mountainous soil; his bleeding fingers clung to another, his grip tiring. How long Hampton had clung there since the rope snapped could have been anywhere from one minute to fifteen.

Where was his Indian guide, Lal? And the Indians carrying the supplies, had they returned to camp? Why did not someone throw another rope?

Below him the mountains dropped to certain death.

Another rock fell away from under him. He heard its echo all the way to the bottom of the canyon. His body ached with weariness and was becoming slippery with sweat. Fear turned his heart into a pounding drum. If he lifted his boot from the one rock to search for a more secure handhold, his fingers might weaken.

He might yell out again to the others, but they should have heard him the first time. Had they felt the rope break—or had someone cut it?

There was no hope. Should he survive, it would be by the Almighty's help alone. As that realization struck Hampton, it eased his fears. He could not hold on like this much longer. He must move.

Cautiously he brought his boot along the rocks and felt for a wider hold, and the leg that now held him was trembling.

"Good Shepherd," he gasped hoarsely, "have mercy . . . come to the aid of this old wandering sheep . . ."

Fighting away the fear that seemed to blind him, Hampton shut his eyes and breathed deeply, concentrating on his next move, one that could bring his death.

His toe touched some obstruction, not more than several inches wide. In order to rest his weight on it he must let go of the rock his fingers clutched.

He held himself flat against the soil, gathering courage, then slid his hand across the dirt and bits of rock and weeds to grasp a mound. His legs were beginning to tremble uncontrollably, and the old familiar pain in the area of his heart began to throb with spasms that brought shortness of breath.

I am going to die, he thought. *This is the end.* Elizabeth flashed into his mind, and tears mingled with his sweat. Guilt supplanted his fear as he thought of how he had never been the husband he should have been. Though he loved her dearly, he had never been the spiritual head he knew she would have wanted. And his daughters . . . what would become of them? Hugo would be their guardian until their marriages, and Kingscote . . . somehow the plantation, once all that his heart feasted upon, seemed insignificant as he stared into the face of death.

Nothing mattered as eternity opened its doors to bid him to enter, ready or not. . . . Nothing mattered as he saw his failures looming larger and larger like shadows prepared to bury him.

Sweat ran into his dimmed vision, the thatch of hair tinged with gray was glued to his forehead. He shut his eyes, feeling his strength leaving his body, as though death were saying, "Here am I."

The pain in his heart eased. He released the small mound, his fingers numb, and as his body slid down he found that his boot was on a larger rock firmly lodged into the soil. *The Lord is my Rock, my Fortress* came the words from a psalm he could not remember. He could rest now, leaning all his weight against the mountain, the side of his face feeling the pebbles dig into his skin. Slowly his heart ceased its drumbeat, and a small breeze cooled him. He was safe for the moment.

Then he heard a sound, a whisper of movement hardly detectable. Some pebbles from above rolled down over him. Who was coming? Someone from the trekking party to help, or the man who had cut the rope?

"Sahib?"

Hampton strained to distinguish the voice. It was Lal.

Should he trust him? Yet if he did not answer, and Lal had come to help. . . .

"I am here!" he called weakly into the wind. "Throw a rope!"

He waited, then heard a sound that turned his blood cold. Lal was chipping away to loosen a boulder that would come crushing down upon him.

———

Seward lay upon a rocky slope less than sixty yards from where Hampton clung for life. Seward had been waiting nearly twenty minutes. He could have fired his rifle several times. . . . he could have killed one, perhaps more, but he waited, for they were beginning to leave. The Burmese warrior had stayed behind alone to finish the evil work of killing Sir Hampton.

Now at last . . . Seward moved.

He made no sound as he came up behind the warrior busy loosening the boulder.

Warned by some instinct, Lal turned suddenly, and Seward fired his pistol. The Burmese slumped to the ground.

Seward had little time to save Hampton. The gunfire would have alerted the others, who might come back. Seward took a rope from the dying warrior and staggered to the mountain's rim.

"Hampton!" called Seward as he quickly tied the end of the rope into a secure loop.

From below, where he clung, Hampton heard the familiar voice and would have shouted had he the strength.

"Hampton!"

"Here—" managed Hampton. It seemed an eternity passed before he saw the rope sliding down the mountain toward him. As it slid beside him, he cautiously moved his stiff hand across the rock and latched hold. He then carefully released his other handhold as he placed the loop over his head and under both arms.

Slowly he was eased up, and as the thought of safety possessed him, Hampton's energy revived, and he struggled to climb upward as Seward hauled on the rope.

Perhaps five minutes had passed before Hampton's eyes could fix on Seward straining above him on the rim. His reddish gray hair was plastered across his sweating forehead, his stark blue eyes riveted upon him.

Hampton thought he was grinning but could not be sure until he felt Seward's big hands pulling him to safety.

In a moment of relief they knelt together, gasping for air, staring up at the heavens, their minds united in offering thanksgiving.

"We best get out of here, quick. Roxbury's men be coming back, 'tis my guess."

"Roxbury!"

Seward scowled. " 'Twas naught but an evil plot to see you dead. Me and the major be thinking Roxbury and Natine worked together. We best get ourselves back to Kingscote. I've a dark feeling they be needin' us. An' I wouldn't be worrying about Alex. More chances than not, ye'll be hearing from him safe and sound, and find the lad never laid eyes on the tea plantation."

"What a fool I've been! Thank God you came, Seward. You've saved my life as you did in the past."

" 'Twas nothing, Sir Hampton. But if we don't get a move, we both may end up over the mountain."

"If Hugo has lifted a finger to harm my wife or daughters—I shall have the man sent to Newgate, brother-in-law or not."

"Are you all right? Ye be limping. . . ."

"Only an injured knee. Do you have a horse?"

"I was smart enough to bring two," said Seward with a grin. "Always did believe the Almighty would aid us."

21

Ethan heard Sir Hugo walk away from the palanquin
as the others followed. Their low voices carried in the
silence. He listened intently to the plan of attack. Sunil
had ten thousand fighting men and many war elephants.
Somehow he must locate the major and alert him. But
where was he!

The Burmese nurse was dying. She sensed this as he
worked to save her. Her feeble fingers reached for the
front of his vest. "M-must say nothing," she rasped.

"Your secret is safe. I am a friend of Prince Adesh. An
Englishman named Major Buckley went to Burma to rescue the boy. Did he arrive? Have you heard anything? I
must find him!"

Her glassy eyes stared. "Zin t-tell English friend—"

"Where!" He brought his ear close to her mouth.

Her words came as a faint whisper, garbled, but they
rang through—"Felix Carey . . . prince there—"

She went limp. His own breathing came more rapidly. Felix Carey? Son of William?

Ethan glanced out the palanquin door into the night
and saw his uncle huddled in low conversation with the
prime minister of Guwahati. The rajputs were busy

279

watching the road again, while others had carried off Sanjay to bury him. *They must not see the child was Burmese!*

Ethan wrapped him in the blanket and climbed down to the dusty road. Sir Hugo looked over at him.

"What are you doing?"

"I will bury the child myself. Gem was deeply loved by Coral."

Sir Hugo said nothing and stood watching. Ethan felt the man's eyes on his back as he walked off the road into the trees. He stopped short, confronted by a rajput guard.

Ethan showed indignation. "I am a doctor who saves lives, yet I have witnessed the murder of an innocent boy. If you will bury a fiend like Sanjay, you must also dig a grave for the son of Prince Rajiv."

At the mention of Rajiv, the one prince beloved by the rajputs of Guwahati, Ethan saw the first flicker of emotion in the dark bearded face of the warrior.

"For the rajkumar's son," he said.

They had lain the boy to rest and were in the process of covering him with soil when dry twigs snapped. Ethan turned sharply. The dark silhouette of Sir Hugo stood silently. Ethan had the horrid notion he would hear his emotionless voice demanding to produce the child.

"We have little time. We will ride north to Sibsagar."

"Yes, of course. Give me only another minute."

He watched his uncle walk back into the darkness. The rajput had buried the child and now waited to make certain Ethan returned to Roxbury.

I must escape! I must find Jace and warn him about Sibsagar.

Ethan's mind worked swiftly now. He said firmly, "Both Rajiv and Jemani accepted the Christian belief. Leave me alone to pray and quote words from the Bible."

The rajput scowled. "Rajiv was not a Christian."

"He was. He and Jemani were baptized on Kingscote. They entrusted their child to the English Kendalls. Now leave me. I wish to pray!"

The rajput, obviously displeased, hesitated, but when Ethan began quoting the Lord's Prayer the warrior left quickly.

Ethan listened until the rajput's heavy steps died away. When he was certain the guard was gone, he darted into the trees. He must hide until his uncle and the rajputs gave up searching for him. They would sooner or later, for Hugo was anxious to reach Sibsagar. He thought of his medical bag and felt a jab of dismay.

No matter . . . as much as he hated to leave it in the dak-bungalow he could not take the chance of returning for it, even if he was certain his uncle and the rajputs had ridden on. It would be like Sir Hugo to leave a guard, knowing how much he cherished his medical supplies.

He strode swiftly forward in the darkness, trees and vines closing in about him, knowing he risked himself to poisonous serpents. He was soon drenched with sweat, and mosquitoes buzzed. Was he a fool? He could not go on this way for any length of time, and he did not know how far he must journey to reach the Burmese border. It would take weeks! And he had no notion where to find the missionary compound of Felix Carey. He might even be killed on the way by Burmese infiltrators. And where could he get supplies?

Emotionally exhausted and breathing heavily in the humid heat, he sank to the ground beneath the dark overhang of the trees to rest a few minutes before going on. He must think!

If Sibsagar was some twenty miles to the northeast, then the British outpost of Jorhat must lie behind him to the south. Dare he go there? Would Sir Hugo send

281

men to search for him? Yet the thought of an Englishman in uniform seemed like an oasis amid the desert of Indian and Burmese soldiers.

Jorhat—and beyond that, Kingscote . . . but no, he must not go back. He could not bring himself to enter the same house where only weeks ago Coral had lived and walked and laughed. The memory of the school came to haunt him. He could see himself working . . . and Coral coming in the ghari, so alive, so happy to see her wishes coming true. . . .

Dead. . . . He had failed her. He had risked them all because he had not stood up to Hugo sooner. No, he could not go forward to either Burma or Sibsagar, nor could he go back to Kingscote. Jorhat was his one chance, and alone on the road, with Burmese infiltrators prowling in the jungle, that chance was slim.

He must have a horse!

That noise—what was it? He scrambled to his feet. Footsteps! There was no time to rest, no time to think. He must run!

———

Coral awoke to a house wrapped in afternoon silence. The fever and loss of blood that had kept her in bed for over a week was gone. Dreary weeks since then had passed, and she wished to forget the nightmarish ordeal with the cobra.

Almost at once the old anxieties confronting her and Kingscote came crowding into her consciousness. Like frightened children, the questions clamored for answers, but she had none.

If Jan-Lee went for Ethan, why have they not returned?

Dressed in cool muslin, her hair braided and looped at the back of her neck, she came down the stairs to an empty house. She sat down on the bottom step holding her arms and staring out the front window where the carriageway was in view.

Would her mother survive? Worse yet, what if she did not regain her mind? Again she thought of what Charles Peddington had told her in Calcutta about Mrs. William Carey: *"Her mind hangs in a delicate balance."*

As Coral sat there in the empty hall she remembered back to the night that now seemed a thousand winters ago. She had newly turned sixteen and came down the stairs to speak to her mother about Jemani's baptism. Her mother and father were talking in anxious tones, and in her memory she could see them again standing there in an embrace, hearing her father say: *"Tales of abductions, of druggings permanently affecting the mind, are not exaggerations."*

Coral frowned. The mental state of her mother was not so unlike what Charles had described when he had discussed Mrs. Carey's mental aberrations. Now that she had experienced some of the fear that came with watching her mother lose her disciplined mind, she was amazed at how William Carey in the midst of such trial was able to work on the translation of Scripture in the next room. Only the grace of God could be sufficient for such ordeals, she thought.

Coral closed her eyes and tried not to imagine the worst. "Mother will get well again. She must."

But always the ugly head of doubt arose. What if she did not? What if she lived for many years deranged?

Even if Jan-Lee arrived with Ethan, could he cure her? Was her brain permanently damaged? If it was only temporary why did she not improve?

"I will not cry!" She shut her eyes tightly and kept back the tears.

When she opened them again she stared intently out the window as though expecting to see Ethan. Had Mrs.

Carey ever recovered? she wondered. Charles Peddington had implied she only grew worse.

Coral was more convinced than ever that Mrs. Carey, much maligned for her mental weakness and inability to adjust to the hardship of missionary life, had been maliciously drugged by some ghazi furious with Carey's missionary work. It could have happened when he managed the indigo plantation in Mudnabatti. When his son Peter died, he had forced several workers to break caste and bury his child—afterward, they had been angry toward him.

Natine! It is not enough that he put the cobra in my room, he had to hurt my mother too!

Her heart suddenly welled with bitterness and hate, and it frightened her more than their circumstances. "God forbids me to hate others. But where is the grace to forgive him? And Gem . . . was Natine not also to blame? He and Sir Hugo!"

She buried her face in her hands. "No. I cannot forgive what you did to my mother! She will never be the same again because of you, never."

Her mother had been so gracious, so intelligent—now she was deranged! And what will we tell Father when he comes home? How will he bear the news?

Oh, Jace, if only you were here, she thought, suddenly longing for his protective embrace.

Wistfully she recalled the song of joy that had been hers only months ago when she had received the message from Jace that Gem was alive, and that he would bring him to Kingscote for the Christmas holidays. All that too was gone. There would be no Christmas. Gem did not exist—there lived instead Prince Adesh Singh, heir to a throne of India.

There was Jace. She had his love, she thought. Would this cause for happiness also die?

"I can take no more now," she murmured. It seemed that trouble had come to settle over Kingscote, like black vultures awaiting a harvest of death.

"What a dark mood I am in! *Vultures . . . harvest of death.*"

She stood up from the step and walked out onto the front verandah facing the lawn and the river. The day was hot and still; the water appeared like gray glass.

Could she not find some reasons for thankfulness among the trials allowed by God for good? For good. . . . Were they? How could the terrible things that were happening on Kingscote ever produce spiritual *good*? Yet the promises of God said they would. Coral was reminded that trouble was a part of each new day and would always be a part of life. To expect anything different was to deny the Scriptures and shipwreck one's faith. Had not the Lord said, "In the world ye shall have tribulation"? Only the presence of the One who was Life himself could sweeten the bitter, could divide the hour into minutes of joy as well as sadness.

Perhaps, she thought, *God allows these so we never lose sight that we are not citizens of time but children of eternity, where no disappointment or sorrow will ever sting.*

At least she had recovered from the cobra bite with little ill effect. She looked at her arm. The wound Preetah's knife had made was healing well.

As she looked down the carriageway toward the road lined with trees, a movement caught her eye. Her heart wanted to stop. Had she imagined it? A Burmese soldier!

She forced herself to not turn and run, screaming. She stood without moving as though watching the river but strained to see through the trees.

There was another movement, and she saw him clearly this time. A ripple of fear went up her back. She had not imagined it—Burmese soldiers on Kingscote!

Do not panic, she told herself. *They must not know you saw them lest they attack at once.*

She turned her back and walked slowly inside the house. Once inside, she slammed the heavy door, her fingers trembling as she fumbled to shove into place the several bolts her father had installed.

She whirled, racing toward the kitchen. "Mera! Rosa!"

Mera came at once, attune to the cries of alarm that seemed to constantly fill the mansion. "Yes, what is it?"

Coral held her, shaking, briefly taking solace in her arms. "Burmese soldiers! Tell Hareesh to lock the doors. Have the other servants do the same. Hurry, Mera!"

Marianna had come down the stairs, and she now clutched the banister as though she would faint. "Burmese warriors?"

"Yes! Quick! Go about the house. Warn the others. Bolt every window and every door. Then come back here!"

Marianna stared at her.

"Don't panic," gritted Coral, deliberately gripping Marianna's arm so hard that she winced. "You will need to keep your wits."

Marianna was shaking, her teeth chattering. She nodded yes, then hurried into the parlor.

As Coral raced up the stairs she heard the servants running everywhere. She threw open the door to her mother's room. Kathleen turned from her mother's bedside and hurried across the room. "What is all the noise? What's happening?"

"There are Burmese soldiers on the road. I just saw them in the trees. I doubt if they will attack the house now, since they don't know what to expect. We need to be prepared. The servants are going about locking up now."

"Father's pistol," said Kathleen. "I put it back in his desk drawer after Natine left. I'll get it." She rushed toward the door. "But we will need more than one!"

Kathleen disappeared down the hall and Coral went swiftly to the side of her mother's bed and looked at her. She was sleeping, looking peaceful. For once, the sight of her ill mother did not affect her.

Coral rushed to the wardrobe and removed her mother's pistol. There was also the rifle that she carried with her in the ghari. Coral found it leaning in one corner against the wall. There were other guns in the house which her father had kept against attack. . . . There had been many frightening times in the past.

But she had been a child then and had been sent with her sisters and the servants' children to hide with the women. Now there was no place to hide, and after the attack on herself and her mother, there were few men she would trust to be their protectors. Thilak was one, and any worker from the hatchery that Thilak trusted. There were also the mercenaries, but could they be reached in time to return to the house?

Coral was surprised at how calm she felt. Her fingers trembled as she carefully checked the pistol. When her father had insisted his wife and three daughters learn to use a gun, Coral had thought it unpleasant. Now she was glad that he had insisted. Kathleen could be depended upon too. Only Marianna was likely to faint!

Coral bolted the locks on the bedroom window and verandah doors and turned to leave the room, glancing back at her mother. She had not stirred from her sleep.

She must send a message to the hatcheries to Yanna and Thilak. Thilak must somehow get past the infiltrators to alert the armed mercenaries guarding Kingscote's border.

Out in the hall she met Preetah, her dark eyes frightened but her voice calm. "I have locked the doors and windows in the upper rooms, Miss Coral, and Reena has gone to warn Rosa in the dispensary and Yanna in the hatchery. I have told her to send for Thilak."

"Good. Can you shoot?"

Preetah raised her chin and drew in a breath. "I can."

"Come with me. My father has weapons in his office."

Thilak arrived secretly through the kitchen door, and his determined expression added to Coral's and Kathleen's courage. Yanna was with him and went immediately to take a rifle.

Coral gave weapons to Thilak as Kathleen gave him his orders.

His face turned grave. "I shall do my best to get past the infiltrators," he told them. "Then I shall go to Jorhat for more help."

"Take my horse," said Kathleen. "He is more swift than the stable horses. He's tethered by the smokehouse."

The child Reena came to cling to Preetah's skirts as Thilak hurried from the front hall.

"Godspeed," whispered Coral.

22

Jorhat Outpost

Jace waited, listening intently to the night noises: a sigh of wind rippling the tall grasses near the marsh, the lone belch of a frog, swiftly followed by the splash of a waterfowl catching its midnight delicacy.

On the far side of the marsh, he and Gokul led their horses down the well-trodden lane, hooves muffled in the powdery dust. A mile ahead, looming against the black jungle, torchlight flickered on the stone walls of the lone British outpost.

He frowned, his old irritation at the sight goading him again. He had always disapproved of allowing trees to grow so near the command post. Time and again he had requested of his commander that the outpost be surrounded by a wide clearing and cannon mounted outside the wall. Like everything in the military he disliked, the simple project of cutting down trees had been buried under mounds of mundane paperwork. And cannon, said Calcutta, was quite impossible on the frontier. It made no matter that every petty raja in the northeast had at least one—the British outpost must make do with muskets!

As they neared, Jace noticed that the ensign had at least restored the breached wall and repaired the gate. A single sepoy stood guard, the white on his uniform showing, belted with the cavalry saber. Jace unpleasantly wondered who would own the soldier's allegiance when fighting erupted. Did his allegiance belong to Sunil or to the raja at Sibsagar? Cynically, he doubted if the soldier were steadfastly loyal to the British flag that hung limp on the pole, with the colors of the 21st Bengal Light Infantry just below.

Again in the uniform of a major, Jace saluted and spoke in Hindi, and the sepoy crisply greeted him and signaled for the sentries to open the gate.

As he rode into the post with Gokul following, Jace scanned the dozen sowars who stood guard about the wall. How much did they know of what was being planned now in Guwahati?

Lights shone in the windows of the barracks and in the small residency of the officer in command—now a mere ensign—until Captain Gavin MacKay arrived. Militarily, Jace remained under orders from the governor-general as captain of Roxbury's security guard in Guwahati. A miserable jest!

He dismounted and gave the reins to Gokul to bring their horses to the stables. "See what you can discover among the ranks. I'll speak with the ensign."

He turned to walk across the yard to the residency when its door opened and a soldier stepped out. The shadows hid his rank, and Jace could not see if he were Indian or English. Jace watched the soldier nervously glance about and settle his helmet on his head, then come down the steps. The uncertain manner in which the man carried himself alerted Jace. *Something is wrong.* "Hut! You! Halt!"

The soldier hesitated, and Jace walked toward him. He should have stated his rank and name. Jace's hand reached for his pistol, but he stopped when he saw the man's face.

"Ethan!" Jace let out an exasperated breath.

Ethan recognized his voice and started with surprise, then hurried toward him, losing his hat in the process with a clatter. He stooped to pick it up, catching it by the plume.

Jace winced. "You make a lamentable sepoy."

"Abominable gadget." He shoved it back on his head, then straightened. "Good heavens, Major! I did not expect the luck of finding you here!"

"What are you doing here in masquerade? I thought that was my specialty." He added wryly, "And by the way, this is not Darjeeling."

Ethan came up, and seeing his tension, Jace sobered. "Trouble?"

"Extraordinarily so! I just left speaking with your Commander in Chief."

"The proper term is ensign," said Jace lazily, his eyes amused. "Come, I will need your report."

Inside the military office Ensign Niles was busily writing when Jace and Ethan entered. Hearing them he glanced up. "Sit down. I shall get to you in—"

Niles jumped to his feet and crisply saluted. "Major!"

"What are you writing?" Jace asked flatly.

Niles, realizing he clutched his pencil, set it down on the worn wooden desk. "A detailed report on the crucial information Doctor Boswell has given to me, sir. I intend to send one of the sepoys with the dispatch—"

"Detailed?" repeated Jace. "Crucial? You thought you would *write* it all out in flowing hand to deliver to a sepoy—is that it, Ensign?"

"Well, sir, actually—yes, that was my first thought, Major."

"Think again."

"Yes, sir!"

Jace held out his hand. The ensign snatched up his report and handed it to him.

"I had a bit more to er—fill in, sir."

"Good." Jace took the piece of paper and, meeting his eyes evenly, tore it into pieces, dropping them in the trash urn. The ensign flushed.

"Just between you and me, Ensign, we are but a handful of brave and dedicated soldiers of His Majesty amid twenty thousand heavily armed soldiers of Sunil. Let's keep the doctor's report a bit of a secret. Just in case."

"Yes, sir!"

Jace turned to Ethan. "Where is Roxbury?"

"On his way to Sibsagar."

As the ensign brewed the last of his coffee, Jace listened while Ethan quietly explained all that had occurred since Jace left Kingscote.

"You are certain Roxbury didn't suspect the child wasn't Gem?"

"He was utterly deceived."

Jace noted the look of vengeful triumph in Ethan's face. Much had changed between Ethan and his father, he thought.

Jace mused over the news Ethan brought. So Sir Hugo and Sunil had intended to use Gem for ransom in order to force the Raja Singh to abdicate his throne to Sunil. "Are you telling me the raja at Sibsagar does not know Jemani had a son?"

"He believes the infant died with her."

"And both Roxbury and Sunil thought they would be successful in using Gem for ransom," Jace said thoughtfully.

"Quite. What they truly planned for the child once the raja capitulated is anyone's guess," said Ethan distastefully.

Jace was not thinking of that but of the difference between Sunil and the raja. "Unlike Sunil, who wishes his contenders dead, Sibsagar would welcome the son of Rajkumari Jemani."

"So it seems, Major. At least Sir Hugo believed it enough to gamble on. Why do you ask? What do you have in mind?"

"Where is Roxbury now?"

"Once they gave up searching for me they must have journeyed on toward Sibsagar as planned."

"Without Gem they have lost their prized jewel with which to bargain. Sunil will now fight. How many in his army? Did you hear any discussion?"

"Ten thousand soldiers and over a hundred war elephants."

Then Zin had spoken the truth. "That is likely to be doubled. Burma has promised the individual armies of the border warlords to Sunil."

"Then there is no hope," said Ethan. "I do not know how long it will take for Sunil to move his army northeast from Guwahati, but it is obvious to me that we are all sitting like ducks in their path. After the rebellion at Guwahati and my introduction to war elephants, I've no wish for further contact."

He stood, looking uncomfortable in the uniform and anxious to mount and ride. "There is nothing we can do here, Major. You yourself informed Ensign Niles you were but a handful of English soldiers. If we stay, we will either be trampled to death or end up prisoners of Sunil."

Still, Jace lounged in the chair, thinking.

"Major!"

"I heard you, Doctor. Your coffee is getting cold." Jace

lifted his tin mug and drank. "How large of an army does Sibsagar have?" he asked the ensign.

Ensign Niles began searching through the desk drawers.

"If I recall," said Jace, "after the treaty with the Company, the raja was to reduce his standing army considerably."

"Yes, sir, since Sibsagar is under British protection, the governor-general felt a large contingency would only make the raja's neighbors worry, especially Burma, which makes no sense to me, sir, since the number of infiltrators has tripled in the last weeks. We lost Scottie only yesterday."

"Scottie?"

"McKilton. From Edinburgh. He was on patrol south of here when his squad was set upon. Only five men made it back."

Jace covered his frown. South of Jorhat, the independent lands belonging to Sir Hampton Kendall joined close to the border with Burma. It had been that tract of jungle that Jace and his troop had traversed when tracking the man-eating tiger for Sir Hampton, the time he first laid eyes on Coral. Remembering, he had to force his mind back on the problem at hand. "Near Kingscote? Sir Hampton Kendall and his dependable men are gone. We have an English family there."

"Yes, sir. I sent out another scout in that direction this morning."

"The plantation at Kingscote must be protected," Ethan said, his voice quavering.

Jace looked at Ethan and could have sworn his eyes misted. Jace scowled. *Does he truly love Coral?* The fact that he had come out the winner in the battle with Ethan for her heart caused him a twinge. The man looked positively sick!

Jace's eyes narrowed under his lashes, and he emptied his cup and stood. "Forget the official document on the size of the raja's army," he told the ensign wearily, who still searched diligently, having emptied an entire drawer.

"Major?" said Ethan.

"Yes?"

Ethan stared at him intently, then ran a defeated hand through his sandy hair. "Nothing, Major. I was going to ask if you would be riding to Kingscote."

His behavior was curious, but Jace pretended he did not notice. "No. And since you are in uniform"—he smiled slightly—"you are under orders not to do so either. I have another mission for you."

"Mission?"

"I've a plan. It may work, and most likely it will fail miserably, but in light of impossible circumstances it is the route we shall take—unless either of you unexpectedly comes up with a solution. How many trustworthy soldiers do you have, Niles?—and do not count the sepoys and sowars."

"Without the native infantry and cavalry, sir, about seventeen men."

"About? You mean you do not know?"

"Dougan is having trouble with his eyes, sir. Blackouts."

Jace was unreadable, but an illogical sense of panic swept over him. What if his own blindness reoccurred now? What would he do? "Ensign, until MacKay arrives with the 13th, I am taking command of the troops here."

The ensign showed surprise, then confusion.

Jace affected an unflinching demeanor. "Do you have reason to contest that decision, Ensign?"

"No, sir. In fact I am quite relieved."

Jace left his chair and walked behind the desk, and

Ensign Niles relinquished the chair behind the desk. Jace sat down and stretched his legs. "Your first order, Ensign."

"Yes, sir?"

"I want those seventeen soldiers—including Dougan!—placed under your command. You will ride out tonight for the Kendall plantation and stay there until you hear from me. Under no circumstances are you to venture forth on the road once you arrive there. Is that clear?"

Ensign Niles struggled not to show his emotion. "Understood, Major."

"I will give you two letters to deliver. One is to a trusty old warrior named Seward. Make certain he receives it when he arrives."

"Yes, sir."

"The other letter is to Miss Kendall."

"Major—" began Ethan softly.

"If Kingscote comes under attack you are to defend it with your lives. Go now and get your command ready to ride. Take the best of the horses. And I want the muskets brought with you."

"The muskets! But sir!"

"Load the munition wagons with all the weapons you can carry. I want to hear you riding out before dawn. Then make straight for Kingscote. That is an order, Ensign!"

"Yes, sir!" Ensign Niles hesitated. "May I speak an opposing word, sir?"

"You may, but it will do no good."

"An all-English command is most unusual. And taking the guns will leave you and the native infantry a bit short."

Jace smiled faintly. "We will manage. Anything else?"

"No, Major."

"Do this undercover with as little fanfare as possible. At the same time as you form your command, give orders to the native officer in charge to prepare his sowars for battle."

The ensign was thoroughly bewildered but saluted and went out.

Jace had made up his mind to abandon the outpost—an action that would see him called before the military court in Calcutta. At the moment, it no longer mattered. The sepoys were all a pack of traitors ready to rip open British bellies at the first order of Sunil, and if there were two or three loyal and brave men among them—and no doubt there were—they would have their opportunity to battle with honor when Sunil used his mammoth war elephants to tear down the walls of the outpost. For Jace had no question in his mind but that Sunil would destroy Jorhat. However, Jace did not plan to be around to watch, and he certainly did not intend to allow English and Scottish soldiers to be massacred for nothing. If anything was left of the outpost when MacKay arrived with the 13th, the ensign and his men could return.

There was a rap on the door, and Gokul entered.

"Any news?" asked Jace, refilling his mug with coffee.

"It smells of treachery to me, sahib. The sooner we get out of here, the happier I will be. Sunil will come sooner than we thought. He is near, perhaps a week away."

"What are our plans, Major?" Ethan asked. "Sending the English soldiers to Kingscote is a wise move. Should we not ride out with them?"

"The Raja of Sibsagar must be warned that Sunil will advance with an army, strengthened by soldiers from Burma." Leaning against the desk, he looked at Ethan. "I take it your willingness to escape Sir Hugo on the road means you've broken your ties to his plans and wishes, that you no longer intend for him to manipulate your life, and the lives of others."

"That is a blunt way to put it, but yes. I shall never return to the relationship I had with him until tonight. You might as well know, Major, that I have no desire to remain in India, least of all on Kingscote. I have thought I might return to London to Roxbury House and resume my practice. Or even travel for a time—perhaps, if war with Burma does not break out, to Rangoon. The fauna and insects available for scientific experimentation are remarkably rare indeed. I thought that I might eventually set up a lab somewhere thereabout. I—I can never go back to Kingscote again," he said. "I have many regrets."

Jace folded his arms across his chest and regarded him. "You cannot undo the past, but you may be able to help change the future of Kingscote, and Assam."

Ethan looked skeptical.

"Go back to Roxbury," said Jace.

"Go back—! Have you lost your senses?"

"I hope not. . . . You say he went to Sibsagar to seek audience with the raja. He will have one purpose on his mind: to deceive him by treachery. Go back, as though to align yourself with him. At Sibsagar warn the raja of what is planned, and tell him that Rajkumari Jemani had a son—and that son lives."

"How do you expect me to speak in the raja's ear when Sir Hugo will be there!"

"Come, Ethan! You outwitted him long enough to arrive here at Jorhat. Once there look for any opportunity—a servant girl, perhaps, one who might remember Jemani and who was loyal to her. You will think of a way."

"I have no doubt Hugo will kill me if he discovers I am your spy."

"Think not of yourself as serving me but England . . . and India. Much depends on Gem being received by his people as Prince Adesh Singh."

Ethan paced. "I don't know. The thought of going back to speak peaceably to him after he—I shall need to think about it."

"There is no time. Sunil will arrive with his army, and to survive, the Raja of Sibsagar must fight. His men are far fewer, and he will not be able to hold out for long. If he is left alone to face certain defeat, he may listen to the treachery of Sir Hugo. But if you are there to promise the arrival of Prince Adesh, I am certain the raja will fight to the death."

Ethan's eyes began to take on warmth. "Can you bring Gem in time? You heard Gokul's words."

"We can try," said Jace and wondered at his own determination. "But the fighting may begin before I arrive. That is where your persistence must come in. You must keep the raja fighting Sunil and thwart Roxbury's counsel to surrender."

"But if fighting erupts before you arrive I see no way for either the raja or the people to see their future maharaja."

"There is only one way. I will need to risk him on the raja's own royal elephant at the right moment in the battle—and hope that the rajputs fighting for Sunil might get an overwhelming dose of emotional frenzy for a change."

"Royal elephant? Good heavens, man, what do I know of such matters!"

"You don't need to. Gokul knows exactly what to do. Follow his directions. Bring that particular elephant to me at a location I will later give Gokul. If all goes well, I shall have Gem with me."

Ethan let out a breath. "I will do as you say, Major.

But so many details coming together at one time—" He shook his head. "It could mean the death of us all."

"If you will not risk yourself for the future of Assam, then do this for Coral."

Ethan's lips tightened.

"Gem is as much her son as Jemani's," said Jace. "She has invested her soul and heart in this child."

"Well said. I will go to Sibsagar and convince Sir Hugo I've had a change of mind. And somehow I will manage to warn the raja."

Jace turned to Gokul. "Go with him as far as you can. But do not let Roxbury see you with Ethan. He is clever enough to know something is in the making."

"But what of you, sahib? You will journey to the missionary alone?"

"I must. Everything depends on your getting that royal elephant."

Gokul's eyes shone. "The mammoth elephant painted black," he said with awe. "The maharaja's 'Black Royal Elephant'!"

"Yes, and if our plan works to bring Prince Adesh on his back—the eyes of the warrior rajputs will shine as yours. A cry from Gem may be our one chance of getting them to come to his side."

"A great task you give old Gokul, one he may not be able to do, sahib. The royal elephant is like a child to the raja, and the trainers, they treat the elephant as a lesser king. They eat and sleep with the royal elephant."

"You are once again the Swami Gokul Sankar Punditji—his holiness Sri Baba of Lankali," Jace told him. "You go to Sibsagar to bring your blessings to the funeral of some guru."

"Which one?"

Jace smirked. "How do I know, Gokul? There are thousands crawling about! Use your imagination. And remember, if you do not get the elephant to me, you might be scattering posies on my grave instead."

23

Burma

Jace dismounted, and taking his horse's reins he walked slowly toward the thatched-roof house surrounded by a number of smaller bungalows. He paused, glancing about the mission station. A boy stood under a wide-branched tree watching his approach. The child was dressed not in Indian garb but in white trousers cut off at the knees and a baggy white shirt. He wore a big straw hat and held a pet monkey on a rope, his gaze fixed on Jace.

Instinctively Jace knew that it was Gem. So this was the baby of the monsoon . . . the child who had brought him and Coral together in riveting emotion, the child they had all risked their lives to find again, who was yet at risk, as were those whose hearts mingled together in a long pursuit to rescue him. Did Gem understand that men wished to kill him, while others fought to save him?

Perhaps, thought Jace, it was only his emotions, but he sensed that there was a haunted, lonely spirit in this child who was starved for affection, for security—like a fawn racing from the arrows of determined hunters.

He was slim, small boned, his complexion olive, his facial features fine, almost delicate. Jace was struck by his handsome appearance, and he was drawn to the almost shy, studious expression.

Jace lowered his hat against the sun, but he did not feel its glare. In his mind he saw Coral standing in the steamy rain outside the little hut belonging to Jemani, holding the infant whom she would eventually adopt. He remembered how he had helped her into the carriage, and how she had been so protective of Rajiv and Jemani's child.

And Gem . . . did he remember anything of Coral? Or were all the childhood memories hidden in his soul?

He must. I will make him remember. Before Gem becomes Raja Adesh Singh it is essential that he knows the story of a beautiful young Englishwoman who risked her life to adopt him, to make him her own son—even only for a summer's morning in time . . . before life turned harsh and cruel.

This boy will make a fine raja, he thought.

Gem did not run away. He stood motionless, showing no fear, simply watching him. Then to Jace's surprise, Gem walked toward his horse and looked up at him, squinting beneath his lashes.

"Master Felix told me that His Excellency Zin would send a friend to bring me to my great-uncle, the maharaja. Are you the friend?"

His manners and use of the English language took Jace off guard. "I am," he said simply, and remembered that he would need to tell Gem that the old Maharaja of Guwahati was dead. Another unpleasant task, even though Gem had never met him.

"I am Prince Adesh Singh, a guest of Felix." His brown eyes unexpectedly glimmered with some excitement that brought a shy smile. "Did you know that the

God of Felix Carey speaks Hindi!"

Felix Carey had been eight years old when he went to India with his missionary father, William. He had learned Bengali even faster than his father did. In Calcutta, Felix had once carried the casket of an untouchable with two high-caste Indians, and the unprecedented act had begun the breakdown of the caste system among Christians in the area. At twenty-one, Felix had been commissioned by his father and the mission station at Serampore to journey to Burma as a missionary.

Although not a physician by degree, Felix was gifted in medicine, and Jace learned that he had introduced the smallpox vaccination into Burma.

The small compound was thriving, yet beset with trials and sorrows. He was impressed with Felix's tenacity; the man had already lost his wife in the missionary venture.

Many would have given up in discouragement and gone home, thought Jace. Felix remained, translating the Scriptures into Burmese.

During his brief stay with Felix, Jace wondered how he could spend time alone with Gem to begin preparing him for all that was ahead, including the battle at Sibsagar, but he need not have wondered how to win his friendship. From the beginning, Gem seemed to be drawn to him, taking keen interest in his wanderings as a youth in China and in Darjeeling. Gem was also curious about the English military and knew something of the British rule in Calcutta. He was just as interested in Jace's love of the sea, of his intentions to build a tea plantation in Darjeeling . . . and of his planned marriage to Coral Kendall, the silk heiress.

Gem's dark eyes, fringed with thick lashes, blinked

hard as he tried to take in all the adult information. He was quite intelligent and well educated, and Jace decided his years of captivity had not injured his ability to learn.

He startled Jace with his question: "The memsahib Coral Kendall—she is the Englishwoman who adopted me when my mother died giving me birth?"

"Who told you?"

Gem rarely smiled, but he did so now, almost shyly. "My Burmese nurse. She has a sister who serves the English family. Her name is Jan-Lee."

Jan-Lee? Jace remembered back to the Burmese ayah . . . was it possible? During all these years could Jan-Lee have known about Gem but kept it from Coral and the Kendall family? And just how much of a friend was the so-called faithful ayah? Had she kept silent for fear of harm to the family, or because she served Warlord Zin?

"I would like to meet my English mother," said Gem quietly, then with intensity—"I wish very much to meet her. I must thank her, not for me only but for my Indian mother and father, Rajkumar Rajiv and Rajkumari Jemani. You will take me to the plantation you call Kingscote?"

Jace saw the tender pleading in the solemn eyes and realized how the years of captivity had made him hungry for contact with those who had cared for him. The thought moved Jace. He placed his hand on the child's dark head.

"One day perhaps. Now your safety and hers are threatened by your father's brother."

"My uncle, yes. He hates me."

"His hate is born of greed and pride. He does not see you as you are but as an obstacle to keep him from fulfilling his desire to rule northern India."

Gem stirred uneasily. "Is it wrong that I do not even care if I am a raja?"

Jace picked up a twig and drew it in the dusty earth. "If you believe God rules the affairs of kingdoms, yes. You might have been born the son of an English sailor and meant to shimmy up ropes to grease the tackle." He looked at Gem and frowned when his words brought the opposite reaction than he had intended. The boy's eyes lit up.

"What is the sea like?"

Jace stood from the porch step and tossed aside the twig. "You were born a prince. You have a calling, a great and noble task to accomplish for your people. Who knows the good you might accomplish? All would be lost if you do not accept the calling of your birth."

Gem watched Jace intensely but said nothing, and as though to divert Jace, he caught sight of his pet monkey and clapped his hands to call him. The brown monkey came quickly, expecting a treat.

Jace regarded him thoughtfully, tilting his head. "Sunil will fight to keep you from the throne. He has an army of ten thousand, many of them disciplined rajputs, men who think of little but fighting and dying for the cause of their maharaja. Sunil plans to attack Sibsagar, the capital of Assam, the ancient city of kings—the home of your mother—your destined home where you can rule and bring honor to the One who gave you this earthly scepter. It is no light thing to turn away as though it is nothing, to look off toward the sunset and think you will keep running from the greed and pride of evil men.

"Your uncle Sunil is evil. If good men do nothing to stand against darkness, the darkness will swallow up the light that remains. Warriors of light battle not because they love the smell of war but because they must. Sometimes warriors must stand alone and trust that if they should die in fighting for what is the best, it was a worthy thing to do.

"We have few warriors on our side, Gem, not even the Burmese warlord—"

"You called me Gem."

"I meant to call you Prince Adesh."

"I like you to call me Gem."

"Gem—Warlord Zin will support your uncle in the battle because it is the wish of his government."

"He took much treasure from my father's uncle in Guwahati. Sometimes he was my friend, sometimes he wore a second face, an enemy."

"I told you, many men are hungry for riches and power."

"Do they ever get full?"

"No. The hunger I speak of cannot be satisfied. It is like a great pit. Not all the gold and pearls in India can fill it. Only God is big enough to fill it with himself and bring satisfaction."

Gem said nothing for a long time. He turned his monkey free and picked up the twig Jace had tossed aside. He too began to draw in the dusty earth.

"Many in India wish the English to leave, and Burma wishes to rule Assam. English soldiers from the military in Calcutta would fight to protect you, and Sibsagar, but they will not arrive in time."

"The English are my friends." He looked at Jace. "Do you fight well?"

Jace smiled a little. "Well enough. At the moment I am your bodyguard. You are my first and only responsibility."

"But I do not wish others to fight and die for me."

"You must not think so. Would you have Sunil rule?"

"No." His mouth went tight to cover a quaver. "You said he murdered my great-uncle at Guwahati with an elephant." His eyes widened. "But Sunil is also my uncle, my father's younger brother!"

It was time to let him know, thought Jace. However much it would hurt him. . . .

"Your father was a friend of mine."

Gem came alert, his eyes clinging to Jace.

"I watched him train with the war elephants at Guwahati. Sunil hired an assassin to kill your father. Because of Rajiv's death your mother Jemani gave birth to you before she was ready, and she died too. Sunil is your uncle by blood, but he is your enemy too. You must stop him. If not for yourself, for the memory of your father and mother, for Assam. You must let me and others fight, and destroy him."

Gem was pale and shaking. It wounded Jace to see the pain in his eyes, to see his small mouth tremble, but the emotional moment reinforced his own determination to bring Sunil down to defeat.

Gem threw the stick aside, and a faint color came to his cheeks. His small shoulders straightened beneath the thin white baggy shirt of a peasant.

"I know it is said that the rajputs will fight with great bravery for the true royal heir!" Jace recalled the dedication of the royal guards who fought for the old maharaja.

Quickly now the thoughts raced through his mind. He had one, possibly two friends among the rajputs at Guwahati, men who were associated with Gokul's brother at Sualkashi, men who were high in command of the warriors. Even among the dozen rajputs who were now with Roxbury there was a man, Nadir, a warrior who had alerted him at Kingscote that Sunil had discovered Gem's place of hiding with Zin. If he could get a message to these few rajputs that Rajiv's son was not

dead but heir to the ancient throne of Sibsagar, perhaps. . . .

"I have a plan. It is risky, for both of us will face a
moment when failure stares us in the face. You must be
brave and believe that what you do is worth the world.
Can you do it, Gem?"

"I am afraid!"

"All men fear. They lie if they boast they do not. It is
not fear itself but surrender to its mastery that destroys.
If a man believes his breath is in the hand of God, he
leaves his fears at the foot of the throne above all earthly
thrones. If God is for us, who can be against us? And if
He is not for us—then nothing matters."

Gem's brown eyes glistened with excitement. "I am
to be the raja. When Felix told me of the living God who
also speaks Hindi, I asked Him for a friend. I awoke at
night to see many men chasing me with tulwars. God
heard me. He sent you to be my friend. I will do as you
say. I fight for the throne of my father and mother. I will
tell Uncle Sunil that he is a bad man."

Suddenly, Gem turned and ran for the hut. "I have
something to show you, Jace!"

Troubled, Jace watched him disappear into the house.
He scowled, his eyes narrowing, as the weight of responsibility suddenly grew heavy. Placing Gem on the royal
elephant and bringing him to the battle for the rajputs
to see could bring unrest. A moment of doubt penetrated
his armor. *What if the boy's appearance as king of both
Guwahati and Sibsagar fails to rally the rajputs?* "Well,
Buckley, you spoke fine words of faith and courage. Did
you mean them?"

His blue-black eyes sought the horizon painted with
orange. "Maybe," he murmured wryly, "I can convince
myself that boarding the *Madras* with both Gem and
Coral and taking to the sea is the voice of God after all."

He was smiling as Gem returned and handed him a black book. "Felix gave it to me. He brought it from his father William Carey. It is written in Hindi, but Felix insists God can even speak these words in Assamese! Even in Bengali! I was told He was only English!"

Jace put a bridle on his emotions. He stooped until their eyes were level, then placed both hands on the small shoulders.

Gem stared at him, then suddenly the boy's eyes welled with tears. They ran down his cheeks, and he threw himself into Jace's arms, starved for affection. "You will always be my friend, Jace, promise!"

Jace held him tightly, feeling the small arms clinging desperately around his neck.

"Did I not willingly become your bodyguard? What better friend could you have than one willing to lay down his life for you?"

Gem looked up, tears wetting his cheeks. He held Jace.

Jace took the Bible and opened it to the Gospel of John, chapter fifteen. He read in Hindi: " 'Greater love hath no man than this, that a man lay down his life for his friends.'

"Christ laid down His life for us. Only He was the King of all kings dying for His subjects. He asks us to be willing to do the same for our brothers."

"B-but I do not want you to die, Jace."

Jace smiled. "I will not die—not yet. I have too much to live for. Both of us do."

"Let us both run away, Jace! Let us find your ship, the one you told me of, with big white sails that reach to the sky! We can sail to many places!"

"Do not tempt me," he said with a faint smile, and stood. "Come. We have a long way to journey, Adesh."

"To you I am Gem—and to my English mother."

"Your mother Jemani would approve of the name. Gem was the name your English mother gave you the night of the monsoon. Gem Ranek Kendall. 'Like a jewel, the one bright moment in all that has happened,' she had said."

Jace placed the book back into his hand and closed the boy's fingers about it. "Never forget. Others will seek to change your mind. But hold to it tightly."

24

Sibsagar

Where's Gokul! He should have been here waiting for me with the royal elephant!

Concealed in the jungle trees on the perimeter of the Brahmaputra valley, Jace beheld Sunil's camp some distance out on the plain that stretched before the ancient city of Sibsagar. He felt his palms sweating. As far as the eye could see, Sunil's tents, infantry, elephants, and horses filled his vision. He had spent the last day concealed with Gem, waiting for a message from Gokul, waiting for the trumpeting of the arrival of the Black Royal Elephant, debating the risk of bringing Gem into the scene of battle.

Would the mighty rajput army from Guwahati, now loyal to Sunil, break their allegiance and turn to Gem? If not, the plan that called for Raja Singh to meet Sunil in head-to-head battle would fail. Jace must produce Gem on the elephant early in the initial stage of battle, for Raja Singh could not hope to outlast the waves of warriors and war elephants that Sunil would hurl against him.

313

If he could not quickly produce Gem on the black elephant, Raja Singh would face certain death. His smaller rajput army and prized elephants would be slaughtered in a noble but fruitless attempt to hold Sunil back from a sweeping victory.

He must! But even then, would it work?

Where is Gokul?

A thousand things could go wrong, but everything depended upon one thing going right! The elephant!

Jace wiped his palms on the front of his rough trousers and touched his scabbard. He glanced toward Gem, who pretended to play with a bag of smooth rocks he had collected. In reality Jace knew the boy was almost sick with anxiety—waiting, wondering—and as much as Jace tried to mask his own feelings of uncertainty, he knew that Gem had picked up his tension.

I can take him and ride out, he thought. The two of us can get through Burma to Rangoon. From there we can catch a ship in the Bay of Bengal and sail up the Ganges Delta to Calcutta.

But Coral waited at Kingscote, and Sunil would easily defeat Raja Singh, and his army of victorious warriors would swarm over the area in jubilant victory. He could not take Gem and ride out leaving Coral alone at Kingscote, but then, perhaps she was not alone. He hoped that Sir Hampton and Seward had arrived by now.

Seward! Bless the old grizzly. He would take care of Coral if he had to battle all of Sunil's army single-handed.

Ensign Niles and his eighteen British soldiers, had they made it?

Jace could feel the anticipation of battle in the early morning. Seasoned warriors, elephants, and horses alike knew instinctively that this was the day, the hour, when their destiny would be decided in the roll call of war drums.

Could he hope to kill Sunil unguarded in his tent?

Disguised as a servant, Jace neared Sunil's compound. The first cluster of tents that formed the edge of the huge village-size camp met him without suspicion. His face was smeared with dust, and he wore a soiled puggari as he mingled with the untouchables who were leading elephants and horses and carrying large bundles of fodder along the lanes between the warriors' tents.

The perimeter of Sunil's royal headquarters was in the center of the camp, surrounded by a high barricade of billowing purple silk embroidered with a black border and supported with decorated poles spaced evenly apart.

Was Sunil there now?

Camped around the royal tent were the smaller tents of his officials and nobles.

An unexpected cheer erupted from a rajput, and Jace saw the warriors line the sides of the lane leading to Sunil's headquarters. Too late. Sunil was riding out on the princely horse, prepared to enter the armored howdah on the royal elephant while the rajputs beat their swords against their shields.

The elephant knelt and Sunil entered, seated beneath the wide umbrella, prepared to show himself on the battlefield as the rallying point of his army.

The captains of the rajput riders shouted staccato orders. The heavy bull elephants, their foreheads padded, began shoving the gun carriages forward as infantry marched beside them beating the kettledrums. The cannons, looped together with twisted bull hide, were rolled into fighting position on the field to target the smaller army of Raja Singh, who moved his rajputs and elephants into battle position. Jace saw a hundred cannons along the outskirts of the camp. Placed behind each cannon were the firepots, linstocks, and leather barrels of powder.

The great elephants were winding their way through Sunil's camp, waving their trunks and trumpeting proudly, knowing that they were at last being readied for the battle. Distinct from the huge war elephants, and smaller, these were tiger seizing, and considered by the trainers to be second rank, yet of admirable temperament befitting the hellish environment of battle.

How many of these animal-warriors did Sunil have with him, five hundred?

Jace admired their beauty in the murky light of dawn as they proudly marched through. Did they know they fought for kings? Somehow he thought they did.

The grand war elephants, kings in their own right, were being harnessed for battle. These would have the honor of leading the vanguard of the mighty rajput cavalry.

Fit for combat with horn bows and arrows, swords, clubs, and saddle-axes, the thousands of rajput warriors wore their unique fighting armor: a woven mesh of steel over a quilted garment, and a round shield of impenetrable rhino skin.

Was there anything he could do other than entertain the insane notion of slipping past thousands of warriors to attack Sunil in the armored howdah on the back of the royal elephant? He would have to be mad on opium to try such a stunt.

The Black Royal Elephant of the house of Singh carrying Gem was the only chance.

The sun began to climb. His tension mounted with it. He returned to the trees where he had hidden Gem. As he looked toward the walled city of Sibsagar, he saw with relief that the gate remained shut. Raja Singh had not yet decided whether to risk battle. Jace was certain

Sir Hugo was doing everything to convince him to surrender. Would Ethan be able to convince the raja to ride forth on the uncertain hope that Jemani had a son who was heir to both thrones?

The imperial forces of Raja Singh were outnumbered four to one in the foot infantry. Sunil's rajput officers were also better trained, in the pinnacle of strength, and primed for battle. Even before Sunil had his uncle assassinated, he had been secretly preparing the maharaja's army for war.

Raja Singh's elephants were also fewer. The most Raja Singh could do was to meet Sunil in a skirmish of blood and death.

That night Jace fell asleep with Gem beside him, hearing the child's quiet breathing. The stars above were shrouded by the thickening clouds.

The next morning dawned with the rumble of thunder—but no, not thunder, thought Jace, sitting up from his blanket. He stood, belting on his scabbard. Drums!

Gem jumped in his sleep and bolted up with a frightened whimper. "What is it, Jace?"

"The call for battle. Stay here on the blanket. I'm going to take a look. If the war cry is what I think, it comes not from Sunil but from your grandfather."

The solemn roll of the drums surged like waves across the darkened Brahmaputra valley. The beat spiraled into a frenzy, filling the plain with a foreboding call to the warriors to march for their maharaja in the certain face of overwhelming odds. Raja Singh, father-in-law of Jemani, grandfather of Gem, was telling Sunil he would confront him with only a few loyal men. The beat slowed into the war call of the rajputs: "Ram. Ram. Ram. Ram. Ram. Ram. . . ." Then it faded slowly. Silence.

Jace looked down at Gem with a confident smile. "This is your day, Gem. Your grandfather believes you live. He sends the black elephant. It must be on its way now with his royal rajput guard."

Gem stared up at him, his teeth chattering with fear and excitement.

Jace reached down and lifted him above his head, then down to his feet. "Quickly, into your royal garb! Today you lay claim to two thrones!"

Gem groped into his bag for the gold cloth, the purple satin turban, the ruby, the small curved tulwar. His teeth continued to chatter, and his little fingers were stiff with cold. "The God who also speaks Hindi, help me! Help me! Help me!" he kept repeating.

Jace went swiftly to the edge of his position and saw a thousand winking lights from the smoldering fires in Sunil's village-camp. He too was ready. Today he hoped to kill the father of Jemani.

In the east, the first tinges of light brought a sullen hue, and in the valley where the two armies somberly converged, darkness yet clung to the dust that would turn blood red before the sun set on both victory and defeat, life and death.

As the sun advanced over the thick jungle, a chorus of battle horns cut through the morning, followed again by the awesome drums. The steady pulse beat rumbled through the ground and through the hills, erupting into a passion. The sound pulled Jace forward like a magnet as though he too must battle! It was the signal for the elite rajput cavalry in both armies to encircle their raja and fight to the death.

The drums stopped, and the Brahmaputra valley was transfixed with portentous quiet. Jace felt himself sweating even in the dawn air.

Where was the royal elephant!

In the light of day the battlefield was clearly visible now with its warriors, bull elephants, cannons, drummers, and rajputs. Like some pageant of tragedy, the act would soon commence.

The gate of Sibsagar was wide open, Raja Singh's smaller army, infantry, and elephants moving out to their death.

"I am ready," breathed Gem hoarsely, tugging at his sleeve. "Where is the elephant?"

Good question! Where was Gokul and the Black Royal Elephant!

From the edge of Sunil's camp, volleys of cannon fire exploded; the earth ripped and spat showers of debris toward the gate of Sibsagar and the raja's small but elite army. The cannons belched forth their hatred again. Rounds of slow-burning fire rained down on Raja Singh's elephants but bounced off the rhino-hide armor that straddled the mammoth beasts. The elephants trumpeted their scorn, and with their trunks encased in royal armor, they began their heavy march forward to meet Sunil's war elephants.

In Sunil's camp, the infantry standing beside the cannons pounded drums, their yellow turbans clear in the bright morning. A second volley from the cannons exploded, the impact more deadly as forty-pound shot ripped into the raja's infantry, and elephants fell and men were trampled.

Now the harsh chant from Sunil's rajputs began to echo as wave after wave of warriors moved forward toward the old raja.

But the raja's big elephants, manned by armored mahouts and carrying warriors in steel-plated howdahs, moved to encircle their king.

Jace watched, tensely gripping the handle of his sword. "Gokul! We are all dead men if you do not arrive quickly!"

Sunil's force of steel-armored elephants advanced,

their armor plate reflecting the sunlight. Five-pound cannons protruded from the armored howdahs carrying the rajputs. Other elephants carried kneeling archers who expertly shot volleys of arrows through the howdah's slits. Behind came walls of foot infantry in companies. Jace heard the ring of steel as barbs bounced off the elephants' armor.

But the faithful elephants surrounding the raja were trained to guard his particular howdah, and they reared out their magnificent trunks and snatched enemy warriors from their positions, hurling them to the ground, then crushing them.

Jace came alert as Gem tugged at his arm. He looked down, and the child's face was pale, his eyes wide and glistening. "My grandfather! He will die, Jace! Where is my black elephant?"

Jace clamped his jaw. Again his eyes searched the plain, then the perimeter of the trees. Nothing! He whistled for his horse. The stallion came and whinnied nervously, alert to the smell of battle.

"Wait here," breathed Jace. "There may be a slight chance I can get through now that the gate is open. I must find Gokul. I want you to hide in that hollowed tree, understand? Do not come out until I return. And if I do not come back, stay there. Do not go to Sibsagar. Ride your horse south to Kingscote. If you cannot find it, keep searching."

"Do not go. You too will be killed!"

"He is right," came an unexpected mocking voice.

Jace turned, sword in hand. *Sunil!*

He stood, lean and muscled in his royal garb, his dark eyes triumphant, a smile on his handsome face.

"Greetings, Javed Kasam. I would not wish you to die without first paying your greetings to me, the Maharaja of Assam." His eyes left Jace to fix on Gem. Sunil's smile faded. For one breathtaking moment Jace saw the bravado sink from his expression.

"Your brother's son," said Jace. "Your nephew, Prince Adesh."

The words, though deliberately quiet, had more effect than a shout.

"Adesh is not dead," Jace continued. "The child Sanjay murdered in the palanquin was a Burmese peasant boy too sick to know what happened. I advise you to stay back, Sunil, or I will kill you."

"Hardly, Major. Drop your sword and unbelt your scabbard. You have no hope. Take one step toward me and the twenty rajputs who have their horn bows aimed at the child will strike him down at once."

Was he lying? But no, Sunil would not come alone. Jace turned his head as the warriors stepped from the trees, their bows directed at Gem.

"I need not tell you they are expert shots," boasted Sunil.

Jace wondered what Gem would do. Would he cry, seek to hide?

Gem did not move. He stood staring at Sunil, and in his royal garb Prince Adesh never looked more noble, Jace thought with a pang of pride.

Jace scanned the rajputs, seeking some glimmer, some passion of loyalty toward Gem in their black eyes, but their rugged black-bearded faces were like flint.

He spoke to them in Hindi: "You behold the full-blooded son of Rajkumar Rajiv Singh! And Rajkumari Jemani Singh of Sibsagar! This is your future Maharaja Adesh Singh of Assam!"

Gem unexpectedly called out, pointing a small finger. "You must arrest my uncle Sunil for killing my father and mother! He is bad!"

As though lightning flashed, Jace saw the confused

expression on the warriors' faces.

"Lies!" said Sunil. "The child is an impostor brought by the English to deceive the Hindus. Kill them both!"

Jace lifted the gold chain around Gem's neck, where he had placed the royal rings of the old maharaja from Guwahati. "The boy's hand will grow strong to fit the power these rings represent. Look! They are your maharaja's!"

The rajputs recognized them and stood frozen, still uncertain of their action.

"He stole them," said Sunil with disdain.

"He entrusted them to me the night you had him assassinated."

The royal rajput guards would either bow the knee to the son of Rajiv or remain loyal to Sunil and kill them both. He acted swiftly to avert their immediate decision, fearing it would be the wrong one.

"You, Sunil! You are a coward and a murderer. You hide behind the strength of these warriors instead of fighting your own battles! Why are you not in the howdah so the warriors who die for you can see you? You break the law of your own people. A raja must be in sight at all times during a battle. Step forth. I intend to kill you for the mutiny at Plassey and for the assassination of the maharaja!"

"Kill him!" gritted Sunil to the chief rajput.

"He is my friend!" cried Gem.

A shout came from the trees, followed by a trumpeting elephant—two majestic beasts crashed forward, one carrying Gokul, the other with an empty howdah. *The Black Royal Elephant!*

In the brief moment when all eyes turned, Jace snatched Gem from the line of the archers and flung him into the bushes, retrieving his sword.

While the guards with Sunil hesitated, Gem crawled

out of sight. Six rajput guards with Gokul rode into the open, their bows taut and ready to shoot. Two were his friendly acquaintances from Sualkashi, another was Nadir, who had been among the dozen warriors riding with Sir Hugo, and who had warned Jace at Kingscote.

Nadir, a rajput captain and respected warrior, shouted to the men with Sunil, withdrawing his katar and lifting it high. "Are you of the warrior blood, but fools? Would you die for the traitor-prince who killed Rajiv? Our future maharaja lives in the blood of the son of Rajiv! Where is your love for honor? Adesh must live!"

The warriors lowered their bows.

"Adesh lives!"

Jace seized the moment. He went after Gem and returned holding the boy high overhead against the backdrop of the raging battle. The warriors removed their swords and beat them against their leather shields amid a crescendo of cheers.

Jace carried him to the royal elephant. Nadir rode up and, bowing, fist at heart, took Gem and placed him inside the howdah seat. "Prince Adesh!"

The mahout signaled the elephant to trumpet on cue, displaying all its royal beauty and power. Jace wondered if Gem would be frightened, but he was not and gazed down bravely. Jace smiled his encouragement, and Gem touched the ruby dangling below his royal turban to make certain it was in place.

Jace had never seen such a large and majestic beast. Shining with black paint, it lumbered forward, driven by a royal mahout with a red turban. The elephant's royal covering was glittering gold cloth, and its howdah was sprinkled with jewels and boasted the standard of Raja Singh. The rajputs gave another shout of allegiance. With swift precision they fell into a disciplined line, the royal entourage leading out toward the battlefield, toward danger, but toward hope—if only the thousands would hear the drums blaring, the horns sounding, and turn to see the Black Royal Elephant arriving.

Gem had turned to glance back at Jace, his eyes pleading for the major's presence. Jace went to mount his horse when suddenly he whirled. Sunil was gone!

Gokul came huffing from the jungle trees. "Over there, sahib! Behind the trees!"

Jace ran after him. He did not go far before he saw Sunil.

Alone and abandoned, he stood with rage on his face, gripping his weapon. "Do you think I run like a rat scampering for its hole? I came to don the tunic of a warrior!" Sunil stepped toward him, deadly cold. "You, Major! Come! We will do our battle here. I will kill you."

"Yes," breathed Jace. "It is fitting. Just you and I!"

25

Sunil slipped the deadly katar from his belt, and his smile was vicious. "No swords, Javed Kasam. That is too simple for warriors such as we." In contempt, he tossed him the Indian blade designed for thrusting.

"Take heed, sahib!" hissed Gokul to Jace.

Jace picked up the blade and made certain it would not fail him.

"Would I deceive you?" mocked Sunil, removing a second katar.

Gokul took position behind a rock.

Jace had used the thrusting dagger before, but he knew Sunil was far more adept. Perhaps he was a fool to give him even the slightest advantage. Sunil, however, was already unbelting his scabbard and tossing aside his sword and cumbersome turban and jewels. In minutes he was a stranger, a ruthless, deadly warrior determined to kill him.

Jace started to remove his jacket while Sunil, still wearing his terrible smile, waited with exaggerated condescension.

Jace stood within fifty feet of Sunil. He took his time, slowly removing his jacket, then his scabbard, and finally his hat, tossing it aside.

He could see the delay was getting to Sunil. "How does it feel to know that you have lost all possibility of ruling Assam, Sunil? Instead of you, your brother's son, Adesh, will sit on the throne. He looks much like the lovely Jemani, does he not? You say you loved her, but she bore Rajiv's child. It is *his* son who will reign."

"We will fight, Major. Save your words!"

Jace now matched Sunil's previous mocking smile with one of his own.

Across the plain the noise of battle continued, adding to their tension.

"Hear, Sunil? Soon your entire army will be acclaiming Prince Adesh. How that must rankle after all your meticulous scheming. Years of searching for him, foiled. You murdered your own brother . . . and your own uncle in Guwahati. The plans with Roxbury, the mutiny at Plassey—all for nothing."

At last Jace saw sweat stand out on Sunil's forehead . . . and he moved toward him.

"And now you will die. How fitting I should use the same kind of dagger that was thrust into my friend Rajiv."

His words were having their effect—he would need that emotional edge. He had no illusions about the fighting ability of Sunil, who was stronger than most of the soft and spoiled princes. Broad through the shoulders and chest, his arms and legs were powerfully muscled.

Sunil approached, and the two men circled warily.

Jace held his katar low, cutting edge up. Sunil thought he had the advantage, and Jace knew it, but his own ability rested in his fighting experience in Burma with Zin, and when he had fought for survival after escaping China on the Old Silk Road.

Sunil moved in suddenly, his blade darting with a stabbing thrust like the strike of a cobra, and the point ripped a gash in the buckskin of Jace's breeches.

Jace struck back, and they both went down, rolling over on the rocks, stabbing and thrusting. Coming up, they faced each other again. Flecks of blood spattered Jace's shirt front. He sprang suddenly, and Sunil leaped back to escape his thrust, then circling, thrusting . . . another spot of blood appeared, this time on Sunil's arm.

Sunil was incredibly swift, agile, his hard face like a mask, showing no emotion.

Jace moved, seemed to slip, and Sunil sprang in. Instantly Jace turned and swung with a chop of his left hand, catching Sunil on the side of the neck and smashing him to the ground.

Sunil, unaccustomed to Oriental fighting, seemed surprised—yet quickly recovered. He came up, lunged low, but Jace stepped aside and thrust, his katar entering Sunil's shoulder. Sunil swung around swiftly to strike back. Jace struck again with a vicious chop and Sunil fell—dazed. He stomped on his wrist and Sunil's grip on his weapon loosened. Jace viciously kicked it out of his fingers, and it landed in the brush.

"Get up."

Sunil sprang at him, knocking Jace backward, but he rolled over and came to his feet. Sunil was searching for his blade. Jace tossed his aside with disgust.

"Come, Sunil."

Sunil stood with a wide stance, staring at him.

Around them the sky churned with the monsoon clouds. Lightning flashed and rumbled above the jungle trees; below them death opened its jaws to receive the rajputs in hand-to-hand fighting.

Sunil gripped and ungripped his fists, then moved

toward him again. Jace circled to the right, causing Sunil to turn to keep in front of him. Jace feinted a move, but Sunil only watched and was not fooled. Sweat ran down their bodies and Jace's lips tasted salt.

Jace moved his left foot forward, gaining a few inches, crouching a little. Sunil feinted, then came in fast. Jace struck his hand down and, catching his wrist, swung the arm back and under, then up Sunil's back. He forced the wrist higher, toward the other shoulder. Sunil's face went white as he tried to twist out of the hold, but Jace kept his grip and heaved upward with all his strength, until he heard bone crack.

Jace released him. Sunil staggered, lost his footing, and fell. Jace turned, exhausted, and walked away, while Sunil crawled toward his horse where he had left his scabbard . . . and his pistol.

Jace sank to the earth, sweating and breathing heavily, staring up at the monsoon clouds.

A pistol shot cracked suddenly. Jace turned to see Gokul standing over the dying body of Sunil.

26

When Jace arrived near the battlefield it had become a nightmare of hand-to-hand combat. Raja Singh's loyal forces were outnumbered.

"I do not see the royal elephant," murmured Gokul worriedly.

The rajput soldiers guarding Raja Singh wore heavy leather helmets and skirts of armor. Steel netting covered their faces and necks. They fired volleys of arrows at the equally armored rajputs fighting for Sunil, whom they did not know was dead. Elephants were everywhere carrying howdahs of rajput archers; some carried two-pound swivel guns mounted on the elephants' backs.

"I fear for the raja," said Jace. "He is the focus of the fighting. Soon he will be surrounded, and there is no way to halt the battle."

Where was Nadir with the royal elephant?

Sunil's infantry massed to encircle Raja Singh. His protective wall of elephants and rajputs were coming under fierce attack. Sibsagar was on the defensive, the number of imperial forces diminishing.

"Look," breathed Gokul.

Jace watched the raja's royal war elephants with respect. Trained to protect the raja, they seemed oblivious to their own danger. The armored trunks reached and seized warrior after warrior, flinging them down to the bloody dust and crushing them beneath their feet.

"But they cannot protect him much longer, sahib."

Then Jace heard what he had longed for. The kettle-drums were rolling, swelling to a crescendo, rolling like waves over the battle scene. The battle horns pierced the morning, then the drums again, pounding the steady pulsating beat.

"Sahib! There! It is well!"

Jace had seen the Black Royal Elephant coming from the trees, led by Nadir and the rajputs sworn to Gem.

"Ram! Ram!" they cried. "Ram! Ram!"

In the center moved the mammoth black elephant, now armored and carrying Gem in a steel howdah decorated with gold. Jace caught his breath and was on his feet, intent on mounting his horse to gallop to the elephant's side. Gem was standing erect inside the howdah, beneath a huge crimson umbrella.

Gokul caught his arm. "No, sahib! No! Do not go! You will be killed in seconds!"

But he need not have worried, for Jace paused and stared. Sunil's rajputs from Guwahati saw the standard of Rajiv carried by Gem on the big black elephant. They saw the boy in royal turban and gold cloth standing erect as though to hold back the very arrows of death.

Slowly, Sibsagar's chant of "Ram! Ram!" was taken up by the rajputs of Sunil. With a swiftness that left him breathless, they turned like fierce tigers to rally to the side of their new maharaja.

Gokul looked at Jace and laughed. "It worked, sahib! God has been merciful to us, to all of us."

Jace, exhausted, let the horse's reins slip from his fingers and watched in silence as the battle turned from certain defeat to great rejoicing.

The Black Royal Elephant carrying Gem lumbered forward to the cheers of the warriors. Nadir was leading the way toward Raja Singh, who, in stunned and tearful disbelief, stood in royal garb inside his howdah to glimpse his first sight of Jemani's son, and to welcome him to the royal palace of Sibsagar.

Inside the palace of Raja Singh, Jace found Ethan. Sir Hugo, where was he? wondered Jace. It was evening in Sibsagar, and the ancient city was lit with ten thousand torches, celebrating the unexpected good fortune of getting their first glimpse of the boy who would be maharaja.

"Where is Roxbury?" demanded Jace.

"Gone," said Ethan wearily, slumping into a gilded chair in a chamber with crimson and gold hangings and black and silver-veined marble walls and floor. "I have not seen him since the battle first began. I am sure he is in hiding. He must know by now that he is defeated and his ambitions in ruin."

Jace wondered. He had no peace despite the good outcome of the battle and the homecoming of Gem. He could think of little now except reaching Kingscote. *Was all well?*

"Maybe Sahib Roxbury went to Kingscote."

Gokul's uneasy words only forced Jace onto his feet, and although exhausted, he was determined to ride out that night.

"Yes," breathed Ethan, his gray eyes coming swiftly to Jace. "He would go there first, then perhaps back to England."

"And you?" asked Jace.

"I think, Major, that I shall take advantage for a time

of His Excellency's hospitality. Then, perhaps, I will journey to Burma."

Jace reached into his jacket and drew out the soiled
drawing that Zin's official had given him showing the
route to the mission station of Felix Carey. Jace handed
it to Ethan and smiled wearily.

"It so happens that Carey is in desperate need of a
physician. He has introduced the smallpox vaccination
into Burma, and he is gifted in medicine, but he is no
doctor. You could be the answer to his prayers."

Ethan took the map and scanned the drawing. He
said nothing for a moment. "An interesting proposition,
Jace. Perhaps I shall do just that."

Ethan stood facing Jace. Their gaze met briefly, and
Ethan seemed about to say something but changed his
mind. "I wish you well, Major."

"Yes." Jace took his hand firmly. "You did well, Ethan.
Without your help here in the palace the outcome would
have been very different."

Ethan's eyes flickered with appreciation.

They stood for a moment saying nothing, then with
a slight smile Jace touched his shoulder and walked out.
Gokul turned to Ethan, salaamed, and followed.

Out in the hall Jace was surprised to see Gem now
surrounded by muscled royal guards.

Jace smiled and bowed. "Your Excellency!"

"I have a gift for you, Jace."

Almost shy again, the boy walked forward on gold
sandals and handed him a poorly wrapped present. "I
wrapped it myself," he said.

Jace took the small box, turning it over in his hand.
"Whatever it is, I shall cherish it."

"You will come often to see me?"

"I will come."

"And bring my English mother?"

"I am certain nothing will be able to keep her away."

Gem smiled, and Jace saw the first sign of happiness in his eyes.

"I will send a royal elephant for her—and you! My grandfather wishes to meet you both and to reward you for your bravery today."

"Your own bravery was something to behold."

"I remembered your words in Burma . . . your words about God . . . then I was no longer afraid."

The royal guards hovered over the boy, anxious to get him safely into the raja's royal chambers. Jace bowed to the young boy, and was escorted down the hall and into the courtyard, where Gokul waited with their horses.

"Kingscote shall be a welcome sight, sahib."

"You do not know how welcome. Come, our work here is done. We have exceptionally good news for Coral."

"I am sure the lovely English damsel waits, pining for you," said Gokul with glinting black eyes.

Jace arched a dark brow as he placed the wrapped present from Gem in his pocket. Then he turned the reins of his horse to ride out the gate of Sibsagar to Kingscote.

27

Kingscote

The nightmare has only begun, thought Coral, clutching the loaded pistol as she backed toward the stairway. Yanna's friend Thilak had not gotten through to warn the mercenaries her father had hired to guard the plantation—or were they all dead, including Thilak?

As night settled, the Burmese renegades were everywhere, closing in about the mansion. She heard windows breaking. The wood was splintering on the heavy front door, and she watched the bolts weakening. From behind her in the kitchen, a shot rang out as the old cook Piroo fired at an intruder, the sound followed by a woman's cry.

Rosa! thought Coral.

Out front on the lawn, she heard the Indian workers loyal to the Kendall family fighting to guard the front entrance. Old men, women, even children, had all come rushing from the hatcheries, and although outnumbered, they defended their positions with whatever weapons they had. Dazed, Coral found herself thinking of how proud she was of their heroic effort to save the feringhis.

Into her mind stabbed the words coming from the Indian who guarded the front door. "Run, sahiba! Run! We will try to stop them!"

"Where are Yanna and Preetah?" shouted Coral.

"We are here!" came their call from the upper hallway.

Behind her on the stairway, Kathleen stood with a pistol. Coral felt her older sister tugging at her arm, and Marianna, pale but coldly determined for one time in her life, stood staring toward the door giving way under the machetes.

"Coral!" demanded Kathleen.

Coral turned and rushed up the stairs, glancing back into the hallway. The door was caving in. Male servants converged in the hall to guard the stairway. Old Piroo stood with his gun in his hands still white with bread flour, his apron now soiled with blood. He took his stand on the lower stair to guard their retreat.

The door broke and heaved open. She saw a rugged warrior, his hand clutching a short curved blade. Piroo fired. The Burmese stumbled backward. As the servants sought to push the door in place, there were other determined footsteps rushing up the porch steps, and warriors entering through broken windows. She heard a scream from the back of the house—from her mother's room! Coral whirled toward the hallway. Someone had reached the top floor!

Her strength flowed back into her body. Her heart thudded in her ears. *Marianna!*

Coral raced up the stairs, each step too slow, hearing her sister's hysterical voice and the sound of furniture breaking. There was no one to help. The men servants were fighting in the hall, the silk workers battled on the lawn, and in the garden near the cook room door, they were trying desperately to hold the marauders back.

Coral saw the door to her mother's room standing open. Preetah was on the hall floor, unconscious; Yanna was struggling to reload her rifle, her black hair streaming wildly about her face.

"In there!" she screamed at Coral.

Coral rushed through the door, raising her pistol to see Kathleen in the grip of a renegade. But Marianna had already grabbed Sir Hampton's war saber on display in the hall. Just as Coral reached the door with the pistol, Marianna gripped the saber handle with both hands and brought it down with a whack. The man released Kathleen and stumbled onto his knees. Marianna struck him again and he fell face forward.

Kathleen stared at the unconscious warrior and slumped into a faint.

Marianna stood white-faced and still, both small hands still gripping the saber, its point resting on the carpet in front of her. Her wide eyes met Coral's.

"Quick! Get Yanna and Preetah in here! Bolt the door! I'll lock the verandah—" Coral's voice stopped abruptly. Outside in the carriageway, horse hooves pounded. There was more shouting, more gunfire, and the added sound of steel striking steel.

"Help has come!" cried Yanna from the broken verandah door. "Thilak did get through. Soldiers! No—it is not him—they look to be from Jorhat! Many of them, maybe fifty! Thank God!"

Jorhat! Was it Jace? Coral ran across her mother's room out onto the verandah and peered below, her eyes anxiously scanning the darkened lawn. In the flaring torchlight she saw men fighting, while one man in command sat astride his strong muscled horse. He looked up toward the verandah and saw her. As the glow from the firelight fell across his face, her heart paused with disappointment and alarm.

337

He is Burmese! These are not British soldiers from Jor-hat!

Below, a woman rushed forward from the shadows and stood looking up. "Miss Coral! It is me, Jan-Lee! I bring friends!"

Friends! "Jan-Lee," cried Coral with joy. She ran from the bedchamber into the hall. Preetah was being attended by Mera while the child Reena hovered like a nervous bird, wringing her tiny hands in despair. Coral stopped long enough to draw the child into her arms. "It is all right now, Reena! Jan-Lee has come and brought friends to help us. The fighting will be over."

Coral hurried down the stairs to the ugly sight of the door hanging on broken hinges. There were dead and wounded on the hall floor and out on the porch, but the Burmese fighters Jan-Lee had brought were bringing the assault to an end.

Her knees weak, the pistol held loosely against the side of her skirt, Coral saw Jan-Lee enter through the door in a soiled hooded cloak, making her way over bodies and broken furniture.

Coral looked into the dark eyes welling with tears, a face lined with care and streaked with dust, her black hair speckled with gray hanging limp and gnarled. Jan-Lee glanced about with dismay, then looked toward Coral, her hands outstretched, and Coral met her in an embrace.

"Thank God," murmured Coral, "you came in time."

She opened her eyes to confront a strong Burmese warrior standing in the doorway, his black eyes cold, his long gray-black hair drawn back and tied with animal skin.

Jan-Lee must have felt her stiffen, for she turned toward the doorway, where the man stood motionless.

338

"This—this is my husband, Warrior Sun Li, nephew of Warlord Zin."

Coral held back her surprise. Zin—the man who held Gem. And Jan-Lee's husband was his nephew. But had not Jan-Lee informed them soon after Emerald was born that her husband had died in the skirmish at Jorhat defending the British? She looked at Sun Li with caution.

"He has come in peace," said Jan-Lee softly.

When Coral looked at her for explanation, Jan-Lee said quietly, "There is much to explain. My husband and I have been long separated, but when Miss Elizabeth was so sick I knew I must take a risk. I went to him in the jungle near Kingscote for help." She turned to him. "This is the daughter of the Master of Kingscote, the Kendall daughter I told you about."

Sun Li stepped forward, and with precision he lowered his head. "My humble apology for the devil renegades who trespassed your land. Those men who came once served me but were worthless dogs who acted against my wishes. My honorable soldiers are now making a quick end to their troublesome ways."

Coral rallied her strength. "Yes, thank you. Without your arrival we would all have been killed."

"It will bring you pleasure to know that the battle for Sibsagar has failed to bring Maharaja Sunil to power."

So Sibsagar had been the destination of the massive army that the mercenaries on Kingscote had seen on the road, moving northeast. She had feared Sunil was on his way to fight Warlord Zin and capture Gem. Sunil was defeated! Her thoughts raced to Sir Hugo. Where was he? Was he alive?

"And Sunil's army?" she asked worriedly.

"A courier brought us word today that Sunil's warriors have vowed loyalty to Prince Adesh Singh. The prince is safe and in loyal care."

For a moment she could think of nothing else, and her relief spiraled upward in silent thanksgiving to God. If Gem was safe, then Jace too would probably be alive.

Jan-Lee had turned to her husband and spoke in low tones. He stepped out onto the porch and gave an order in Burmese, and a man wearing a worn leather tunic with an ankle-length cloak stepped into the hall.

"I present Kung yu Tei, a wise man in the lore of Eastern drugs, both good and evil. He has come to look upon Madame Kendall."

Coral's heart leaped with joy. "Oh, yes, please, do come. This way."

The man bowed with silent dignity and followed her up the stairs.

Inside Elizabeth's chamber, Kathleen and Marianna showed surprise to see him but remained silent. Coral was about to follow him to her mother's bedside, when Jan-Lee took hold of her arm and drew her to the other side of the room.

"Jan-Lee, you risked your life to venture into the jungle for help; how can we ever thank you?"

"I did what I must to help Miss Elizabeth, who has long been a friend to me and Emerald, and to save Kingscote."

"When you did not return with Doctor Boswell we feared something had happened on the road. And Emerald has been asking for you daily!"

"I could not find your cousin or uncle on the road toward Darjeeling, so I went to the secret jungle camp of my husband. He sent a message to me only days before Natine tried to harm you both. Natine knew that my husband was not dead as I said, that I had written him several messages, and he threatened to tell your father. But I was not a spy! I wrote him pleading, asking him not to attack. I have always been loyal to you!"

Confused, Coral said, "It would take more than Na-tine's lies to turn the family against you. You need not have feared his threats. But I don't understand about your husband. You told my mother he had been killed at Jorhat."

Her haggard face turned sorrowful. "I must confess past sins to you, to Miss Elizabeth and Sir Hampton. My husband—I said he was killed when Emerald was born, but as you now see, it is not so. Sorrowfully, he served with Zin these treacherous years, and I feared to let your mother and father know. I had to think of Emerald."

Coral shook her head. "You need not have feared bearing the reputation of your husband. My parents would have understood."

"No, Miss Coral, there is—is more. My husband was a spy for Burma, for his uncle Warlord Zin. It was my husband who helped steal Gem away that ugly night."

Coral stared, stunned.

Tears showed in Jan-Lee's eyes. "I tried to stop him, but he would not listen."

"You knew?" whispered Coral, devastated.

"No, no, only when fire started in the hatcheries I guessed and feared what would happen. I rushed to the nursery to hide Gem, but the sepoy serving Zin was already there. I told him I would also go with Gem to wherever my husband waited to bring Gem to Warlord Zin, but he would not let me. He told me Zin had my sister and her child too, and that all would be killed if I said anything. Then he hit me, and I remember nothing else."

"Jan-Lee. . . ."

"My sister, she—she was Gem's nurse these years at Zin's palace. I feared not only for you and Gem but for her and her boy if you went to Zin demanding Gem's release. Sunil was also involved with my husband, promising him that the English presence in Assam would be

341

no more, that he would give Burma the land on the border. I guessed that Sunil had an assassin kill Rajiv the night you brought Gem home from the hut, but I knew that enemies prowled in the jungle. If I said anything, all of Kingscote might have been burned."

Coral could say nothing, feeling her own dismay and seeing the pain in Jan-Lee's face.

"Tonight I learned from my husband that my sister and her son are dead. But you rejoice, Miss Coral. You be happy because Gem—Prince Adesh lives. And my husband . . . he is no longer your enemy. Sunil has lost the war, and Burma knows that with two thrones united in Gem, Assam is too strong for war now. And soon the English will arrive. My husband listened to me in the jungle as I pled for your life and Miss Elizabeth. He is a man tired of the jungle, of running and hiding. Warlord Zin sent him a message to come back, to not fight against Kingscote because of a man named Javed Kasam. Zin said you would marry this man who is his friend. That, Miss Coral, I do not understand."

Coral managed a weary smile. Javed Kasam. If only that particular warrior would walk through the door now and hold her tightly in his embrace. "Perhaps you will understand one day. I can say nothing now."

Jan-Lee nodded. "My husband will leave the jungle near Kingscote and return to his uncle. I will take Emerald and go with him."

Coral was overwhelmed with all the information, and her silence must have been mistaken by Jan-Lee for anger. "Forgive me, Miss Coral. Yet—I did tell you Gem was not dead so you would not sorrow. I told you of a scar on the child's foot."

"Oh, Jan-Lee, I am not angry. I understand the reason for your silence. You were afraid for all of us. You too were held ransom all these years. But it is over now." She took hold of the woman's shoulders. "Gem is safe. He is a prince who will rule in Guwahati."

Jan-Lee's eyes flickered with sudden emotion. "Not only Guwahati but Sibsagar."

"Sibsagar?" asked Coral curiously.

"So Sun Li tells me. You will learn soon. I know little more. I must go to Emerald now, to get her ready to ride with her father."

"Oh, but you need not go," cried Coral. "Your loyalty is not questioned. And it was you who risked your life to find your husband in the jungle camp. You saved us all. And you brought the wise man to treat my mother. I am in your debt. We all are."

Jan-Lee took hold of her. For the first time a small smile touched the ayah's lips. "It is enough that you say so. I will hold those words to my heart. But I must go. It is time for Emerald to look upon the face of her father. And now with peace coming—perhaps we will find our own peace in Burma in the house of his uncle, Warlord Zin."

"I hope so for your sake and Emerald's. And if not, remember you are always welcome to return."

"I will remember."

When Sun Li mounted his horse to ride out the next morning with his followers, the dead had been buried in the jungle, and the windows and doors were temporarily repaired.

Coral stood on the steps as they prepared to ride away. Jan-Lee was mounted with Emerald in front of her. It was the girl's eyes that held Coral's attention, for they shone with silent adoration as they fixed proudly upon her father.

Sun Li leaned from his horse and handed Coral a long

item wrapped in red cloth. "Zin has sent this. It is to be given to Javed Kasam on his wedding day."

Coral took the gift. It was heavy and she guessed it to be a sword.

"Tell him it is a gift from the Zin. He first thought to use it against the English at Sibsagar when he fought beside Sunil, but Zin has listened to Javed Kasam's words. My uncle now returns this gift in peace, and I also return across the border to my own place."

He turned his horse to ride, glancing at Jan-Lee and Emerald. She brought her horse beside him, the warriors following. As Jan-Lee left she turned her head, and there was a faint smile on her face. She said something to Emerald, who tore her eyes from her father to smile and lift her hand toward Coral. Then glimpsing Kathleen and Marianna on the upper verandah with Reena, she waved goodbye.

Reena brought her fingers to her forehead.

Below on the steps, Coral watched until they were out of sight behind the trees. Only a trail of dust lingered beneath the lowering sky.

Inside the house, she climbed the stairs to the upper hall and heard the excited voices of her sisters coming from her mother's chambers. Coral laid the gift from Zin on the hall table beneath her father's war saber hanging again on the wall and hurried into the room.

Kathleen and Marianna turned with the first smiles she had seen on their faces in weeks.

"Is she awake?" asked Coral expectantly.

"No, but she does seem to be moving in her sleep. And Marianna is sure she heard her whisper Father's name."

Coral came to the bedside. Though her hopes had momentarily soared with the excitement of her sisters, she saw only her mother's stillness.

"When Father arrives he may be the one able to reach her," said Kathleen.

Coral said nothing.

28

It was nearly a week later. The morning sun momentarily broke through the clouds, and peacocks strutted across the lawn, making shrill calls. Coral placed a red rose on her mother's breakfast tray held by Kathleen, while Mera looked on, smiling. Elizabeth was not well, but her condition had improved, and however feeble the ray of light, it was a cause for celebration. Suddenly, from Kings Road a company of some twenty men mounted on horses turned onto the carriageway and came riding toward the mansion. Marianna came alert and walked toward the window to look out.

As Marianna watched them, the tension in her face broke into a delighted smile. She let out a high-pitched squeal, nearly causing Kathleen to drop the tray. Coral turned to see Marianna throw open the door, and lifting her skirts, she ran down the steps to meet the riders.

Coral hurried out, scanning the riders as they approached. She caught a glimpse of the two men in front, rugged men in hats and riding cloaks. As she recognized their faces her breath paused. "It is Father and Seward!"

She ran to meet them.

"Father," Kathleen whispered and, pushing the tray toward Mera, rushed out the door.

Sir Hampton dismounted and swept Marianna into his arms, and Coral and Kathleen were quickly at his side, both trying to embrace him at the same time while Seward looked on grinning.

"Now that be a sight worth it all."

"Yes, sir," said Ensign Niles, smiling. "Makes me anxious to get home to England."

"England, he says! Nae, but Scotland it is!" said Seward good-naturedly.

The ensign and his small troop from Jorhat had met Hampton and Seward on the road toward Kingscote. The ensign, who had already given Seward the letter entrusted to him by the major, now reached into his jacket and pulled out a second letter. He waited for an appropriate lull in the exchange of tears and greetings between the Kendall daughters and their father. When he at last had an opportunity, he cleared his voice. "Miss Kendall?"

Three women turned and looked up at him. He scanned their faces and found himself growing warm. "Ah . . . Miss Coral?"

She smiled, and her eyes went to the letter. Her heart beat faster as somehow she suspected that it was from Jace. "I am Coral."

"Major Buckley asked me to give this to you before he rode to Burma."

In Elizabeth's dim chamber, Sir Hampton knelt beside her bed and held her thin hand between his strong ones.

"Liza?" he whispered for the third time. " 'Tis me,

Hampton." He leaned toward the pale face, and found the once-lovely features now gaunt. "Dear God," he lamented. "Liza, my love, can you hear me?" he rasped, reaching bronzed fingers to smooth away her dark hair now streaked with gray. He leaned and kissed her, then buried his head into her neck as his emotions cracked. "Liza, don't leave me. Nothing means anything without you. Not Kingscote, not all my tomorrows. Liza—"

Coral quietly shut the bedchamber door on the scene and stood in the hallway, feeling the familiar ache in her throat. The warm homecoming had quickly been shrouded by the news of Elizabeth's condition.

Her sisters stood waiting, hoping for good news. They had thought the voice of their father might bring her out of the peaceful but deep sleep. Seward hung back with a slight frown, and Coral suspected he was thinking of Natine, perhaps even blaming himself for her mother's tragedy.

"She did not respond?" asked Kathleen after seeing Coral's expression.

Coral shook her head. The gloom that hung in the hall only made her wish to get alone in her room and read Jace's letter again. At least the news of Gem was wonderful, she reminded herself.

Before going to bed she walked over to where Seward stood. "She seemed a trifle better this morning and we had hoped. . . . The Burmese doctor did what he could and left a powder. You must not feel bad, Seward. If you had stayed here instead of going to Darjeeling, Father would have been killed."

He nodded but said nothing. She laid a hand on his arm, then turned and walked to her chamber.

If only the voice of Hampton would bring Mother back to consciousness. But what if she did hear him? What if she *could not* respond?

The thought tormented her, and she clutched Jace's letter tightly, as though by doing so she received comfort. "Please, Lord, make her come out of this stupor."

———

Seward watched Coral walk down the hall. There was no more he could do here, he thought, depressed. What could he say to Hampton, to any of them? He turned to leave, to make his bunk with the small troop from Jorhat that was bedded down near the stables. In the hall his gaze bumped against a long object wrapped in red silk. He stopped and squinted.

That embroidered dragon! That be the sign of Warlord Zin.

And just what was it doing here?

He carefully lifted it and turned to Kathleen. "Lass, this is a sword—from Zin."

Kathleen's disinterest showed. "Oh? I've never seen it before. Maybe it belonged to Jan-Lee's husband."

Seward's suspicions were rising. "Might I look at it?"

"Why, of course, Seward."

She and Marianna turned to walk to their rooms. "Good-night," they echoed.

"Aye, lassies, good-night. I'll be with the troop near the stables if ye be needin' me."

He unwrapped the red silk and stifled a cry of jubilation. The Mogul sword!

His face broke into a smile. "Aye, Jace be happy to see this again."

He wondered that it had sat on the hall table for a week since Sun Li and his Burmese warriors had ridden back—it was worth a fortune. So it was Zin who had somehow ended up with the sword stolen from Jace in Calcutta, he thought, frowning. He hesitated as he weighed it in his sturdy hand, then his bushy brows came together. *Best be guardin' this myself until he returns.*

Wrapping it again, and still frowning, he left the mansion. He walked in the darkness in the direction of the stables, glancing up at the clouds. The monsoon would be breaking. *The lad ought to be arrivin' soon now from Sibsagar. And Roxbury, where might that conniving blackguard be lurking?*

He paused and glanced back at the mansion with the golden light burning in the upper windows, then walked on.

Seward chuckled as he imagined Jace's exuberance when he saw the prized blade. "It may be we will have us a fine mansion in Darjeeling after all."

Seated on the satin-covered chair, Coral listened to the grumbles of thunder announcing the monsoon. The clouds would soon open and the drenching rain would pour. Kingscote rested in stillness beneath the canopy of dense clouds. Nothing moved, nothing stirred amid the jungle. Palm fronds were etched darkly against zigzag flashes of lightning. She spread the sheet of paper to read Jace's letter again.

He wrote briefly of all that had happened since leaving Kingscote to ride to Burma in search of Gem. It came as a delightful surprise that the Lord had worked out circumstances whereby Gem had been able to spend time with Felix Carey.

Through Jace's words, she relived the tension he must have experienced when he told her of his plan to thwart Sunil in his effort to rule Sibsagar and Guwahati by introducing Gem on the Black Royal Elephant.

Coral already knew through Jan-Lee's husband that

the feat had been successful, and so she could without fear read about the risk Jace had taken. She felt pride in him as she tried to imagine how he had managed to bring Gem to Sibsagar at the right time to defeat Sunil's plot.

"Gem, an heir to two thrones. And Jemani had been the daughter of the Raja of Sibsagar!"

Coral remembered her saying at her baptism: *"My Rajiv is a prince. There is no one better among men."*

A prince! Of course! Why had she not thought of what she said before? And Jemani was a rajkumari, a princess from Sibsagar! And Gem—

"Gem is to be maharaja," whispered Coral, and laughter welled up in her heart. "God allowed Jace and me to protect him from Sunil."

She lingered again over Jace's farewell: "I shall soon return to claim Roxbury's promise of a Christmas wedding on Kingscote."

She smiled, her heart pounding; then her smile faded as feminine vanity stole over her. "Whatever will I wear? No one in the family even knows yet!"

In her own happy but disjointed thoughts tinged with nervous excitement, she did not hear the lone horse ride up in the carriageway below the open verandah. She sat in the chair holding the letter, lost in her thoughts.

———

Sir Hugo Roxbury entered the silent house. He did not know that Hampton and Seward had arrived safely from Darjeeling, nor that Coral had shared the letter from Alex with her father and sisters telling of his voyage to London.

As though a harbinger of what was to come, a blinding streak of lightning stabbed the blackness above the mansion, followed by a loud clap of thunder that rattled the broken glass in the downstairs windows. Hugo climbed the stairs to his room.

Coral heard quiet footsteps in the hall, and they seemed to slow, then abruptly stop outside her door. She wondered at the odd reaction and expected it to be followed by a knock. Her light was on and the golden glow showed beneath the door . . . but no knock sounded and the steps moved on.

Strange, she thought, and peered out her door down the hall.

Sir Hugo's chamber door was slightly ajar, and a light burned.

Her heart thudded. He was back. How dare he show his face in the house? Did he think they did not know how he had used Natine in his vile plan with the cobra and drugs? And what of the trap set for her father in Darjeeling! Did he think he could lie his way out again?

She left her room and walked quietly down the hall until she came to his door. She knocked. There was no answer. She hesitated, then pushed the door open and looked in.

Sir Hugo had his back toward her, his bags open on the bed, and he was quickly packing.

Anger filled Coral, and she said with sarcasm, "What! Uncle! You are leaving so soon? You have not yet made Kingscote your own."

At the sound of her voice he turned, startled. Coral wanted to flinch under his dark eyes.

"You," he said so quietly that she shivered. His surprise revealed that he knew about the cobra. For a moment their eyes locked, and she wanted to scream with terror and run. Perhaps because the reality struck with such awful clarity, she could only stand and meet his gaze.

"No," she whispered. "I am not dead yet, Uncle. Natine's niece Preetah was able to bleed my arm. But my mother is very ill. She may never recover the use of her mind. My father is with her now. Seward rescued him from your treachery in Darjeeling."

Sir Hugo said nothing and only looked down at her, his face and eyes too still and deep to reveal the thoughts racing through his mind.

"Where is Ethan?" she demanded. "What have you done to him? Did you try to kill him too?"

He seemed to recover from his daze and returned to his packing. "You are beginning to sound like a hysterical woman, my dear. I would have thought that emotion fitting your sisters but not you. Ethan is at Sibsagar. Do pull yourself together. As for the cobra, it was merely meant to frighten you. To keep you from stubbornly pressing ahead in your ambition with the school."

"You would know best about the ugly side of ambition. Was burning my school and my Hindi New Testament also meant to frighten me? If you think you can return to London as though nothing has happened, and simply lie your way back into Aunt Margaret's arms, you are mistaken. I shall write her of your evil. You are a wicked and dangerous man, Uncle."

He laughed softly but went on packing. "If I am so wretchedly vile and dangerous, my dear, you had best alert Seward I am here. You should not remain alone in my presence for long. I may try to make good on Natine's failure."

"More threats, dear Uncle?"

"I have no time to waste on words, Coral. I am leaving tonight, and I shall no longer hinder you or your plans. Are you not relieved?" His words held a sudden tone of sarcasm. "As for London, I have every intention of returning to my wife and daughter. I advise you not to be foolish enough to write her—lest I be forced to intercept the letter." He turned, and his dark eyes were cool. "I should hate for something to happen to Margaret."

A chill ran through her. "Are you threatening Margaret or me?"

"I am telling you to be wise and keep all your wild suspicions to yourself. Hampton and I shall work this matter out together by correspondence."

"So you can think of new schemes with which to blind him? You will never give up, will you, Uncle?"

His mouth curved beneath the dark mustache. He turned away, then paused to look at her. "I admit I am relieved to see you alive. Your wit has come to be appreciated. If Margaret had half of your ability, she would have seen through me years ago."

"Maybe she found it easier to pretend that she did not."

"Yes . . . perhaps she was wise after all. And she will be both well and safe when you and Buckley show up in London—if her mind is not pained by your suspicions."

He truly believes he can get away with this, she thought. "There are British troops here from Jorhat. And if I tell either my father or Seward you are here, they will order the ensign to arrest you."

"On what charges? Your suspicions? You have no evidence."

"No. But the major has proof of your involvement in the mutiny at Plassey and the assassination at Guwahati. And he knows how Harrington and Zameem worked with you. He suspected you even at Manali and sent word to Colonel Warbeck in Calcutta."

Sir Hugo searched her face, and she hoped her fear did not show.

"Jace Buckley is dead," he said. "He was killed by Sunil at Sibsagar."

For a moment horror gripped her. Then she drew in a breath. "No, he is quite alive, and so is Gem. I am becoming accustomed to your lies. The battle at Sibsagar is over. That is the reason you are running. You know Jace will come."

He snapped his bags shut and picked them up from the bed. A smirk lingered on his face. "Goodbye, Coral."

He strode past her and walked down the hall to the stairway. Sir Hugo had never allowed anything to trap him before. Was it a mistake to let him leave Kingscote?

Coral followed. She might have alerted Seward and her father, but Hugo was not a man to apprehend at a desperate moment. It was best to let Jace bring the matter of his guilt to the governor-general in Calcutta, where he would receive a fair trial.

At the stairway she looked down into the hall, but he had already gone out the front door.

———

Outside on the front verandah, Sir Hugo stood in the darkness. Where was the horse he had ordered the groom to saddle? He looked down the carriageway and saw no sign of the Indian boy. Impatiently he set his two bags down. The sky churned with thick clouds. The Brahmaputra River flowed by, obscure and silent. He would travel south to Guwahati before Sunil's army returned. Was Sunil dead? It no longer mattered. All plans and schemes were now like broken pottery, fit for nothing but the dump heap. Perhaps tomorrow new plans would rise from the ashes, but now he must escape. When he returned, matters would be different. He would think of some way to start over, to rebuild his dreams.

He snapped out of his reverie. A manji was walking toward him from the river. Sir Hugo could see his white puggari.

A *boat*, he thought suddenly. *Yes, to Guwahati.* "You! Get the boat ready. I am going downriver. Be quick about it."

"Yes, sahib."

Sir Hugo picked up his bags and left the porch. He followed the boatman down the sloping lawn to the ghat steps.

Hugo entered the boat and settled himself on the seat, glancing back at Kingscote. The golden light in the high windows seemed to stare back at him, and for one strange moment he sensed he would never walk across the lawn again, and never mount the verandah steps to enter its hall.

"Perfect nonsense," he murmured. "Of course I shall come back. I am not yet defeated."

A movement from the manji caught his attention. He drew back in a moment of surprise as he looked into the face of Natine. "Natine, you startled me. I thought you were yet in the village."

"News has come from Sibsagar, Sahib Roxbury. Maharaja Sunil is dead. Rajiv's son is alive and will rule one day. You vowed to me it would not be so."

"Do I control the outcome of battles? If Sunil is dead, it is because he blundered badly."

"No. It is you who has made the mistake. You promised me if I help you, Gem will die. That you will be burra-sahib of Kingscote. No more feringhi religion, no more school, and Kali reigns supreme. Now Sunil is dead. I am told Gem will be the maharaja of all Assam! He will serve Miss Coral's God! Now the major comes to Kingscote. The school will be rebuilt, and more feringhis will come! It is you, Sahib Roxbury, who has done all this evil."

"Do not be a fool, Natine."

"I am a fool. I believed you. Were better that I stayed Sir Hampton's friend than listen to your lies. There will be no more lies."

Sir Hugo did not like the wild gleam in the servant's eyes. His hand moved slowly under his black coat to reach for his pistol.

Natine stood, his eyes cold. Slowly he lifted the lid from a small basket at his feet.

Hugo's eyes widened. "No, you fool—"

The cobra landed on his chest. Hugo caught only a glimpse of its flat, weaving head, its beady eyes glowing yellow. He felt the fangs sink into his throat. He cried out, trying to fling it from him into the river.

From out of the darkness the priest came, and Hugo screamed at the face of death. "Get away . . . you filthy murderer. . . ."

They lifted him from the boat and Hugo struggled to wrench free, but already the venom was working.

"God," he tried to call, but the word would go no further than his tongue. Instead he heard "Kali" chanted in his ears. Darkness was coming to swallow him up. Horror and fear seized him. Too late . . . too late. . . .

The two men threw him into the river, and Hugo felt the dark water dragging him down.

The first drops of rain began to fall and landed on the worn ghat steps as Natine and the sadhu hurried up to the lawn.

———

Coral tossed restlessly in her sleep. The familiar nightmare had returned. She was running, and the trees were on fire; the hatcheries were going up in billowing flames that reached toward the sky. *Jace!*

A brilliant streak of lightning startled her awake. She sat up and looked toward the open window, her heart pounding. Fire! She threw aside her covers, intent on reaching the verandah. The hatcheries were burning—

No! What was that odor?—smoke. The mansion was burning! She raced into the hall, banging on the other bedchamber doors as she went. "Father! Kathleen, Marianna, get up! Hurry! Fire! Get out!"

She heard them stirring in a moment of muddled confusion, but ran on. She must warn the servants downstairs. As she ran for the stairway she heard breaking glass coming from her sisters' rooms. She stopped, horrified. The parlor was burning, and her father's office. Smoke crept like evil fog ready to smother and blind its victims. Coral screamed below for the ensign, for Piroo, for Mera, Rosa, and the other servants. She heard nothing. Had they been able to get out the back door?

"Please, God, help us!"

She turned to go back down the hall to help her father with Elizabeth when a feeble wail reached her ears from somewhere downstairs in the smoke.

Reena! Why was she not with Preetah?

Cold fear gripped her stomach. Coral clutched the banister and stared below. "Reena!" she shouted. "Where are you? Can you hear me?"

Nothing. Only the crackle of fire, the stench of acrid fumes, the sputter of rich draperies going up in flames, the crystal chandelier crashing to the marble floor. The expensive family paintings from Roxbury House toppled from the parlor walls and melted in the heat.

"Miss Coral!" Reena screamed. "Here! I'm caught!"

The sound came from the ballroom.

Coral refused to think of the hopelessness of her cause. She went down the stairs holding her dressing gown over her mouth and nose. Suddenly she stopped! A man appeared in the hallway, but he did not see her, so intent was he on reaching Reena.

"Reena! It is me, Uncle Natine! Where are you!"

Coral froze. Natine stumbled through the ballroom doors.

The plantation was awake, and in the hatcheries and out on the lawn there were shouting voices looming like dying shadows in the firelight. Horses raced by, and she heard the voice of Ensign Niles shouting orders, followed by the trumpeting of elephants.

Something crashed in the direction of the ballroom. A moment later she heard Reena outside shouting: "Uncle, where are you? Are you still in there?"

There was the horrible sound of sizzling wood, and the heat was becoming unbearable. *Reena is outside safe*, thought Coral. *But Natine and I are both trapped.*

She heard his voice in the ballroom, but it seemed that it was consumed in the roar of fire. She tried to retreat in the direction of the stairs, but there was so much smoke she could not see, and her eyes and lungs burned. She crawled toward the stairs and bumped into the divan. She struggled in the direction of where she thought the front door should be. Everything was too hot to touch.

She reached her hand out. "Help me!"

———

"Sahib!" whispered Gokul, pointing.

The night air smelled of smoke, and flames were leaping into the darkness, defying the gentle rain that had begun to fall. Jace raced his horse down the car-

360

riageway, his gaze searching the crowd that was gathering on the wide lawn for a glimpse of Coral. She was not there! For a moment his emotions gave way to panic.

He maneuvered his horse through the crowd, searching. Marianna saw him and ran toward his horse, grabbing his booted leg. "Major! Coral is missing! Kathleen and I went to her room before we crawled down from the verandah, and she wasn't there! She is somewhere downstairs!"

Jace galloped the horse toward the front of the house, reining him in as the animal shied from the flames. The door was open and smoke swirled, burning his throat. *A fool's death*, he thought, but he entered.

"Coral!"

Sir Hampton had opened the windows in the bedchamber where Elizabeth lay moaning in her sleep. Below he saw men on horses and workers running in all directions. His daughters, had they climbed down through the verandah? He could only trust God that they had, for the hall was now dark with smoke seeping under the door.

He ran back to the bed and picked up Elizabeth, carrying her toward the verandah. Already the fire was spreading. He could see the hatcheries billowing up into clouds. Everything was aflame. Kingscote would be nothing but ashes by morning.

His heart was beating, but he felt nothing but deadness. "Elizabeth," he repeated, holding her in his arms and gazing out, numb. "Elizabeth! Kingscote is being destroyed."

The firelight fell upon them as he stood transfixed on

the verandah, staring out at what once had been his life, his pride, his passion.

Seward was shouting up at him to come down quickly. He heard the shouts of Kathleen and Marianna.

Coral. Where was his sweet Coral?

Panic gripped him. His eyes filled with tears as he looked back helplessly at the smoking door.

"She's trapped! Dear God! Coral is trapped in the fire!"

Elizabeth moaned. At the desperate wail of Hampton, she stirred, her eyes blinking. "Coral!" cried Elizabeth. "Coral!"

Hampton looked down into the drawn face of the woman in his arms and saw fear in her eyes. A surge of joy flooded through him. She understood! Her mind was not destroyed!

"Sir Hampton!" shouted Seward from below. "Aye, man, the rope, the rope! Before it burns!"

Hampton's strength of will rallied. He moved swiftly now, and holding Elizabeth with one arm, he grasped the rope that Seward had thrown to the rail.

Kingscote was on fire but his beloved was awake. All was not lost. He had her. And he had a new, more powerful love for God. Hope burned more brightly than did the flames, more enduring than a family dynasty, more lasting than brick and mortar. Casting aside all restraint he shouted upward into the cascading rain: "Almighty God! I give you thanks!"

His body was worn and hurting, but with a light heart he managed to climb down, holding on to Elizabeth. Then—rain! It was pouring!

"Beautiful monsoon!" he choked with delight, looking up at the dark clouds. "Sweet silver drops! Come!"

The lightning streaked hot white against black; thunder uttered its dominance; the huge fat drops broke in a tumultuous downpour beating against the fire in the mansion, the hatcheries, the jungle trees. Hampton laughed. Elephants trumpeted. And the fire struggled to survive. . . .

Coral heard Jace, and the sound of his strong, urgent voice shot through her like a bright arrow. She crawled in the direction of his voice, seeing nothing but the smoke that burned her lungs and parched her throat.

"Jace!" The call was feeble. Did he hear it?

She heard his steps and struggled to move in his direction.

He advanced to where she was, and Coral reached out both hands. "Jace!"

He swept her into his arms and ran back in the direction from which he had come, and soon they emerged into the drenching rain, warm and steamy. He carried her away from the house toward the cooler shrubs, where Coral coughed and gasped, filling her lungs with fresh air.

Preetah had found her sister Reena and knelt on the grass embracing her. Reena was pointing back toward the house. "Natine!"

Her cries were lost in the joy from her father and sisters as they saw Coral safely with Jace.

Only vaguely aware of the others spread out on the lawn, Coral met the penetrating blue-black eyes while the rain soaked him. "I—I thought I would never see you again."

"My dear Miss Kendall," he said with mock decorum. "Did you think I would settle for losing you to mere fire and smoke after all I've gone through to get you?"

Emotionally spent, she gave in to laughter, leaning her head against his wet chest.

The rain was pouring, soaking her through to the skin, washing the smell of smoke from her hair and face. Her head lifted, her eyes growing languid as the firelight flickered against his wet skin.

"I—I don't look or feel like a bride," she whispered, her eyes clinging to his.

"Ah! But you will!" he whispered. He smiled faintly, and she loved the glimmer of warmth in the depths of his eyes. He smoothed the wet strands of golden hair from her face and throat.

His lips met hers . . . and the moment merged with the intensity of the fire.

They were oblivious to the downpour, the trumpeting elephants, the shouting voices.

————————

Across the lawn, Seward stood where Hampton knelt, Elizabeth's head on his lap. "The monsoon be putting the fire out! The Almighty be good to us this day, Hampton! Not all be lost after all."

"No, all is not lost," said Sir Hampton, cradling Elizabeth against his chest. As the rain poured upon them, Elizabeth lifted a weak hand to draw Hampton's creased face down to hers.

"You are safe."

"Yes, Liza!"

"The—the hatcheries, the house—"

"I have you, nothing else matters. But look, Liza! Seward is right!" He gestured toward the hatcheries. God has sent the monsoon for Kingscote! The blessed rains are putting the flames out. Not all is ashes! Out of what is left, we will build again!"

"C-Coral—"

"She is with the major. And Kathleen and Marianna are here—" He turned his head and held out his arm to include them. They came, kneeling, embracing their mother.

"Oh, Mama, you are all right," wept Marianna.

"Yes. . . ."

29

Convincing Sir Hampton to let him marry his daughter instead of giving her to Ethan, whom the family now knew to be with Felix Carey in Burma, had proven a simpler task than Jace had anticipated.

There was a break in the rains, and the two men stood by the banks of the Brahmaputra, looking toward the charred ruin of the Kendall mansion.

"It will take years, but we will build again," said Hampton. "The caterpillars and mulberry orchard, thank God, were not all destroyed."

Jace wrestled with his own desires. He knew Hampton wanted him to stay permanently at Kingscote. Jace was in the same position he'd been in with the colonel when it came to the expectation of having a son or daughter by his side in the family enterprise. With the colonel it was the military, with Hampton, the silk.

Jace's infatuation with Darjeeling had been too long in progress to lay it aside, yet he respected this man enough to find it difficult to take Coral and leave to chart his own course. Especially now.

He lowered his hat and looked past the sloping lawn at the Kendall ruin, but in his mind he saw another mansion, white against the backdrop of the Himalayas. The ruling rajas of Sikkim called Darjeeling *Dorje Ling*, meaning "Place of Thunderbolts." On a summit at 2123 meters, Darjeeling straddled a large ridge and was forested with lush green, offering breathtaking views of the snowy mountain peaks and down to the swollen rivers in the valley bottoms. During the monsoon season thick clouds obscured the eastern Himalaya mountain region like a crown of white, but the rest of the year the sight was majestic. His plantation would sit on soft rolling hills of tea bushes for as far as he could see, and there would be workers from Nepal, hundreds of them to cultivate and harvest, and to load the *Madras* and other ships for the voyage to Europe.

Sir Hampton studied Jace as though he recognized something akin to himself. He sighed. "I lost Michael through my stubbornness to accept what he was, what he wanted in life. I should have backed his endeavor financially. I've a feeling, Jace, you and Michael were right. Your interest in the mountainous region was farsighted. One day the East India Company may find it a crucial location."

Jace had thought he and Seward were the only ones to have thought of that. "Darjeeling could become an important pass into Nepal and Tibet. It could know rapid development as a trading center and tea-growing area along the trade route leading from Sikkim to the plains of India."

"Aye, and the climate is perfect for tea. I know a pang of regret, thinking of Michael."

"If Michael were here, I think I know what he would say."

Hampton looked at him, and it was obvious he already felt pleased that the young man would become his son-in-law. His eyes misted. "And what would my son say?"

Jace looked up the grassy slope and saw Coral walk toward them, the hem of her billowing skirts ruffling in the breeze. She stopped, one hand holding her hat. Jace thought not only of Kingscote but her school.

"He would say your dream lives on in the ashes, only waiting for you to find the strength to try again. The past bleeds with the prayers and tears of many who hold Kingscote in their heart."

Sir Hampton laid a strong hand on his shoulder and looked not at the ruin but at Jace. "Aye, he would. And he would tell you to do the same, my son. Go to Darjeeling. Take Coral, and Seward. Someday the family will have both a silk and tea dynasty in Assam."

Jace thought of Alex and said smoothly, "You may find yourself unexpectedly converged upon by a number of marriages. I can think of only one reason why Alex would go to London. A Roxbury may end up your daughter-in-law after all."

Hampton frowned. Jace tried not to smile, for he knew Belinda was looked upon as frivolous. "You might want to prepare Mrs. Kendall for the surprise. I feel certain Alex will return with Belinda as his bride."

Hampton only grunted.

"Kathleen will back me up on my suspicion. She too guessed he went to save her from Sir George. Later she found the small box she had asked Elizabeth about. It contained a ring that Alex had once secretly given to Belinda. She sent it back to Alex as a distress call. It was that ring that Natine stole and used to lure you to Darjeeling."

"Ah. . . ."

Hampton squinted toward the house, and it seemed to Jace that he was visualizing grandsons and granddaughters romping on the lawn. Jace smiled. "I think you will have a small army to carry on Kingscote in the years to come."

"And Darjeeling," Hampton was swift to add.

"The monsoon will make trekking to Darjeeling impossible for months. I have already spoken to Coral, and Seward and I would like to serve you here until Kingscote is repaired. Then, for Coral's sake, it is best she remain here until we have a residence on the Darjeeling land that can offer her what she needs," said Jace, thinking of her health. "She will also want to rebuild the school with your permission, this time in stone."

Hampton smiled his pleasure. "I shall take you up on that. It may be I shall have my first grandson born on Kingscote after all."

"Sahib," came a sober interruption.

Jace and Hampton turned to look downriver, where Gokul was returning from his walk along the banks. "What is it, Gokul?" called Jace.

"I believe the river is unhappy. It has returned the remains of Sir Hugo Roxbury."

Jace and Hampton exchanged glances. "The storm maybe," said Hampton tonelessly, his jaw hard. "His boat may have overturned."

Jace had his own suspicions. "I think Natine caught up with him. Coral said Roxbury left in haste not long before the fire."

"Aye, you may be right. Natine may have felt betrayed when their schemes did not work out."

Gokul was holding something. "This ruby ring I saw many times on his hand. The crocodiles didn't leave much, but this proves that the remains are indeed Roxbury's."

Hampton sighed as he took it between his fingers and

stared at it, remembering the many years that were forever past. "It is his ring all right. Margaret, I think, will not grieve too deeply."

———

Amid the downpour, the task of building appropriate shelter for them all proved formidable. With the help of Jace, Seward, Ensign Niles, and the troopers, extra bungalows were constructed. Thilak and men from the hatcheries worked to put up a makeshift roof over the mansion's cook room, where Piroo morosely searched through the ashes for his precious cooking utensils, grumbling against Natine and the sadhu from morning till evening when he departed with a long face for the stables.

Nearly a month had passed since the fire. Neither Coral nor Jace had discussed the wedding. She knew why, of course.

At noon he stopped at her meager bungalow, standing in the doorway, drenching wet with a cynical lopsided smirk. "You could always run away with a derelict sea captain. At least you'll be dry in the Great Cabin. However, I cannot promise smooth sailing."

A brow arched when she said nothing. He scanned her. "Need I remind you that Christmas draweth nigh? True, we are not exactly in a merry countenance, but if I am going to live in perpetual rain, I might as well share my muddy hut with a fair damsel."

"But, Jace, a wedding here? How? I've not even a decent dress to wear and—"

He took her elbow. "Come. It is time we had a cozy gathering with your family to discuss more important matters than aching backs and sore thumbs."

"And just where, sir, do you advise we have this 'comfortable' little gathering?"

"The cook room, of course. I happen to be hungry and Piroo has baked my favorite delicacy—chupatti bread."

She smiled at his good-natured sarcasm, for their food had been as boring as their shelters. In the company of her glum sisters, she walked with Jace in the rain to the mansion shell.

They had all gathered at his request, somewhat amused, and Seward grinned as they entered. "The cook room be the most important room in the house," and his eyes twinkled as he helped himself to one of Piroo's breads.

"Indeed?" said Coral wryly. "With my wedding due on Christmas?"

"Aye, lass, but the major be willing to take you aboard the *Madras* and marry you anytime," teased Seward.

Coral heard the constant plop, plop of water splashing in the vessels Piroo and Rosa had set about the room. It was anything but romantic, thought Coral grimly.

"Christmas wedding, indeed," she said, folding her arms. "I shall stand ankle deep in water."

"We could all sail on Jace's ship for London," said Kathleen baitingly. "What a wedding you would have at Roxbury House. Granny V would think herself in heaven between you and Cousin Belinda."

"Just think," said Marianna. "Alex and Belinda. So that was why you kept asking Mother about him receiving a letter and a small box."

Coral too remembered, and had wondered, but events had kept her too occupied until now to ask about Kathleen's suspicions. It wasn't until she had produced the letter to her father and sisters that Kathleen had admitted finding an empty box in Alex's bedchamber.

"I recognized the ornate box at once as belonging to

Belinda," said Kathleen. "She showed it to me in Calcutta. Alex had given her his family ring as a token of engagement, but later changed his plans for Austria. It wasn't until she sent the letter to him telling of a forced marriage in London to Sir George that Alex decided he truly loved her."

Marianna sighed wistfully. "I wish someone would decide he loved me like that."

"You mean Charles Peddington?" teased Kathleen.

"Maybe Captain Gavin MacKay," said Marianna with a smile, and then laughed when Kathleen unexpectedly blushed.

"London, and Roxbury House," said Coral thoughtfully, and glanced sideways at Jace. She knew a grand wedding meant nothing to him. He had already remarked that waltzing his wedding night away in the stiff company of London's earls and lords at the Roxbury ballroom was the last thing he wanted. She knew, however, that if she truly wished for the wedding to be held in London he would agree. Under his even stare she smiled and pretended to be serious.

"Yes, and a wedding dress from the Silk House, created by Jacques! What more could I want?"

"It is two months from Assam to Diamond Harbor, and six months to London from Calcutta," remarked Jace smoothly. "And knowing your grandmother, it will take three more months to get ready for the wedding. Are you suggesting we wait another year to marry?"

Coral smiled at Kathleen. "Going to London for the wedding would suit me fine; however, the major is somewhat difficult to hold on to. If I delay a year he may decide to disappear again with Gokul. Or worse yet—set sail for some distant port."

She walked over to Jace and placed a protective hand on his arm. "No, I think I'd better marry you now. A girl never knows about seafarers."

He regarded her. "A wise decision, madam." He turned toward Elizabeth. "And you, Mrs. Kendall? What do you suggest for your daughter? If you would have us wait and voyage to London, both Coral and I will consider."

Coral was pleased to see the kindness in his eyes when he looked at her mother.

Elizabeth rallied and came alert. "You said something, Jace?"

He quietly repeated his question.

Every head turned toward Elizabeth. She had been silent for some time, and Coral and the others thought it trying for her to make much comment about the upcoming marriage. Although she had agreed to the wedding and was happy to welcome Jace into the family, she had offered little advice concerning the dilemma.

"Perhaps you can marry at Sibsagar. Prince Adesh would welcome the idea. I think we all would." Her brown eyes gleamed unexpectedly and a smile showed on her thin face. "I think it would prove fitting to your relationship with Gem."

Coral caught her breath and went to her, stooping beside her chair. She picked up the cool hand that rested on the shawl over her lap. "Why, Mother, what an exciting idea. It is perfect." She turned her head toward Jace, her eyes pleading.

"I think it can be arranged," he said. "Both Gem and his ruling grandfather expect to meet with you. In light of what has happened on Kingscote, a wedding in the palace isn't likely to offend Raja Singh."

Coral felt her excitement growing. A wedding in the royal palace—the home of Jemani! "Yes, that is what I want."

Jace offered a light bow. "As you wish. A royal wedding it shall be."

He left to find Gokul, and Coral turned to her mother and laughed. "No one but you would have thought of it. But a dress—why, everything in my room is either ruined by smoke or rain!"

Marianna asked dubiously, "What about an Indian wedding dress?"

Coral shook her head. "No. I want to carry on Mother's tradition and marry in white silk, with a veil and satin slippers and—"

"Maybe . . ." cried Kathleen and turned to her mother. "*Your* wedding dress! The trunk was salvaged, and if I could take the dress apart and redesign it— maybe Coral can have her white dress."

"Yes!" cried Coral, on her feet. She looked at her mother, whose brown eyes shone. "Oh, Mother, can we?"

Elizabeth smiled up at Hampton, who came and took her hand in his. "I can think of no finer use for your mother's wedding dress."

Coral and her sisters raced toward the charred remains of the back room where the goods that had been recovered were stored. Many items in the process of being sorted through by Mera and Rosa were stacked high. Coral searched for the trunk that her mother had brought from Roxbury House.

"Here it is," cried Marianna.

Coral opened the trunk, and her hopes were shattered. She groaned. She drew out various discolored objects until she came to the carefully wrapped wedding dress. She lifted it out.

"How dreadful! The cloth is scorched, and even the pearls look discolored," groaned Marianna.

"Well," said Coral, completely disheartened. "It was

silk at one time—definitely expensive and boasting that Mother was a Roxbury from London."

They stared at the remains in silence while the rain ran off the edges of the partial roof.

Coral folded it back into the trunk. "Do not say anything to Mother yet."

———————

Sibsagar

Jace sat on cushions in the royal chamber of the palace. Before him was a large display of various-size diamonds, rubies, emeralds, sapphires, and other gems. There were dozens of rings, bracelets, necklaces, nose rings, anklets, and a host of other ornaments.

Jace studied them carefully. Opposite him, Raja Singh sat cross-legged studying the Mogul sword with bright, eager eyes. Jace knew the sword's value. His primary interest at the moment was a wedding ring for Coral, but there was a residence to build at Darjeeling and many future expenses. He had intended to sell the *Madras*—his pride and joy—in order to buy her a ring, but now he would not need to. He was even pleased enough to feel kindly toward Zin. Zin had placed a short message inside the red silk cover: "A wedding gift to my friend Javed Kasam."

Jace, however, had no doubt that the "thief" he had come across in Calcutta had been one of Zin's men from the bazaars. No matter . . . he had the heirloom back—and just in time. If Seward had not taken it upon himself to safeguard it, it would have been destroyed in the fire.

Jace held up the diamond and ruby ring he wanted and a matching necklace, thinking of the one Ethan had given to Coral. This one was far more delicate, and exquisite.

"I will take these," he said. "But the sword is worth more. It is from the Mogul's palace at Agra."

"Indeed, indeed," said Raja Singh. He gestured to the servant, then smiled at Jace. "I have many gifts for you, Major Buckley. How could I ever show gratitude enough for returning Prince Adesh, son of my daughter Jemani, to his home safely? You are much in our favor!"

Servants brought in several small bags of jewels, several jewel-handled weapons, silk and satin cloaks, turbans, and all manner of ornate garb, each also adorned with jewels.

"Your generosity, Excellency, humbles me. But one thing more I do ask: I need silk cloth for a wedding dress. Would any woman in your zenana have this?"

"I feel assured we can oblige you, Major. I shall have a servant see to it at once."

"And slippers," added Jace.

"Anything you may wish."

An hour later, Jace, Seward, and Gokul gathered up the treasure, and with the wedding arranged, they departed for the humble huts of Kingscote.

"Ah, sahib," said Gokul with a grin. "This is one time silk heiress is poor, and future tea plantation master is very rich."

"Javed Kasam would be highly pleased," quipped Jace, thinking back to that moment in the ghari in Calcutta when Coral had tried to buy him with the Roxbury ring. *"I'll buy you that tea plantation,"* she had said. He would now bring her silk to make a wedding dress. He held up the diamond and ruby wedding ring to let it catch the light.

Someday the family would finish sorting through the rubble and hopefully find most of their treasures, including that Roxbury ring, but for now, the only ring Coral would own was the one Jace Buckley had placed on her finger himself.

———

Felix Carey's Mission Station
Burma

So Hugo is dead but Coral is alive.

Ethan sat on the bunk in his bamboo hut reading the letter Coral had written him explaining the death of his father. Knowing that she lived brought him joy and a new sense of freedom. Until this moment he had not understood how thoughts of her death had burdened him with false guilt. Thank God she was well—and happy in her coming marriage to the major.

Ethan's gray eyes showed no emotion, then unexpectedly he gave a laugh. "How fitting an end," he murmured.

Slowly he folded the letter and walked to his makeshift desk to file it where he might read it again when he thought of her, but he paused. The words came to mind that Felix Carey had spoke that rainy morning in chapel from the Apostle Paul's Epistle to the Philippians: ". . . forgetting those things which are behind, and reaching forth unto those things which are before . . ."

Yes, thought Ethan.

Felix would know well about forgetting yesterday and pressing toward tomorrow. A young man also, he had already lost his wife to illness here in Burma.

Ethan's decision came quietly. He would stay in Burma and dedicate himself to his medical work, aiding Felix. Someday he might wish to return to London, but for the foreseeable future he was content to lose himself in his work.

He stood in silence listening to the rain, then held the letter to the flame on the candle and watched it curl and wither into ash.

30

Coral sighed as she held up the yards of silk for Kathleen to study. "What do you think? Can you make the wedding dress?"

Kathleen held it to her cheek. "It is gorgeous."

"Oh, I want to get married too!" moaned Marianna.

"I can make a fine wedding dress—if I receive the help I will need," said Kathleen. "We haven't much time and no place to work that isn't smudged with soot."

"We will all help," said Marianna. "Preetah is good with cloth."

The girl smiled. "Oh, I would like to very much."

Preetah had not grieved over the death of her uncle Natine, whose charred body had been found in the rubble. Thinking of it now brought Coral a small shudder. What had been his reason for coming in the house once he had set the fire? Had he intended to bolt her in her room? The thought that she had come within feet of him on the stairway after she had gone down to try to find Reena was chilling. Yet Natine had performed one act of mercy in his death. He *had* saved Reena, and Coral had not been able to reach her.

The news about Sir Hugo had not been so pleasant.

Jace had informed Coral that morning that his body had been found in the river.

"Then we will begin work immediately" said Kathleen, bringing Coral's mind back to the present. Her sister frowned. "If I could only find my sewing things, but there is no chance of that. We'll do the best we can with what we have."

"Yanna said her bungalow is larger and dry," said Preetah. "You can work there. I will care for the children and let them stay with Reena."

"And I previously gave her needles and silk thread so she could make Devi a sari for Christmas," said Kathleen.

"Then I will go tell her," said Preetah and ran out.

"Christmas will not be so dreadfully disappointing after all," said Marianna.

Coral lifted her new slippers with their tiny sparkling diamonds and scrutinized them thoughtfully. More important than the slippers was the man who had thought enough of her to come back from Sibsagar with them. She was learning even more about the adventurous seafarer as the days past. Jace, she decided, was a very romantic man.

On a rainy afternoon a surprising entourage arrived at Kingscote. The 13th rode up the carriageway under Colonel John Warbeck and Captain Gavin MacKay. A lone civilian journeyed with them, Charles Peddington.

"And look at us," groaned Kathleen, staring down at her soiled Indian sari.

Marianna picked up the disfigured mirror they had found in the ash rubble and looked at herself with horror. Gone was the elaborate hairdo of curls and ribbons, and her hair was wound simply into a chignon with the strands hanging limp. Her blue eyes came tragically to

Kathleen. "Mister Peddington will never recognize me."

Kathleen was smarting under her own injured pride. The last time she had seen Gavin MacKay she had been dressed in an expensive frock at Manali, and boasting of her disinterest in anything but returning to the Silk House at London. The truth was, after all the loss and heartache they had been through recently, she was not so certain she wished to go to London. Perhaps she was ready for marriage herself.

"Well," she said wryly to Marianna, who stood disconsolately as the rain dripped through the thatch roof. "It is time we ate humble pie."

———

Jace was surprised to see his adoptive father, Colonel John Warbeck. He raced to his bungalow, where Gokul was already rushing about to produce Jace's military uniform. While Jace threw off his leather jerkins and Indian tunic, Gokul tried to polish the buttons.

"What is *he* doing here?" murmured Jace, snatching his report on the mutiny at Jorhat from a waterproof trunk under his bedroll.

"Ah, Sahib-Major, the Colonel, he will never relent until you stay in the wondrous Bengal army."

Jace cast him a wry glance as he buttoned the top collar on his jacket. "My hat."

"Here!"

Jace placed it precisely on his head, and with the report under his arm to protect it from the rain, he walked across the mud to meet Colonel John Warbeck.

Ensign Niles and the troop from Jorhat were forming a military line to receive the colonel. The colonel saw Jace and rode up, drawing his horse to a stop. The rain pelted on the colonel's hat and black raincoat, and the steely gray eyes swept Jace. "Congratulations on a mission well done," he said. "I expect a full report."

Jace saluted. "As you say, Colonel, a full report." He handed the thick volume to his father.

The colonel took the papers and glanced toward the bungalow.

Jace stepped aside. "Gokul! Send up to Piroo! Have him brew some of that coffee we brought back from the bazaar at Sibsagar!"

"At once, Sahib-Major!"

The colonel smiled for the first time, and his eyes showed a mellowed amusement as he dismounted. "Coffee, is it? What happened to your Darjeeling tea?"

Jace too smiled. "Just as soon as you release me from this uniform I shall have time enough to send plenty to your office in Calcutta."

In the bungalow the colonel leafed through the report. "I'll send this to the governor-general. You can fill me in on what has happened."

Several hours had passed while the colonel sat musing over the details and drinking the coffee that Gokul now brewed on a small fire in the corner of the hut.

"That Roxbury was involved does not surprise me. When I received your message from MacKay about Harrington and Zameen, I guessed there might be trouble against the maharaja at Guwahati. We came as quickly as we could."

"What about Harrington and Zameen?"

The colonel chuckled. "They are warming the jail at Fort William, awaiting trial. I had anticipated returning with Roxbury and Sanjay as well. It is a relief that Sanjay is dead, and I should have hated to be in attendance when Roxbury was shot."

Jace noticed an odd look in his father's eyes. Suddenly he remembered . . . Lady Margaret Roxbury—had not the colonel once been engaged to marry her?

"Roxbury's ring is the only proof the man is dead. The crocodiles got most of the rest."

"Sir Hampton has the ring?"

"He was thinking of sending it to Margaret."

Jace saw the subdued interest in the gray eyes. "She is not here?"

"She is in London at Roxbury House." He added smoothly, "You might wish to bring her the ring and the news of Hugo's unfortunate death."

The colonel smiled faintly. "Yes, a military duty, of course."

"Yes, of course. She will need words of sympathy, someone to offer a hand of encouragement. I will speak to Hampton about your upcoming voyage to London to make certain he entrusts the ring and a letter of condolence to you."

The colonel arched a brow of curiosity over Jace's influence.

Jace smiled and folded his arms. "I am going to marry his daughter Coral."

"The one with the green eyes at the ball in Calcutta?"

"You remember."

"I am certain you would also. We both have fine taste in women."

The colonel seemed to be thinking more of London than he was of military matters. "About my mission," Jace pressed. "It is complete now. Did you bring my discharge papers from the governor-general?"

The colonel smiled and reached into his pocket. "Now, Jace, would I forget anything so important?"

"I was thinking you might."

The colonel smiled and handed them to him in an official envelope. "With a marriage on the horizon and a tea plantation to make successful, I would not want to stifle you in that uniform. As of the new year you are released from the office of major."

Jace took the envelope. Their eyes met. The colonel laughed and they gripped each other by the shoulders.

"I am proud of you, Jace. I always was, even when you were off on that ship."

"I hope to keep that respect, Father."

"You will. And now . . . where is the beautiful damsel with the green eyes? I wish to meet my future daughter-in-law."

———

Coral watched Marianna and Charles Peddington huddle under the thatch roof, deep in conversation. Charles was doing all the talking and Marianna was all eyes. *She has found her hero*, thought Coral with pleasure.

But it was days later when Charles approached Sir Hampton with a breathless Marianna on his arm to ask for her hand in marriage.

"Of course we plan to wait an entire year, sir," said Charles, his face flushed under Sir Hampton's smile.

"And Charles wants to stay here permanently, Father," added Marianna.

"I hope to assist Coral with the new school. I've brought her teaching resources and the Scriptures in the Assamese language."

Sir Hampton pretended to be thoughtful. He rubbed his chin. "Of course, Charles, I will need to discuss this matter with Elizabeth."

"Yes, sir!" said Charles with a beaming smile and looked at Marianna. They both guessed they had already won.

Elizabeth, who yet had difficulty in walking, laughed when Hampton told her the news. "Well, darling, you must admit your fears about our daughters producing no heirs has proven groundless. Two marriages announced! And I am certain Kathleen and Gavin will soon come to an agreement."

"Aye, 'tis about time. And Gavin being a Scot at that."

The announcement did come. But it was not what the family expected. Coral was the first to hear about it from Jace.

"He has decided Kathleen should work at Silk House after all. While she works with your aunt Margaret and the man they call Jacques, Gavin intends to try to win Sir Hugo's old seat in Parliament. Politics seem an odd choice where Gavin is concerned, but he is adamant. He will do all he can to win the support of your grandmother."

"Granny V? She will adore him! If she has anything to say about it, he will sit in Parliament. I wonder about Alex and Belinda. . . ."

Jace scowled up at the dripping thatch roof. "How is your wedding dress coming?"

"It is nearly finished."

He looked at her. "When Alex returns with Belinda I have a suspicion he will settle down and be content to play his music in the new ballroom at Kingscote. And he should prove more of an asset to the silk than Hampton would have guessed."

"Did you hear? Colonel Warbeck will go to London with Gavin and Kathleen."

Jace smiled a little. "Yes, he wishes to return Roxbury's ring to your aunt." He stood and walked toward her. "And now, what about you and me?"

31

Sibsagar

Torchbearers marched four abreast of Jace's royal elephant. His wedding garb had been sent by Prince Adesh, no doubt carefully chosen under the scrutinizing eye of the raja himself. Jace wore immaculate black with a smoke blue sash and a jeweled tulwar. Across from him sat Seward and Gokul, also adorned for the occasion.

Seward sighed. "Well, lad, this be the best day in a long while. Never thought you'd be claiming Hampton's prized daughter, though I did suspect back in Manali that the lass was caring for you. Nothing else but love could have made her come with me and Boswell that night." He chuckled. "Darjeeling will be a bit more interesting now. Always did think some children running about would brighten the tea patch."

Jace's mouth turned. "Not a 'tea patch,' Seward—acres of tea. Containing all the miserable brew that English ladies could yearn for."

"Ah, sahib," said Gokul, settling his silk turban more carefully. "What bothers old Gokul is how we grow this

389

'miserable brew' when Sahib Hampton thinks only of silkworms."

"Don't worry, old man, I will think of something—just as soon as the Kendall mansion is livable again. We can't leave them now. But Alex is bound to arrive soon with Belinda, and that will give me a way out."

Gokul scratched his chin dubiously.

Seward's reddish gray brows came together. "Aye, we'll find us a way all right. Be anxious to turn our partnership into a rich and prosperous plantation before Burma gets new notions of trying to annex Assam. A new war will ruin everything. Be assured England will send an entire army to enter Burma if it comes to it."

"That is one war I intend to stay out of," said Jace dryly.

"Aye, if we can—and if your sons and daughters can."

Jace looked at him thoughtfully but said nothing.

"I have one thing on my mind now. And I believe we have arrived at the palace, gentlemen."

Through the flickering light emerged the vision of hundreds of spectators. Jace's elephant proceeded instinctively to the very entry, where it knelt for them to dismount. He saw the raja in royal garb and beside him, Gem—Prince Adesh Singh.

As Jace stood waiting for Coral he became aware that her elephant was coming. He watched through the myriads of bright torches lining the avenue, and another elephant slowly emerged. In the firelight he could see that it was of royal lineage and carried a golden howdah and a wide crimson silk umbrella. It came toward them, elaborately decorated, and tinkling with bells.

Jace watched as Coral's elephant neared the center of the royal court. While the rajput guards stood around him in military splendor, the elephant knelt. Several guards walked forward to help her alight. His breath paused as he saw Coral. . . .

———

Gokul wiped his eyes as he watched unobtrusively from the royal pavilion, where he had chosen the best view possible. He straddled a limb that extended out over the courtyard. Sahib would be proud of him if he could see how he had managed to "shimmy" up the tree, he thought with a smile. He glanced at little Prince Adesh. He had managed to have a big surprise waiting for sahib and sahiba, and it was he, Gokul, who had told him what would make his two friends happy.

Gokul watched now, intently.

Coral came from the torchlight, veiled and surrounded by her sisters and the memsahib herself. There was also Preetah, Yanna, and little Reena—all wearing cloth of gold. Reena carried white flowers in a woven basket.

Coral stopped and salaamed to Raja Singh and Prince Adesh, and a hush fell for a moment over the crowd. Then she turned and walked toward Jace.

He came to meet her. He stared at her for a long moment, then whispered something in her ear. She turned and looked, and from the shadows walked a young man plainly dressed and carrying a black book.

Gokul smiled. This was Prince Adesh's surprise.

Felix Carey stopped in front of them, holding open his Bible, and began to perform the marriage ceremony.

At the conclusion of the brief service, Jace reached out and lifted Coral's veil. Again he whispered something, then enfolded her in his arms.

"Ah . . ." sighed Gokul with deep satisfaction.

A cheer went up from the spectators and guests.

———

Coral stood with Jace and turned to face again the raja and Prince Adesh. Her eyes feasted on Gem. How handsome he was! How princely. He walked toward her, and Coral felt Jace's hand on the small of her back edging her forward.

Misted brown eyes looked up at her, then a shy smile. He handed her a present. "For you, Mother," he said.

Mother. . . .

Coral swallowed back the emotion and knelt so she could meet him face-to-face. "A present for me, Excellency?"

"To you, I will be Gem. To you and to Jace. He too is my friend." He handed her the present.

Coral accepted it, the gold wrapping winking in the torchlight.

"Please open it now," urged Gem anxiously.

She gently removed the wrapping and stared. *A Bible.* She opened it and saw the words were in Hindi.

Gem smiled at her pleasure. "Jace said bad men burned your first one. I gave him this one when he left for Kingscote, but he wished me to give it to you now."

"Gem, I shall treasure it forever. It is all the more precious because it came from your hand."

"I have another gift. This one I chose when I knew you and Jace would marry here at Sibsagar."

He motioned toward the elephant. "It is yours, Mother. Jace told me about an elephant named Rani. I think I remember such an elephant. This one is now Rani too."

Coral smiled and could not speak.

The guards had come for him. The winsome child was now Prince Adesh again. His smile left, and he took on a serious expression and stepped back. They walked him back to the side of his grandfather, and Coral watched as he sat down on the dais. For a moment their eyes held;

Gem blinked, then lowered his gaze. Coral swallowed back the cramp in her throat and felt Jace's gentle hand on her elbow telling her it was time to stand to her feet and walk away.

She stood, and something in his gaze brought a smile to her lips.

"We will see Gem again," he said. "Many times. But now, Mrs. Buckley, it is *our* time."

Her eyes whispered her love, and they turned to be escorted toward the royal howdah. The wedding feast was laid out in the palace, and then a royal apartment awaited, beautifully prepared for a king and his queen. A long journey of tomorrows also waited. . . .

With one hand Coral held to Jace's arm; with the other she held the Hindi Bible from Gem. In her heart, Coral held the promise that each tomorrow would first pass through the wise and loving hand of their God.

GLOSSARY

AYAH: A child's nurse.

BRAHMIN: Highest Hindu caste.

BURRA-SAHIB: A great man.

CANTONMENT: British administrative and military area.

CHA-CHA: Uncle.

CHUNNI: A light head-covering; a scarf.

DAK-BUNGALOW: A resting house for travelers.

DEKHO: "Look."

DEWAN: The chief minister of an Indian ruler.

DURBAR: Royal public audience.

FERINGHI: A foreigner.

GHAT: Steps or a platform on the river.

GHARI: A horse-drawn vehicle; a carriage.

GHAZI: A fanatic; usually with religious overtones, but also referring to political beliefs.

HOWDAH: A framework with a seat for carrying passengers on the back of an elephant.

HOOKAH: A water pipe for tobacco.

HUZOOR: Your honor.

JAI RAM: A Hindu greeting.

KANSAMAH: A cook.

KATAR: A thrusting knife.

KOTWAL: A headman.

MAHARAJA: A Hindu king.

MAHOUT: An elephant driver.

MANJI: A boatman.

NAMASTE: A respectful gesture of fingers to the forehead with palms together.

PALANQUIN: A boxlike enclosure carried on poles.

PUGGARI: A turban.

PUNKAH: A fan made of heavy matting or canvas, sometimes wet, and pulled by a rope to make a breeze.

RAJA: A king.

RAJKUMAR: A prince.

RAJKUMARI: A princess.

RANI: A queen.

RAJPUT: A warrior cast of the Hindus, a rank below the *brahmins*.

SADHU: Hindu holy man.

SEPOY: An infantry soldier.

SOWAR: A cavalry trooper.

TEHSILDAR: The village headman.

TONGA: A two-wheel vehicle.

TOPIWALLAH: A man who wears a hat; a foreigner.

TULWAR: A curved sword.

UNTOUCHABLE: One that is below the Hindu caste system, condemned as unclean in this life.

WALLAH: A driver.

ZENANA: Women's quarters.